KILL BAXTER

D0062023

Also available from Charlie Human and Titan Books

APOCALYPSE NOW NOW

KILL BAXTER

CHARLIE HUMAN

TITAN BOOKS

Kill Baxter
Print edition ISBN: 9781783294763
E-book edition ISBN: 9781783294787

Published by Titan Books
A division of Titan Publishing Group Ltd
144 Southwark Street, London SE1 0UP

First edition: November 2015
2 4 6 8 10 9 7 5 3 1

A CIP catalogue record for this title is available from the British Library.

Printed and bound in the USA.

For Georgia

I place the barrel of the handgun in my mouth. I have lost everything and there's no real point in going on. Karma is a bitch. Karma doesn't care that I wanted to change my ways. Karma doesn't believe in good intentions.

I have failed miserably at being good. I couldn't even get that right. I'm the same nasty piece of work that I've always been, except now I can't be happy with it. What has been felt cannot be unfelt. Even having saved the world doesn't make me feel good about myself. Perhaps it's something you get habituated to; each new world-saving moment has to be bigger and better than the last to give you that same dopamine and serotonin kick. Maybe heroes are just junkies.

I've killed everything in this life worth living for, so the only thing left to do is kill Baxter. They say suicide is a selfish, egotistical thing to do. It suits me perfectly. It all seems so clear now. This is going to be great. The steely taste of the gun. The explosion. The oblivion. I can't wait.

Hexpoort Admissions Procedure Document XH03
Security Clearance Level: Impi

APPLICANT: BAXTER ZEVCENKO
AGE: 16

Baxter was brought to the attention of the Hexpoort admissions faculty by the MK6 agent codenamed Tone. As with any potential student, careful attention must be paid to his genetic history, magical skills and psychological make-up profile. The following profile was compiled from extensive MK6 surveillance of the subject and interviews with all involved in his case.

HISTORY
Baxter is a unique case. His genetic lineage is a strange hybrid of Siener, the Afrikaner mystics active primarily during the Boer wars, and the Murder, the shape-shifting giant Crows that have been responsible for the deaths of many in the Hidden community.

  We believe Baxter was first introduced to the existence of

the Murder by his grandfather, 'Grandpa Zev', but that Baxter initially did not believe him. Grandpa Zev was of Siener descent but had none of their abilities. It is only in Baxter that the Siener powers of clairvoyant sight have fully manifested.

However, the reality of Baxter's heritage goes further than that. At the centre of Baxter's strange tale is the former head of MK6 Kobus 'Mirth' Basson, who went rogue and attempted to twist the organisation to his own nefarious purposes. Basson himself was part Crow and was implicated in a plan to gain control of two ancient inter-dimensional vehicles that had the power to rend space and time.

There has been speculation that these vehicles served to imprison two old gods, but this has not been definitively proven by subsequent investigations. Whatever the truth of their history, these vehicles were undeniably powerful and in Basson's hands they posed an unparalleled threat to the safety and security of our world.

Baxter was the pawn that was meant to cement Basson's control of the vehicles' ability to traverse time and space. We believe that Baxter himself is the result of Basson altering timelines to create a perfect combination of Crow and Siener, a mixture potent enough to pilot these inter-dimensional craft. To this end Basson captured Baxter's girlfriend Esmé, posed as Baxter's psychologist and managed to briefly convince Baxter that he was a serial killer.

These events culminated in a battle in an alternate dimension that destroyed an alternate version of Cape Town city and resulted in Basson's death. This was ruled by the MK6 Blood Kraal as acceptable collateral damage in ending the threat of such a dangerous rogue agent.

PSYCHOLOGICAL PROFILE

The combination of this Crow and Siener genetic inheritance has resulted in extreme internal tension within Baxter's psychological make-up.

Baxter displays elements of the so-called Dark Triad of personality traits: narcissism, Machiavellianism and psychopathy, and his leadership of a porn-dealing high-school gang called the Spider allowed him full expression of these traits.

However, the kidnapping of his girlfriend Esmé resulted in a late blossoming of conscience and ignited in him a desire to follow a more virtuous path.

Only time will tell whether this will be a permanent personality change, but a panel of MK6 psychologists has predicted that he will soon revert to his old ways. A leopard does not change its spots, after all.

FIELD APPRAISALS

Thorough interviews have been conducted with every agent who came into contact with Baxter during the Basson episode. We have included statements from the three agents who had the most interaction with him:

Agent: Jackson 'Jackie' Ronin

Notes: Agent Ronin works as a supernatural bounty hunter, a position that gives him great access to the Hidden community. He has been suspended on numerous occasions for wanton violence and alcohol abuse and has more cautions, violations and disciplinary reviews on his record than any other agent in history. It is this committee's understanding that he suffers from PTSD from his involvement in the Border War during apartheid.

Statement: 'Baxter? Why don't you go ask the little shit yourself? OK, OK, fine. He can be a dumb little punk but the kid has real potential. Thing is he's conflicted, you can see it sometimes on his face, the two sides of him battling it out. If he can sort out the shit he's got going on in his head he could be a real force to be reckoned with.'

Agent: Dr Pat (retired)

Notes: Pat runs the Haven, a facility that takes in Hidden creatures that are under threat. Her record is full of disciplinary cautions for placing the needs of the Hidden above her work as an agent.

Statement: 'A very sweet boy, but with a lot on his mind. The bond he had with Klipspringer, an Ndiru bok-boy he met at the Haven, was very special as Klipspringer likes very few humans.'

Agent: Katinka

Notes: A member of the all-female Hidden race known as The Flock, Katinka was born male and barely escaped execution. Now living as a transsexual, Katinka is the subject of a bitter political battle between The Flock and MK6.

Statement: 'He's a cool kid, with a lot of power in that cute little head of his. If he'd just go a little easier on himself he'd realise he's not as bad and hardcore as he thinks he is. But that's teenagers, right?'

RECOMMENDATIONS
The committee accepts Baxter as a student of the Hexpoort

magical education facility with reservations. He seems unable to fully control his abilities, sometimes displaying extreme competence at directing his sight, and at other times seemingly unable to use it at all.

Our primary recommendation is to have Baxter tested as soon as possible to determine the extent of his abilities. The kind of tension that Baxter experiences as a result of his genetics can result in either a total, permanent blockage of abilities or the almost unconscious mastering of new spells and abilities. Either way he must be treated with extreme caution.

BROWSER HISTORY

It's my fifth session at Pornography Anonymous and I still can't shake the feeling that the world owes me something. This despite the copious amounts of 'sharing', 'talking about feelings' and 'apologising' that I've been forced into as part of my rehabilitation.

'Good morning, everybody,' says Harold Emly, compulsive masturbator, reformed porn addict and leader of this little group of cinematic sex aficionados. Harold has a large moon-shaped face and strawberry-blond hair that is going white at the temples. He's wearing a lime-green golf shirt and has a sparkly stud in his left ear lobe. He chews his lip as he speaks, which gives his words a slight slurring quality and makes it sound as if he's on his fourth glass of cheap red wine for the night.

Harold was once a famous radio sports commentator, beloved by the nation, before he was disgraced when he accidentally left the microphone on while he indulged in his favourite compulsion during an ad break and treated cricket fans everywhere to a short but noisy performance.

'Good morning, Harold,' the weird little group intones solemnly, thus initiating the opening of yet another session. I see the smiles and nods of solidarity and I feel a wave of disgust pass over me. I've been accepted into the sordid, sweaty ranks of PA and they look on me as one of their own.

I should be a hero. I should be interviewed by newspapers, I should be considering competing offers by publishers and establishing a healthy social media following by being retweeted by minor celebrities. I should have my own meme, for fuck's sake.

No. There's no denying the world has been massively unappreciative. I mean – and I'm not fishing for hero-worship here – I struggled against my own inner demons, fought an inter-dimensional battle in a vehicle that was actually a prison for an elder god, and ended up saving the world from certain domination. No biggie. Does the world care? The unfortunate answer to that question is no. Not even a little bit. Now I know how Jesus and Ultraman must have felt.

I rub the stub of my little finger. It has become my signature move: rubbing my finger stump philosophically and thinking about everything the world owes me.

I look up and see the rest of the group looking at me. The rumour is that I cut off my own finger to stop myself from jerking off. They nod sympathetically and I quickly pull my hands apart.

'Baxter,' Harold says, hunching forward in his chair, causing the gold zodiac-sign pendant around his neck to swing back and forth hypnotically. 'Why don't you share with the group first today?'

Yes, why don't I share? I should tell them that getting into a new school has been impossible despite considerable effort on my part to prove I've been 'reformed'. Pornography Anonymous is just the tip of the iceberg. I've been to several psychologists and have been diagnosed with everything from bipolar disorder to ADHD to PTSD. I've been prescribed a rainbow spectrum of drugs to help me deal with my problems. Since my last psychologist tried to convince me that I was a serial killer and then attempted to murder me with a giant Octopus exoskeleton, I don't think it's unreasonable that I'm a little sceptical.

The truth is that I do need to reform, but pornography has never been a problem for me. I'm a businessman and porn just happened to be the product that I traded in. The habit I really need to kick is manipulation. The problem is that I've decided to care but my personality seems thoroughly unsuited to it.

I itch like a junkie to manipulate people. My puppetmaster's fingers tingle for the strings. Oh Lord, just one more hit of that sweet, sweet strategy.

But I now have a conscience and there's no use denying it, and it won't let me return to my old manipulative ways. It's not easy. Trying to reform in everyday life is like trying to lose weight by working in a doughnut shop.

The thing that keeps me going is that Esmé now thinks I'm 'noble', which may also have something to do with the fact that I detached a mind-controlling arachnid parasite from her brain stem, but still, I'm determined to hang on to her good graces.

It's hard. My hero Niccolò Machiavelli would laugh at me: 'For a man who strives after goodness in all his acts is sure to come to ruin, since there are so many men who are not good,' he said. Amen, Niccolò, but I'm willing to bet he didn't have a touchy-feely little Boer mystic metrosexual on his shoulder that had something to say about everything.

'Baxter,' Harold prompts. I've been trying, really trying, to play this self-help game, but today I've had enough. 'I used to deal porn,' I say irritably. 'Very profitably. But then I was press-ganged into caring by the slave-driver in my chest and harried into submission by the little metrosexual on my shoulder. Then I dragged a giant Octopus into another dimension and killed it so that it wouldn't destroy the world.'

'Yes!' Harold says. 'Yes, yes, yes! Which of us isn't attacked every day by the giant Octopus of porn wanting to drag us into another dimension?' There are murmurs of agreement from the group. 'The world may not appreciate you, Baxter, but we do. It's your three-month anniversary. You have earned the honour of wearing this. Let's give Baxter three cheers!' He hands me a yellow plastic key ring with PORNOGRAPHY ANONYMOUS emblazoned across it while the others applaud and cheer.

'Wow, thanks,' I say, shoving the key ring into my pocket.

I zone out for the rest of the meeting, periodically regaining consciousness to half-heartedly clap as someone recounts their weird little porn story.

Finally we say the PA serenity prayer to end the session. 'God grant me the strength to use safe search, the serenity to know that deleting your browser history doesn't make it OK, and the wisdom to understand that nobody reads *Playboy* for the articles any more, et cetera, et cetera. Kumbaya!'

The meeting ends and I shove my hands into the pockets of my black hoodie and slouch in the direction of the exit.

'Baxter?' Harold calls and shambles towards me. I push my hair out of my face, adjust my glasses and resist the urge to run.

'Glad I caught you!' Harold says. 'A few of us from PA stay afterwards for another group. I thought it might be beneficial for you if you joined.'

'Is this some kind of Pornography Fight Club?' I ask. 'Because I'm really not interested.'

'Ha ha. No, no,' Harold says with a light, jovial punch to my shoulder.

'Will it count towards my rehab?'

Harold considers this for a second. 'Well, yes, I suppose I could sign off on it counting towards your mandatory rehabilitation hours.'

'OK,' I say. 'Fine. Count me in.' Porn rehab is like a Band-Aid;

it's best just to rip it off all at once.

Harold breaks into a huge grin and pats my shoulder. I try not to think about where those hands have been. 'You'll like this, Baxter. I'm certain.'

'I really doubt it,' I say.

Harold guides me back to the circle of scuffed plastic chairs and I slide back into one with a feeling of resignation and despair hanging over me like a cloud. This was not how I imagined my life would turn out.

One of the PA members – Tom, I think – has stayed behind too. I've had to sit through his stories about the type of porn he's into, so I pretend he doesn't exist.

Gradually new people begin to trickle into the community centre. Harold greets everybody with a handshake or hug and ticks names off a list. The circle of chairs fills up.

'Right, I think that's everybody,' he says. 'I want to welcome you all, and also extend a warm welcome to someone new. Baxter Zevcenko is a young man from another group who I'm certain will fit right in here. Although he does not exactly meet the criteria, I feel that his experience of loss is close to our own. Let's give Baxter a warm ritual welcome.'

The group begin to click their fingers above their heads and stamp their feet in a weird, syncopated rhythm. Cultists, definitely cultists.

'Welcome to the Inner Sanctum, Baxter,' Harold says proudly. 'Although we don't have an official name, we call ourselves The Fallen. We're mostly professionals: media personalities, businessmen, doctors and lawyers. The common thread that joins us is that we have fallen from grace, so offended society that we're for evermore forced to live on the periphery, to be the butts of a thousand jokes, the targets of a million whispered comments. Group, would you like to introduce yourselves and say why you're here?'

'Tom Weston,' says the guy that stayed behind from PA. 'Former radio DJ. Sexist remarks on late-night radio.'

'Darryl Melkin,' says a black guy in skinny jeans and thick glasses. 'Geek-chic poster boy and best-selling popular science author. Plagiarism and fabricating quotes. Oh, and Malcolm Gladwell is not even a real scientist and can go fuck himself with a rusty nail.'

'Darryl.' Harold's tone is fatherly. 'You know what we said about that. Let's keep all the bottled-up hate for expression time.'

'Well done to Malcolm Gladwell. He should be commended for his strong narratives that are accessible to the general public. I'm happy for his success,' Darryl says through gritted teeth.

'That's better,' Harold replies with a smile.

'Sissy van der Spuy,' says a tall blonde as she dabs at her lipstick. 'I tweeted a racist joke. But I'm not racist, I know lots of black people.'

'Of course you do, Sissy,' Harold says, patting her on the shoulder.

Round the group they go. People who have disgraced and humiliated themselves and been shunned by society.

'You see,' Harold says, spreading his arms wide. 'We're all the same. The Internet turned its harsh, cruel, outraged eye upon us. The world hates us now, Baxter. But at least we're all in it together. Listening to your stories, I realised that in a way you're just like us. You too have lost your position in the world.'

I am in no way like these people. I am in NO WAY LIKE THESE PEOPLE.

'We do creative therapy mostly,' Harold says. 'Responding creatively to a traumatic situation has tremendous potential to heal.'

'I made these.' Sissy proudly shows me a pair of earrings.

'I don't know if papier mâché earrings in the colours of the old South African flag are inherently therapeutic for someone accused of racism,' I say.

Darryl raises a finger. 'That's where you're mistaken. It doesn't matter if it's wrong or inappropriate. It's expressive; it's like flushing poison from your system.' He holds up a beautifully rendered picture of Malcolm Gladwell with his hair alight and his eyes bleeding.

'Right,' I say.

'I understand that this will be your last session before you leave for your new school. I urge you to channel your frustration into some kind of project. Perhaps throwing yourself into your studies will help?' Harold says.

'OK,' I say, tired and wanting to get as far away from this group as possible. 'I'll try.'

Ronin is slumped in the driver's seat of the Cortina, picking his fingernails with a knife. 'God, what took you so long? You cured yet? I could wait while you knock one out in the bushes.'

'Thanks, but I'm OK,' I say with a sarcastic smile. 'Besides, nobody is apparently ever cured of addiction. Only in remission.'

The bounty hunter has become a closer friend than I could ever have anticipated. Thanks largely to the fact that he helped me rescue Esmé. He's the only one that I can really talk to about all the strange creeping, crawling, screeching, roaring things that cling to Cape Town's underbelly. Plus he always has drugs and alcohol.

'Well, rather you than me,' he says. 'Sitting around in groups with a bunch of slack-jawed morons would drive me insane.'

'I thought acid, booze and monsters already drove you insane.'

He purses his lips and nods. 'True. Speaking of.' He takes a sip from his hip flask. 'I've got a little therapeutic announcement of my own. This is my last drink. Ever.'

'Da-dum tish,' I say. 'Good one.'

He gives me his serial-killer look that he usually reserves for scaring small children. 'Do I look like I'm joking?'

'You're giving up drinking?' I say, raising my eyebrows. 'That's like anyone else saying they're giving up breathing.'

'Yeah, I've been thinking that maybe I should try and change my life too. Being back with Sue has made me think about stuff. Deep stuff, you know?'

'You're talking to the definitive example of how love fucked someone up,' I say. 'So yeah, I get it. But what prompted this little lifestyle change?'

He shrugs. 'Sue's off on a smuggling trip and I want to be clean by the time she gets back.'

'Why? She drinks the same amount as you, probably more.'

'I left her at the altar because I was running away from stuff, you know, running away from myself and shit.' He looks at me. 'Go ahead, make a snarky comment. I fucking dare you.'

I hold up my hands. 'Wasn't going to.'

'I even bought a book.' He closes his knife, reaches into his trench coat and pulls out a bright yellow paperback with a grinning idiot on the cover giving a thumbs-up sign: *The New You: Tips For a Happier, Healthier Lifestyle*.

'You're serious?'

'Serious as ball cancer, sparky,' he says.

'Well, good luck to both of us.' I grab the hip flask from Ronin and take a swig. 'We're both going to need it.' I hold up the hip flask. 'You might want to get rid of this then.'

He grabs it out of my hand and shoves it back into his coat. 'I'm going to keep it right here with me. It'll remind me to resist the temptation.' He taps his temple. 'Reverse psychology, sparky.'

'Right,' I say. I lean back in the passenger seat as Ronin starts the car. 'So where we going today anyway?'

'School shopping for you. Gun shopping for me,' he says.

School shopping because I've been forced to accept Tone's offer and enrol in Hexpoort, a magical training facility in the middle of nowhere. It sucks, but it's my only real option, my preference for not being stabbed and sexually assaulted precluding any involvement in the South African penal system. That and the fact that I honestly have no other prospects for the future. While other kids my age were off interning in law firms and media houses, I was gaining valuable work experience catching elementals and fighting things that go bump in the night.

'So what's Hexpoort like anyway?' I ask as we drive. I tried googling it but I got one ominous website before my laptop went nuts with malware warnings and the browser shut down.

'Oh,' Ronin says, and I catch the involuntary grimace on his face. 'Fine, just fine.'

'Right.' A cold drop of fear slides down my throat and settles in my belly. If it makes Ronin grimace, then it must be bad. Really bad.

We weave through the traffic, as usual Ronin using the rules of the road as more of a rough guideline than an absolute fact.

'Jesus, slow down,' I say, gripping the dashboard. 'Do you always have to go so fast?' I'll be pissed if I survived the apocalypse only to be killed by Ronin's bad driving.

'Yes,' he grunts and speeds up a little.

'Such a child,' I mutter as we hurtle through a red light.

'So where are we gonna be buying these books and guns?' I ask.

'Hidden Designation Zone Four.' Ronin cuts in front of a taxi and responds to the blaring of a horn with the middle finger.

'Catchy name,' I say.

'That's official. Mostly it's just called the Freak Quarter.'

The Cortina slides into the chaos of Wynberg station. Fruit

vendors and guys selling bric-a-brac compete with taxi drivers in a war of who can shout the loudest. A guy with a pit bull on a leash is arguing with a skinny security guard, and two huge Nigerian bodybuilders are flexing for ladies getting their hair braided in a sidewalk hair salon.

We pull into a side road in front of an old factory with a large picture of a boot on it that says 'Osmans Shoe Manufacture'. Ronin leans on the hooter and a guy selling fruit in front of the building waves his hand irritably and limps over to a large tarpaulin covering the entrance. With a flourish he pulls it aside and Ronin eases the car through, stopping briefly to deposit a couple of coins into the fruit seller's open palm. He gives us a gold-fronted smile and ushers us in like we're royalty.

Inside, the factory is huge, and empty except for dozens of cars parked around the entrance. Ronin pulls in next to a silver Jeep and we get out.

We walk over to a red diamond painted on the bare floor. Ronin spits on the ground, cuts his thumb with his knife and chants a few sentences in Xhosa. I pick out something about 'blood' and 'fence'. He grabs me by the sleeve and yanks me through a murky translucent barrier that I didn't even know was there. It feels like walking through a wall of sewer water and I instinctively hold my breath. The world shimmers and sparkles like when you stand up too quickly. The dancing sparkles in my vision start to solidify and the empty building becomes an undulating ocean of colour, sound and smell.

'Armmerghh,' I mutter. A moment of nausea rises as my vision adjusts to the sudden switch.

'I see you're your usual eloquent self when we do anything magical,' Ronin says. 'You'd think you'd be used to it by now.'

The truth is, I'm not. It still hurts to use my fledgling Siener ability and I've tried to avoid it as much as possible. But my general perception of reality has definitely shifted and I now have a sort of general anxiety about the world. After the whole battling giant Crows and mutants experience, I find myself gloomily wondering whether there are even worse things out there.

We push our way through the throng. The Freak Quarter is part market, part festival, part shopping district. I see bearded dwarven kids getting rides on grumpy-looking unicorns. A Tokoloshe wearing an American flag bandanna trying to hustle a trio of heavily made up elven women in stilettos. An anthropomorphic snake in a Mexican poncho busks with a battered guitar and a harmonica.

A dirty-looking dwarf approaches us with a handful of jewellery. 'Looking for real dwarven gold?' he murmurs. 'I'll make you a special deal because I like the look of your faces.'

'Ah, very nice,' Ronin says, turning over a gold ring in his fingers.

The guy grins, showing a mouthful of brown teeth. 'Only the best.'

Ronin draws a shape over the handful of shiny jewellery with his finger. It shimmers like ice cream melting in the sun, revealing a small pile of rusted bolts and screws.

'I think we'll pass,' he says.

'Fokken poes,' the dwarf hisses as he scuttles away.

'Street conjurors used to be all over the place,' Ronin says. 'But they were successfully regulated in the Hidden community. Now they tend to stick to working for banks and for medical insurance companies.'

'Boys?' a bright voice calls.

I turn around. 'Pat?'

'Baxter!' she says and gives me a hug, inadvertently spiking me in the cheek with a sharp crystal earring. She holds my shoulders and looks at me with her kindly eyes, her curly white hair bouncing up and down.

'Right,' I say. But I shove the pamphlet into my pocket. Fuck the Man.

We skirt the crowd and make our way up the old iron staircase in the corner of the factory to the second floor, which is a maze of shops and stalls. Ronin leads me to a huge corrugated-iron shop that occupies a quarter of the floor space. DEMENTERTAINMENT says a sign in lurid pink neon, and the entrance is flanked by huge wooden speakers blasting weird disjointed seventies psychedelic rock.

'Everything we need is in here,' Ronin says with a grin.

I look doubtfully at the skulls, crystals, feathers, rock posters, herbs, incense and old vinyl. Easing my way past a stuffed cat wearing battle armour, I follow Ronin inside.

'Edred Blackheath, scumbag sorcerer, former grave-robber and collector of all things magical,' he calls out as we approach the counter. The guy behind it is leaning on his elbows and flicking through a magazine. He has long grey-streaked black hair, and is wearing a dirty pink Hello Kitty T-shirt, a leather waistcoat and a tacky turquoise faux Native American choker around his neck. A tattoo of a waterfall flows from his left eye down his cheekbone to his chin, and two large gold hoop earrings hang from his ears.

'Jackie Ronin,' Edred says. 'Just plain scumbag.'

'C'mon, Ed.' Ronin leans forward and grips the man's hand. 'Be nice.'

'When was I ever nice?' Edred says and pulls Ronin into a gruff hug. 'Who's your friend?'

'Baxter Zevcenko,' I say.

'This is Zevcenko?' Edred raises an eyebrow. 'This is the tyke that took on Basson? Well, well, I must admit I thought he'd be more … impressive.'

'You and me both,' Ronin says with a grin, grabbing a stool

Pat runs the Haven, a shelter for the strange things that exist in the realm of the Hidden. She was the first one to explain something of this world that I found myself thrust into. Basically, entire races of weird creatures exist in the dark and shadowy corners of life and MK6 spends all their time making sure the majority of people don't find out. By any means necessary.

'How lovely to see you!' Before I can reply, she turns away. 'Adopt a sprite. Save a life!' She shoves a pamphlet into the hand of an old dwarf, who tries desperately not to take it. Pat persists and eventually he gives up, grunts and shoves it into his pocket.

'The little darlings need good homes.'

'You're too fussy, Pat,' Ronin says good-naturedly. 'If people want to adopt, just let them have one of the little bastards.'

Pat's bright face turns instantly stormy. 'Jackson Ronin, I will not have one of my babies in an unfit home!'

'He's just winding you up,' I say. 'Ignore him.'

Pat glares at Ronin and then gives me a big smile. 'Tone says you're going to Hexpoort.'

'Don't remind me.'

'Oh, you'll love the Draken there. Beautiful creatures,' she says. 'Such charming natures.'

Ronin makes a noise like he's choking on a chicken bone.

'Well, we'd better get going,' he says. 'Got a lot to do.'

'Have fun, Baxter,' Pat says. 'I know you'll love it there. I just know it.'

'Adopt a sprite,' she says to a man with a scaled face in a suit as we walk away. 'Make a difference!'

We jostle our way back through the market towards a set of iron steps that lead to the second floor. A crowd of the Hidden has gathered in the market's central area, where a stage made out of plastic crates has been set up. The hippie that stands on it has a brown and black snout and a set of powerful jaws.

'Is that an anthropomorphic hyena dressed in tie-dye and yoga pants?' I ask.

'Kholomodumo,' Ronin says. 'Real mean bastards.'

'How long do we have to put up with this?' it shouts as it shuffles up and down on the crates. 'Project Staal is taking our children, destroying our families.'

A guy with wild hair, no front teeth and a non-standard approach to personal hygiene shoves a pamphlet into my hand. Ronin grunts as he grabs the guy by the collar and propels him forcefully out of our way.

The pamphlet is typeset in a garish bright green font. 'Manifesto of the Bone Kraal,' I read out loud.

'Put that down,' Ronin says, trying to grab it from me.

'Um, why?' I say, jerking it out of reach.

'Because that kind of shit can land you in an MK6 interrogation room, and you don't want to be there, trust me.'

'MK6 is scared of these clowns?' I scan the page. 'Blah, blah, oppression, transparency, et cetera, et cetera.'

'Not exactly scared,' Ronin says, scratching his beard. 'But those clowns are on the MK shit list.'

'Why?' I ask. 'This is my world now too. I should know about this stuff.'

'Your world?' Ronin chuckles and shakes his head. 'I wouldn't be getting all possessive about it, sparky. But OK. The Bone Kraal are agitators. They want transparency, accountability, democracy in the way the Hidden are treated.'

'Sounds, you know, righteous and noble,' I say.

Ronin raises an eyebrow. 'Oh, the naivety of the young and stupid. It's not righteous and noble when you're part of a black ops government agency that is conspiring to hide the fact that monsters and magic are real. Then it's terrorism. THAT is your world.'

and sitting down in front of the counter.

I give them a sarcastic smile and then raise both my middle fingers.

Edred laughs. 'That's the spirit, my boy.'

'How's things, Ed?' Ronin asks.

'Well, I've been attending so many funerals lately, you'd think I was living in a fucking old-age home.'

'Yeah, I've been hearing things,' Ronin says.

'More agents dead, their teeth taken for Muti.' Ed shakes his head. 'MK6 agents being hunted like dogs. Never thought I'd see the day.'

'Come on, you don't believe this Muti Man urban legend, do you?'

Ed looks at Ronin. 'Well, someone or something is killing those agents,' he says. 'And the Blood Kraal are doing fuck all to find out who.'

'There are enough things out there that want to do that without inventing some bogeyman.'

Ed shrugs. 'Suit yourself. If you want to stick your head in the sand, there's nothing I can do about it.'

'C'mon …' Ronin says.

Ed raises a hand. 'Conversation closed. I know what Ronin's here for, but what can I do for you, young Master Zevcenko?'

'I need whatever's on the Hexpoort curriculum for this year,' I say.

'Ah, a Poort initiate, eh?' He smiles at me with tobacco-stained teeth. 'They get younger every year.' He pulls a fat brown folder from beneath the counter. 'Hexpoort, Hexpoort,' he says as he flicks through it. 'Perhaps not the most prestigious occult educator out there, but certainly still one of the best. Here we go, the Hexpoort first-year curriculum.' He sucks his teeth. 'This is going to cost you.'

'I have to buy textbooks?' I say. 'MK6 are a government agency, aren't they, like, government-sponsored?'

'The government can't even get enough textbooks for basic education. You really think they're going to spring for a couple of hundred copies of Crowley's *Magick Without Tears* every year?'

'I'm guessing no?'

'You guess right. Some of the stuff you can find online for free, but the rarer things you have to get from me.'

'OK, so what else is going on there? I'm gonna need what, a wand and a spellbook or something?'

Ed sighs and slams his hand down on the counter. 'Popular culture has ruined magic. Utterly ruined it.'

'Here we go,' Ronin mutters and pulls a cigarette from his pocket.

'All wands and fucking "you shall not pass" and "wingardium fucking leviosa". Students become fixated on that shit and never progress. They never take the time to investigate the real bones, the real blood of magic. You're not gonna be Hendrix if all you listen to is Bieber, you know what I'm saying?'

'I think so,' I reply, not having a clue what he's going on about.

'Magic is just a tool,' he says. 'A spade. You're not going to dig a good hole if you don't put your back into it.'

'Last time I was here, magic was a spanner,' Ronin says. 'And before that it was a hammer. Pick a metaphor and stick with it, Ed, that's all I'm saying.'

'Well, I'm not wrong, am I? Props, Ronin, it has all become about props. I preferred magic when it wasn't so mainstream.'

His rant continues as he browses the bookshelves, unceremoniously pulling out books and dumping them into a plastic supermarket basket. 'You know what I heard the other day? You can get a degree in magic online. ONLINE! If ever there were a recipe for disaster …'

He eventually hands me the basket. 'I'm adding one of my own essential magical texts free of charge,' he says as he shows me a vaguely recognisable picture of a crazy-looking old guy with a beard.

'What's this?'

'A picture of Alan Moore's face,' Ed says.

'A picture of Alan Moore's face is on my curriculum?'

Edred gives me the crazy eye. 'No, but sometimes it's all you need.'

'OK, OK,' Ronin says. 'The kid's got what he came for. Now do you have what I want?' He licks his lips in anticipation.

'Hmmm, what was it you were looking for again? My memory isn't what it used to be.' Ed taps his chin with the tips of his fingers.

'Don't fuck with me, Ed,' Ronin says, his eyes all wide like a junkie's. 'You said you had it.'

'Easy, calm down.' Ed grins and holds up his hands. 'Just messing with you. I've got it.' He retrieves a battered wooden case from underneath a pile of books. 'The Blackfish,' he says, opening the case.

The gun inside is about the size of an Uzi, squat and a metallic grey-black, like it's made from hematite. The muzzle is shaped like the mouth of some kind of prehistoric fish, with huge teeth that protrude like tusks.

'It's beautiful,' Ronin whispers. This is as close to religious as I've ever seen him.

'One of a kind,' Edred agrees, hefting it to his shoulder and sighting down the odd barrel. 'A worthy successor to Warchild.'

Ronin holds out his hands pleadingly. 'Let me see it, Ed.'

'I'm not sure you can afford it,' Edred says. 'Last I heard, you weren't exactly in the black.'

'We can make a plan, can't we?' Ronin is like a kid begging for candyfloss. 'I can pay it off.'

'Not this time.' Ed replaces the weapon carefully in the case. 'Sorry, buddy, but business is business.'

'Surely there's something I can do?' Ronin says. 'C'mon, man.'

Ed steeples his fingers. 'Well, there is … no, no, I couldn't ask you to do that.'

'What?' Ronin says. 'You can ask me, man.'

'No, nothing.'

'Seriously, Ed, just ask.'

'Well, it's just that Norrd is putting pressure on me, forcing me to pay protection money,' Ed says. 'He's really muscled in on the Freak Quarter and your lot at MK aren't stopping him.'

Ronin shrugs. 'No need to interfere when the Hidden are regulating themselves is the dominant philosophy over at HQ.'

'Yeah, except when it interferes with government turning a profit,' Ed replies.

'That's the way it's always been and you know it. But why do you need me? You can handle yourself.'

Ed nods. 'Sure, maybe once or twice when they come knocking. But you know Norrd. He's got serious muscle. He'll just keep coming after me until I pay him, or I'm dead.'

'Yeah, Norrd's a bastard all right.'

'So hypothetically, what if you were to pay Norrd a visit? Off the books,' Ed says. 'Tell him to back off?'

Ronin grimaces and tugs at his beard braid. 'I don't know, Ed. Doing stuff off the books can land me in shit. MK doesn't exactly encourage us to fuck with power-players for our own personal gain.'

'Give me a break. Half the stuff you do is off the books. The Dwarven Legion hates Norrd, so they won't give a shit. And the way I hear it, the Legion is calling a lot of the shots in MK these days.'

'I'm not your enforcer, Ed. If he decides to come after you, I can't stop him.'

'And I'm not your personal armourer, Ronin,' Ed says. 'Want that terrible naked feeling you get when you don't have a custom weapon under that filthy coat of yours to disappear?'

Ronin's eyes narrow. 'If I do this, you'll give me the Blackfish?'

Ed smiles like a used-car salesman. 'You do it and she's all yours. I'll throw in your little buddy's textbooks for free too.'

Ronin looks at Ed, looks at the gun and sighs. 'ok, fine. I'll go speak to the goddamn goblin.'

GOBLIN TAP-OUT

The Bowelfong Muay Thai and MMA Gym is situated in the nether regions of Sea Point's main road. It occupies the entire top floor of a building that also houses a Greek diner, a tattoo parlour, an adult shop and a trendy dog-grooming 'creative studio' that offers an endless variety of mullets and mohawks with which to humiliate your canine friends.

We climb the stairs amid the smashing, screeching, buzzing and yelping noises (not necessarily in that order) and push through a pair of swinging doors.

The gym smells like cheap deodorant. There are a couple of muscular dwarves kicking pads with their tree-trunk legs. The *oooooooof* that explodes from a pad being struck by dwarven shin bone makes me mentally note 'being kicked by a dwarf' as something that I really, really don't want to happen to me.

But I've seen dwarves before. It's the huge grey-skinned creatures in board shorts rolling, grappling and choking each other out on the blue gym mats that catch my attention. They're ugly on a scale I never thought possible: bipedal bull terriers with fat necks, no noses and mouths that split their bullet-shaped heads open like wounds.

One of these things sits cross-legged on a cushion, flanked by two of his kind dressed in red Adidas tracksuits and watching the fighters throw each other about the mat. He takes ugliness to the next level, as if his face is trying to prove some point about the futility of beauty and happiness in a cruel world. He has a misshapen head, bulging eyes, and thick, coarse hair, like a shower cap made of pubes tugged over his scalp. His eyebrows are ridiculously sculpted like a geisha's and one of them is pierced by several thick iron rings. He gives us a lopsided smile as we approach, revealing large jagged canines.

'A goblin who wants to be a samurai. Norrd, you're cute, has anybody ever told you that?' Ronin says.

'My concubines,' Norrd replies in a rumbling hiss. 'But they might be biased. Who's your little friend?' He reaches down and delicately pours a cup of tea from a Japanese tea set.

'An agent.'

Norrd raises a manicured eyebrow. 'A little young for an MK fascist, wouldn't you say?'

'Magic doesn't have an age restriction,' Ronin says. 'He's a child prodigy.'

Norrd fixes me with a stare. I force myself to return it and try to put on a suitable powerful magician face but probably only succeed in looking constipated.

'So,' Norrd says in between sips of tea. 'Shall I try and guess why you're here, or do you just want to tell me?'

'Ed says you're squeezing him for protection money.'

'Insurance,' Norrd says. 'That's not illegal, is it?'

Ronin laughs. 'Well, I grant you you're only slightly worse than regular insurers, but let's not get into semantics. You're squeezing Ed. I want you to stop.'

'Oh well, if YOU want me to stop …' Norrd picks imaginary lint off his kimono.

'You don't need the small change Ed pays you,' Ronin says. 'So why don't we come to some sort of agreement?'

'What can I say? My regular business has been disrupted by the internal politics of the Obayifo. They're not producing things for me like they used to. It's forced me to fall back on my more basic streams of income.'

'Come on, Norrd, the faeries are probably trying to up payments again. Give them a little more and they'll be producing your Fae-kong counterfeits again in no time.'

Norrd shakes his head. 'Not this time. Ed's just going to have to suck it up.'

'Well then, why not start offering Pilates?' Ronin says. 'That's what a lot of the other gyms are doing.'

I imagine lines of grunting goblin moms toning their post-natal core muscles. Not a nice thought.

'Funny,' Norrd says. 'Almost as funny as what happened at the Flesh Palace. Is that what you're here for, Ronin? To destroy a legitimate business?'

'That was Basson,' Ronin says.

'Basson was part of MK6, was he not? And if the MK can't control its employees, then why should we respect its authority?'

'Because it will come in here and raze the place to the ground if you push it.'

Norrd smiles, his pointed little teeth shining with saliva. 'That's exactly what he said you'd say. He's right. Humans are all the same: bullying, cowardly worms.'

'Who is right?' Ronin asks.

'The one who is going to pay me for your teeth.'

He waves his hand and his goblin guards surround us. Up close, they smell of fungus and AXE deodorant.

Ronin's hand is under his coat and he pulls out two handguns. In a heartbeat a goblin has a meaty forearm around my neck with a knife a millimetre away from my eyeball. Two of the tracksuited goblins step in front of Norrd, forming a protective barrier of grey flesh.

'Well, now you have a choice,' Norrd says. 'You can try shooting through them to get to me, but your little friend will be on the receiving end of an unfortunate brain puncture. Or you can put those guns down and come with me.'

Personally I don't see much of a choice, but Ronin hesitates for several long moments before dropping the guns. The goblins strip him of the rest of his weapons and give me an invasive pat-down that I can't help but think is karma for some of the terrible porn scenarios I've sold.

Norrd stands and beckons. 'Please. Follow me.' He leads us through the gym to an elevator surrounded by scratch-like runes. We pile in, Ronin and me in the middle surrounded by a phalanx of goblins. The lift descends and we stand silently listening to the pan-pipe version of 'Sympathy for the Devil'.

We reach the basement and carry on going.

'An outing to a goblin lair,' Ronin says. 'My, my, what did we do to deserve such an honour?'

'You're MK6.' Norrd's tongue licks his bottom lip. 'You deserve far more than this.'

Eventually the elevator stops and the doors open to a darkness that seems to stretch for ever. I can hear the rough breath of the guards and the sound of my own heartbeat in my ears. I'm pushed forward through a series of turns. Finally light appears and I'm pathetically glad to see it.

We step out on to a walkway that spirals down into the earth. The walls are lined with dwellings, like high-rise flats in reverse. There are large grassy balconies that act as communal spaces. Goblin kids play among washing lines. A fat goblin in tight shorts and a Hawaiian shirt lying on a recliner in his front yard gives me a thumbs-up as we pass.

We descend into the goblin lair, passing shops, markets and even what looks like a hotel. The spiral walkway ends at a large stone amphitheatre plastered with posters for old movies. There's a giant screen, and a thick wooden pole wrapped in razor wire with sharp steel spikes driven into it at regular intervals. It looks like some kind of industrial cactus.

'Welcome to the Crimson Courtyard,' Norrd says with a grin. 'We mostly use it to watch music videos and TV series.' He gestures to the wire-wrapped pole. 'Although it does have other uses.'

An old Celine Dion concert is playing on the giant screen as we enter, and Norrd makes a kill-it motion, slashing his hand across his throat. The concert is paused and Celine is stopped mid-song, her face contorted like she's caught in a perpetual scream.

'I think I'll pass,' Ronin says.

'Unfortunately your attendance is compulsory,' Norrd says. 'Please come and take your seats of honour.'

We're led to the centre of the amphitheatre, next to the pole, and forced to our knees. Goblins begin to filter into the seats and fear starts to tingle in my fingers like little silver sparks. The audience chatters away, nudging, pushing, and imitating Celine's screaming mouth with much amusement.

'Now what?' Ronin asks. 'This goblin stink is going to make me throw up soon.'

'Now we're going to take your teeth,' says Norrd. 'And then your heads, as punishment for your complicity in the systematic oppression of the Hidden.'

'Lovely. I take it your sudden interest in extreme dentistry has to do with this Muti Man degenerate?'

Norrd gives us a nasty little grin. 'The Muti Man. Yes. I admit I was sceptical at first. He fucked with my business and I wasn't happy about that. But he is very … persuasive.'

'Rich, you mean?' Ronin says.

'The two tend to go hand in hand,' Norrd replies. 'That and he makes a lot of sense. He and his Bone Kraal have been organising us against the oppression of humans and dwarves. Like he says, separately we're weak but together we're strong.'

'Do you want a bunch of pencils so that you can visually demonstrate what you mean?' Ronin says.

A tracksuited goblin backhands him across the face and he sprawls on the bloody amphitheatre floor with a grunt. He pushes himself back to his knees and spits a mixture of blood and saliva at Norrd, but unfortunately the body-fluid cocktail falls short and splatters at the goblin's pedicured feet.

'Take their teeth,' Norrd orders, and the goblin crowd begins to hoot and stamp in appreciation.

The goblin heavies grab us and Norrd produces a pair of ugly pliers and holds them up. The crowd roars with approval.

'Fuck it, Ronin,' I hiss, struggling to keep a dirty goblin hand from prising open my jaws. 'Please tell me you didn't bring me here just so that I could get my teeth ripped out and then be decapitated. Please, please, please, with motherfucking cherries on top, tell me that you have a reason for manoeuvring yourself into the middle of a goblin stronghold.'

'I invoke Mazrech Sutial,' Ronin shouts.

The crowd goes deathly silent, as if a mute button has been hit.

'Tsk, tsk, tsk,' Norrd says, coming to stand in front of us. His kimono starts to slip open and I jerk my head away. Just decapitate me now. The very last thing I need in this situation is full-frontal goblin. 'Humans cannot invoke trial by combat.'

'I believe you'll find we can if we are on goblin land,' Ronin says. 'I'm certain the Kebra Bik, skral four, is pretty clear about this.'

Norrd frowns, and thankfully wraps his kimono tighter around his waist.

'Consult the Kebra Bik,' Ronin says like a schoolteacher talking to a particularly slow student. 'Bit embarrassing really, a human knowing the goblin gospel better than you do.'

'Shut your fucking mouth.'

'Take their teeth!' shouts a goblin in the crowd.

Norrd grimaces but shakes his head. 'The bounty hunter is correct. They are entitled to trial by combat.'

'What's going on?' I whisper to Ronin.

'They have to let me fight. The Kebra Bik is their highest law.'

'So we're gonna be OK?' I ask.

'Well …' Ronin says.

'Well then, it's a chain battle!' Norrd shouts, and the crowd explodes into a frenzy of shouting, stamping and cackling. Norrd doesn't look particularly pissed off and I'm getting a really, really bad feeling about this. 'Far be it from me to stand in the way of a little friendly competition,' he adds, clapping his hands together.

'What's chain battling?' I whisper to Ronin. 'Ronin! What the hell is chain battling?'

As it turns out, chain battling is the worst fucking idea anybody has ever had. The rules are as simple as they are insane. Two fighters are chained to the pole in the centre of the amphitheatre by one arm and proceed to beat the shit out of one another while trying to impale each other on the spikes and razor wire. Just a little family fun if you're a goblin.

One of the tracksuited goblin bruisers offers Norrd a piece of sushi and he holds it delicately between his knuckly, hairy fingers. 'Ready to meet your opponent?' he asks.

'One of them?' Ronin nods smugly to the goblins flanking Norrd. 'Or perhaps both of them? I don't want it to be unfair. I'll do it blindfolded.'

Norrd drops the sushi into his mouth and chews. 'I'm afraid not, bounty hunter,' he says through a mouthful of salmon.

There's a low moan as a monstrosity is dragged by a chain into the amphitheatre. It's a massive goblin, bluish in colour, with a bear-like snout and a coarse beard caked with ice. Its muscles are twisted and corded like ancient tree roots, arms hanging down with knuckles literally dragging on the floor. A runic sigil surrounded by flames is tattooed on the huge muscular slab of its deformed chest. It looks around, blinking against the light, its eyes rolling wildly in its head and its snout sniffing the air.

'Oh,' Ronin says, the self-confidence sliding off his face.

'A Halzig,' Norrd says. 'I take it that wasn't what you were expecting?'

Ronin attempts a nonchalant shrug and fails dismally.

'Ice goblin,' Norrd says to me. 'Not indigenous to South Africa. I imported him from Greenland to fight and I've never had one second of buyer's remorse.'

'I take it this isn't a good thing?' I whisper to Ronin.

'Let's just say the Halzig are particularly adept at chain battle,' he replies.

'Looks like you haven't been cured of making stupid decisions.'

'You can't be cured of that,' Ronin says. 'You can only go into remission.'

'Don't do this …' I say.

'Listen, there's no getting out of it now.' He puts a hand on my shoulder. 'Watching humans die is a favourite goblin pastime.'

'Why's it always like this with you?' I ask.

'Like I've said before, I'm just a fun, dance-like-nobody-is-watching kinda guy,' he says with a grin.

'Try not to fucking die,' I tell him.

The Halzig's huge left arm is chained to the pole and it suddenly gains a sense of clarity and purpose, looking around for its victim with a murderous snarl.

Ronin, in a black vest and camo fatigues, rolls his shoulders and stretches his neck, then ties his long red hair back into a ponytail. He takes a packet of cigarettes from his pocket as the goblins chain his left arm to the pole.

'Smoke?' he offers, holding the packet out to the Halzig.

It gives a short howl and lunges at him. Ronin spins out of the way and entangles it in the chain long enough to light his smoke.

'I know, I know, lung cancer,' he says, pulling on the chain and trying to drag the Halzig's arm into a nest of razor wire.

But the Halzig hasn't even begun yet. Its animal rage transforms into a cold, lethal cunning. It methodically frees itself from the chain and begins to stalk Ronin around the pole.

Ronin keeps up his usual dumb banter, but I can see the sweat beginning to drip down his face as his attempts to avoid the giant goblin become more and more desperate. He stumbles and it catches him with a long arm and effortlessly slams him into the ground, wrapping the chain around his foot and reeling him in like a fish on a line. With a last brutal yank it drags him into reach and begins to pound on him with its sledgehammer fists.

'Ground and pound' doesn't even begin to describe the Halzig's fighting technique. Ronin covers up valiantly and manages to squirm out of the way like a cockroach from beneath a slipper. He's gasping for air and bleeding from a gash on his cheek. He looks across at me and spits a mouthful of blood on to the floor. I give him an optimistic thumbs-up.

He picks up his cigarette, puts it between his bloody lips and drags himself to his feet.

'Bravo,' Norrd says, with a sarcastic little clap. 'You're giving it one hundred and ten per cent, which is the most important thing.'

Ronin grabs the chain, wraps part of it around his fist and forearm and runs straight at the ice goblin. He hits it with a series of percussive punches to the ribs and then vaults up on to it, using its knees as stepladders. It roars as he punches it viciously in the face with his chain-wrapped fist but grabs him around the neck and holds him suspended in the air. He struggles against the clawed hand at his throat and his face turns from white to red to purple in a matter of seconds.

'Disappointing,' Norrd says, looking at his nails.

I start preparing myself to make a run for it but then notice Ronin's right arm. He's surreptitiously wrapping the chain around the Halzig's lower limbs. His body is slumping but he manages to swing his feet up and put his whole weight on to the chain.

He slips from the Halzig's grasp and pulls the chain as he falls, dragging the Halzig down with him. They hit the ground and Ronin scrambles across the goblin's chest, wrenches its head backwards and slams his boot into it with a satisfying crunch. Without pausing, he drags the Halzig towards the pole, positions its head against a spike, reconsiders and adjusts the angle, then boots the head into the spike. There's a wet crunch as it punches through, coming out just beneath the left eye.

Ronin drags the body across to Norrd like a dog proudly displaying a pigeon carcass. 'Leave Ed alone,' he says, jabbing towards Norrd with a finger.

The goblins in the tracksuits are suddenly wielding AK-47s.

'Do you know how much that Halzig cost me?' Norrd screeches.

'Surely can't be more than your weekly anal bleaching,' Ronin says, wiping blood out of his eyes.

'The Bone Kraal is coming for you, human. It's coming for all of you,' Norrd screams.

'Really? Brilliant. Then please sign me up for your human genocide newsletter. My email address is Ronin-at-go-fuck-yourself-dot-com.'

He staggers towards me and puts an arm around my

shoulders. He's bleeding from the gash in his head and dragging one of his legs.

'Let's get the hell out of here, sparky.'

The goblins watch us with narrow, menacing eyes as we make the painfully slow shuffle up the walkway to the elevator and out of the goblin lair.

'You drive,' Ronin says, fumbling for the keys as we reach the Cortina. I start the car just as he passes out in the passenger seat.

'Ask for Dr Munro,' Ronin says, his eyes popping open the moment we stop outside the emergency room. I help him through the entrance and we collapse on the uncomfortable plastic chairs next to a guy holding part of his face on with a cloth, and a woman missing a finger. I give her an empathetic nod.

An old doctor with wild brown hair, a series of deep ugly facial scars, and a T-shirt with a cat on a trampoline beneath his white coat turns the corner, takes one look at Ronin and rolls his eyes.

'Schoolgirls beat you up again?'

'That was once!' Ronin says, wincing. 'And they *were* possessed by demonic forces.'

'Right, "possessed".' Munro smiles. 'Come on, let's sew the worst of that up.'

'You're a gent, Doc,' Ronin says.

While I wait, I get a Coke from the vending machine and slouch against the wall watching the various casualties hobble by and trying to guess their origins. It's while I'm trying to figure out how a guy managed to jam a corkscrew into *that* part of his body that I casually look through a window and see Anwar staring sullenly at an episode of *Days of Our Lives* on a flickering TV.

Seeing my arch-nemesis is, like, emotionally challenging and I need to take a moment to process it:

CrowBax:	Could probably still take him out with an overdose. It'll look like an accident.
SienerBax:	You're ridiculous. We saved him. Besides, we're being good from now on, remember. Remember?
CrowBax:	I don't remember having an equal say in that.
SienerBax:	Be good. For Esmé.
CrowBax:	OK, fine. But we don't have to go see him, right?

I walk in through the ward door trying to look nonchalant. Anwar is lying on a bed looking bored, but when his eyes land on me they narrow into daggers of pure malice.

'Zevcenko,' he spits.

'So nice to see you,' I say through gritted teeth.

'Yeah, I bet.'

'I thought you were OK?' I say.

He lifts his pyjama top and shows me the nasty scar on his abdomen.

'The stabbing caused complications. I have to have a colostomy bag.'

'I bet chicks dig it,' I say before I can stop myself.

'Fuck you,' he hisses.

'Yeah, well, just don't forget who saved your life. I could have left you there to marinate in your own bodily fluids.'

'Knowing that hurts more than any of the tubes they've shoved into my orifices.'

'Well, I'm not particularly fond of the decision either,' I say.

We stare at each other in hostile silence.

'What are you into, Zevcenko?' Anwar says eventually.

'What do you mean?'

'I'm trying to figure it out, man,' he says as he jabs the button next to him to lever his bed into a more upright position. 'You give up your porn for a bunch of guns. I thought you were going to use them to secure some kind of new territory, but I don't hear anything further about it. It's like they've just disappeared.'

'They have,' I say. 'I no longer have them.'

'You sold them? I could have found you a buyer if that's what you were after.'

'Traded them,' I say. 'And what I wanted you couldn't get.'

'Hmmm. I always knew you were into some dark shit, Zevcenko. Let me in on it and I'll leave your little flunkies alone.'

'The Spider has disbanded. Kyle, Zikhona and the Kid are all NPCs now. They don't figure in the game any more.'

He laughs. 'I think I'll decide that.'

'Listen,' I say. 'It's over. We're finished. High school isn't like the Mafia.'

'You're really going to stand here and say something like that to me? Did we even go to the same school? It's almost like you're a different person.'

'Just leave them alone,' I say.

'Or what?'

I could jam my thumb into his wound. Twist until he agrees. I could drop an anonymous note to the cops about Central and the guns that Anwar had there.

'Or nothing. I'm just asking you.'

'This whole "nice" thing is wearing really fucking thin, Zevcenko. What's your scheme, what's your angle?'

'No angle,' I say.

He laughs. 'Then you're a fucking idiot.'

For the first time in my life, I think I might actually agree with him.

'He has no internal injuries,' Dr Munro says to me when I find them.

'Forty-seven stitches,' Ronin groans as he stands up, touching the seam that holds his cheek together. 'Not even close to my top score.'

Munro sighs. 'When I first agreed to help you, I was under the impression that my involvement would be of the now-and-again variety.'

'You agreed to help me because you were being hunted by a Kholomodumo. I still have its skull somewhere if you need reminding.'

Munro touches the deep tracks that have been gouged into his face. 'No,' he says. 'I don't need any reminding.'

'Painkillers, then,' Ronin says with a satisfied smile. 'And no skimping. I want the good stuff. I know what cheapskates you doctors are.'

Munro sighs and scrawls him a prescription.

'See you soon, Doc.' Ronin pats Munro on the back and stuffs the prescription into his trench coat.

'One day it's going to catch up with you,' says Munro, shaking his head.

'Not if I keep running fast enough, Doc,' Ronin replies with a grin.

We pick up Ronin's medication at the dispensary and then I help him to stumble through the parking lot to the Cortina. By the time we're on the highway, he's crushed some of his pain pills into a joint and is on a slurry, happy buzz that's immune to pain.

'This quitting alcohol is such a cinch, sparky,' he says. 'All you have to do is just stop. BAM! You don't need any of this twelve-step bullshit.'

'It's been half a day, and you're high.'

'You're undermining my self-esteem,' Ronin says, lying back in the passenger seat and closing his eyes. 'Now put on some Moondog.'

I rummage through his cassettes, keeping one hand on the

wheel. Moondog is Ronin's favourite when he's high, but it annoys the hell out of me. I slam a cassette into the tape player and then try to grab the joint out of Ronin's hand. Without opening his eyes, he pulls it out of reach. I sigh and let the music's orchestral madness envelop me.

PLATFORM AGNOSTIC

I get home to find my brother Rafe sitting on the stairs reading another South African history book. At this point I think there's probably more South African history in Rafe's brain than in any library. They should make my red-haired weirdo brother a national monument.

Rafe is possibly the biggest surprise this whole mess has produced. Far from being the intellectually challenged older brother I thought I had, he exists on a whole other level of Siener mystic power. Where I see visions, he lives in an inner world of wisdom and insight. And what he lacks in conversational ability he makes up for in know-it-allness.

Still, it's good knowing there is someone else whose genetic make-up is as screwed up as mine. I still wish I could talk to Grandpa Zev, though. Just to tell him he was right about giant Crows and to chat some of this stuff through. Rafe isn't exactly the biggest talker.

'Hey,' I say.

He looks up and hits me with the knowing eye. I used to think he looked at me with the knowing eye to annoy me. Now I know he does it to annoy me *and* because he also has Siener abilities.

'Whoa, whoa, give me a chance,' I say, holding up my hands. 'Let me get a word in here, buddy.'

He just stares. Then he puts the book down on the stairs and gets up and opens the door that leads into the garage. He turns to look at me and I sigh. 'OK, Lassie. Where are we going this time?'

My folks are out on a date night, which means an art movie, dinner at the same restaurant they always go to and lots of red wine, so we grab our bikes and head out. In the past I would have mocked Rafe and possibly tried to lock him in a closet. But now I just follow. However much it absolutely grates to admit it, on a certain unknown metaphysical level he's much smarter than I am.

I follow his bike light through the winding back roads of our neighbourhood. The night is cool and dark and there's an eerie mist hanging low over the houses, but I've long since stopped worrying about eerie ambience. The real shit that's out there can kill you just as easily in broad daylight.

I know where we're going before we get there; I can feel the tug of the canal way before I see it. I've tried to avoid it as much as possible lately. There's a strange power in it that pulls at the eye in my forehead, the only part of suburbia that does that, and I'd rather not have anything further exacerbating my mental issues. I can teeter unsteadily on the brink of reality quite fine by myself, thank you very much.

We reach the damp grass surrounding the canal and Rafe throws his bike down. I do the same and follow him into a little hollow of warped and twisted trees. A bed of cardboard boxes has been made up next to a rock and an old rusting chain-link fence.

'You bring me to the nicest places,' I murmur as Rafe sits down in the dank hollow.

I grab a seat next to him and wait for a couple of moments in silence.

'I'm really surprised this didn't make it on to the "Twenty

Things You Have to Do in Cape Town", I say as I catch a whiff of urine from somewhere downriver.

Shut up.

The voice rings clearly in my head like I'm wearing invisible DJ-level, noise-cancelling headphones. I'm so startled that I sort of half stand up, get my foot caught underneath me and topple over into some reeds.

Now who's the retard?

'Rafe?' I say, pushing myself quickly on to my haunches. 'Who the fuck was that?'

He looks at me with a tiny flicker of amusement twitching at his lips.

Who do you think it was, dum-dum?

OK. I know crazy stuff is possible, but I'd sorta drawn a line under it. Creatures? Fine. Ritual magic? OK, I can manage that. Far sight? Not cool, but I guess I'm just going to have to find a way to deal with it. But this far and no further. Telepathy? Come on!

I thought you'd be a little more adult about this.

'Fuck,' I say, running my hands through my hair and then readjusting my glasses and breathing deeply. 'OK, OK. You're telepathic. Please explain this little quirk.'

It's just something I've learnt to do. You can probably do it too.

'I doubt it.'

Try.

He stares at me like he's asking me to tie my shoelaces.

'OK,' I say.

I concentrate really hard on saying something to his mind with mine. Nothing.

This is a Crow thing, not a Siener thing. So you have to open up that part of yourself. It helps if you use your fingers, too.

He twines his fingers together in a weird configuration and

I copy him. My mind begins to throb and twist. Shapes swirl in front of my eyes. I gape as a tiny glowing bridge unfolds from my third eye. It stretches across the gap between us and locks on to Rafe's forehead.

My mind explodes with a rush of foreign memories and sensations. I recognise a lot of them because I have a corresponding set. They're Rafe's memories. I watch a rapid-fire tour of what a dick I've been to him since we were kids. There's me blaming him for stealing from my dad's booze cabinet. There's me almost drowning him in the pool. Yep, there's me taking credit for a picture he drew when he was five.

You really are an asshole.

'Thanks,' I say.

He shakes his head. *Try to speak to me with your mind.*

I concentrate really hard. I picture the words marching across that little bridge like toy soldiers.

Ummmerggaaaa.

'How was that?' I ask.

You sound like that time when you fell and landed with your groin on the crossbar of your bike.

'Thanks.'

You'll get there. Keep your chin up, kiddo.

'Screw you,' I say with a laugh.

There are different parts of all of us.

'Oh, I know all about that.'

He snorts.

You've only just scratched the surface. There's a whole geography in your head that you'll have to explore.

'I can't wait,' I say, and wonder yet again how I could have underestimated my brother for all these years.

* * *

The next day Kyle comes round to help me pack for Hexpoort. Kyle is having a tough time of it all. The end of the Spider has resulted in a kind of crisis for him. He really doesn't know what to do with himself and I'm at a loss as to how to help him. He's been researching supernatural stuff non-stop since he found out it was real. It has become really annoying.

'It just seems strange that the Hidden STAY hidden,' he says, sitting in front of my laptop. 'I mean, it's a fairly major thing. Other creatures live among us. Magic exists. Keeping it secret is undemocratic.'

'All those conspiracy websites and fringe magazines are actually creating a layer of noise,' I tell him. 'The Hidden stay hidden because they're hidden in plain view. That's what Ronin says, at least.'

'This Bone Kraal you were telling me about,' he says. 'I found a video on their YouTube account.'

'THE REVENGE OF THE DOWNTRODDEN,' intones one of those robotic computer voices. 'WE CANNOT STAND BY WHILE THE HIDDEN ARE OPPRESSED ...'

I hit the space bar. 'OK, I think we get it.'

'A secret revolutionary organisation fighting against the system,' Kyle says. 'You think they'd let you join?'

'Goblins tried to pull the teeth from my skull and then decapitate me for them. So no, I don't think they'd let me join. You're forgetting I'm going to Hexpoort and training to *be* the system.'

'Oh yeah,' Kyle says. 'That kinda sucks.'

I've started packing my stuff into a pair of battered borrowed suitcases. I consider taking some of my book collection but then realise that it's no longer really appropriate to my new life path. Ayn Rand, Niccolò Machiavelli, Sun Tzu. None of them have much to say about the value of listening to your inner good guy.

I put the books back on to the shelf. I take my school books. This is what I need to be reading now. I look through them. *The Essence of Magic*. Some of it makes sense in an abstract sort of way. Some of it is complete gibberish.

'You're going to tell me what you learn at this Poort place, though, right?' Kyle says.

'I'm going to do even better. I'm going to write you regular emails describing the stuff I find out.'

Harold is right: maybe focusing on writing about this magical stuff will be a new hobby for me. It'll help me purge my urge to tickle the strings of strategy and caress the keys of corruption. It's like I've been involved in a major car accident and I'm learning to walk again.

Kyle nods. 'That's good. Because I'm probably magic too. I mean, I've always been a late developer; my voice only broke like six months ago. I'm probably heir to this incredible magical lineage too.'

'Yeah,' I say, and try to sound as neutral as possible.

He looks up from the laptop. 'You don't believe that?'

'I do, I do,' I say. 'I just … you know … I don't really know how this stuff works and I don't want you getting your hopes up …'

He stands up. 'It's always like this, Bax. You never believe I can do anything.' He has that hurt expression he gets that makes him look like an oversized puppy.

'It's not always like that.'

I know what to say but it would be manipulative, so it's the wrong thing to do.

'I'll speak to them about getting you into Hexpoort,' I say. 'I'm pretty sure all you need is a little bump and your magical ability will sprout like your late-forming pubes.'

'Really?' His face brightens so much that I just nod and smile. 'Thanks, Bax,' he says.

When he leaves two hours later, I sit in my room and feel guilty. I've lied to my best friend. I have no intention of speaking to anyone at Hexpoort about him. It's the old keep-on-putting-it-off-and-get-him-to-focus-on-something-else strategy. I've used it a thousand times. This is the only time I've ever felt bad about it.

CrowBax:	All communication is persuasive. We just happen to be good at it.
SienerBax:	We agreed. We're going to try to treat people fairly. We're not going to exploit weaknesses.
CrowBax:	Just cut off my fucking hand. I'm already missing a finger, just take the whole thing. Please. Take an eye, take a kidney, but please don't take my beautiful manipulations …

I've fallen off the wagon already. I've manipulated Kyle and I hate myself for it. I realise it's not just the big manipulations I have to stop. It's the small ones too. I have to go completely cold turkey. I have to end this bullshit.

The depression leech is sucking all the happy juices out of my brain, so I shove some more clothes into a bag and then stomp downstairs to get a coffee.

My mother is in the kitchen, playing a game on her phone. She swears and paws viciously at the screen. 'Fucking cocksucking aliens,' she shouts. My mom can swear like a sailor when she gets riled up.

'Hey, Mom,' I say and turn the kettle on. 'I thought games turned you into a psycho?' It's one of her theories. My mother is convinced that me dealing porn is either down to a vaccination I had as a kid, the gluten in my food, or video games. She's not sure which, but definitely one of those.

'Baxter! Sorry, was just replying to an email.' She places her phone face down on the counter.

'Right,' I say.

'What you been doing?' she asks, patting the stool next to her. 'Spending time with Rafe, I hope. He's been really anti-social lately. I wish he wouldn't spend so much time reading his history book and living in his head.'

'Getting school books,' I say, dutifully sitting down. 'And yeah, I've spent some time with Rafe.'

'Good. This is a second chance for you. You don't have to do things like you did at Westridge, you know? There's no shame in trying to change, trying to be good.' She's right, I guess. Unfortunately there's no money, power or prestige either.

My inner change is not the only shifting of paradigms that has happened in our house. My mother used to think I was a normal teenager. But the kind of things she's seen and heard since I was busted have convinced her otherwise. Unfortunately there is nothing in glossy magazines entitled 'So your son is a maimed porn dealer with mental issues? Our experts weigh in.'

'I know things haven't always been easy for you,' she starts.

'Wait, Mom,' I say. I know she wants to understand, to probe the depths of my dysfunction to understand where she went wrong, but I just can't handle it today. 'Our family household income means we're in the top two per cent of the world's population. I was enrolled in one of the top schools in South Africa, which offered an education on a par with the best in the world. I've never wanted for anything. I didn't deal porn because I was repressing some deep psychological issues to do with Rafe. I didn't do it because there was anything wrong. I did it because I wanted to do it, because I chose to do it. And it may have been ethically unsound, antisocial and bordering on the sociopathic, but it was mine, OK? It was mine.'

It's not what my mom wants to hear. Her face crinkles into a mixture of disgust, fear and disappointment. Disfearpointment is an ugly beast that latches on and tugs at her eyebrows and lips. Having your parents experience an overwhelming feeling of disappointment and revulsion at the monster you've become is a really unpleasant thing, no matter how cool you think you are. Trust me.

'And now?' is all she manages to croak.

'Now I'm trying to be better,' I say.

She nods. 'Are you ready for tomorrow?'

I shrug.

'Oh Baxter,' she says, pulling me into a hug that squashes my face against her cheek. 'You really are a strange child. I suppose I always knew that.'

'Thanks, Mom,' I murmur into her neck. 'I think.'

My dad is no longer unemployed. He has recently landed a job as a viral brand activation specialist at an agency, so when he pops his head into my room later, he has swapped his dressing gown for chinos and a loud shirt.

'How's work?' I say.

'Don't ask.' He sighs and sits down on my bed. 'I organised a synchronised twerking flash mob for a car insurance company. But only four of the twerkers showed up and I had to fill in so that I didn't look like an idiot in front of the client.'

I laugh. 'And how'd that work out?'

He sighs again. 'Well, it went viral. But not the way we wanted.'

I laugh and he takes this as his cue to start on why he's really in my room.

'Listen, Bax,' he says.

My dad has never been the most communicative. He hasn't really hit any of the major teenage milestones, so now he tries to get the sex talk, the drug talk, and the you-shouldn't-deal-porn-and-do-whatever-you-did-to-lose-a-finger talk all done in one go.

'When you reach a certain age, you want to experiment;

that's natural.' I know I'm going to have to stop him, but part of me is kinda interested to see where he's going to go with this. 'You kids are bombarded with so many images these days, it's understandable that you'd have some strange ideas about the way the world works.' That's right, Dad, all that inter-dimensional mantis reality TV has really screwed me up.

'It's OK, Dad,' I say. 'Now that Grandpa Zev is gone, it's up to me to be the lizard-tongued, devil-horned black sheep of the family.'

He smiles at that. 'You and he are very alike.'

'Genetics is a bitch,' I say.

'No matter what trouble you get into, you can always tell us,' he says, and then gives me an awkward shoulder hug.

I really wish that were true, Dad.

He's about to launch into another little monologue when Esmé climbs up the side of the house and wriggles through my window. She's wearing a black leather jacket, a weird stoner rock T-shirt, a black beanie, black leggings and bright green boots. My dad nods at her and adopts the cool, hip-and-happening dad persona he uses on all my friends. I've long since stopped being embarrassed by it.

'You're welcome to use the door, Esmé,' he says.

'Thanks, Mr Zee,' she replies through a mouthful of gum.

'Well, I'll leave you two alone. And I won't tell your mother.'

'You're always so cool, Mr Zee,' Esmé says.

'Well …' My dad adjusts his shirt. 'Working in the media industry I—'

'Thanks, Dad,' I say.

He nods and closes the door behind him.

'Hey, magic boy,' Esmé says, flopping down on to my bed.

'Hey. Where you been lately?'

'Oh, I was just hanging out with my friend Troy.'

'Troy?' I say, and wince as a couple of rounds of armour-piercing jealousy are fired into my chest.

'Aww, are you jealous? Cute. He's just a friend, dummy.'

'I'm not jealous,' I say with a sneer.

'Good. Ready for your big day at special school?'

'I prefer "differently gifted",' I say with a laugh.

'Oh, you're different all right. So they're going to teach you how to be a sangoma and shit?'

'I have no idea what they're going to teach me. I'm just going to keep my head down, graduate, have my criminal record cleared and then get the hell away from this supernatural shit for ever.'

'Once you go quack, you never go back,' she says, popping another stick of gum into her mouth.

'Cute.' I lie down next to her. 'How was your day?'

'Someone called me a manic pixie dream girl at school,' she says.

'What did you do?'

'Put her in a headlock and carved "I heart Zooey Deschanel" into her arm with a compass.'

'Nice,' I say.

'I thought so.'

We share a set of headphones and she runs her fingers up and down my arm as we listen to some of the tracks that are in the centre of our musical-taste Venn diagram.

'Did you really believe you were a murderer? That all this shit wasn't real?' she says.

'It seemed pretty believable at the time.'

'And now?'

'No.'

'Really?'

'OK. I don't know. It's weird. I still have moments where I think my life is just made up. Like everything I know is just an illusion.'

'I think everyone has that sometimes, don't they?'

'Yeah, maybe. I'm going to miss you,' I say.

'Me too, magic boy,' she says and leans across to kiss me.

The next morning I get up and pack the last of my stuff. I sit on each of the cases in turn, jiggling their zips and bouncing up and down until they're mostly closed. I start to drag them out of my room, but Rafe stands in the doorway clutching a notebook. His new thing is to wear an orange onesie around the house, which, combined with his wild red hair, makes him look like some kind of demented flaming Pokémon.

'What's up?' I ask.

He shrugs.

'I'm going to miss you. But we'll still talk, OK?' I say.

He scribbles something furiously in his notebook and hands it to me.

In your dreams, it says.

I laugh. 'Asshole.' I give him a hug, which he squirms and wriggles to avoid.

My parents help me carry my bags to the platform. Kyle, Zikhona and the Inhalant Kid are slouching against a pillar waiting for me. Zikhona grabs me and squashes me against her gold bomber jacket. She smells of bubblegum and expensive perfume. I get Kyle and the Inhalant Kid in a group hug that smells of cigarettes, glue and the horrible pheromone deodorant that Kyle bought off the Internet (months later and he swears it's on the brink of actually working).

Kyle sniffles a bit, and I see tears in his eyes.

'I can't believe you're going to magic school,' he says. 'I should be going too.'

'I know,' I say. 'I wish you could.'

'Remember what you promised.'

I feel the guilt throb in my chest.

'I remember,' I say.

'What are we supposed to do during term time?' the Inhalant Kid asks. 'I can't just do schoolwork. I'll go crazy.'

I stand in front of them and give my last speech as head of the brief, beautiful organisation that was the Spider.

'The Spider is gone,' I say seriously. 'You have to stay out of school politics completely or Anwar will crush you.'

Zikhona pounds her fist in her palm. 'Let the fucker try.'

'I mean it. It's the end of an era. I'm trying to be a better person. I suggest you do the same.'

It crushes me the way they look at me. It's like I've reneged on every promise I've ever made. I want to throw stones at them and tell them to 'git'.

'We'll miss you, Bax,' says Kyle.

A terrible lonely feeling descends as I walk away from them, my coven of freaks.

'Do you want us to wait with you?' asks my dad, putting a hand on my shoulder.

'No,' I say. 'It's OK.'

I hug them both and wave and smile as they leave. My mom turns back and fixes me with a look. The meaning is understood: *You promised to be good, Baxter.* I give her a little nod.

I sit down on my cases to wait for the train. I'm preparing myself to belly-flop into a pool of self-pity when a commotion at the far end of the platform interrupts me. A familiar red-bearded shape blunders through the crowd muttering like a madman.

His face is purple around the ugly line of stitches that hold it together. He has his coat clutched about him and he's shivering uncontrollably. He sways, stumbles into a pillar, holds on to it like it's a life raft in stormy seas, and then pushes off and careens towards me.

He collapses on the platform next to me and gives me a thumbs-up. 'Found you,' he mutters.

'You don't look so good,' I tell him. Which is saying a lot considering his appearance is always on a sliding scale from escaped psycho to homeless Viking.

'I need a drink,' he says and lies back on the concrete, his fingers twined in his hair like he's holding the top of his head on.

'I thought you had it beat?' I say a little smugly.

'Almost there.' He smiles wanly.

'Uh-uh.'

'Positive thinking, that's what Dr Femowaqui says in the book. My new self is blossoming like a thousand-petalled lotus.' He is consumed by a racking cough and spits out an oozing wad of black phlegm on to the concrete.

'Yeah, you're blossoming all right,' I say, turning away with a grimace.

'So, you ready for the Poort?' he asks.

'I don't know. Any words of wisdom about your alma mater?'

Even through the alcohol jitters I can see the grimace on his face.

'You need to play the game, build alliances, be savvy, be smart,' he wheezes.

'Well, I'm done with that,' I say.

He laughs and it turns into another round of coughing. 'The problem with you, sparky, is that you always do the wrong thing at the wrong time. You're an asshole when you need to be an angel and an angel when you need to be an asshole.'

'Thanks, Deepak,' I say. 'But this is what I'm doing now.'

He nods. 'One thing I can say about you is that yours is a type of stupidity that I can respect. My only advice is to try and not get fucked up too badly.'

'Thanks,' I say.

Ronin waits with me for a few minutes and then slaps me on the back and stumbles away, sweating like a marathon runner. I'm placing imaginary wagers on how long he'll stay on the wagon when my train arrives.

It's old, rusted and completely trashed, covered in peeling black paint with a thick line of dirty pink down the centre.

I sigh and stand up. A guy my age jogs across the platform towards me. His head is shaved, he has full-sleeve Japanese tattoos on both arms, and he's wearing camo shorts. He's good-looking, except for a crescent-moon scar beneath his left eye.

'Hi, I'm Hekka,' he says. He gives me a warm smile but there's something about him that makes me wary. Easy now, Baxter. You're suspicious of everybody. This guy is just trying to be friendly.

'Hi,' I reply. 'Baxter.'

'Baxter Zevcenko?' he says.

'Um, yeah. How did you …'

'You're a hero, man. Well, I mean, kinda. I heard about Basson.'

'Well, that wasn't only—'

'Are you kidding? That's some heroic shit right there.' He extends his hand. 'I just want to thank you for saving the world.'

I take his hand and shake. I was completely wrong about this guy. He's actually quite cool.

'Wow,' I say. 'Well, that's … I mean, no problem.'

'Always good to meet new people. It can be hard here. Particularly for us …' He touches the scar under his eye.

'Us?'

'Heroes, man,' he says. 'I'm prophesied to be the Chosen One, so I know how it goes. The pressure, am I right?'

'Yeah, I guess …'

'I mean, my parents were both killed in sinister circumstances when I was little. That forges character, right?'

'Shit. I'm sorry,' I say. 'But I wouldn't know. My parents are both still fine. My dad's into viral marketing, so I suppose that's something …'

He raises his eyebrows. 'Your parents are both fine? Well, that sucks for you. But I guess we all have our life-defining challenges.'

'All Hexpoort students please board the train,' a smoothly robotic voice announces.

I grab my cases.

'So what's the deal?' I say. 'Do we just get on the train?'

Hekka drops his voice. 'I know you're new, but you must be somewhat acquainted with … you know …'

'Magic?' I say.

'Uh-uh.' He smiles.

'A little,' I say.

He points to a pillar. 'In order to get to the registration desk, you need to run at that pillar.'

'You're kidding me.'

He laughs and puts a hand on my shoulder. 'I know, I know. Lame, isn't it? It's just a stupid little gimmick that they use to impress new students. There's a lot of stuff they just blatantly copy from books and movies. If I'm honest about it, they're really not very creative.'

'So it's kinda like the veil around the Freak Quarter?' I look at the pillar.

He clicks and points a finger at me. 'Exactly, man. Just run at it,' he says with a smile. 'Trust me.'

Alarms are going off in my head. *Look at the way he's leaning in*, a part of my mind screams. *He's too enthusiastic. He's not just casually giving you information.* I suppress it viciously, like a riot cop pepper-spraying a crowd. 'Sometimes you've got to trust people, Baxter,' I whisper under my breath.

I hold a case in each hand and begin to run. The pillar grows in my vision.

'Faster,' Hekka shouts from behind me. 'It won't work unless it's fast.'

I pick up speed and hurtle towards the pillar, the wheels of the cases thunking on the concrete.

It's at the last moment that I consciously realise what I've known all along. But by then it's too late. I slam into the pillar, ricochet off at an angle, trip over my own feet and fall hard on to the platform.

Laughter explodes from Hekka and a group of cronies who have gathered around him. He saunters over and leans down next to my ear. 'I'm the hero at Hexpoort, Zevcenko,' he says. 'You're a fucking Crow. Did you really think you were going to waltz in here and take over?'

I lie there on the concrete, breathing hard.

CrowBax: Get up! Gouge his fucking eyes out!
SienerBax: You promised. Remember that. You promised.

A figure looms over me and I ball my fists up involuntarily. But it grips my arm and pulls me to my feet.

'Don't worry. Those fuckwits got me with that last term.'

'Thanks,' I say and look at him.

He's a young black guy in a trilby, tweed suit and bow tie, with a fat set of headphones around his neck. There's a restless energy about him that seems familiar. He bounces on his heels as he helps me up. I look over to where Hekka is re-enacting my stupidity, miming hitting the pillar and falling backwards in slow-mo.

'I'm Nom, by the way,' he says and we bump fists. He hands me a card. It features a URL and an illustration of a goat wearing Ray-Bans. 'My street-style blog,' he says.

'And that douche over there is Hekka Jones,' he adds darkly. 'Total asshole.'

'Yeah, I think I picked that up.'

'He thinks he's some big shot because there's a prophecy about him being the Chosen One or some shit. Walks around the school pretending to be all conflicted about his destiny. It's so fucking pretentious it makes me want to throw up.'

'The Chosen One, like for real?'

Nom shrugs. 'Fuck knows. It's all a little vague. Crescent scar, dead parents, born during a certain moon or something.'

'Couldn't happen to a nicer guy,' I say.

'Come on,' Nom says. 'We better get on the train.'

The inside of the train is covered from floor to ceiling in graffiti; generations of Hexpoort students making their mark.

I go to sit down in the first carriage but Nom grabs my arm. 'Nooo, kemosabe,' he says. 'That carriage is Pondscum's.'

'And Pondscum is ...?'

'You don't know about the clans?'

I shake my head.

'Shit, dude, you don't know anything. There are three clans: Pondscum, Broken Teeth and Carrion,' he says as he leads me to the back of the train.

'Wow, very pleasant.'

'Yeah, well, when we get to the Poort, you'll see they're kinda appropriate.'

'Which one are you?'

He lifts his sleeve and shows me a hideous tattoo of a mouth full of smashed teeth on his forearm. 'Broken Teeth for life,' he says, tapping his chest with his fist.

'So you're like the good guys?'

He snorts. 'Hell, no. We're all as bad as each other. All the clans are plentifully supplied with assholes of the highest order, though I'll admit that Hekka being Pondscum does lift their average. Carrion control most of the porn, we have the best alcohol and drugs and Pondscum are like the enforcers.'

He looks at my face and frowns. 'What's the matter?'

'Just a sickening sense of déjà vu,' I say.

He shrugs. 'What did you expect? It *is* high school.'

We find a seat at the back of the train. I slump down on a seat that has been slashed with a knife but Nom can't keep still. He gets up and looks out the window, then sits down again, all the time keeping up an incessant stream of talking that I am forced to just let wash over me.

'You're pretty ... high-energy,' I say eventually.

'Hey, I'm an orphan raised by the bok-people in the Transkei. I can't help it,' he replies with a grin.

'Bok-people, really? Do you know Klipspringer?'

'Oh yeah, sure,' he says. 'All us bok-people know each other.'

'No, it's just—'

'Just kidding, man.' He taps me on the shoulder. 'Relax, relax.'

'So that must have been interesting,' I say. 'Growing up like that.'

'What can I say? I'm the Xhosa Pan.' He gives another huge grin. 'It was like with any other family, it just kinda felt normal, you know. I'm glad, though. I learnt their animal communication magic.'

I laugh. 'Animal communication? That's almost as bad as my stupid abilities.'

Nom shrugs. 'I like it. Look.' He points to a cockroach that is scuttling across the carriage floor and then widens his mouth and emits a soft modulated hissing sound.

The cockroach stops in the middle of the floor and hisses back.

Nom hisses a couple more times and then the cockroach scuttles off beneath one of the bunks.

'Interesting chap,' Nom says. 'Quite philosophical, actually. Most cockroaches are. Something about their—'

He's interrupted by a small kid with long grey hair pulled back into a ponytail. He's clutching a hessian sack, and two white rats scurry across his shoulders and head like they're on a racetrack.

'What's up, Stevo?' Nom asks.

'Lotsa junkies in the batch of newbies,' Stevo says. 'It's going to be a profitable term.'

'Speaking of newbies, this is Baxter. Baxter, this is Stevo, Broken Teeth's chemist.'

'Pleasure,' the kid says. 'Oh, and these two are Hunter and Timothy.' He stretches out his hand and the rats scurry on to it. Their eyes are huge and dark and they stare at me with extreme intensity. He holds out two tiny pieces of paper with the other hand and the rats bolt down his arm to chew on them. 'They've been taking psychedelics since birth. They get a bit pissy if they don't have their daily trip.'

'You talk to them?' I ask Nom.

Nom rolls his eyes. 'I try not to. Always going on about mind expansion and the Buddha and shit. It's tiring.'

Stevo looks at me and holds up the hessian sack. 'What about you, newbie? I got hooch, I got dope, I got the best mushrooms you'll ever have. What's your poison?'

'I'm OK,' I say.

'C'mon,' Nom says. 'Have a drink with us to celebrate your first day. Give us some Runeshine, Stevo.'

Stevo reaches into his sack and pulls out a dirty bottle filled with a clear liquid. He balances two plastic cups on the seat and pours us each a shot.

'To new things!' Nom says and holds up his cup.

I grab the other and pour the liquid into my mouth. It hits the back of my throat like the flame from a propane torch and I begin to splutter. 'Holy shit,' I cough, but instantly a pleasant feeling settles over me.

'It's good, am I right?' Nom says with a grin.

'Yeah.' I mirror his grin. 'You're right.'

Stevo sits down next to us, Timothy and Hunter on each of his shoulders like gargoyles. They look like they're staring through the window at the secrets of the universe.

'So … what happened to your hair?' I ask. 'Was it always like that?'

'Magic happened,' he says. 'I tried a spell to make a marijuana plant grow to four times its natural size. Good idea, but I was punching way above my weight magically and I totally overextended myself. Well, the plant exploded into a fiery ball and I went instantly George Clooney.'

'Wow,' I say.

'Still, it could have been worse.' Stevo shrugs.

'How?' asks Nom. 'You look like an old man. How could it possibly have been worse?'

'I was originally going to use it as a dick enlargement spell,' Stevo says with a grin.

The train starts purring, proceeds to screeching and then shudders violently as it pulls away from the station. Cape Town begins to jog by outside, slowly at first, then rushing by all at once. I lie back on the seat and watch the colours of the city – ash, brown, silver and white – give way to a blurred palette of wheat, viridian, rust, ash and vivid blue. The smells change from oil and cars, underscored by the scent of the sea, to dry earth, brush and manure.

The Runeshine settles like warm sand in my brain and I begin to drift in and out of consciousness to the metronome clacking of the train on the tracks. I feel the familiar throb in my forehead. I'm starting to be able to distinguish the various sensations that spew from my third eye like bilge water during times like these. Sometimes it's just a sensation of the vast emptiness that lies beneath everything, the empty screen on which the icons of life glow and blink reassuringly. At other times it's like my nervous system is a tree of lights and I can watch the electrical impulses complete their circuits and feel the vast miasma of desires and aversions rise and fall within myself. It would be quite cool and Zen if it weren't so utterly terrifying; this experience of being a single entity gurgling and pulsing away in an empty universe.

My eyelids start to flicker and the inside and outside worlds begin to merge, the train feeling like it's travelling down my brain stem and into my spine.

When I open my eyes again, things are different. Very different. The kind of different that makes you wonder whether reality is just a giant game of Twister played by unimaginably powerful beings to keep themselves entertained. Which is one thing to think when you're stoned and looking up at the night sky, but quite another when you're in a place where everything is saying your name. Even the rocks.

'Baxter,' says a small rock in front of me. 'Baxter,' adds another older, chubbier-looking rock conversationally. Next to them trees drip multifaceted pastel jewels into ponds with cherub faces that sing like choirs of angels, 'Baxxxxxteerrrrrrr.'

I rub my eyes confusedly, which, to be frank, is the only really acceptable response in a situation like this. I look into the radiant blue sky above me, where languid waterfalls run backwards through turbines that power the wings of huge bird-shaped flying machines all humming the name 'Baxter'.

The noise rises to an unbearable crescendo and I have no other choice but to huddle down with my hands over my ears and try to block out the thronging chorus. It does absolutely no good. The noise is as much in my head as it is anywhere else. I think I'm about to go mad because I just can't fucking stand my name any more. It's got to stop. Please, it's absolutely got to stop. It really, really, really just has to …

'The Conscious Self,' a deep booming voice says. 'Never thought we'd actually ever meet you.' I'm so pathetically grateful to hear anything that's not 'Baxter' that I open my eyes. Four people are standing in a loose circle around me. Four people in pastel-coloured, rhinestone-studded jumpsuits.

I want to say something, but the Baxters are still ringing in my skull like terrible bells. 'Say your name,' commands the deep-voiced man. He's wearing a peach-coloured jumpsuit, has an unimaginably huge afro, and sports a grey-streaked soul patch on his chin.

'What?' I croak, my head feeling like it's going to split under the pressure.

'Say your name,' the man repeats, 'quickly.'

'Baxter,' I say. The terrible noise stops instantly. There's a silence that is better than anything I've ever experienced. I bask in it, gulping down the sheer lack of Baxters like milk after a hot curry.

I look at the man and he raises an eyebrow.

'What the hell was that?' I ask.

'Feedback,' he says. 'You're the Conscious Self and this is your psyche. It's like you put the microphone too close to the speaker, you dig?'

The truth is, I don't dig. I don't dig one little bit. The man looks at my face and grins. 'Welcome to your own psyche. Take a look around. Enjoy the view.'

I look around. Jewelled trees shuffle down yellow-brick roads humming to themselves. A herd of skeletal mechanical elephants stride past, trumpeting through ornately carved pipe-organ valves that jut from their ribs. An elegant flock of white evening gloves fly overhead, each pair flapping their fingers in perfect unison. In the distance I can see mountains made of a complex of radiant interlocking symbols framed by giggling lavender clouds.

The man walks over to a tree hung with perfectly shaped globules. He pulls one from a branch. It wobbles in his hand. 'Breastfruit,' he says, removing the jewel from the nipple, then putting the fruit to his mouth and sucking out the liquid. 'Try some.'

I shake my head. 'No thanks.'

'Don't get too caught up in it all,' the man says, clapping me on the back. 'It'll drive you crazy.'

'Don't get me wrong,' I say carefully. 'Your world is very beautiful and I have no desire to harm it. But is there any way that I can … leave it?'

The man and his companions all laugh. 'Leave it? You are it! But you're understandably confused.' He extends a large hand. 'I'm Tyrone, your genital phase.'

'Excuse me?'

He points to the rhinestones on his jumpsuit. Up close I see they're arranged to form a picture of a man with a beard smoking a cigar.

'It's Freud, man,' Tyrone says.

'I'm sorry,' I say. 'I really have no idea what you're talking about.'

I'm shaken violently from side to side. Some vast, imageless presence has me in its teeth and is going for the jugular. I fling my arms up in front of my face. 'No,' I say. 'Please, let me go.'

'Whoa there, tiger.' Nom grabs my arms.

I peek through my hands and see his concerned face bouncing up and down in front of me. I rub my eyes. 'How long was I asleep?'

He shrugs. 'An hour? Maybe I should have warned you that Runeshine can be a little hallucinogenic.'

'Yeah, maybe you should have,' I say with an embarrassed smile.

'Well, grab a bunk and have a proper sleep. It's a long ride to the Poort.'

I climb into one of the uncomfortable bunks. Sleep doesn't come easily. I'm a bit homesick already, and whatever the hell that dream was, it has me spooked. I lie staring at the ceiling until sleep eventually gets tired of waiting and just grabs me in a headlock and pulls me under.

THE POORT AT THE END OF THE WORLD

I wake up with a headache and several moments of wide-eyed panic before remembering where I am. But luckily my dreams are dim and insignificant in my memory and didn't involve people in rhinestone jumpsuits.

Nom claps me on the shoulder and hands me a sandwich. Stevo is still asleep, Hunter and Timothy curled up and snuggled together on top of his head.

'Feeling better?' Nom asks as I climb off the bunk.

'Yeah,' I say. 'Don't know what happened there. Sorry.'

Nom waves a hand. 'Don't worry about it. Runeshine hits everyone hard the first time they drink it.'

I bite into the dry sandwich and force myself to chew and swallow.

'If you need to use the toilet, do it now,' Nom says. 'There's always a rush before we get on the buses.'

I take his advice and walk the long corridor to the toilet. On the way I encounter a threesome: a guy and two girls. One is blonde and perfectly made up. The other has raven-black hair, purple eyeshadow and a pierced nose and lip. The blonde looks bored and is scrolling through her phone. The goth is clearly into it. She winks at me over the shoulder of her white-arsed lover. I half smile, avert my eyes and walk quickly past.

Some kids are smoking meth in the toilet and I have to wait until they're finished. I squeeze into the small cubicle, kick a small burnt glass pipe and needle out of the way with the toe of my shoe and sit with my head in my hands. I hate Hexpoort already and I haven't even got there yet.

I take out my phone. I have three bars so I give it a try and dial the number.

'Esmé?' I say.

'Hey, magic boy,' she says. 'Are you there yet?' It's so damn good to hear her voice.

'Nah.' I try to sound nonchalant. 'Still on the train.' I hear a voice in the background and Esmé laughs.

'Who you with?' I say.

'Oh, just my friend Troy.'

'Who is this Troy?' I ask coolly. 'Have I ever met him?'

'I thought you said you weren't jealous?'

'I'm not,' I say. 'Pssht. Me, jealous? Come on. I just like to know what you're doing.'

'Troy and I are hanging out, that's all.'

The voice says something in the background and Esmé laughs.

'Jesus,' I say. 'Do you think you could focus on me for a second?' I instantly regret it.

'Bax, if you're going to be a dick, I'm going to hang up. Call me again if you want to apologise.'

The line goes dead. Shit. I instantly redial the number and then realise that the signal has disappeared.

'Fuck!' I scream and kick the toilet wall repeatedly until I force myself to calm down. Just relax. Wait until you've got signal and then call her back. At least you've got a phone and there is an intermittent signal. It's all going to be OK.

I open the toilet door feeling a Zen-like calm. Which is instantly dispelled by a pair of hands grabbing me and slamming me against the corridor wall.

Hekka's face is right in mine and his forearm is against my throat. 'Well look. It's the boy who wants to be king,' he says, spitting into my eye.

'What the hell are you talking about?' I choke out, struggling against the tattooed forearm that is slowly closing off my airway. 'I don't want to be anything.'

'Well, you shouldn't have saved the world then,' he says. His face is angry and red and the crescent scar is throbbing with his pulse. 'That's my job. I want you to say it. Say "You're the Chosen One".'

'You're the Chosen One,' I gurgle. 'You're the Chosen One.'

'Don't fucking forget it.' He pushes harder on my throat, then pulls my phone from my hand. 'I'll take this.'

I struggle against his arm and grab at the phone. It's my lifeline to the outside world.

'Give it to me,' I hiss.

'Consider it your donation to the cause,' he says with a smile. He raises a fist. 'I'm going to leave you with a little souvenir of your brush with greatness.'

'Leave him alone,' two voices say in unison.

I strain my neck to look over Hekka's shoulder and see the two girls from the threesome. Except they have the same torso. The shirt is white and starched, but one shoulder is ripped, revealing an arm full of tattoos. One leg is wearing a torn fishnet stocking. In one hand is a cheerleading pompom; the other is holding a switchblade delicately between purple nails.

'Siamese monster alert,' Hekka says, taking his forearm off my throat. 'Freaks defending freaks. Perfect.'

'Just get the fuck out of here,' the goth says. 'Go jerk off to your diagram of the Hero's Journey or something.'

Hekka clenches his fists. 'I'm the Chosen One. You and this freak are nothing.'

'You know why men become big heroes?' the goth says.

'Please tell me,' Hekka says.

The twins walk over until they're standing right in front of him. 'Because they have tiny penises,' the goth says with a smile.

Hekka punches the wall next to her and then stalks off down the corridor.

'You OK?' the cheerleader asks.

'Yeah, thanks for that,' I say, rubbing my neck.

'Stop staring, dildo,' the goth says.

'I'm really sorry, it's just …'

'Yeah, we're conjoined twins. Thanks for pointing that out. We wouldn't have noticed otherwise.'

'Technically we're dicephalus twins,' the cheerleader says. 'Which means two heads and one body.'

'Thanks for that, brainiac. I think he may have noticed,' the goth says. 'Anyways, saving your ass has been real but I've really got to go and smoke a joint.'

'Bye!' calls the cheerleader as they saunter off down the corridor.

I stare after them. I haven't even got to Hexpoort yet and already my phone has been jacked by the Chosen One and I've been saved by a knife-wielding set of conjoined twins. Fucking great.

We disembark at a small station that's not marked on the map that I have. It looks like it could be any part of small-town South Africa, a confluence of churches, petrol stations and well-aged shopping centres.

I shield my eyes against the unpleasantly bright sun. A fleet of rusty buses wait for us in the dirt. Nom and Stevo help me carry my cases to an old maroon clunker driven by an equally old grey-haired woman. She's built a small shrine to Elvis on her dashboard, paying tribute to the plastic figurine of the King she has stuck above the speedometer with shells, beads, feathers and hair.

The bus is crammed with teenagers in various stages of inebriation.

'Everyone's just getting it out before we hit the Poort,' Nom says as we find a seat at the back. 'The school term can be a bit brutal.'

'What's it like?' I ask. 'Hexpoort?'

'Oh,' he says with a grin. 'I don't want to spoil it for you.'

We drive for about an hour through a wasteland of dirt and dust. The driver puts on an old Miriam Makeba album; the tape is stretched, giving the recording a warped, hallucinatory quality that does not play nice with my depression. I stare listlessly at the desolate landscape outside. Even the few farm kids that we pass look menacing. The bus judders and shakes as we hit an orange dirt road that leads up into a series of stark hills.

'Beautiful,' I say with a sigh. I lose track of the time as the brown landscape streaks by.

Eventually we grind to a halt. 'Welcome to the Poort,' Nom says with a grand gesture.

I crane my neck to see through the windscreen. Hexpoort squats against brown canyon walls, an old Dutch granite fort in the shape of a pentacle, surrounded by a perimeter of electric fencing and razor wire.

'The points of the star are Malpit, Donkergees, Bokveld, Wintergat and Skaduwee,' Nom says. 'You'll end up living in either Malpit, Donkergees or Wintergat depending on what clan you're in. I'm in Broken Teeth, so I stay in Malpit.'

'How do they decide what clan you're in?' I ask. 'Some kind of magical choosing thing?'

He shrugs. 'Nah, dude, I think it's more a logistical thing: space, beds available, et cetera.'

I stare at the high granite walls and the razor wire.

'Looks like a prison,' I say.

'You can, and should, judge a book by its cover.' Stevo smiles. 'But don't look so glum, Bax. It's not all bad.'

'Yeah,' I say, but I don't believe that for a second.

Hexpoort smells of woodsmoke and herbs. I breathe it in and try to imagine myself staying here. It's difficult.

We're let through the perimeter fence by a couple of grim-faced guards and make our way to the entrance of the fort. Huge steel doors carved with scenes of Zulu warriors fighting strange lizard-like creatures bar our way.

'That's the story of the Battle of Blood River; it doesn't often get told,' Stevo says, nodding to the carvings. 'Crazy shit.'

The doors swing open to admit us to the courtyard. My suitcases clack on the cobbled stones as we enter and I can't stop myself from putting my hand against a granite wall. I feel a deep, shuddering cold, like the fort has roots that sink down into the earth and suck up dark secrets.

We pass an old gallows made of black wood. A frayed noose hangs from the wooden arm and sways in the breeze.

'Apparently the Dutch Hexenmeisters, their mages, used to have sangomas hanged there,' Stevo says. 'They didn't like the competition.'

'Stevo is our little historian,' Nom says. 'Get him stoned and he'll talk about this shit for hours.'

I smile and can't help but think I should introduce him to Rafe.

'Come on,' Nom says. 'We've got opening assembly.'

The crowd of kids gather at the foot of an old stone staircase that winds its way up the side of the fort like a snake. There's no jostling or fighting now. Everyone stands quietly, their eyes flicking nervously up towards the top of the stairs. I'm so prepared for anything – animal, mineral or vegetable – to come sauntering down that when a woman with a painted face and a man in khaki appear, it's a bit of an anticlimax.

The woman is sturdy and muscular, with high cheekbones. Her steel-grey hair is pulled back into a bun pierced by porcupine quills. She's wearing a red leather breastplate, and riding pants with heavy soldier's boots. Her wrists and elbows are bound with white beads and her dark skin is caked with red clay. She carries a cow-tail whisk in one hand and a long, wicked whip in the other. A squat handgun is strapped like a gunslinger's to her upper thigh. 'Newbies assemble next to the gallows,' she says in a cold, commanding voice.

'The rest of you into your dorms and get some rest. You're going to need it; this term's going to be fun,' the guy adds. He's large and beefy, with an epic handlebar moustache, and dark hair held off his face by a black headband with a bright red rising-sun logo. He's wearing all khaki: a two-tone, short-sleeved shirt, very short shorts and long socks. Huge aviator sunglasses perch on his bulbous nose and he has silver rings fashioned into skulls and dragons on every finger.

There are groans and murmurs as the returning students troop off into the fort.

'See you later,' Nom says, and Stevo pats me reassuringly on the back.

A group of fifteen new kids stay behind and look nervously at each other. The woman stands in front of us with her hands on her hips. 'I'm the Red Witch and I'm the head of this little institution. According to traditional law you are all trainee sangomas, my twasas. Which is a euphemism for bitches.'

She walks up and down in front of us, looking less than impressed with her new bunch of recruits.

'There is one simple rule that will make our relationship run smoothly and it's this: you do what I say, when I say it, without questioning, or you'll feel pain like you've never felt before. If you're thinking you can handle it, if there's a little voice in your head that's saying that you can fuck with me and then deal with the consequences, I urge you to silence that little voice forcefully. You *can't* handle it.'

She turns to her khaki companion. 'This is the Shadow Boer. He is my second-in-command and is also to be obeyed without question.'

She spreads her hands and smiles. 'Now that we have got the formalities out of the way, let me tell you about the place where you find yourselves.' She gestures to the surrounding structure. 'Dutch Hexenmeisters built these walls and held them against English warlocks and magic-shielded Zulu impi. The English took the fort and used it for their own purposes. Then the Zulu took it. Then the English again.'

She raises a finger. 'Whether you're Xhosa, Zulu, Dutch, English, Irish, Scottish, Chinese, French, Indian or whatever the fuck fruity combination your ancestors conferred on you, make no mistake: blood has been spilled on these stones. Our ancestors threatened, killed and fucked one another here.' She smiles a dangerous smile. Her teeth are brilliantly white against the red clay. 'And here we stand fucked into one big crucible.'

She pauses for a moment, and during the silence I can feel the roots of the fort threading together, the blood in my veins pulsing, the group of us for one moment a single living organism, a human hivemind, ancient, flawed and bloody.

'Yes,' the Red Witch says with a grin that tells me I've experienced the effect that was intended. 'We're not here to teach you how to impress your little girlfriends and boyfriends with charms or magic potions. No, no. And we're not here to be glamorous secret agents either.'

She stands in front of one of the newbies and swats him across the face with her whisk. 'Oh, we might call ourselves agents, but we're really just cops, policing the borders of reality. And make no mistake: out there we're the worst kind of cops, the kind that everyone wants to kill. Other cops like to see us die because they don't understand who we are. The Hidden like to see us die for daring to enter their worlds.

'The only thing that gives us the edge, that little bit extra that stops us from being splattered all over the streets, is what you'll learn here. This is dirty magic, gutter magic, street-fighting magic. We don't rest on ceremony. Find out what works and use it. I don't care if you pray to Darth Vader and masturbate to torture porn to charge your sigils. If you cut yourself and smoke crystal meth to get into the mood for rituals. We're understaffed, underpaid and unimpressed by your fledgling abilities. In parts of this country people are stoned to death and necklaced for witchcraft. Nobody cares if you use magic outside of the confines of these walls. If you fuck up, you're dead. So don't fuck up.'

She turns to the Shadow Boer. 'Break them up into their clans.'

The Shadow Boer begins calling out names and clans in a booming voice. The crowd starts to dissipate as the newbies are assigned. I feel like I'm the last kid being picked for dodgeball. 'Zevcenko. Broken Teeth,' the Boer says after a long pause.

'Hey, cool, you're with us,' Nom says as I rattle my suitcases into Malpit.

Malpit is a shrine to teenagers left to their own devices. Hundreds of posters line the walls. There's a big one of Gandalf with a big dick drawn on the front of his robe. There's one of Harry Potter with his eyes gouged out and his wand transformed into – yes, you guessed it – a big dick. Beer bottles are piled up in the entrance and a water fountain featuring a statuette of an old wizard has been turned into a giant ashtray.

Stevo is sitting on a dirty couch covered with cigarette burns. He points to the ceiling, where DO WHAT THOU WILT SHALL BE THE WHOLE OF THE LAW has been spray-painted in gold. 'We take that to heart.'

'How was the welcome speech?' Nom asks.

'Not very welcoming,' I say, slumping down on to a beanbag next to Stevo. 'What's her problem?'

'Life, I think,' Nom says with a grin. 'But seriously, she's part of the Blood Kraal, the council that regulates supernatural affairs in Sub-Saharan Africa. Just stay on her good side.'

I sigh, and Nom smiles. 'Here, let me show you around.'

Malpit is an anarcho-commune, an ongoing squat party with its own internal logic. 'There aren't really any proper beds left,' Nom says. 'But there's a mattress on the floor over there that you can use.'

'Great,' I say.

'This is our kitchen. Cleaning roster on the fridge, although some of us take it more to heart than others.' He gives Stevo a look.

'Dude, I said I would clean it later. Get off my case,' Stevo says.

A bunch of kids are playing video games on a huge TV. I recognise the goth and the cheerleader, the conjoined twins who saved me from Hekka on the train.

'Faith and Chastity,' Nom says. 'This is Baxter.'

'I'm Faith,' the cheerleader says. 'And my sister here is Chastity. It's a bit like calling a big guy "Tiny".'

'Screw you, ho-bag,' Chastity says.

'Biologically impossible, otherwise I'm sure you would have tried already,' Faith replies.

'Thanks for helping me with Hekka,' I say.

'She's the one that wanted to help,' Chastity says. 'She whines when she doesn't get her way. It's not like I can get away from it.'

'Nice to meet you, Baxter.' Faith smiles.

'Oooh, she likes you,' Chastity says. 'Why don't you two kiss? I don't mind. I'll let you use my half of the body. I may even try to get in a grope myself.'

I blush, which is unusual for me. Faith rolls her eyes.

'Game of Sanity later?' Nom says.

'Damn straight,' Chastity replies. 'I've been practising. Oh, and bring the newbie. I want to see what he's made of.'

She gives me a wink and they return to their video games.

I dump my stuff next to my mattress as the Shadow Boer comes in. 'Newbies,' he barks. 'Time for your tattoos.'

Nom gives me a half-hearted thumbs-up as I follow the Boer down the long stone staircase.

I've always thought about getting a tattoo. My dad has a tribal band tattooed around his unimpressive bicep. I guess at the time he thought it looked cool, but now it looks like he accidentally spilled the nineties over his arm. But as I stand in line and watch an old guy with greasy hair permanently mark adolescents, I decide that my body is not a temple that needs to be decorated. The old guy wields the tattoo gun like he's in an action movie, and causes almost as much bloodshed.

'Does it have to be there?' I ask as he touches the gun to my forearm.

'Oh no,' the old guy growls. 'Perhaps you'd rather have a nice Chinese symbol for freedom on your lower back?'

'Well no, it's just that—'

'Shut the hell up, kid,' he spits. 'Or this is gonna hurt even more.'

I'm sitting outside dabbing my arm with a tissue when the

reality of my situation hits home. I look down at the gruesome prison-style rendering of a mouth full of smashed teeth. It's still bleeding, which adds to the effect. I'm away from my friends and family in a place that's on no maps and where they freely tattoo minors with magic ink.

'Now you're one of us,' Chastity says, holding out her arm to show an equally mutilated mouth. 'Thankfully we only needed to get one,' adds Faith with a smile.

'Why?' I say. 'Why do we have these?'

'If you try to leave, it hurts like a chemical burn,' Chastity says. 'Like nothing you've ever felt before. They got tired of kids escaping so they made a plan.'

'Fuck.' I touch the bloody mouth gingerly.

'Come on,' Faith says. 'First class of the semester.'

'We're all in the same class?' I whisper as I sit down at a desk next to Nom.

'Well, yeah,' he says. 'No funding, very few teachers. We're all in it together, baby.'

We're in a classroom in the stony belly of Hexpoort. I'm expecting a military instructor, someone with a crew cut and a bad attitude to put us through our paces. What I'm not expecting is a giant bipedal tabby cat wearing a kaftan, Buddhist chanting beads and little circular steel-rimmed glasses.

'Good morning, one and all,' he says in a low, musical voice. 'Many of you know me already, but for the benefit of those who don't, my name is King and I'm the curriculum director here at Hexpoort. And before any of you newbies freak out, let us cut to the chase: I look like a cat.'

He picks up a piece of chalk and scrawls the letters CAT on the board.

'What I am, however, is a Nunda, an ancient race with its roots in Central Africa.' He opens his desk and pulls out several sheaves of paper and holds them up. 'Lolcats, Garfield or Grumpy Cat pinned on my office door may seem like juvenile hijinks, but it's seriously uncool, people.'

There are sniggers from the class.

'I take offence at this specific brand of humour as it only serves to further entrench human privilege.'

He clears his throat. 'Now that we've got that unpleasantness out of the way, I'd like to extend a warm welcome to the new members of Hexpoort. In today's class I'll be assessing the abilities of our new recruits. When I call your name, please come through to my office and I'll administer the tests. The rest of you start reading John Lilly's *The Center of the Cyclone* and think about how it relates to Timothy Leary's ideas about the eight-circuit model of consciousness.'

King calls a kid's name and ushers him to the office adjoining the classroom. I start reading the book.

'Hey, asshole.'

I don't turn around.

'Asshole!'

Something hits me on the back of the head and I swing around.

'You settling in?' Hekka says. He and a bunch of his dumb jock friends are sitting at the back of the classroom. Hekka has his feet up on the desk and his hands interlaced behind his head. 'What abilities do you think the kitteh will find in you? The ability to suck dick?'

I turn back to the book but I feel Hekka come up behind me and lean over my desk.

'I'm the Chosen One, fated by birth to save the world. You know what you are?'

'No,' I say. 'Please enlighten me.'

'You're fucking nothing.'

Time slows down. I feel the Hulk rage build. I could twist him around, squash him like a fly. Destroy him completely and entirely. But I don't. I am Zen. I am a calm pool reflecting the moon. I am gouging out his eyes with a rusty spoon. No. I'm not. I am Zen. I am a calm pool reflecting the moon.

I just nod and continue to flick through my textbook.

'Like I said,' Hekka says, slapping the back of my head so hard that my glasses fall off. 'Nothing.'

'Baxter Zevcenko?' King sticks his large head round the door.

I get up and follow him through, dodging another projectile that comes sailing from the back of the class.

The office smells of incense and cat. There's a large desk made of dark wood, and a sprawling red Persian rug carpets the floor. I brush hairs from the seat in front of the desk and sit down. Several Egyptian-style paintings of cats being worshipped hang on the granite walls.

'Bastet, the cat goddess,' King says with a smile when he sees me looking at them. 'Among the Nunda it's a symbol of empowerment, similar to the black fist.'

'Is it really so bad out there for them? The Hidden, I mean,' I say.

'"Them"? I'm going to stop you there, compadre. Exoticising the other is primary in the discourse around the Hidden Ones. The community is so fragmented and there is a lot of inter-species conflict. I'm considered by many to be a traitor. Working for the Man, quite literally in my case.'

He sits back, places his hands on his generous belly and contemplates me with his strange yellow eyes. 'Besides, your unique history means that speaking of "them" is not really accurate. I know you've got both Crow and Siener blood and that it's not exactly a happy mix. Am I right so far?'

'Yeah,' I say. 'So what?'

'Well, it's a very interesting combination, and I am eager to test what abilities you may have as a result.'

'OK,' I say. 'Knock yourself out.'

He fits a series of electrodes to my head and connects them to a laptop. 'Now I want you to clear your mind and just look at the pictures I show you.' He flashes me a series of images: a phrenologist's diagram of a human head, a scarab beetle, the *Dark Side of the Moon* album cover, sugar skulls, ice cream covered with ants, a sword dripping with honey, a samurai committing hara-kiri, a collection of teen boy-band posters.

'Hmmm,' he says as he taps at the laptop keyboard. 'Very interesting.'

He puts a series of cards face down on the desk and asks me to draw what I think they hold. I quickly sketch the first things that come into my head: interlocking triangles, a house, a sailboat, a smiley face.

'Ah.' He taps the keyboard again. 'And now we're going to play a story-telling game. I'm going to give you prompts and I want you to flesh out the story. Just let your mind go and use your imagination.'

He clears his throat. 'There is a man named …' I stare at him blankly. 'Whatever comes into your head, Baxter,' he says.

'His name is Herbert,' I begin. 'He goes on a yacht and gets into a breakdance battle with penguins …'

We continue like this, and as we talk, his voice begins to lull me.

'You're walking down a passageway,' he says. 'You're looking for a man called Whitey Valke. That's right, Baxter, deeper and deeper …'

And there go my eyes, flickering like dragonfly wings.

'What do you see, Baxter?'

'A child …' I murmur. 'Very scared, in a red room.' It's true. I can see the faint hazy outline of a child in a room.

'Good,' King says. 'Deeper and deeper, Baxter.'

The vision spins out of control and cleaves through my skull. I see a horrible dark figure approaching the child and attacking him.

'Stop!' I scream. 'Stop.'

My eyes jerk open and King is standing over me with his hands on my shoulders. 'It's OK,' he says. 'You're safe. It was just a vision.'

He pours me a glass of water and I gulp it down gratefully.

'Whitey Valke was a serial killer in the eighties. I took a chance on you, Baxter. What you saw was probably his infamous red-room abduction. The last child he took.'

'I probably heard about it somewhere,' I say. 'Read it online or something.'

'I seriously doubt it.' King smiles, making his whiskers twitch. 'It was never released. Whitey Valke was a goblin.'

'So I got a small glimpse of something,' I say. 'I've seen things before …'

'What it means is that I believe you have skill in both Seeing and Dreaming. Remarkable.'

'Well, that's good, right? I thought I was here to learn about this shit.'

He taps one of his claws thoughtfully on the desk. 'Well, yes. But it may cause … problems for you. Dreamwalking is an ancient skill that not many have the aptitude for any more. You have a high degree of potential for it. But your other magical abilities seem … blocked.'

'Blocked?' I say.

'From what I can gather, you'll have difficulty performing even the most basic spells.'

'Great.' I sit back in the chair.

'Don't be despondent. Dreamwalking is a powerful skill. You're a wildcard, Baxter, and if there's anything I've learnt, it's that the MK6 establishment does not like wildcards.'

'Story of my life,' I say.

'I will instruct you as far as I can. But further than that we have to approach a specialised teacher.'

'You have a specialised teacher for this stuff? Well, that's great.'

He shakes his head, which gives the impression that he's chasing a laser pointer. 'Not exactly. She herself is a bit of a … wildcard.' He scratches his chin. 'I'll speak to her. In the meantime …'

He reaches into his desk and hands me a black hard drive with a fraying smiley face sticker on it. 'The entire school info dump is on there, our "library" for want of a better word. That's everything we have clearance to give to students. It's not organised in any meaningful way so you're going to have to sift through it on your own to find mention of Dreamwalking.'

'OK,' I say. 'I can do that.'

He chuckles. 'Easier said than done. There may be a few mentions of Dreamwalking. It may also be referred to as "surfing mercury" or "aethernautics" or simply "exploring". Most often these things are talked about obliquely.'

I sigh.

'Enjoy,' he says with a smile. 'I'll let you know when I've spoken to your potential mentor.'

A GAME OF SANITY

I trudge back through the courtyard from an extra remedial class with King. He's right: I have absolutely no aptitude for magic. He says he's spoken to this 'specialised teacher' but she has yet to give him an answer. It probably won't make a difference. No matter how hard I practise the exercises I'm given, I just can't make it work, and I'm starting to have massive performance anxiety. Failure to produce a flame on your palm in front of the whole class is embarrassing, and there's no Viagra for magic.

I look up and see the Red Witch standing silhouetted against the setting sun on top of the Hexpoort ramparts. A bird, a huge grey and white falcon, watches me from its perch on her thick leather glove. It launches off and swoops across the barren canyon. The Witch turns her eyes on me with the same penetrating gaze as the bird. I hurry away.

My new life has not been going so great. If Westridge was an exercise in attempting to control the raging sea of hormones, chemicals and body parts of delinquent teenagers, then Hexpoort is that plus kids with the ability to bend the fundamental laws of physics. Within my first week I've witnessed a fight using knives of corrosive green fire, an overdose on Stevo's product, and the aftermath of an orgy where a kid from Pondscum broke his penis attempting a reverse cowboy with a girl from Broken Teeth. While they were magically hovering in the air.

I'm just trying to keep my head down and stay the hell out of school politics. Which isn't easy. Hekka struts around with this faux inner conflict showing on his face: the tortured hero trying to come to terms with his fate. It's fucking ridiculous. He engineers all these little situations where he comes across as the noble underdog in class. I saw him fucking plotting them out on an Excel document.

Thankfully Nom lent me an old cell phone and I managed to get hold of Esmé to apologise. She was cool and distant, which made me push harder, which made her angry, which made me angry, which made her angrier which ... It didn't exactly go well.

I feel my old life slipping further and further away from me and I can't seem to stop it. So I've developed coping strategies. I play insane amounts of chess on Nom's crappy phone. It's a bit like manipulator methadone, but I admit it's a cheap substitute. My project to send Kyle emails about magical things has also become a ritual. The sheer amount of information on the Hexpoort hard drive is astounding, and I dive into it nightly. I've gone through scans of diary entries, newspaper clippings, old documents and napkins with whisky stains and formulas written on them. I find obscure people of esoterica and tell him about them, trying to unravel the insanely bizarre shit that the magical community has done over the years. I find a couple of articles about magic and dreamwalking scanned from an old magazine called *The Journal of Occult Practices* that are helpful. Kyle's loving it.

I reach the Malpit stairs and make the long climb up to the dorm. I'm starving, and when Nom brings in a huge pot of stew, I'm pathetically grateful, even though it's cold so we're forced to wait in a line and heat it up in the microwave.

I sit on the couch next to Stevo to eat. The stew is not bad: thick and spicy and filled with vegetables and chunks of stringy meat.

'What is this?' I ask through a mouthful.

'Dassie,' Stevo says as he chews. 'The Witch has had a good hawking day.' He reaches up to give Timothy and Hunter a chunk each. They sit on his head and eat contentedly. Then he produces a bottle of home-made whisky from a brown paper packet at his feet and passes it around.

'Not hallucinogenic, I promise,' Nom says as he hands me the bottle.

'Not unless you drink too much,' Stevo adds with a grin.

I take a grateful swig and feel the liquor burn my throat. My first week at the Poort has been rough and I'm glad to take the edge off. I'm having another swig when Faith and Chastity appear. Chastity grabs the bottle from my hand and takes a long gulp. 'Right, Sanity time, you little bitches,' she says, wiping her mouth with her sleeve.

'All right!' Stevo claps his hands together. 'I've got some new material.'

Chastity laughs. 'Your shit is going to be Disneyland compared to what I've concocted,' she says.

'It's true.' Faith shakes her head. 'She tried it on me.'

We clear the floor and sit down on pillows in a small circle.

'So,' Chastity says. 'Rules for the newbie. Sanity is the official game of Hexpoort and it's simple. We use illusion magic to create the sickest, grossest, most disturbing images we can imagine to freak people out. Call "Sanity!" and the images stop but you lose the round. The one who can last the longest wins.'

'OK,' I say. 'But my magic is not that, you know, great.'

'Oooh.' Chastity puts on a baby voice. 'I forgot the poor little man can't get it up.'

'Ignore her.' Faith turns her head so she's glaring at the side of her twin's face. 'It happens to a lot of people. It's fine. You can just be the victim this time around.'

'Fine,' Chastity says with a cruel smile. 'And I'm the conjuror.'

'No problem,' I say. 'I'm good at games.'

Chastity and Faith sit directly across from me and Chastity begins chanting in Xhosa and making gestures with her hand. My vision starts to shift and images appear in the air in front of me. They become more vivid, like I'm watching something in high definition. It's not pretty. The porno stuff I can manage. I've seen enough creature porn in my young life to be able to run with the big dogs. Then comes the wave of snuff. Some of it is your rudimentary serial-killer schtick. Clowns with butcher knives, dolls coming alive. It's like watching an eighties horror marathon on TV.

I smile and yawn. Chastity looks at me with raised eyebrows and I know I've made a mistake. Truly bizarre stuff starts happening. Monsters and ghouls seem to latch on to my face and shriek with schizophrenic voices, screaming so close to me that I think my eardrums are going to burst.

'Sanity!' I shout, before I know what's happening. 'SANITY, SANITY, SANITY!'

The images and sounds disappear abruptly to reveal Chastity blowing the end of her index finger like it's a smoking six-gun. 'Works every time,' she says.

'Don't worry, man.' Nom puts a hand on my shoulder. 'Not many people can beat her at Sanity. She's the queen.'

That night I lie awake on my mattress listening to the stone around me. I experience a deep, tingling sensation that takes loneliness and puts it through a wah-wah pedal so that it peaks and dips unpredictably in my chest. I've never been suicidal, but for the first time in my life I consider it. I want out. I want out of this goddamn place.

My dreams are thankfully nondescript. Teeth falling out, being late for buses and the occasional feeling of falling – the stuff that counts as banal for me these days. The next day reality is far, far worse than any dream. We're digging pits under the fiery eye of the sun. Sweat drips into my eyes and I blink furiously to stop the stinging. Today's lesson at Hexpoort is hard manual labour. The Shadow Boer walks up and down next to the pit like a drill sergeant.

'This is some insane Mr Miyagi shit,' the kid next to me says, sweat dripping down his dirt-smeared face. 'Why the hell do we have to do this?'

'I'd rather be waxing a car or painting a fence,' I agree as my spade bites into the dry earth.

'I'm going to ask him.'

'Don't,' I say. 'Really, don't.'

He ignores me. 'When do we learn magic?'

The Shadow Boer looks at him. 'Magic? Oh, so you are fokken wanting to be learning magic then, mah sunshine?' He claps the kid on the shoulder. 'Jussus, man, you should have just asked.'

The kid smiles, the Boer smiles back. And then knees him in the groin.

'You are like the clay and I'm going to be moulding you,' he says, making it sound almost sexual. A bearded man in khaki shorts and socks lasciviously showing how he will mould your soul is an awkward moment of note. Everyone looks down. 'You want to learn magic, mah sunshines?' he says. 'Then you must be strong.'

The days in Hexpoort blend into a blur of hard labour, magic lessons, and drinking and drugs at Malpit. I don't seem to be making progress with the magic, but my alcohol and drug tolerance has improved, and my body aches from hard physical exercise.

The carpal tunnel syndrome in my mouse hand has been replaced by calluses. Wiry muscle is beginning to build. My hunched keyboard shoulders are straightening out. My screen eyes are refocusing. It feels like I'm starting to live more in the physical world and less in my mind. I'm hating every second of it.

My finely tuned skills are atrophying. I've worked for years for the stamina and multitasking ability to watch two seasons of a series in one night while following the public destruction of a celebrity on social media and crowd-solving a terrorist attack on Reddit. I was a perfect interface between man and machine. Now I'm just becoming buff.

The nights are filled with deep feelings of emptiness. I grit my teeth and bear it, presumably out of the same insanely masochistic impulse that has me stopping myself from interfering in the politics of the school.

It's five weeks after I first stepped through the Hexpoort gates when the Shadow Boer takes us to a field within the school boundaries. In it is a paintball-splotched fake town complete with junked cars with what look like real bullet holes in them. A metal frame on the side of the field holds dozens of black punching bags swaying in the breeze.

The Boer stops us in front of the bags. 'You are here to be learning Combatives, your real fokken education here at Hexpoort,' he says, scratching his beard. 'Listen here, mah sunshines. Mamma Nature, in her favouritest quest to fuck wif the human race, has given us this limp wet rag for a body and skopped us out into the world with beasts and monsters whose DNA has fokken being pumping iron at the evolution gym.'

He walks up and down in front of us, looking each one of us in the eye as he passes. 'If a bookie looked at us, no claws, fangs, no scaly armour, the oke would have placed odds on us being knocked out in the opening rounds of our evolution. But we didn't just survive, we fokken rocked the party, ek sê. We climbed to the top of the food chain wif a goddamn stone knife between our teeth.' He waggles his thumbs. 'Everyone say "thanks, thumbs". The point, julle klein naaiers, is give up all sense of romance. Your stupid little spaghetti bodies are not well designed for kicking ass. Too many soft spots.' He jabs a kid in the neck with his finger and the kid collapses in a heap on the ground. The Boer grabs him by the shirt, hauls him to his feet and pats him on the back.

'The only trick to fighting is to find the soft spots in your enemy and then stab, gouge, crush and bite them until the fokken thing stops moving. And then stamp on his head just to be sure. Any questions?'

One kid raises a trembling hand.

'Ja, you,' the Boer says.

'Why do we have to learn fighting?' the kid says. 'Why can't we just use magic?'

I grit my teeth and wait for him to get hit in the throat, but the Boer nods.

'The first rule, mah sunshines, is to keep the energy you have like you're on the last bar of your cell-phone battery. Magic takes energy to use. If it's easier to club something to the ground with a spade and then stomp on its head, then you do that rather. But the best is a combination of the two.'

He grabs the kid who asked the question. 'Boom, flash spell to the eyes, grab him by the throat, headbutt. Nighty-night.' He doesn't hit the kid hard but he drops too. The Boer sighs, then leans down and pulls him back up to his feet.

'Ja, mah sunshines. Demons, elementals, Treskulls, Obayifo, Nahuda and a thousand other fokken nasties are out there, and these okes are really not nice. I'm going to teach you how to fight them with whatever you have. No offence, but those namby-pamby magic theorist bookworms might be teaching you all that "oooh, let's get in touch wif our feelings" magic shit, but you meet a demon, they gonna fuck you up six–love if you try to get all philomasophical with them. We'll do Musangwe boxing, Zulu stick fighting, Cape Flats knife fighting, and street-fighting magic. We'll fokken do muay thai and you thai and everyone thai. We'll do ju-jitsu, karate, kung-fok-you and every other fokken chop suey thing you can imagine. By the time I'm done with you, you'll have a fighting chance against the terrible things that stalk the night, do you unnerstand me?'

'Yes, Boer,' the class mumbles.

'No, you don't. Do you fokken unnerstand me?'

'Yes, Boer,' we shout.

'Ja, well you better. Now start punching those fokken bags.'

I put on a pair of dirty gloves and start hitting the bag half-heartedly. I'm really not in the mood for this.

'You!' The Boer strides over to me. 'You're not giving it a fokken detoxifying face mask.' He takes the bag between his thick hands and strokes. 'Would you like a nice massage now, bag?' he says in a falsetto voice. 'How about some lekker chamomile tea?' Then he steps back and hits it so hard that everyone flinches. 'Ag, ja, sorry, bag. That's not going to happen.' He leans across so that his face is right next to mine. 'Hit it!' he shouts, so loud that my ears ring.

So I punch and continue punching. I hit the bag until my arms hurt. I picture everyone I hate: Anwar, Hekka, even Basson. My face is streaming with sweat, my T-shirt is soaked and I feel like my arms have been jolted from their sockets. The Boer looks at me with his dark eyes. 'Better,' he says with a nod. 'Now kick.'

By the time I head back to the showers in Malpit, my body feels like melted plasticine. I step gingerly into the stream of water and it knocks the breath out of me. I look at the taps miserably. No hot water. The cold digs deep into my cells like cancer. I hate it here. I hate it with so much force that it scares me.

It's right then that I decide I'm going to escape. If I stay here any longer, my resolve to be good is going to crumble. I look through the stream of cold water at my arm. This ugly tattoo may be magical, but it'll probably hurt less than staying here. I'll find somewhere to lie low in Cape Town and make a little money. I'll start another business, legit this time. At least I'll be able to see Esmé and Kyle and the rest of my crew.

King intercepts me as I'm heading back to my mattress. 'Your specialised teacher has agreed to meet with you.'

'Now?' I say. 'Please, I need to sleep. I'm exhausted.'

He shakes his head. 'She's not someone you keep waiting.'

I sigh, throw my stuff down on to my mattress and follow him down the Malpit stairs.

He takes me into a part of Hexpoort I've never been: the point of the pentacle called Bokveld. This is where the teacher's apartments are. It's not somewhere you want to be called at the best of times. The apartments are minimalist, with a central common room and a huge communal kitchen. The Boer is sprawled on a leather couch in the common room watching reality TV as we pass. He doesn't look up.

King leads me to a large set of wooden doors right at the back. 'Here you go,' he says. 'She's waiting for you.'

'You're not coming in?' I ask nervously.

'Oh no,' he says with a small purring smile. 'You're on your own.'

I push open the wooden doors and find myself in a large apartment. The granite walls have been decorated with large canvases of bright abstract art, and there are dozens of pot plants of various sizes scattered around. A huge window has been set into the heavy granite wall, giving a panoramic view of the surrounding canyon. The sun is setting, and the tan and brown of the rocks contrasts brilliantly with the intense oranges and velvety purples of the clouds.

'Nice, isn't it?'

I turn to see the Red Witch striding across the living room towelling her wet hair. She's wearing a torn black Nine Inch Nails T-shirt ornamented by two strings of multicoloured beads, and a pair of ripped jeans. It's strange seeing her face without its usual covering of red clay. If anything, it's more intimidating.

She walks across to the huge window and knocks on it. 'Bulletproof,' she says. 'But that hasn't stopped people from trying.' She steps between two cacti and pulls out a wooden chair, flips it around and straddles it, her arms hanging over the back. 'King has apprised me of your situation, Zevcenko,' she says. 'Take a seat.'

I quickly head to the colourful couch and sit with my hands on my lap like I'm waiting for punishment. 'King said I was meeting my new teacher here,' I say.

The Witch smiles. 'You are: me.'

'You?' I croak. 'No disrespect, Red Witch …'

'You can call me ma,' she says. 'It's traditional for a twasa. But the answer to your question is yes, me. You have a problem and I intend to help you solve it.'

'The thing is, I really have no background in magic,' I say. 'I've been looking at the books, but I—'

'You seem to be mistaken about the nature of this conversation, Zevcenko,' she says. 'Let me correct your obvious confusion. This is me telling you what's happening. There is no discussion involved. Understand?'

'Yes.'

She shoots me a hard look. 'Yes, ma.'

'Sorry. Yes, ma.'

'You have the potential to become a Dreamwalker. That's a skill that hasn't been seen in a long, long time. It's also what is probably stopping your general magical progress.'

'Great,' I say. 'One question: what is Dreamwalking? I've looked at the hard drive that King gave me, but it's all pretty vague.'

She removes the two intertwined strings of beads from around her neck and hands them to me.

'These were passed down to me by my teacher. He had some skill in Dreamwalking, but I never could get the hang of it.'

'So what am I supposed to do with them? Look pretty?'

She smacks me across the back of the head.

'Stop being a smartass.'

'Sorry, ma,' I say.

'Dreamwalking allows you free access into your own psyche. It allows you access to other people's dreams, and in certain cases into the depths of someone else's mind. It may not sound like much, but properly utilised, it can be an incredibly powerful tool. Or weapon. There are tales of great dream battles between sangomas, like psychic games of chess, with the winner capturing the loser's True Will and being able to control him completely. Those beads are the key to the White Ways, the world of the dream. The White Ways are the strands of the web of being, and each bead represents an axis within your own psyche.

'I can't tell you any more than that; like I say, I had no talent for Dreamwalking. All I can tell you is what my teacher told me: seek an inner guide, a part or even several parts of yourself that can teach you how to traverse the world of the dream.'

'You mean like travel inside my own mind?' I say.

'Well yes, bright spark. I'm not talking about going to Umhlanga Rocks for a holiday.'

'How?' I say.

'That's up to you,' she says. 'My teacher said that weaving the beads was the key to Dreamwalking.'

She gets up and points to the door. 'I expect you to have made progress by the next time I see you, Zevcenko.'

Everyone is asleep when I get back to Malpit except for a couple of kids smoking a bong. I sit on my mattress with the two strands of beads in my hands. What the fuck am I supposed to do with a bunch of touristy jewellery? I weave them between my hands like I'm playing that game that girls play when they're kids. Nothing.

'Useless,' I say and put them in a pile next to my bed. I lay my head on the pillow and skydive gratefully into unconsciousness.

I'm in a featureless city, grey, gloomy and massive. The street sign up ahead of me says 'Glowstick', which is suitably obtuse for a dream.

'Hey,' a voice says. 'Welcome back, daddio.'

I turn to see the guy with the massive afro and his group of rhinestone-studded dream weirdos behind me.

'You again? Jesus, I have the strangest dreams.'

'No, man,' he says. 'Not Jesus. Tyrone, your genital phase.'

One of his friends, with garish red lips and blonde hair piled high in a beehive, quickly powders her face in an antique hand mirror and strolls over to me. 'Light me up, won't you, honey?' she drawls. She holds out a lighter and places her long cigarette delicately between her lips.

I sigh and light the cigarette. She scratches me under the chin with a nail. 'Ain't you just the cutest thing?'

'Stop seducing the Conscious Self,' Tyrone says.

'Oh shush.' She flaps a hand at him.

'OK,' Tyrone says slowly. 'I can tell that you're not really grasping what's going on.' He touches his chest. 'I'm your genital stage.' He points to the woman with the cigarette. 'This is your oral phase.'

'Please, honey,' she says. 'Call me Junebug.'

'That's your phallic stage,' Tyrone continues, jerking his head to indicate a guy in a baby-blue jumpsuit wearing a giant white Stetson. He has a straw in his mouth and a massive Smith & Wesson revolver holstered at his hip.

'Hey, motherfucker,' he drawls.

'Oh shush,' Junebug says again, slapping his shoulder. 'It's his standard Freudian joke. He doesn't mean anything by it. You can call him Richard.'

'This over here ...' Tyrone nods at a South American-looking guy with a bone through his nose who scratches at his lime-green jumpsuit like it doesn't fit, 'is your anal stage, Cabales.' Cabales raises a hand in greeting. 'And last but not least is your latency stage. Now where the hell did Chester get to?'

There's a yapping noise and a little chihuahua with a silver rhinestone-studded bow tie trots out from behind Junebug and starts sniffing my leg.

'That's great,' I say. 'Lovely to meet you all. But why are you here?'

'Well, together we are Psychosexual Development,' Tyrone says. 'The basic phases your libidinal drive goes through on its dance-floor shuffle towards maturity, as proposed by Sigmund Freud. We also moonlight as your psyche's first and only funk band.'

I frown at him. 'So what you're saying is that you're all parts of me.'

'Yes!' Tyrone says, like I'm finally understanding a particularly complex maths problem. 'Well, except your anal stage. Your natural anal stage didn't develop. Cabales over there is a novice Peruvian shaman who accidentally blundered into your psyche while high on ayahuasca, so we trapped him and made him perform the functions of your anal stage.' He snaps his fingers. 'Improvisation. That's what I like about being part of your psyche.'

I hold up my hand. 'So, just so we're clear, you replaced a stage of my internal development with a Peruvian shaman? Of all the things I've heard in my life, that's possibly the most fucking demented.'

Cabales gives me a hurt look. 'Hey, you surely remember all the unfortunate toilet-related accidents you had when you were younger?'

My face goes red just thinking about it. My mother said it was because I was a very anxious child. 'Yeah,' I mumble.

'Well, those stopped, didn't they?'

'Eventually.'

He snaps his fingers. 'Well, that's when we recruited Cabales.'

'This is all really fascinating, in an incredibly, ridiculously fucked up sort of way,' I say. 'But why are you here, in my dreams?'

'We're here to teach you to Dreamwalk, honey,' Junebug says. 'Some people get totem animals, some get holy guardian angels, some get daemons. You get your libidinal phases as a seventies funk band. Everyone is different, just remember that.'

'It's a lot to take in,' Tyrone adds. 'We get that. But we're here to help you.'

'Yeah, it's a lot to take in,' I say sarcastically.

Richard strides across to me, lifts his Stetson and looks me in the eye. 'So how about you quit your bellyaching and we teach you something?' *he drawls. Chester the chihuahua yaps his approval.*

'OK, fine,' I say with a sigh. 'What are you going to teach me?'

'Let's start with travelling into other people's dreams.' *Tyrone gestures to the dark, empty city around us.* 'This is what we like to call a dreamsaver. It's just a kind of empty stock image that your brain conjures up to house things. Once you start to manipulate the dream, you can use whatever dreamsaver you find yourself in to access whatever state of mind you want.'

'What about the beads?' I ask. 'How do those fit in?'

'Those are just an interface, honey,' Junebug says, dabbing at her lipstick. 'Different cultures use different things: sticks with symbols carved into them, statuettes, pendants. It's a short cut into the dreamworld. If you get good enough with those pretty beads, you won't have to go through the motions of going to sleep.'

'But let's start slow,' Tyrone says. 'I want you to try and change this dreamsaver to something else. Think you can do that?'

I look around. The city is menacing and claustrophobic and I start to feel the paranoia taking over. 'Sure,' I say nervously. 'This place sucks anyway.'

'Focus,' Tyrone tells me. 'And make the dream respond to your will.'

I focus on the street, the buildings, the dark sky. I feel like I'm slowly being crushed by them. Birds, black pigeons with red eyes, begin to appear, fluttering down and landing on the buildings around me. More arrive, hundreds of them, cooing and scratching with their evil little feet. This is not good at all. I need desperately to get away from this place.

'Easy,' Tyrone says, looking at the birds nervously. 'You want to just let your mind become calm. Those birds won't be dangerous unless you make them dangerous. Think of a good memory.'

It's not exactly the most calming thing he could have said. I search my mind for something reassuring and hit an image of Kyle and me playing video games in his room. OK, so it's not the most epic memory, but it's comforting because it was a simpler time, before I knew about all the things in the world that want to kill me.

I focus so hard on that memory that I think my head is going to split open. I feel the world shift around me, and when I open my eyes I'm in a giant cage. Kyle is riding a unicorn with the face of Nettie Harrison, the girl that died of leukaemia when we were in grade two. He's squealing with terror as a man smoking a cigar orders him to serve an eternity of detention.

'Good,' Tyrone says with a satisfied smile. 'We're in Kyle's dreams now.'

'We're in Kyle's dreams?' I say. 'So can he see and hear me?'

Junebug nods. 'Uh-uh. It's better than Skype, honey.'

'Kyle!' I shout. 'Kyle!'

Kyle's bizarre unicorn ride disappears and he drops to the ground. He sits on the floor staring at me.

'It's Baxter,' I say.

'What the hell is going on?' He looks frantically from side to side.

'You're dreaming.'

'That explains the man with the cigar.' He breathes a sigh of relief.

'Yeah, partially,' I say. 'What the fuck, dude? Are your dreams always like this?'

'No. Well, yes,' he says, rubbing his face.

'Jesus. No wonder you always look tired.'

'What are you doing here, Bax?' he asks. 'Are you real?'

'Yeah, it's really me.' I laugh. 'It's a magical thing that I'm learning from those guys over there.' I point towards Psychosexual Development. They wave.

'You're learning to hack into other people's dreams from a funk band?' he asks.

'Er, yeah,' I say. 'Don't ask how that happened.'

'This is awesome, man.' He stands up. 'Think what we could do in here. IN OUR MINDS! This is like the best thing that's ever happened.' He grabs my shoulders. 'Teach me how to do it, Bax. I'm gonna go into Anwar's brain and fuck shit up.'

'No,' I say. 'I mean, I don't really know how. This is the first time I've done it.'

Kyle frowns. 'You're not holding out on me, are you, Bax? I mean, this is like gold and you won't teach me? That's bullshit.'

'No,' I say. 'Of course not, man. I'm just trying to get a handle on it first so I can teach you better.'

He looks at me suspiciously. 'You've talked to the honchos at Hexpoort, though, right? About getting me in?'

'Yeah, of course,' I lie. 'They say they'll get back to me.'

That's the second time I've lied to Kyle. The guilt rises in me like grey water. Unfortunately, because I'm in a dream, that means it rises in here too. Grey bilge water begins rushing into the cage, and

Kyle and I are instantly up to our necks in it. Worse, there are things swimming in it, black shapes that writhe and twist. Something bites my left arm and I jerk it back. Blood stains the water.

'You've got to control it,' Tyrone says, paddling up next to me. 'Think of something else. QUICKLY! THINK OF SOMETHING ELSE.' *His head goes beneath the water and I reach out for another memory. Something. Anything.*

Ronin is crouched against an old gnarled oak tree, shivering. 'Can't get away from it. Even in my dreams,' he says.

'Get away from what?' I ask. 'Ronin, are you OK?'

'Alcohol,' he says, pointing a shaking hand.

There's a low growling sound as a wolf steps out from a forest that I didn't even know was there. Its eyes are red and its coat is sodden. It smells of pure alcohol. It growls again and whisky pours from its mouth in a torrent that pools around our feet.

'Get away,' Ronin whimpers, looking down at the whisky. 'Get away from me.'

'What do we do?' I ask as the wolf edges closer, its jaws shuddering and snapping like those old plastic wind-up teeth toys.

Ronin sighs, draws himself up and pushes me out the way. 'We do nothing, sparky,' he says. 'I've got to beat this myself.' He turns and stumbles off into the dark forest, his trench coat flapping and the wolf loping after him.

'Right,' says Tyrone, putting a hand on my shoulder as he shakes grey water out of his afro. 'I think that's enough learning for today.'

'Definitely enough learning,' Junebug says, drying her hands. 'We'll try again, don't you worry. You'll get it.' She reaches across and touches me on the forehead. 'See you soon, honey.'

I wake up feeling like I've been mauled in my sleep. My Broken Teeth room-mates are sitting around eating breakfast, playing video games and smoking joints. Nom hands me a bowl of porridge and sits on the end of my mattress. 'Thought I'd let you sleep in a little,' he says. Even his usual hyperactive self has been muted by the brutal Hexpoort curriculum.

'Thanks,' I say, sitting up and rubbing my eyes. 'I had the weirdest dreams.'

'Nightmares more like. Looks like you scratched yourself.' He nods to my left arm.

I look down and see a dark red wound. 'Yeah. Must have scratched myself.'

'I'll get you a bandage,' he says, standing up. 'The Boer says he's got something special planned for us today. Better make sure you're fighting fit.'

I groan and put my head back against the cold stone.

I follow Nom, Faith and Chastity and Stevo through the Hexpoort courtyard to the east end of the perimeter fence. 'Wait,' I say, stopping. 'I thought our tattoos would burn us if we went further than this.'

'Are you scared, newbie?' Chastity says, flicking her dark hair out of her face. She looks at me with those kohl-lined eyes and I draw myself up manfully.

'The perimeter is extended here,' Faith tells me. 'We can go all the way up to the back of the canyon without getting tatburns.'

Tatburns. The painful experience that apparently happens when you step outside the Hexpoort boundaries without permission. Something I've been thinking about a lot lately. Something I've been thinking about testing.

'There's a dam at the top of the canyon, newbie,' Chastity says. 'We sometimes go skinny-dipping there.'

I feel myself blushing. Goddammit, Baxter, you promised you would be nice. You never promised you'd be a socially awkward nerd.

'Yeah,' I say, nonchalantly. 'Sure.'

'We need to get to the Boer's lesson.' Nom is bouncing up and down on his heels. 'Or you know what happens.'

That thought has all of us jogging quickly up the canyon.

'Those are new,' Stevo says, pointing to a set of steel cages that line the canyon walls. They're covered with a huge black tarpaulin that doesn't keep the stench from escaping. It's a thick, animal stench, part wet dog, part rotting meat.

Faith holds her nose. 'What *is* that?'

'No worse than that perfume you insist on spraying on us, princess,' Chastity says, folding her arms. We have reached the edge of the group of kids gathered around the Boer.

'Ja, mah sunshines.' He rubs his hands together. 'We've got a kief surprise for you today. Newly imported to Hexpoort in order to teach you little naaiers some discipline and respect.' He pulls the tarpaulin from the cages. 'Say hello to your Draken.'

The things in the cages are like long pink mammalian snakes with short muscular legs. They shudder as they walk, like giant rolls of polony left on the bass bin of a speaker. Their eyes are slits and they have dragon-like snouts with long whiskers that hang down their faces. One of them stops in front of the group of students and hisses, its face filled with nothing but hatred for humanity.

'Draken,' the Boer says with a satisfied smile. 'We got these from a gang we bust. They used them to dispose of bodies.'

'Oh Christ,' Stevo says. 'He's not going to make us—'

'You will be assigned a Draken and you will fokken look after it like your own mamma,' the Boer says, clapping his hands together. 'So, mah sunshines. Are you ready to meet your new BFF?'

We gingerly follow him to the cages. As we're stepping inside, I grab the edge of his khaki shirt. He spins around ready to drive the edge of his palm into my throat. I put my hands up and flinch.

'What?' the Boer says.

'It's just, I'm not really an animal person,' I say. 'The worst thing is when people post pictures of their cats online, am I right?' He looks at me with his dark, unblinking eyes. 'I mean, some people are able to find solace in the company of animals, while others are happy to enjoy their higher intelligence functions without lowering themselves to the babbling, infantile, sentimental idiocy of animal ownership.'

'I've got just the one for you,' the Boer says with a smile, and propels me into the cage towards an old Draken that is lying curled up and glowering in the corner. One eye has been gouged out, clearly the result of a fight. Its tongue lolls out of its mouth and its remaining pink piggy eye glares at me with pure, naked hatred. 'Baxter, meet Gigli. You and him make the perfect fokken couple.' He hands me a leash and an electric cattle prod. 'The Draken pack works according to power. If you don't show them who the alpha is, they'll rip your head from your body.' He turns around to help some of the other kids get acquainted. 'Have fokken fun,' he calls over his shoulder.

I look at Gigli. The scarred old bastard hates me already. That much is plain.

'Make your Draken trust you, sunshines,' the Boer shouts. 'Talk to them, let them hear your voice.'

I clear my throat and Gigli begins to hiss.

'Baxter, I don't hear you talking,' the Boer says.

'Um, hi,' I begin.

Gigli hisses again, a terrifying guttural sound that makes my nervous system tingle.

'What am I supposed to say?' I shout to the Boer.

'Anything. Speak from the fokken heart.'

I hold the leash in one hand and the cattle prod in the other and consider my options. Gigli looks at me, his single eye narrowed and his double row of teeth bared.

'Listen,' I say. 'I don't like this any more than you do. We don't have to be BFFs, but maybe we can come to a mutually beneficial arrangement?'

Gigli gets up and walks towards me.

'That's it,' I tell him.

He stands in front of me and sniffs at my jeans.

'Good boy,' I say.

He wraps his tail around my legs and drags me to the ground with ease. Then he stands over me, his face close to mine, his terrible monster breath in my nostrils.

'You two seem to be getting along fokken well,' the Boer says with an unpleasant chuckle. 'Don't worry. They don't really seem to like the taste of humans. Our ultimate goal is to have you and your Draken work as a fighting machine, two minds functioning as one to bring destruction to your enemies.'

I look up at Gigli's face breathing down on me. Somehow I don't think this is a mutual partnership.

I stay that way for the rest of the class. Everybody else gradually develops a bond with their Draken. Gigli remains steadfast in his withering, virulent hatred of everything that I am.

Nom, of course, has no problems. With his animal communication ability he chitters and growls his way through a quick conversation, and suddenly he and his Draken, Boris, are buddies for life.

'Hey,' I whisper from beneath Gigli. 'Help me out here. Talk to him, would you?'

Nom looks around quickly and then nods. He stands in front of Gigli and utters a low rumbling growl followed by several high-pitched hisses.

Gigli responds with a single bark that sends fear coursing

through my body and almost makes me wet myself.

'He says you are human excrement. When he looks at you he sees nothing but a pus-filled bag of weakness that he can't even be bothered to kill because it would be absolutely no challenge. He says that even if the Great Draken himself came down from the sky and ordered him to undergo the bonding ceremony, he would rather defy his own deity than be in any way linked to you.'

'Jesus, you got all of that from one bark?'

Nom nods. 'The Draken language is really quite efficient. Its syntax is remarkable. For instance, when he said you were excrement—'

'OK, yeah. That's great,' I say.

Gigli gets off me and lopes away to sit and glower in the corner.

'This is ridiculous. That fugly thing is never going to like me.'

'Don't worry, Bax.' Nom puts a hand on my shoulder. 'He may still come round.'

From: Bax (baxter@hexpoort.com)
To: Kyle (wordflex@gmail.com)

Yo

So here's another hit of that sweet, sweet magical theory you love so much.
I'm still sucking at it so don't ask me for any pointers. How things with you?
Gotten laid yet? Wait, don't answer that. I know the answer. BURN!

Oh, and send me something interesting/funny. This place is
seriously getting to me.

Bax

'South African Magic in Context' by Si Konyela
The Journal of Occult Practices 2002

South African magic is a confluence of magical influences: Xhosa and Zulu
shamanism, the magic of the Dutch Hexenmeisters (from which the
American Pennsylvania Dutch Pow Wow magic also derived), English
High Ceremonial Magic, Vodun from West Africa, as well as the ecstatic
practices of the Khoisan people.

The resultant discipline is a hybrid magical form that combines both high magic and folk magic from the oral tradition into an effective magical style that is eminently suitable for the South African context.

Although there are many regional variances and specialisations, certain core principles within the broader Southern African magical system remain constant.

!Num

!Num is a traditional term for energy in magic. The South African system places emphasis on achieving a balance between the aim of the spell and the energy it takes to achieve this end. For instance, using magic to pick up an object is possible but far less energy is used by simply using one's hand to achieve the same goal. Thus ways of controlling and amplifying magical energy are important to the system, particularly for more complex spells.

Muti

Muti is the generic term for the ingredients of magical spells. The term includes herbs and plants but has increasingly come to refer to the blood and body parts used to amplify magical workings. Some examples of traditional muti are powdered vulture bones, hyena jaws, the teeth of various animals (including humans), organs and skin.

Blood is perhaps the most important muti in African magic. Magical ability is determined by the blood of the user (hence the importance of genetic lineage) and drawing magical power from the spilled blood of other creatures is central to creating magic that doesn't totally deplete the user.

The Mojo Bag

Traditionally called a wanga bag, but almost universally referred to as a mojo bag, this set of talismans is central to the South African practice of magic, an ancient technology that allows the interface of mind and energy.

A sangoma's mojo bag is as individual as a set of fingerprints and consists of a set of seven magical items accumulated over many years. Some of these magical items have become as famous as the magicians that wielded them: the White Ant carving of Eugène Nielen Marais, the bronze beetle of Miriam Makeba and the Coke bottle of Oom Dawid Kruiper.

Nobody understands the process of how an object links to a particular mage but one thing is clear: you don't get the talismans you want. Many a mage has hoped for a tiger claw and ended up with a coffee-shop loyalty card.

Masters and Apprentices

'Twasa' is a term denoting a person undertaking the study of South African magic. In the South African system a twasa may have many teachers but only one master. As with many European systems of magic, the apprentice is bonded to the master and shares a lifelong mental bond. This is not always a happy arrangement and there are many instances of students murdering their masters, and vice versa, in the dark history of South African magic.

Conclusion

South African magic has primarily been transmitted as part of the oral traditions of the many disparate cultures that occupy Southern Africa. The attempts to formalise it have largely failed and it remains to be seen whether this raw, powerful art will be able to maintain its distinct identity in an age of globalised magical practices.

MUMBLEROCK

'The thing is, we've barely spoken since you've been there,' Esmé says.

I'm huddled in a cold granite corridor with my hoodie over my head and Nom's cheap phone pressed to my ear.

'I know,' I say. 'I'm sorry. It's just been a little intense here. It's not going very well.'

'Why?'

'I suck at magic, I'm not an animal person, and not getting involved in school politics is like having a part of my personality amputated.'

'Bax. You are doing that for yourself, right? The good thing, I mean.'

'Yeah,' I lie. My glasses start to slip down my nose and I push them up with the back of my hand.

'OK. Because you shouldn't try to be something you're not.'

'It's just that—'

'Hey, asshole,' a voice calls down the corridor.

'Shit,' I say into the phone. 'I've got to go. But I've found out a cool thing I can do. I'll, umm, show you later.'

'OK,' Esmé says. 'Later.'

'I, umm, lov—' I begin, but the phone goes dead.

'Hey, asshole. I'm talking to you.'

I sigh and turn around to face Hekka and one of his cronies.

'I see you have another phone for me,' he says with a grin.

'Yeah, come and get it.' I smile and stick the phone down the front of my jeans and into my boxers.

'Jesus,' Hekka says with a grimace. 'You can keep the fucking thing.'

I shrug. 'Suit yourself.'

He covers the gap between us in an instant and pins me against the wall. I feel the weight of his arms on mine and I know I could slip them easily. I've watched him fighting in the Boer's classes. He's strong but he's dumb. My new-found muscles ache to wrap themselves around his neck and squeeze the life out of him. But I don't let them.

'What's going on here?' King calls out, striding down the corridor. He's wearing what looks like a blue toga today, revealing one furry shoulder.

Hekka dips his head. 'I didn't ask for this, Baxter,' he says softly. 'I don't want to be different, I don't want to be special.' He turns his head to the side and gives a wink that only I can see.

'Baxter,' King says sternly. 'Leave Hekka alone. He's got enough to deal with.'

The rage burns so hot inside me that I feel like I could boil water just by touching it.

'OK,' I say through gritted teeth. 'Sorry.'

King nods and continues down the corridor. Hekka gives the middle finger to his back and then shoves me up against the wall again. I clench my fists at my sides.

'I hear you think you're a Dreamwalker,' he says. 'Well, aren't you fucking special?'

I look directly into his eyes. 'Listen, man, I genuinely don't want any of your glory. You go ahead and be the hero. Seriously. I'm really, really not interested.'

'So what you're saying is that you think that being the Chosen One is unimportant?'

I sigh. 'I think that if Fate really wanted to maintain the status quo or bring balance to the force or whatever, then many thousands of small processes running in the background, kinda like apps, would be better than investing all that world-saving in a single individual.'

He reaches out a hand and grabs me by the throat. 'Well, that's how it works. The world doesn't want your nerd opinions.'

I force myself to nod.

He raises a fist as if to punch me. 'You better watch your hero-hating, Zevcenko,' he says, then drops his hand, shoves me against the wall one last time and jerks his head for his crony to follow him.

I stand with my fists still clenched, staring at their backs.

CrowBax:	DESTROY!
SienerBax:	OK, I know you're upset, but—
CrowBax:	That was humiliating. Have you never heard of self-defence? This wouldn't be being bad; it'd just be defending ourselves.
SienerBax:	We can't. We're on the wagon. Thirty-five days clean. Manipulation-free.
CrowBax:	Please, just the one. One gambit, one act of psychological terrorism. Just give me Hekka. Please, I just need one. Pleassssse.

Pangs of loneliness burrow through my chest. My fingers are itching, my head is pounding. I don't know what to do.

I quickly retrieve the phone from my boxers and dial a

number that I never thought I'd dial.

'Harold Emly,' says the slightly slurry voice on the other end.

'Harold, hi, it's, um, Baxter Zevcenko. From Pornography Anonymous?'

'Baxter! It's so great to hear your voice. How's your new school going?'

'Not so good. Um, I think I'm going to relapse.' I don't tell him that I mean relapsing into manipulating people, rather than porn.

'It's OK, Baxter,' he says soothingly. 'Tell me what happened.'

I take a deep breath. 'OK. But this is going to sound really, really weird to you.'

I tell him about Hexpoort and about not being magical enough. I tell him about the seventies funk band that is teaching me to Dreamwalk. I tell him about my giant tabby-cat teacher and the Chosen One who is bullying me.

Harold is quiet for a long moment. Eventually he speaks. 'I have to tell you that that's not even in the top ten weirdest things someone from Pornography Anonymous has told me.'

'Really?'

'Don't worry, it's all confidential with me,' he says. 'You need to hang in there, Baxter. These times of stress are when relapses happen. You need to reaffirm your intention to stay clean. Don't throw away all the progress you've made.'

I take another deep breath. 'Thanks, Harold. I feel better already.'

'Of course. And Baxter, if you ever need any other help, the Fallen and I would be happy to assist.'

'Thanks, Harold,' I say.

'Any time. I've got to run now. I've got a PA meeting starting.'

I hang up the phone and stand in the corridor. I think of Esmé and I think of my mom. 'Be strong, Baxter,' I whisper to myself. 'Just be strong.'

I sit through my next class with stoic aloofness. Hekka tries to get under my skin but I let wads of paper and insults bounce off me like I'm bulletproof.

'Baxter,' King says when the class ends. 'Can I speak to you in my office?'

I sigh and follow him in, coughing at the strong smell of incense as I sit down.

'Sorry. I'll put that out.' He takes an incense stick from a holder and stubs it out.

'Listen,' I say. 'I'm sorry about Hekka. It won't happen again.'

He stares at me with his large yellow eyes, and one of his pointy ears twitches. 'I know you weren't harassing Hekka Jones in the corridor,' he says. 'That kid is an asshole. But it's easier to keep him happy.'

I laugh. 'Well, we agree on that. But why? Why does everyone tiptoe around that motherfucker?'

'You've heard the rumour?' he asks.

'It's a little more than a rumour,' I say. 'He basically walks around with a trucker cap that says "Chosen One" on it.'

King laughs, a sharp hacking and snorting like he's coughing up a hairball. 'He's not the most humble student we have. Unfortunately we have reason to believe that the prophecy is very real.'

'What *is* this prophecy?' I say. 'Where did it come from?'

'It's an old Siener one,' he says. 'Your ancestry is the reason why I want to share it with you.' He adjusts his spectacles, clears his throat and starts to read.

> *He will be branded with the crescent moon*
> *An orphan bred in fear and chaos*
> *The Muti Man*
> *Half angel, half devil*

He will erase the line
Between the Known and the Hidden.

He finishes reading, slides his spectacles on to the tip of his nose and looks at me.

'That's it?' I say.

He nods.

'You're fucking kidding me. You're giving Hekka special treatment because of that bullshit?'

He reaches into his desk and takes out a file. 'Since you've arrived at Hexpoort, several more agents have been killed and their teeth taken.' He pulls photos from the files and hands them to me. Crime scenes. People sprawled at awkward angles with bloody mouths and no teeth.

'Yeah,' I say with a grimace. 'Goblins tried to rip my teeth out for the Muti Man. I believe he's real.' I hand back the photos. 'But I certainly don't believe this bullshit prophecy. It's what they do in horoscopes: make it vague enough to apply to anyone. I mean, come on. Half angel and half devil? Doesn't that basically describe human nature? I mean, don't you ever wonder why prophecies don't just say "The Chosen One's name is Bob, here is his telephone number and GPS coordinates"?'

'It's not that simple,' King says, raising a bushy feline eyebrow.

'No, because it's bullshit. Kids here can create fire out of nothing and they're only learning. If the power of prophecy actually existed, it would be more accurate.'

'MK6 agents are dying and that's becoming an increasing concern.'

'You wanted my official half-Siener opinion on that prophecy?' I say.

King nods.

'Well, I've just given it to you.'

King sighs. 'Well, thank you, Baxter.' He puts the file back in his desk drawer. 'I think we're done here.'

I get up and walk to the door.

'Baxter?'

I turn around to look at him.

'How is your magical progress going?'

'Badly,' I say.

'Well, I suggest you try and make some progress before your next lesson with the Witch. She's a big fan of results.'

'Thanks,' I say and slam the door behind me.

I use my lunch break to put in some quality time with Gigli. He uses it to lie in his pen and glare at me with that piggy eye. I squat down next to the cage with my palms showing. *I come in peace, you Draken psycho.*

'Come on,' I say in a soft, cooing voice. 'We can do this.'

He pricks his ears up and cocks his head to the side.

'That's it.' I stick my hand through the bars. 'Come on over and say hello. There's no need to fight about this.'

He gets up and starts to walk towards me. He looks curious, sniffing the ground and pricking his ears up.

'That's it, boy,' I say. 'Now we're getting somewhere.'

He smiles lopsidedly, letting his long tongue hang out of his mouth. Hell yeah. I'm the goddamn Draken-whisperer.

In an instant he's across the cage with a snarling hiss. I jerk my hand back just before his teeth snap shut on the space it occupied. I tumble backwards on to my ass and scrabble through the dirt away from the cage.

Gigli presses his nose against the bars and gives a long, wheezing chuckle. I stare at him with hatred. What a fucking asshole.

* * *

The rest of the day happens around me like time-lapse photography. I'm a complete magical failure, a single, solitary point that exists outside of everything else. I have one thing, and only one thing, going for me in this place. I wait until early evening and then slip away and find a quiet spot in one of the corridors; an alcove that houses a small stone gargoyle. I give it the middle finger as I sit down with my back to the wall.

The Witch's next lesson is scheduled for tomorrow morning and I seriously need to make some progress. I take a deep breath and weave the beads between my fingers. The world shimmers and I dive into unconsciousness.

'You're getting the hang of the beads, daddio,' Tyrone says. 'Nice going.'

'Still got a long way to go,' Richard drawls, pushing back his Stetson. 'Best we get started.'

'Long way to go to where?' I look around. The dreamsaver this time is a peaceful meadow.

'To there, honey,' Junebug says, gesturing with her ever-present cigarette.

I look to where she's pointing. There are mountains in the distance, with a city in front of them. From the middle of the city a pagoda rises like something out of a samurai movie. 'What's that?' I say, shading my eyes.

'That's where you go to meet your True Self, honey,' Junebug says. 'He's the one that sent us here to help you.'

'My True Self? Aren't I my True Self?'

'You're the Conscious Self,' Tyrone says, and Cabales grunts in agreement.

'So I'm like the king around here?'

Richard lifts the collar of his rhinestone jumpsuit and shakes his pelvis a little. 'Ain't nobody but the king is the king, baby.'

'The king?' Tyrone says. 'Get a load of this kid. No, you're not the king. You're the poster boy, the figurehead. You have very little executive power. I mean, technically we're ALL Baxter, you're just the one that tells yourself that in the mirror in the morning. The only way to unlock your magical potential is for you, the Conscious Self, to meet your True Self.'

'So let's get going,' Richard says. 'We're wasting time. We have to cross the underworld of your unconscious to get there.'

'OK,' I say. 'That's not going to be too much of a problem, is it? I mean, it is my mind.'

Tyrone chuckles. 'If only it were that simple. Think of your unconscious as the browser history of your psyche. All your secret desires, taboo images and unhealthy intentions exist here.'

'Shit,' I say.

'Yeah,' Tyrone agrees. 'Exactly.'

We follow a winding gravel path through the meadow, me in the centre of the group of funksters and Chester, my Freudian latency-phase chihuahua, trotting along behind.

After a long time we reach the edge of the city. The path becomes pavement and we follow it along a winding street. As we walk, the neighbourhood grows increasingly dilapidated. 'This is where your prejudices hang out,' Tyrone whispers to me. 'Play it cool.'

'I'm not prejudiced,' I say defensively.

Tyrone raises an eyebrow. 'Of course you're not.'

The neighbourhood becomes a sprawling slum. Groups of people hang in doorways and look at us as we pass. 'Hey, toots,' a big skinhead guy shouts to Junebug. 'Quit hanging out with those homos and come and hang out with us.'

She gives him a friendly wave and we carry on walking.

'It's your mind, remember?' Tyrone says. 'They won't be a problem unless you make them a problem.'

We pass an old house with a fat guy sitting on a couch on the porch drinking beer. The stench of Cheetos, sweat and farts wafts from him.

'That's your toxic masculinity,' Junebug says.

'Fuck you, bitch,' the fat man shouts. 'Why don't you come over and have a ride.' He gestures towards his sweat-stained crotch.

'No thanks!' she calls back. 'But thank you.'

'Nice guy,' I say, as we hurry past.

She laughs. 'He's not so bad once you look past the impotent animal rage.'

I focus on staying calm. It's my mind. It's my mind. It's my mind. I keep repeating that until we exit the slum.

Tyrone pats me on the shoulder. 'You did well. They could have torn us apart.'

'What?' I say.

He smiles. 'Like I said, you did well.'

The slum opens up on to a big park. It looks like an outdoor music festival has been happening here. There are empty beer cans scattered everywhere. People are wandering around aimlessly, depressed, make-up smeared, perpetually trying to piece together what happened the night before. They've run out of cigarettes, but they keep searching for packets that never appear. They look at each other with disgust.

'The Asphodel Meadows,' Richard says, and he puts a hand on the huge revolver at his hip. 'Dangerous place.'

We walk through the dismal end of the party. I feel I'm coming down from a drug I didn't take. The further we go, the more the world is drained of colour.

'Fight it, honey,' Junebug says, stroking my cheek. 'Just keep going.'

I feel like the air has become molasses. I fight against it, every step a struggle. Esmé is going to leave me for Troy. I can see that now. The rest of my life is going to be this terrifying battle against my need to manipulate. I may eventually succeed at acting like I'm good, but I'm never going to feel good. The self-loathing is always going to be there.

I stumble and sit down in what looks like a chill tent at the end of a party. Dirty beanbags and empty plastic bank bags are scattered everywhere. It smells of incense, sex and stale beer. I grab a beanbag and lie down.

'You've got to get through this,' Junebug says, sitting down next to me.

'Nooo,' I whisper, burying my face in the beanbag. 'I can't go on.'

Cabales, my surrogate anal-phase shaman, squats down and stares at me.

'What does he want?' I murmur into my beanbag.

He starts talking in Spanish, punctuating each point by prodding me in the arm with a hard finger.

'He says the great feathered serpent god will eventually destroy the world in a hail of cosmic fire. All your problems are nothing. Until the end comes we should all just do what we can.'

I turn my head and look at him. His dark eyes bore into me.

'OK,' I say with a sniff. 'Let's go.'

I let the shaman help me up and he puts an arm around my shoulder. He utters a couple more words of Spanish.

'He says you smell like shit,' Junebug says with a smile. 'He's right: that beanbag was really dirty, honey.'

I wipe the side of my face with my sleeve and follow them out of the chill tent.

'Almost there,' Tyrone says, pointing to the pagoda that juts up a few blocks away from us. 'You're doing really, really well.'

'Thanks,' I murmur, and I let them lead me the rest of the way out of the park. As soon as we are out on the streets again, I feel better. Much, much better.

'That was horrible,' I say. 'I never want to go back there.'

'You don't have to, honey,' Junebug says with a smile.

The streets are clean and wide here and there's a refreshing breeze blowing. Up ahead a fire hydrant has burst and the street has flooded. We splash through the water. 'The shallows,' Tyrone says. 'Try not to look at it too long.'

I glance down as I walk, and I can see thousands of online articles: Wikipedia entries on Marxism, pieces about Syrian politics, radical feminism, nutrition; half-articles that I didn't finish, things I skimmed. I stare into them, the colourful ideas, ideologies and opinions streaming past. I'm mesmerised. 'Whoa there,' Tyrone says, grabbing my shoulder. 'I said don't look too long. You can still drown in the shallows.'

I force myself to look ahead as we walk. 'Almost there.' Tyrone points to the pagoda. 'We're really almost—'

'Hey! Bax. Wake up!'

I open my eyes. 'What? What's going on?' I look up groggily to see Nom standing over me, shaking my shoulders.

'I've been looking everywhere for you,' he says. 'Why are you lurking in an empty corridor?'

'Just getting some peace and quiet,' I say, trying to massage the kinks out of my neck. 'I was kinda busy, man. What's up?'

'I want you to come check something out.' He hauls me from the alcove and up the stairs to Malpit.

'Come on,' I say. 'I've got stuff to do.' I need to visit Esmé's dreams. Or at least give her another call.

He drags me to the window and points out into the night. At first my eyes find it difficult to focus, but gradually they adjust and I see the unmistakable form of Gigli slipping from his cage.

'What is that slithery bastard doing?' I whisper.

Nom shrugs. 'Maybe we should follow him.'

'What the hell for? He almost took my hand off earlier.'

'Find out where he's going. Maybe it'll help you to figure him out. You need to do something, Bax.'

I rub my eyes. 'You think so?'

He shrugs. 'Beasties of any kind, humans included, just want to be understood.'

'If you say so.'

'Come on,' he says, throwing me my hoodie. 'We'll just check it out and then you can come back and do whatever you have to do. What do you have to lose?'

'Sleep,' I mumble as I follow him down the Malpit staircase.

The night is cool. I pull my hoodie up as we slip across the courtyard and past the gallows, which is even creepier at night-time. We trek up through the canyon, following the vague pink shape of Gigli against the purple, dark blue and black of the night. The moon is full and bright and I can see the landscape stretching out down below us as we climb. An English teacher once tried to tell our class about the tradition of describing the landscape in South African literature. Man, was that a boring lesson. I guess the Sieners saw this landscape as their spiritual homeland. The rugged hills and rasping scrubland chipped and filed away at the European to form the Afrikaner. The fact that that is all part of me is as strange as having the oil-spill of Crow blood in my veins.

'What was it like growing up with the bok-people? I mean really,' I ask as we walk.

'The Ndiru is what we call ourselves,' he says. 'It was good. Bit weird for me now, though, because I have to consciously shift between the human world and that world; it's like having two parts of myself.'

I laugh. 'Yeah, I can sympathise with that.'

'My people don't understand why I came to Hexpoort,' he says. 'They think I've joined the enemy.'

'Really?'

'Humans haven't exactly been good to the Ndiru. Even now my family is forced to live in a designated area and can be killed if they leave it.'

'What?' I say. 'That's bullshit.'

He shrugs. 'That's the way it is. But that's why I came to Hexpoort. Maybe I can change things.'

'Yeah, maybe.' I shove my hands in my hoodie pockets.

'Well, we've got to do something,' Nom says. 'It's bad and it's getting worse.'

Along the path we come across an old rusted tractor that a family of badgers had made into a badger mansion. Nom barks a greeting and the male badger chitters something in return. The female immediately attacks him ferociously. After a quick one-sided fight, the male limps off into the scrubland.

'Jesus, what was that all about?'

'Little bastard tried to sell me one of his kids. Badgers, man. They've got some serious issues. Now otters, on the other hand, those guys have things sorted.'

I follow Nom past the dam at the top of the canyon.

'We're getting close to the perimeter,' he says. 'If he goes past it, we're going to have to call it a night.'

But Gigli stops just short of the Hexpoort perimeter. There's a small cave in the side of the canyon and he ducks into it. A soft mewling sound emanates from within. We creep closer, crouch behind a rock and peek round into the cave.

'The old horndog,' I whisper. Gigli has his pink form wrapped around a female leopard in a loving embrace. In front of them three weird little cubs mewl and play with each other.

'They're tiny. So cute,' Nom says. 'A Draken mating with a leopard. Who thought that'd be possible?'

'God, imagine what they're going to look like when they're older,' I whisper. 'They'll make some fugly safari pictures. What do we call 'em? Drakpards?'

'Leodraks,' Nom replies.

'Yeah, that's better.'

We watch the little cubs frolicking while their proud parents look on.

'So damn cute,' Nom repeats. 'Wish I had my camera …'

A snuffling sound comes from the path leading up the canyon.

'What was that?' I whisper.

Nom shrugs and puts his finger to his lips.

Gigli heard it too, because he's up and standing protectively in front of the cave. A low hissing erupts from his throat and is answered by a deep rumbling growl.

'Oh Jesus,' Nom says, scrambling backwards and almost knocking me over.

'What?' I ask. 'What is it?'

Six creatures emerge into the rocky area surrounding the cave. They're big and muscled, with hunched shoulders, hyena snouts and two long canines jutting from their jaws. They circle around, their huge mouths dripping saliva on to the ground.

'Kholomodumo,' Nom whispers.

'Wonderful. What are they doing here?'

'Goblins sometimes use them as dogs, but right now I'd say they're looking for a snack.'

The Kholomodumo prowl around, sniffing and slavering and looking at the cubs like they're on a buffet table. Gigli coils and uncoils, his piggy eye fixed on them and his mouth curled in a snarl. He's a mean motherfucker for sure, but I'm not convinced even he can take on six of the things at the same time.

'We have to help him,' I say.

'Yeah.' Nom sighs. 'We do.'

We scrabble around in the dirt and find two decent-sized sticks. Nom sets them alight with a spell, because I can't even do that yet.

'OK,' I say. 'Here goes.'

We jump out from behind the rock brandishing the flaming

sticks in front of us like swords. It seemed like a sound plan at the time, but close up to six of these hyena beasts, I realise that I might have overestimated its efficacy.

They turn towards us, snarling. One of them lunges forward and I bring my stick down in a flaming arc on to its snout. It yelps and jumps back, then immediately springs forward again. I vault off one of the rocks out of the way. The Boer's teaching comes so naturally to me that I don't even have to think about it. All those hours punching bags, hauling logs and practising moves makes my body respond as if it's on automatic.

Out of the corner of my eye I see Nom firing off spells. Gigli is locked in mortal combat with two of the Kholomodumo and the mother leopard is stalking back and forth in front of her babies as two more slink towards her.

I charge towards them and catch one with a well-timed shot to the neck. It goes down, and without thinking about it I jump as high as I can and plant both of my feet on one of its legs. It snaps like firewood and the thing yelps and twists out of the way. I swipe at the other one and then stumble backwards as it lunges. It misses me, but carries on and smashes into Gigli's side. He's thrown against a rock and spins around hissing at the three beasts that now surround him.

I run towards him and stab one of them in the side with my stick. It's a glancing blow but it draws blood and the thing turns towards me. In a heartbeat Gigli lurches forward and rips its throat out. Blood gushes on to the dirt and the thing drops to the ground. Gigli gulps down a mouthful of oesophagus and gives me a lopsided bloody grin.

And just like that it happens. The mind-meld that the Boer was talking about, that special connection between man and Draken, snaps together like a completed Rubik's cube, and like a whirling dervish of pain and destruction we plough into the

Kholomodumo. Gigli wraps and unwraps his body around me like a pink mammalian nunchaku, ripping into flesh and bone with glee. I slip into the gaps that he leaves and jab with my flaming stick like it's a spear until it shatters and all I'm left with is a bloody shard of wood.

Three of the Kholomodumo are dead and the remaining three decide that the pickings aren't as easy as they'd hoped. They lope off into the night, chased by a nasty fire spell from Nom.

I drop to my knees, breathing hard. There's blood all over me and I'm not sure how much of it is mine. I touch my side gingerly. There are a couple of lacerations but I think I'm OK. Gigli walks up to me and presses his head against mine. His breath smells like blood and decaying food, but I don't mind. He hisses something.

Nom is lying back against a rock, wiping blood from his face.

'He says you're his brother,' he translates. 'And that if the Great Draken himself came down from the sky and ordered him to abandon you, he would rather defy his own deity than not be linked to you.'

Gigli nuzzles his nose against my hand and then retreats back to the cave to his lady love and their fugly little cubs.

Nom helps me up and we walk slowly away from the cave.

'What the fuck were those things doing here?' I ask.

'No idea,' Nom says. 'But they've gone past the Hexpoort perimeter, so we can't follow them.'

'Oh damn,' I say.

We stand and look at the hole that the Kholomodumo ripped in the perimeter fence.

'Come on.' Nom puts a hand on my shoulder.

I carry on looking at the fence.

He sighs. 'Don't. You're already in enough pain.'

I hold up my hands. 'Perfect time, then,' I say.

He shrugs. 'Go ahead. Everyone has to test it once.'

I look at the hole. I could get out of here. If I could find a road and if there's somebody driving along it and if that somebody is not a murderer, then maybe I could make it to a town and then buy a bus ticket back to Cape Town. I duck through the hole and stand on the other side of the fence, looking back at Nom.

Just as I thought. The whole 'magical tattoo' thing is a ruse, a way of keeping us in line. They don't even need to police us, because we're policing ourselves. It's so fucking indicative of our culture that we have internalised that kind of— UUHHHRGH, JESUS!

The pain is like nothing I've ever felt before. I'm simultaneously on fire and drowning, having my tongue ripped out while tasting hydrochloric acid. My skin sloughs off my body and I'm a bleached skeleton bare to the thousand icy knives of the semi-desert air.

I stumble backwards, gasping, choking, whimpering. Nom grabs my arm and pulls me back through the hole. The pain disappears instantly. I look down at my arms to make sure the skin is still there.

'Told you,' a voice says from behind us. I turn to see Faith and Chastity watching me, a towel slung over their shoulder. Chastity blows a bubble with her gum. 'What the fuck happened to you two suckers?'

We tell her about the Kholomodumo but leave out the part about Gigli and his cubs. He's my friend now and he deserves a little privacy.

'We're going to the dam to swim,' Faith says. 'You want to come?'

'Yeah,' Chastity adds. 'You tried to escape, you felt the pain. It's like a rite of passage. You're one of us now.'

I'm so hopped up on adrenalin that I feel I can do anything.

'Sure,' I say.

We walk slowly up to the dam. We find Stevo rolling a joint on the bank. 'You get tatburn?' he asks as we approach.

I rub my arms and shudder at the memory. 'Yeah.'

He shakes his head. 'Hurts like a motherfucker, doesn't it?'

'Got something to take the edge off for the newbie, Stevo?' Chastity says.

Stevo grins. 'When do I not have something to take the edge off? Mumblerock.' He opens his palm to show us a handful of purplish crystals. One of his rats runs down his arm and stands on his hind legs, little paws waving and nose sniffing the air. 'Quit it, Hunter,' Stevo says. 'You're such a goddamn junkie.

'There are these weeds that grow around the boundary fence of the Poort. I found out that if you put them through an intense alchemical process you get these resinous crystals that you can smoke.'

'Why's it called Mumblerock?'

'You'll see.'

He pulls out a glass pipe, puts some of the crystals inside. Chastity produces a Zippo with a flourish and holds it under the bulb. Stevo takes a couple of hits and then passes it to Faith.

'I don't do drugs,' Faith says, pursing her lips.

'Pity we share the same bloodstream,' Chastity says, grabbing the pipe and taking a hit.

Faith rolls her eyes. 'Teen angst is so unattractive on you.'

I look at them. It must be tough. Two such individual people sharing the same body.

'Is that pity I see in your eyes, Baxter? Because if it is, cut it the fuck out,' Chastity says.

'For once we agree,' Faith says.

'Bad move,' Nom says shaking his head. 'Especially because she's high. You're going to get it now.'

They stand up unsteadily.

'Together we're the cheerleader and the goth,' Chastity says.

'The popular and the unpopular. She writes in her fluffy pink diary about boys, while I cut myself. We're the top and bottom of the social hierarchy, the yin-yang, the alpha and omega of high school.' She hands me the pipe. 'So fuck your pity.'

'Sorry,' I say. 'It won't happen again.'

'Just smoke the damn drugs, Zevcenko,' Chastity says.

I take a hit. It tastes vile, like burning plastic.

'Good, eh?' Stevo says.

'No,' I reply. 'Not good at all.'

He laughs. 'You'll come to love it, trust me.'

A pleasant buzzing starts in my temples, like wasps flying in formation through my frontal lobes.

'Let's swim,' Chastity says.

My head is thudding and everything looks weird. Weirder than usual. The stars are splattered across the sky and the cool night air fills my lungs like they're helium balloons. I feel elated, inflated, and I'm pretty sure my pupils are heavily dilated.

I strip down without thinking and follow the procession of naked bodies into the tea-coloured water of the dam. I dive in and the coldness punches me in the sternum, but I don't care. It soothes the lacerations on my side and the water is filled with glorious streaming fractals pulsing to the thudding of my heart.

I break through the surface of the water and watch as Faith and Chastity stand waist-deep in the water like a beautiful dual mermaid. They simultaneously scoop water in their hands and splash it at me. I watch it falling in slow motion like multifaceted jewels that have been suspended in the jelly-like substance of time.

We lie back on the grass and watch the stars dance. I feel like I've been holding my breath since I got to Hexpoort. I finally let it out and watch it spiralling up into the galaxy.

'Why did you want to escape?' asks Faith. Her blonde hair looks silvery in the moonlight.

'There's this girl …' I start, but my mouth feels rubbery. 'There's this …' I start again, but my mouth is seriously hanging open now and I can't shut it. An involuntary purring comes from my throat. I begin to splutter and mumble like I'm insane. I shoot Nom a panicked look and try to speak again, but he holds his hand up and makes a circular motion with it.

'Just ride it out.'

The others start to mumble and chatter too, and it's like we're some kind of insane congregation on the hill, speaking in tongues, muttering incoherently. It lasts for about five minutes before I regain some measure of control over my organs of articulation.

'And that, kids,' Stevo says in a slurred monotone, 'is why it's called Mumblerock.'

We burst out in hysterical laughter. It's another five minutes before any of us can actually talk.

From: Bax (baxter@hexpoort.com)
To: Kyle (wordflex@gmail.com)

Hey man

Yeah, thanks for cat gifs, douche. If King sees them he'll probably scratch me to death. So here's another article from the Journal since you liked the other one so much. #dreamwalking #yolo

Don't miss me too much

Bax

'The Lost Art of Dreamwalking' by Frater D.X.
The Journal of Occult Practices 1995

Dreamwalking is the term for a cluster of skills and abilities that have largely been lost in the modern practice of magic. Simply put, dreamwalking is the ability to consciously travel into one's own psyche and into the psyches of others at will.

It is the purpose of this article to explore the little we know of dreamwalking with the aim of helping to preserve the theoretical understanding of thisfascinating art for future generations.

The Nature of Dreams

Sigmund Freud called dreams the 'royal road to the unconscious'. The Freudian theory of psychosexual development, being the theory of how the human libido develops in five stages, is integral to how we understand repression and expression in dreaming.

According to Freud, dreams are a way of symbolically projecting desire, acting out repressed urges, and facing fears in a way that makes sense to the dreamer. So however crazy, bizarre or incoherent the dream seems, the pattern is there and the dreamer need only look deeper in order to discern what it means.

Occult interpretations of Freud's (and his student Jung's) work take further this idea of the meaning of the symbols of the psyche. According to occultists, the main task the dreamer undertakes in dreamwalking is the defeat of the False Ego and the connection to one's True Self, an act that can unlock a dreamer's true potential.

The False Ego is depicted in many mythologies as a beast – the dragon that St George slays or the snake in the Garden of Eden – that the Conscious Self (the hero) must defeat in order to progress to the True Self. This can only be done through achieving holism or unity in the psyche.

The Guides of the Dream

Those who, thanks to their genetic heritage, are predisposed to the skill of dreamwalking are often able to slip naturally into the dreamworld with little help. Drugs, alcohol or repetitive sensory experiences such as long drives will often catapult them into the dreamworld, although practices such as the Mongolian use of bird entrails, the European use of throwing sticks and the African way of weaving beads were traditionally used as a conscious interface between a dreamwalker and his psyche.

The dreamworld, however, can be a confusing and dangerous place, and the psyche of the dreamwalker often provides guides to ferry the conscious mind safely through the dream. Call them spirit guides, totem animals or guardian angels, these guides often take on a strange, ridiculous or terrifying form to shock the conscious mind out of complacency.

The Dangers of Dreamwalking

We are psychologically more vulnerable when we dream. Most dreams happen at a shallow level and expose the dreamer to very little danger, but the deeper one travels the more dangerous it becomes.

Records exist from the golden age of dreamwalking (AD 1000–1115) when much was gained from the dreamworld but many dreamwalkers were also lost. In fact, more dreamwalkers died during this period than during any other period in history. Entire dream-wars were fought by dream-walkers from the comfort of their own beds, and dream espionage and assassinations were rife.

Even more politically dangerous were dream kidnappings. Capturing the True Self of somebody allows direct control of that person, and there are records of extreme acts of political control perpetrated by dreamwalkers.

Thankfully, the only way to access another's True Will is to be invited in by an aspect of the psyche. (There are instances where the psyche of a recently deceased dreamwalker can be invited into the psyche of another person but these are rarely a happy union and most often result in the rejection of the host psyche, and hostility or even destructive behaviour by the psyche in limbo.)

The excesses of this so-called golden age resulted in the Church purges of the Middle Ages whereby dreamwalking was restricted to elite members of the clergy, and most of the accumulated knowledge of dreamwalking was destroyed in an effort to keep its power out of the hands of the common people.

There are rumours of certain genetic lines that retain the ability, but sadly most of the knowledge of dreamwalking has been lost in the mists of time. It is the hope of the author that through careful research some of this forgotten art can be restored to its former glory.

DOGS OF WAR

'Tell me again about your spirit guides,' the Witch says. She's wearing a black Iron Maiden T-shirt, a pair of camo shorts and a thin line of beads that circles her head. She sits cross-legged on the couch in her apartment and I sit on a cushion on the floor. She says that particular seating arrangement is traditional. The Mumblerock hangover is throbbing in my temples and my lacerated side hurts like hell.

'Psychosexual Development,' I say. 'That's what they call themselves.'

She stares at me.

'Ma,' I add.

She nods. 'And they're …'

'My libidinal phases,' I say with a sigh. 'I know what it sounds like, ma.'

'The fact that you are able to enter other people's dreams is positive,' she says. 'And the quest you're undertaking through your own mind is talked about often in magical literature.'

She gets up and walks over to the ceiling-high bookcase that dominates the back of the room. She locates a book with a really terrible cover of a muscular shirtless man riding a dragon.

Apparently some self-publishing magicians do their own covers.

'"The journey to find one's True Will, or True Self, is the most important journey that a magician will ever undertake."' She leans against the bookcase and reads. '"The True Will is protected by various psychic processes from attack by rival magicians. One must never allow any outside influence into one's psyche."'

'Yes, ma,' I say, suppressing a yawn and then wincing as pain shoots through my ribs.

'Am I boring you, Zevcenko?' the Witch says, her eyes fixing on me like rifle scopes.

'No, ma,' I say quickly.

'Well, whatever blocks you have are all in your own psyche. Meeting your True Will can hopefully release them,' the Witch says, snapping the book shut. 'Nevertheless, on to your next lesson. You have your mojo bag?'

I nod and retrieve a small blue canvas bag from my pocket. All the newbies were given one by King, but so far they've remained empty. She reseats herself on the couch and produces a bag of her own. Hers is made of blue shwcshwe fabric.

'Your mojo bag is fundamental to your practice of the art,' she says, opening the mouth of her bag and delicately retrieving a dead jewel-encrusted spider. She lays it in her open palm. 'The seven items that you keep in it are your totems. They'll allow you to interface with the mental state necessary for you to effect changes in the world.'

'I don't have any totems,' I say, opening my bag and shaking it.

The Witch looks at me like I'm a special brand of stupid. 'Your totems are not tradeable stickers, Zevcenko,' she says. 'It takes years to build up a full set. Mine took ten years.'

'It took ten years to find seven trinkets, ma?' I say.

The Witch raises her hand as if to swat me. I flinch.

'Are you trying to test my patience?' she says. 'You don't find your totems, they find you. You'll know when it happens. It feels like a puzzle piece fitting into place.'

So I guess I shouldn't bother looking on eBay.

The Witch dismisses me with a wave of her hand and I walk quickly to the door.

'Go get your side looked at in the infirmary, Zevcenko,' she says as I put my hand on the doorknob. 'If you miss a lesson because of whatever stupid shit you get up to, it's not going to be happy times for you.'

'Yes, ma,' I say and get the hell out of there as quickly as I can.

I make a pass at the infirmary and get the tough, beefy tattooed nurse to disinfect and bandage my side. She barely bats an eyelid at the lacerations. I'm sure she's seen a lot worse. Back at Malpit, I lock myself in the bathroom. I've got a short break before my next class and I really need to wake up. I rub my eyes and stare into the mirror. My eyes are bloodshot and have that stinging, sandy feeling. I feel permanently hung-over. Someone bangs on the door. 'Chill the fuck out,' I scream. The communal nature of Malpit is also really starting to work on my nerves.

My phone vibrates in my pocket and I yank it out. 'Bax!' Kyle says. He sounds nervous and on edge, and for some reason that instantly annoys the hell out of me. He's there in Cape Town living it up and I'm stuck here. What's he got to be on edge about?

'Hey, man,' I say, stifling a yawn. 'What's up?'

'Listen, I phoned because something weird is happening in Cape Town,' he says.

'People are arriving to events on time?' I say.

'Funny,' he says. 'No. It's … I don't know how to explain it, but it's like a feeling, something in the air. It feels wrong.'

'OK, Sherlock Holmes,' I say. 'Step away from the paranoia.'

'I'm telling you,' he says. 'There's something off.'

'Dude,' I say. 'There's nothing off in Cape Town. Seriously, don't worry about it.'

'Oh well, if the Amazing Zevcenko says so, then I guess it must be true. Stupid me.'

'Come on,' I say. 'It's just that you don't really have an aptitude for this kind of stuff. There's nothing wrong with that.'

There's a long pause.

'You haven't even spoken to anyone at Hexpoort about me, have you?' he says eventually.

'What?' I say. 'You're getting all worked up and—'

'Just answer the fucking question,' he says. 'Yes or no. Have you spoken to anyone about getting me in there?'

Maybe I'm just hung-over and annoyed, maybe I know that at some stage I need to tell him, or maybe I just feel bad about lying to my best friend, but I go and do it. I tell the truth.

'No,' I say.

There's another silence.

'Fuck you,' he says eventually.

'Kyle,' I say. 'I'm just trying to—'

'No, you're not,' he says. 'You don't care about what I want. You fucking go around like you're Supreme Lord Commander—'

'Kyle …'

'You want to know the truth?' he says. 'The truth is that even when you're trying to be good, you're a dick.'

That hurts.

'Please,' I say.

'Since we're being truthful,' he says, 'Esmé has been spending way too much time with that Troy guy. You might want to look into that, Supreme Lord Commander.'

The phone goes dead.

Someone bangs on the door again. I get up, fling it open and face the pimply kid outside, who still has his fist raised. 'What the fuck is your problem?' I shout. He looks at me like I'm insane.

I push past him and storm down the Malpit stairs. The anger burns white-hot inside me. I'm sick of it all. I'm sick of Hexpoort, I'm sick of Kyle and his whiny bullshit, I'm sick of Esmé and this fucking Troy. I reach for Nom's phone and dial her number.

'Hey, magic boy,' she says. 'You didn't call me last night. You said you would.'

'Tell me about Troy,' I say tersely.

'What?'

'Troy,' I repeat. 'Who is he? What is your relationship with him?'

'I told you,' she says. 'He's a friend, we hang out.'

'I don't believe you. I can't believe you would do this to me. I fucking saved you. I save you and this is what I get.'

'Oh, so you saved me, did you?' she says sarcastically. 'All hail the hero.'

Shit. This isn't exactly going as I had hoped.

'Wow,' she continues. 'Baxter Zevcenko, you take emotional blackmail to another level. May I remind you that I wouldn't have HAD A FUCKING ARACHNID ATTACHED TO MY BRAIN STEM had it not been for the fact that some psycho had a massive occult crush on you.'

'OK,' I say. 'You're right. I'm sorry. It's just I've been—'

'Let me make this easier for you.' Her voice drips acid. 'Remember what I said about long-distance relationships? Well, I don't think this one is going to work. Goodbye, Baxter.'

She hangs up.

I throw it against the granite wall and it explodes in a shower of cheap plastic and electronics.

'Fuck!' I scream down the corridor. 'FUCK!!!'

My screams of self-pity are cut short by a massive explosion outside. The aftershock throbs in my solar plexus. A siren begins to wail, and in the distance I can hear the *dukka-dukka-dukka* of gunfire. There's more gunfire and it's closer now. I begin to walk down a corridor, and then my something-bad-is-happening sense kicks into full gear and I break into a flat sprint.

I hurtle back towards the Malpit staircase and slam into a bunch of kids milling uncertainly at the bottom. 'What's going on?' I shout.

'The siren for when we're under attack,' says one of them, a short, stocky kid that I know from Magical Design.

'Attack? What kind of attack?'

He shrugs. Another bunch of kids come hurtling down the stairs and I'm relieved to see Nom among them.

'Hey.' I grab his arm. 'What's happening?'

'Don't know,' he says with a frown. 'We've done a drill like this before. We should congregate in the courtyard. Have you got the phone I lent you? We can call Stevo.'

'No,' I say. 'I, um, left it somewhere. That sounds like gunfire, though. Are you sure this is a drill?'

'Well, if this aren't the biggest bunch of fokken cry babies I has ever seen.' The Boer strides down the corridor towards us. 'This are not a drill,' he shouts. 'I repeat, this are not a fokken drill. We are under attack.'

'Jesus,' Nom whispers. 'Who would be dumb enough to attack this place?'

'Fall into line and follow me,' the Boer orders.

We jog down the corridors like soldiers marching. The Boer heads straight for the armoury and flings open the heavy steel door. Inside, it's like something out of a video game. Racks and racks of guns, knives, swords, spears and halberds line the walls. The Boer begins handing out weapons. He shoves an assault rifle, a handgun and a long, ugly pig-sticking knife into my hands. I fumble with the holster, and the Boer grabs it and straps it around my waist, then slaps me on the back.

My palms are feeling clammy and the back of my throat is very, very dry. I'm getting a pretty strong WWI fighting-in-the-trenches feeling about this, and I'm not incredibly keen to be cannon fodder.

'What do we do?' I say hoarsely.

'Kill anything that bloody tries to kill you,' the Boer replies. Well, at least it's not complicated.

Nom and I follow a bunch of kids into the courtyard. The Witch is on top of the wall. She has her breastplate on and her face is painted. Her falcon perches on her glove and she holds an assault rifle in the other hand.

'Everyone up on to the walls,' she shouts. 'Take firing positions.'

We zigzag up the staircase to the battlements. Teachers and students are crouched down to avoid the barrage of machine-gun fire that is tearing holes in the granite. I squeeze my way in between a bunch of Pondscum kids and risk a peek over the wall.

'Might be a training exercise,' Stevo says nervously.

It's an attractive thought, right up until the Pondscum kid next to me is thrown backwards by a bullet. He clutches manically at the wound in his throat, kicks a couple of times and then goes still. The blood pools at our feet.

'Oh God,' I say, pressing my back against the wall.

'Return fire,' the Witch shouts, aiming her rifle over the wall and squeezing off a burst.

I take a deep breath, expel it forcefully and then pop up and point my rifle over the edge.

Down below, a dozen black Humvees are parked in formation. Their fifty-cal turret guns are rattling and spraying the wall. I duck again without firing. This is insane. I look up and see black shapes circling above us.

'Crows,' I spit.

'And golems, goblins, Kholomodumo and narlfa,' Nom says.

'It's an army,' I reply.

The Boer crouch-runs down the wall and stops next to us. 'Flammables,' he says, as he pumps another magazine into his gun. 'If those fokken birdies attack, we need something to braai them with.'

As if on cue, the Crows start spiralling down and dive-bombing the walls. Nom and I scramble down into the courtyard.

'Emergency generators,' I say. 'They must have fuel.'

We're running across the courtyard when there's another explosion. I get hit in the back by a piece of masonry and stumble to my knees. I kneel there on the cobblestones trying to assess how badly injured I am.

I don't have much time to think. The explosion has opened up a hole in the wall and Kholomodumo come snarling through it, their snouts to the ground and their red eyes rolling about in their heads. One of them catches my scent and heads for me like a heat-seeking missile. I scrabble for the rifle on the strap around my neck but I fumble it. The creature's maw is inches from my face when something slams into it and sprays me with its blood. Gigli gives me a big grin and then spins around and finishes it off. I've never been so happy to see that demented smile in my life.

The hole in the wall is crawling with enemies. Goblins stream through, and I brace the rifle against my shoulder, point it in their general direction and squeeze the trigger. The gun bucks against my shoulder and one of the goblins drops. Another returns fire, and I scramble backwards desperately behind the gallows. Wood splinters fly past my face as gunfire rips into it.

I glance across to the generators. I'm not fast enough to make it to them without getting shot. Gigli looks at me and then jerks his head for me to climb on to his back. I swing my leg over his body. It's like riding a really bad-tempered, foul-smelling Luck Dragon, but I'll take it.

With a snort, he pushes off and hurtles across the courtyard. Bullets zing around us, but we make it to the generators without being aerated. Two goblin commandos run towards us but are engaged by King, and I don't mean in a critical discourse about the Hidden. His chubby tabby body reveals a foundation of corded muscles that ripple beneath his fur as he attacks them. A claw rips through a goblin face. The other one throws a vicious punch; King catches it in his teeth and with a shake of his head rips the hand right off. Nunda are warriors, I no longer doubt that.

The generators are surrounded by jerrycans filled with petrol. I'm gathering them up when I see Nom hurtling across the courtyard followed by three Kholomodumo. I take aim with the rifle and catch one right between the eyes. It skids to a halt. Nom turns and fires wildly but misses the remaining two. I try to get a bead on one of them, but Nom keeps obscuring my line of fire. The things close on him and he stumbles on a cobblestone and falls to his knees.

Faith and Chastity appear, blonde and black hair streaming behind them, an Uzi in each hand. They gun down the Kholomodumo, emptying their clips into the muscular bodies, and grab Nom, as red dots dance across the courtyard looking for targets. Fuck, there are snipers at the top of the canyon. A *clak-clak-clak* bounces off the canyon wall and the cobblestones next to my friends are ripped up by bullets.

I duck out from behind the generator and spray a line of fire across the canyon. Nom and Faith and Chastity sprint for the generators and drop behind them. I spray another haphazard burst of fire and then follow them. Stone and masonry explodes near us, but we're safe. For the moment.

'Holy fuck,' Chastity says. 'They're not messing around.'

We watch as Crows pick figures off the wall, lift them up and drop them on to the stony ground below.

'We need to get this petrol to them,' I say. 'Fast.'

'I've got a plan,' Nom says, handing me his gun.

He puts his face to the cobblestones of the courtyard and begins hissing and chirruping.

'Not sure an insanity defence is the best tactic here,' Chastity says.

'No,' I say. 'I think he's—'

Cockroaches begin pouring from the walls around us. I get an instant tingling-spine feeling and resist the urge to scream and scramble up on to the generator. 'There's a whole nest of them here,' Nom says, lifting his head. 'We sometimes get together and talk Derrida and Foucault.'

The cockroaches scuttle around us, climbing over each other. Nom holds up his hands and issues a series of hisses. The roaches respond, and I close my eyes and grit my teeth as the sound washes over me. With a final salutary hiss they break away and swarm over the jerrycans. I flatten myself against the generators as a wave of brown chitin starts to ferry the petrol across the cobblestoned courtyard. Sniper bullets rip into them, but the mass of roaches absorbs them and keeps going. I sneak the barrel of my rifle out from behind the generators and provide covering fire.

The roaches reach the wall and the Boer gives us the thumbs-up across the courtyard and starts overseeing the making of Molotovs.

'Nicely done, Nom,' Faith says with a sweet smile.

He shrugs nonchalantly. 'It was really just a question of engaging their philosophical understanding of freedom ...'

'OK, nerd,' Chastity says. 'Save the wordwank for later.'

The thudding of a helicopter circling above, the sound amplified by the surrounding canyon, drags our attention from the walls. I swing my rifle up towards it and pull the trigger. *Click*. Shit. I throw it down and draw the handgun from its holster. A bright spotlight strafes the ground and we press ourselves up against the generators. The chopper circles downward, banking sharply out of the way of an RPG fired from the walls and responding with a heavy burst of gunfire, before dropping sharply and landing neatly next to the gallows.

A platoon of goblins in balaclavas and flak jackets disembark and take up positions around the chopper. They are followed by a tall, hunched figure wearing a frayed black cloak with a cowl that covers his face, and leaning on a gnarled staff. A tall, teetering crown is balanced on top of his head. A crown made of teeth.

'You don't think that's …' Nom starts.

'The Muti Man,' I whisper.

'We need to kill that creepy mofo,' Chastity says, checking the clip in her Uzi.

'Where's Gigli?' I look around for his long pink shape.

'I saw him go through the hole in the wall with some of the other Draken,' Nom says.

'Shit. If we start firing at those goblins, we're dead.'

'How about a game of Sanity?' Chastity says with a grin.

'You're good, Chas,' Nom says, 'but you can't take them all on.'

'That's why Faith is going to help me,' Chastity says. The conjoined twins can't really look each other in the eye, but each turns her head a little.

'I'm not,' Faith says. 'That's your thing.'

'Come on,' Chastity replies. 'You've seen me do it a thousand times. And we share the same central nervous system, so I know you know how to do it. Plus I reckon all that repressed stuff going on in that little Barbie head of yours will make for some pretty scary shit.'

Faith scowls. 'OK. But if we get out of this alive, we're doing facials and pedicures together. Both of us, not just my half of the body.'

'Fine,' Chastity says. 'I'll goddamn vajazzle us if it gets you to Sanity those ugly fucks.'

'That won't be necessary,' Faith says primly.

They each put a hand out and begin chanting, Afrikaans, Xhosa, Zulu flowing into each other. Shapes start to form around the goblins, misty, incoherent shapes that begin to yelp and scream. The shapes solidify into images of goblins cutting their own throats, goblins eating each other, goblins collapsing in rivers of blood. The terrifying screams warp and pitch in a pure cacophony of terror and helplessness. I have to admit, it's a masterpiece.

The real commando goblins start firing wildly. Some shoot at each other; some clutch their heads, whimpering; the rest just run.

The Muti Man turns towards us, and beneath his cowl I can see nothing but small bright eyes. His raises his staff, and Faith and Chastity fall to the ground, both holding their heads.

'Illusion is a dangerous game,' he calls across the courtyard. His voice is reedy and wheezing. 'And I play it better than most.'

He walks slowly, painfully towards us, his staff clacking on the cobbles. I raise my gun and fire. The bullet takes him in the shoulder. He grunts but carries on walking.

'A Dreamwalker playing with guns like he's a minion,' he says. He flicks his staff and my hand spasms in pain, the gun clattering to the stones. I clutch it to my chest and use the other hand to drag the long, ugly knife out of its sheath. 'Please,' the Muti Man says. 'You're embarrassing us both.'

He is right in front of me now, at least two feet taller than I am, and looming over me like the Grim Reaper.

'When my informants told me of a Dreamwalker at Hexpoort, I had to investigate. And here he is hiding away in a dark corner.' He leans down, and I can see those bright little eyes shining in the depths of his hood. 'Hexpoort and its masters have insulted me beyond my ability to bear. They harbour a false Chosen One, one who they say bears the marks of prophecy, and a

Dreamwalker who they claim rivals my power.'

He reaches up and throws back his cowl. His face is distorted, half human and half Crow, lined with folds of scarred flesh. It's the beak that is the worst, a mangled crescent that dangles down, revealing the twisted mouth beneath.

'Marked with the crescent,' he wheezes. 'The Muti Man come to erase the lines between Known and Hidden. So show me, Dreamwalker,' he says. 'Show me your power.'

I scrabble for the beads in my pocket and drop them on the ground. The Muti Man laughs, a horrible hacking sound. 'A boy playing with a toy from a Christmas cracker. More human lies.'

There's the whooping sound of battle cries above us. I look up to see creatures with white wings and dark skin scything through Crows with flaming swords. They're part of the Flock, African Valkyries like Katinka, and they're on our side.

'Remember this moment, Dreamwalker,' the Muti Man says. 'Remember the moment I let you and your friends live.'

He turns on his heel and walks back towards the chopper.

The fight in the skies is raging, and between the battling white and black wings I see a huge ship ponderously cutting through the air. It's black, sleek and angular, like one of those stealth bombers, but shaped like an old frigate, the black sails marked with a red pentagram surrounded by runes.

'Dwarven airship,' says Nom.

'We're saved,' Chastity adds. She and Faith are both pale-faced. I can only shudder at the thought of what the Muti Man made them see.

The dwarven airship turns and its gun turrets open fire, tearing through the escaping chopper, which spins around frantically like a bird trapped in a room and then slams into the side of the canyon and explodes.

'Yes!' says Faith, pumping her fist in victory. 'What?' she asks when we look at her. 'That was some sadistic stuff he forced into my head.'

We run up on to the walls. The Humvees are retreating but are being picked off by the airship's superior firepower. A pack of Draken are chasing the fleeing goblins, and I see Gigli run down a commando and snack on its face.

The airship turns and hovers above us, a rush of air whipping my hair and clothes about me like I'm in a wind tunnel. It docks against the wall and a metal gangplank opens up and clangs on the granite. Dwarven legionnaires in black combat fatigues and yellow berets, carrying heavy assault rifles, jog down the gangplank and take up positions along the wall. A dwarf in a long black coat appears and follows them slowly, hands clasped behind his back. His coat has a high collar marked with a turquoise insignia of a forked tongue. He has a sabre at his waist and a rifle in a scabbard on his back. As he gets closer, I can see that his black-bearded face is ragged with scars, one eye white, the other dark and menacing.

Stevo joins us on the wall, breathing heavily. Timothy and Hunter are peeking out from his shirt pockets, still not convinced that the fighting is over.

'That's a Samnite,' Stevo whispers. 'From Dwarven High Command.'

'You all right, Stevo?' I ask.

'Yeah.' He nods. 'Managed to keep away from most of the fighting.'

'What a hero,' Chastity says.

Stevo shrugs. 'I'll leave that to other people.'

The Samnite steps on to the Hexpoort walls and looks around disdainfully. The Witch approaches and inclines her head, which in Witch terms is the equivalent of a curtsey.

'We thank you for your assistance, Malachi.'

'Assistance?' he says, in a cold voice. 'Deliverance more like. You were almost overrun.'

The Witch's mouth twitches. I step back. She's going to throw this guy from the walls.

'Yes, of course,' she says through gritted teeth. 'We thank you again.'

'I'm commandeering the teachers' quarters for my men,' he says. 'I trust you can take care of the clean-up? Or should we help you with that too?'

'Thank you. We have it under control.' I can see the Witch's fists clenching and unclenching at her sides.

'Right,' she shouts as the dwarves descend from the walls. Her eyes are burning with anger and frustration. 'I want clean-up units formed. If you find any enemy survivors, alert the Boer. We need them for interrogation. If you are badly hurt, make your way to the infirmary. The rest of you, I want to see action, or there will be hell to pay.'

The adrenalin is wearing off and my hands start to shake. Nom turns away and throws up against the wall. Chastity is shaking her head and opening and closing her eyes like she's trying to flush something from her memory. Faith is staring down at where students' bodies are being dragged out of the courtyard and covered with sheets.

'How many do you think we lost?' she says softly.

I scan the walls and the courtyard. 'Lots,' I reply.

'What the hell just happened? Why did they do this?'

It's a question I'm not sure I want an answer to.

THE APPRENTICE

The clean-up is almost as brutal as the fight. We drag bodies into the middle of the courtyard: kids to the left of the gallows and goblins to the right. We work mechanically, dragging people we know from class across the cobblestones with a kind of methodical intensity that's our only protection against their vacant wide-eyed stares and garish wounds.

The pile of goblin bodies is huge, a tower of grey limbs and sagging faces. The Boer drags several goblins, burnt and bleeding but still alive, into Hexpoort for questioning. The torched Crow bodies are torched even further until they're nothing but black lumps of smouldering ash. There is no sign of the Muti Man in the wreckage of the helicopter.

The Flock, dozens of dark-skinned Valkyries wearing shining metal faceplates that show only the intense eyes beneath, help us. The tall, white-winged women talk to each other in a combination of Afrikaans and flickering hand gestures, but ignore the rest of us completely.

I find myself staring down at the corpse of the kid from Magical Design that I spoke to when the attack started. He has a bullet hole through his cheek. I have my hand wrapped in his shirt collar, ready to drag him to our growing pile of bodies, but I can't seem to move.

'Zevcenko,' the Boer says, coming to stand next to me. 'Get your fokken ass moving.'

'I …' I say, staring down at the body.

'Ja, I know.' The Boer's face is caked with blood and his khaki shirt is burnt and slashed. 'In all my years here I've never lost a fokken student. Now I've lost twenty.'

The official count is twenty-two. The Boer helps me drag the corpse of the kid on to the pile and we stand back staring at it. 'Go wash yourself,' the Boer says. 'The Witch wants to convene everybody in fifteen minutes.'

I find Stevo, Nom, Faith and Chastity and we help each other clean the blood and grime off. The bandage around my ribs is stuck, and Faith helps me peel it off and dab at the lacerations. We replace the bandage and then I go in search of a clean T-shirt.

By the time we're ready, the rest of Hexpoort has gathered in front of the gallows. The dead kids have been covered with blankets but the goblins remain open to the air, a giant shrine of grinning mouths and glassy eyes. The Flock stand at the back, lounging against the Hexpoort walls, but the dwarven Samnite and several of his men have ascended the gallows platform with the Witch. They stand looking over the assembled students with hard expressions.

The Witch steps forward and begins to speak. 'We have been attacked in full force by an unknown enemy. Thanks to Hekka Jones sending out an emergency distress signal, our allies managed to respond quickly enough to stop Hexpoort from being taken.'

Hekka is at the front of the crowd and dips his head as if he dislikes the attention.

'Probably because he was hiding in the communications room,' Nom whispers in my ear.

'I would like to thank our allies for their swift response. Malachi and the Dwarven Legion, and Naebril and her Flock.'

A tall member of the Flock has shifted her faceplate on to her head. Her face is lean and hard but has a look of detached amusement. She raises a hand in acknowledgement.

'We need to regroup,' the Witch says, 'and—'

The Samnite moves forward and holds up a hand. 'We are at war,' he declares. 'And war is not a time for empty platitudes.'

He flicks his hand and several dwarven legionnaires drag a hooded figure on to the platform. It's a goblin, burnt and injured, with his hands cuffed behind him. Another legionnaire follows them, recording with a top-of-the-range camera.

'War is a time for decisive action and swift retribution,' the Samnite says, his voice loud and resonant, reverberating across the courtyard. The legionnaires strip the combat jacket from the goblin and bare his grey chest. 'War is a time for punishing those that stand against us.'

One of the legionnaires draws a knife from his boot and carves the scratch-like goblin script into the prisoner's chest. Blood streams from the wounds and the goblin grunts in pain.

King pushes through the crowd. 'I object,' he says, his eyes wide and shocked. 'That is a symbol of desecration! According to the Kebra Bik, his soul will never find peace.'

The Samnite looks down at him. 'War is a time to send a message.'

The legionnaires drag the goblin across the platform and loop the gallows noose around his neck.

The Witch turns to the Samnite, a look of outrage on her face. 'He needs to be interrogated. We need to find whoever organised this attack.'

The Samnite looks at her with contempt. 'We already know who we're at war with. Not just those that attacked us, not just the goblin race, but the whole of the Hidden.'

He flicks his hand again and the gallows platform opens, dropping the goblin through. There's a pop as his neck breaks.

Naebril of the Flock saunters forward and the students part to give her a path to the platform. She raises her hands and claps, a slow, sarcastic gesture that makes the Samnite bristle.

'Well done,' she says in a strong voice, a voice used to command. 'That was a brilliant piece of theatre. But we're not here to listen to your xenophobic threats.' She turns to the Witch. 'We have helped you, and now it is time for you to repay us.'

The Witch's outrage is raised another notch. She stands there, her body taut like a guitar string tuned too tight. 'You know our stance.' Her voice is flat. 'Katinka is an MK6 agent. We will not hand her over to be killed.'

'The thing you call Katinka is an abomination,' Naebril says. 'A male member of the Flock that should have been killed at birth. The fact that he attempts to hide in a female persona does not exempt him from the dictates of our culture.'

The Samnite looks down at her like she's a particularly disgusting bug that he's about to squash.

'Your "culture" has no right to make demands of the rulership,' he says. 'Personally I'd prefer it if that confused cross-dressing member of your species were cleansed from this planet. But the Dwarven Legion, and by extension its interest in MK6, will not tolerate the questioning of its authority.'

There's a shifting at the back of the assembled groups, and I turn to see the Flock donning faceplates and drawing swords. The dwarven legionnaires have their hands on their guns, and red dots appear in the courtyard as snipers on the airship take aim.

Naebril shakes her head and laughs. 'Perhaps a time is coming when the Hidden will no longer bend a knee to the Legion and its lackeys.'

She flickers a hand gesture and the Flock take flight, dozens of huge white wings unfolding and transporting dark bodies up and away from the Hexpoort walls. Naebril points a finger at the Samnite and then follows them, scattering students as she takes to the air.

The Samnite's face is a mask of hate and anger. He looks down at us.

'You object?' he says to King.

'Well, the Hidden are disparate. There is no unified front. Dwarves themselves fall under the category—'

'You are removed from your post as teacher at this institution.'

Two dwarven legionnaires approach. King smiles, and his sharp teeth glint in the firelight. 'Lay a hand on me, my friends, and you'll lose it.' They hang back.

'With all due respect, you cannot make changes to my staff,' the Witch says.

'With all due respect,' the Samnite replies with a smile, 'Dwarven High Command has invested more money in this institution than your human government. Every inch of this facility has been purchased with dwarven gold, and we have the final say in any decision.'

'The Blood Kraal will hear about this,' the Witch says furiously.

'Yes, of course. Please contact the MK6 council. Let them convince you of the veracity of what I'm saying.'

The Witch stares at him, and then spins on her heel and stalks away down the gallows stairs.

King is sitting in his office smoking. He nods to the chair in front of the desk when I enter. I slide into it and watch him. He offers me the cigarette and I take a drag. It tastes of cat.

'Malachi is right,' he says. 'MK6 leadership in the Blood Kraal has confirmed that he is acting steward of Hexpoort.'

'Why?' I ask. 'He's a total dick.'

King gives a low purring chuckle. 'You have a way with words, Zevcenko, no doubt. Yes, he's a dick. But he represents the interests of a very powerful organisation.'

'So what happens now?'

'I am relieved of my teaching post pending an investigation into where my loyalties lie.' He shakes his head. 'Fifteen fucking years in this place and I need a dwarf to tell me who and what I'm loyal to.'

I hand back the cigarette.

'You students are going to be apprenticed immediately to whatever agents are available.'

'I thought apprenticeship was only—'

'In your fourth year of study at Hexpoort? Yes. And the majority of you are in your first and second years. But according to our esteemed Samnite steward, "the Dwarven Legion is committed to many freedom operations across the globe and cannot be expected to shoulder the burden of this alone". He snorts. 'Freedom operations. That's what they call mercenary wars these days.'

'Jesus,' I say. 'Are we really at war? Is that what the Muti Man wants?'

King shrugs and blows a plume of smoke from beneath his whiskers. 'I saw the crown in the courtyard. You were the only one who got a good look at him.'

I shudder when I think about that twisted face and beak. I describe the whole thing to King: the way he brushed aside Faith and Chastity.

'An injured Crow,' King says, and scratches his chin with a claw. 'And one that can perform magic. It sounds like we were attacked by a Tengu.'

He reaches across and pulls a scroll from a drawer in his desk. He unrolls it and plants an incense holder and a pen on the corners to keep it open. The scroll is made of red fabric and is marked in ink with a mandala annotated in Sanskrit. In the centre is a man with black wings and a long nose, holding a staff.

'Tengu are Crow shamans,' King says. 'From what we understand, they are the Murder's ruling class, although the Murder is thought to have splintered after the pact with Basson and the betrayal of Sabian Dober.'

'So this could be revenge?'

King nods. 'Maybe. Although if this Tengu is the Muti Man, then his alliance with the Bone Kraal suggests different interests.'

'OK,' I say. 'But who are the Bone Kraal? I've heard them mentioned before, but everyone seems to think they're a joke.'

King sighs. 'The Blood Kraal and the Bone Kraal were two sides of the same coin, two ancient organisations that were formed to govern the magical world. The Blood Kraal was made up of humans and the Bone Kraal of members of the Hidden.'

'Right,' I say. 'So what happened?'

'The human Blood Kraal formed an alliance with the Dwarven Legion hundreds of years ago. The Bone Kraal was gradually stripped of power until it was nothing more than a figurehead.'

'And now it's back? But why would a Crow be working with a Hidden organisation? I thought it was their mission to hunt down the Hidden?'

'It was,' King says. 'But maybe they're working together on the understanding that humans and dwarves are the real problem. And you know what?' He stubs out his cigarette and looks at me with those strange yellow eyes. 'Part of me doesn't blame them.'

Over the next few days, MK6 agents arrive at Hexpoort in a flood. There are tall Masai warriors carrying spears, short Somalian witches with painted faces, ageing long-haired metal-heads, rotund businessmen smoking cigars, lean police detectives and tough-looking uniformed cops. A scary guy with prison tattoos on his face throws a creepy smile and a gang sign as he passes, and a soccer mom reaches up to tie her hair in a ponytail and reveals a Glock nestled in the waistband of her granny panties. MK6, it seems, has reached into all areas of South African life.

I can't stop thinking about Esmé and what an idiot I am. I said things that I really, really regret. The kind of things that shot the possibility of a second chance in the back of the head execution-style. I've never been dumped before. All those pop songs are surprisingly accurate. It does hurt that bad. I should be lying in bed listening to tragic love songs and crying into my pillow, but unfortunately nobody has written a song about getting over a broken heart while clearing up dead goblins. Yet.

I'm humming softly and rhyming 'can't get you out of my head' with 'clearing up the goblin dead' when I see a Cortina brake hard, reverse into a parking space next to a black van, and then slam unsteadily into the Hexpoort perimeter fence. Ronin climbs out, a brown beanie pulled low over his red hair and an army duffel bag slung over his shoulder. He's talking to himself as he stumbles towards the gate. He looks terrible; his face is pasty and his beard wild.

'Be your best self,' he mutters, and walks right past me.

'Ronin!' I shout. 'Hey, Ronin!'

He turns and sees me. 'Jesus, sparky. Have they turned you into a fucking ninja? Didn't even see you.' He claps a hand on my shoulder and then uses it for support as he fumbles for a cigarette in his pocket.

'How you been?' he mumbles through the ciggie. 'You been touched by the miracle of education yet?'

'Oh yeah. It's been like one big TED talk up here.'

'Heard about the trouble you had,' he says. He's sweating, but his blue eyes are as intense as ever. 'You OK?'

'Kinda. I think.' The adrenalin has long since been replaced by an ever-present horror at the violence I've seen, which competes with the more mundane horror I feel at being dumped by both my girlfriend and my best friend on the same day.

'Kinda is sometimes as good as it gets,' Ronin says. 'Come on. Help me put my stuff in one of the dank little rat holes they call rooms here.'

I help him with his bag to the Skaduwee point of the Hexpoort pentacle, and then we make our way to the gallows. The goblin's body is still swinging in the breeze and Ronin raises his eyebrows. 'I didn't know Hexpoort was into executions.'

'The Samnite,' I say. 'He says he wants to send a message.'

'Malachi?' Ronin asks, and I nod. He shakes his head. 'That's one sick puppy. I knew him on the Border and still wish I had put a bullet in his head when I had the chance.'

'Well, let me give you another opportunity,' a commanding voice says.

Ronin laughs and turns around. 'We missed a great he's-right-behind-me-isn't-he? moment there, pal.'

'Pal.' The Samnite flexes his black-gloved hands and purses his lips. 'Pal. That would imply a kind of equality between the two of us, wouldn't it? Is that what you think, Ronin? That we're colleagues?'

'I remember a little dwarf mercenary in his first combat deployment shitting himself with the rest of us on the Border,' Ronin says.

Malachi smiles, showing very white teeth in the black forest of his beard. 'The first act, and what happened in the second? You fell into the gutter and had to be rescued by that cock-loving failure of a dwarf.'

'Baresh was the best battle shaman the Legion ever had,'

Ronin says, his eyes burning. 'You're not fit to bow in front of his memory.'

The Samnite clasps his hands behind his back and leans in to Ronin's ear. 'Soon it's time for the third act, Ronin. You might not like how the story ends.'

He turns and walks away and Ronin lets out a low breath. 'There are only two people I've ever thought had a chance of taking me in a fight,' he says. 'One of them is your combatives teacher, the Shadow Boer. The other is that homophobic, xenophobic motherfucker walking away from us.'

Malachi and the Witch ascend the platform again. The Witch is clenching her jaw and staring daggers at anyone who looks at her, but she nods for the Samnite to speak.

'We are entering a new era,' he says. 'You are not children. You are soldiers in a war and it is time that you had a chance to fight.' He gestures to the Witch, who steps forward.

'We would obviously have preferred to give you all more training before this. But with things as they are, we are drastically undermanned, so we will be fast-tracking your education. Some of our agents will now give short talks about what it'll be like out there in the field. Consider this a final lesson, and listen well.'

Agents take to the gallows one by one to give words of advice. Most keep it short and simple: always check your weapons, the importance of making your contacts trust you, the value of knowing something of the cultural specifics of different Hidden communities.

Malachi snorts at that last one. Rule with an iron fist seems to be his approach to diplomacy.

When his turn comes, Ronin clambers up on to the platform and stands looking over the assembled students like a dog deciding which tree to piss on. 'I once saw an agent suck on an assault rifle and pull the trigger,' he starts. 'At the time I thought he was an idiot, but I wonder daily whether he was, in fact, the smart one.' He rubs his face. 'There's a particular blend of antidepressants and Jack Daniel's that'll get you through the first year. I'll post the recipe on Google or whatever. OK, over and out.'

He stumbles back down and nudges me with his shoulder. 'Always had a natural gift for public speaking,' he says.

The Witch calls us to her apartment later that day.

'Jackie Ronin,' she says, shaking her head. 'The last time you were here, you were suspended for stealing hallucinogenics from the test lab.'

I sit on the floor – it's traditional – but Ronin's an agent so he sits on the couch.

'Actually I was tripping on hallucinogenics,' he says. 'Has anyone ever told you that you're not the most calming influence for someone who is high?'

'You were here when Ronin was here, ma?' I ask. 'Wow, you must be really—'

Ronin kicks my foot and gives a quick shake of his head.

'I mean … never mind.'

She stares hard at both of us, and even Ronin averts his eyes.

'We're apprenticing students tonight,' the Witch says. 'I know you two have a certain amount of history together. Will you be bonding? I need to make sure each student is matched with an appropriate master, and I can't think of any more matched than you two.'

'Thanks, ma. I think.'

'Right,' she says. 'That's settled. Next is your assignment. The Legion is insisting on sending out agents to shake down the Hidden communities and flush out the Bone Kraal.'

'You think that's the best strategy?' Ronin asks.

'I don't think anything,' she says with a snarl. 'The Legion thinks it, says it, and I obey.'

'Not really your style,' Ronin says.

The Witch slams her fist into the couch next to him. 'What's not my style is losing everything I've worked so hard for in this school to a bunch of dwarves,' she barks. 'What's not my style is burying twenty-two students, twenty-two more than have ever died at Hexpoort on my watch. That's not my style.'

Ronin nods meekly like he's back at school. 'Yes, ma.'

'I'm divvying up assignments. You get the Obayifo.'

'Really? Obayifo patrol? You know I hate those little bastards and their fat Slugmothers.'

She gives him another hard stare. 'We've contacted the cartel. One of the Obayifo families has gone rogue and cut off all communication.'

Which one?'

'Squirrelskull.'

'Of course it's Squirrelskull,' Ronin says. 'Why wouldn't it be the most bloodthirsty?'

'They've moved their hive. So you're going to have to find them.'

'I'm not happy about this,' Ronin says.

'My heart breaks for you,' the Witch replies. 'Now get the fuck out of my apartment.'

Later that night, we're led into the depths of Hexpoort, a procession of agents and students carrying flaming torches. Hekka gives me a shove, but I can feel his heart is not in it. The students are all subdued and nervous, each recovering from the attack in their own way and coming to terms with the agent that the Witch has paired them with.

'It's bullshit,' Chastity whispers as we walk. 'Faith and I are two people but we're paired with one agent, some fucking dude whose cover is as a middle-level manager.'

'It's logistics,' Faith hisses, but Chastity rolls her eyes. 'Who'd you get?'

'Ronin,' I whisper. 'The—'

'The homeless guy.' Chastity nods. 'What an inspiration. OK, I take it back. You got the worst deal.'

I laugh.

The stairs lead down into what used to be the dungeons. We walk past old cells with rusting bars and dark stains on the walls. The dungeons open out into a massive circular space. It's cold and dank and the flickering torches make sinister shadowplay. A massive bonfire has been built in the centre of the room and the Boer throws his torch on to it. We stand around it in a circle and it becomes pleasantly warm, then hot, then like an unbearable furnace.

'Strip down to your underwear,' the Witch calls out. I curse the fact that I decided to wear yellow Y-fronts today. I have a horrible vest tan from digging in the sun and the bandage around my ribs is stained with blood. Sweat pours down my body. It feels like we're in hell.

We're given white beads to wear as a headdress. 'The apprentice ceremony is where you are bonded to your master,' the Witch shouts over the roar of the fire. 'It is a sacred bond that will last throughout your life. You will honour. You will obey. This is a bond of blood. There are no half-measures.'

The Boer leads a chilled-looking goat into the centre of the circle. It chews lazily on a stalk and looks around curiously. The Boer cuts its throat with a large knife. It drops to the floor, still gazing around with a bemused expression on its face.

The Witch lights a bundle of imphepho, African sage, and the pungent smell fills my nostrils. The bonding begins. Students step forward one by one with their masters, and the Witch facilitates the ritual between them. Their faces are smeared with white clay from a bucket, their arms are tied together with rawhide, and the Witch fills her mouth with goat blood and spits it on to them.

The smell and the heat are too much for me, and in the flickering light I think I can see Grandpa Zev and Klara, my great grandmother, smiling at me. The flag of the Sieners flaps in the wind behind them, planted in the dusty landscape. A storm rolls across the land. I can see stones shaped by ancient sculptors; symbols of the Mantis abound, carved into the rock. The place hums and clicks with energy. I find a rooibos-coloured pool. A waterfall plummets into it. I dive in. The hallucinatory quality of it surrounds me, bubbles rising, fractalised rainbows. The brown lake seems to hum with natural minerals and a godless, unconscious, ancient power – a pool of glistening life force. I dive down, the icy water causing an instant headache that travels through my skull into my jaw and the nerves in my teeth. There is the swishing almost-silence of my limbs, and then I surface, breaking the water with a gasp.

Words form in my mind. A poem in Afrikaans:

> O koud is die windjie
> en skraal.
> En blink in die dof-lig
> en kaal,
> so wyd as die Heer se genade,
> lê die velde in sterlig en skade
> En hoog in die rande,
> versprei in die brande,
> is die grassaad aan roere
> soos winkende hande.
> O treurig die wysie
> op die ooswind se maat,

soos die lied van 'n meisie
in haar liefde verlaat.
In elk' grashalm se vou
blink 'n druppel van dou,
en vinnig verbleek dit
tot ryp in die kou!

The words rattle through me. A deep melancholy. Loss and ache. A thousand whispering fissures of ancestors' voices. The beloved country not only cries but whispers, moans, aches, dreams, giggles, laughs, wiggles, shakes and dances. The Siener part of me strafes the sky with a light show of temporal lobe insight. Poetry is just magic without the dressing up.

I see strange black pillars scratched with symbols. A young Crow child undergoing his first transformation into Crow form. His first hunt. The fear, the blood, the power; I understand it.

I find myself standing in front of the Witch, my arms bound to Ronin's. I feel the connection between me and Ronin and between Ronin and his master Baresh and between Baresh and his master Elmat and between Elmat and his master Gremos. Stretching back into prehistory.

My small individual ego washes away like dirt in the shower. I see Ronin when he was younger: the portrait of the bounty hunter as a young man. He is at art school, his hair pulled back into a neat ponytail and wearing a clean denim shirt. I see him attending class, going to poetry recitals, sit-ins, protests against the apartheid government. It's weird seeing him like this. He looks almost … happy.

I see him with the tiny microdots of LSD, sitting up on a hillside, ready to feign madness to get out of the draft. He takes them, and his drug-fuelled trance and my magic-fuelled one become intertwined, our consciousness splashing together like paint on a canvas.

I see him still messed up from a bad trip and going through the brutal boot camp of Basson's Special Weapons Unit. I see him on the Border with rage in his eyes and killing, and I see more of the darkness in him than I've ever known.

I watch in horrified fascination as Ronin is transformed from an idealistic young artist into a stone-cold killer. He was a mediocre artist, but he is a genius killer.

I see his face change. The alcohol and drugs claw at his skin and leave ragged marks. Countless fights contort and twist his features, his nose broken and reset.

At his best he is a warrior and at his worst he is a monster. I see him drinking and drinking and drinking until the monster subsides into the murky, muddy recesses of his unconscious.

I see Baresh finding him and helping him, putting him back together, still massively cracked, still massively flawed, but in one piece. I see Ronin finding the pieces in his mojo bag and finally becoming a battle shaman in his own right.

I see the pressures of being an agent forming the dark, hard diamond of personality that is Ronin today, and in that moment I see that he is the most dangerous man I've ever met. A shiver runs down my spine. Ronin and I are stuck together, bonded by the power of magic, and I'm not exactly sure how I feel about that.

I look at him, both of us bloody, our hands bound together by a rawhide cord so tight that it's cutting off my circulation. His eye twitches and I can see him clenching his jaw.

That awkward moment when you've been magically bonded as an apprentice to a lethal alcoholic who is trying to get clean.

WEAPON OF CHOICE

*T*he ziggurat is directly in our path, an angular pyramid made of a strange fungal material; spongy turquoise, red and yellow.

I stand with the funk band and look up at the stairs that zigzag to the top.

'Is this it?'

'Nope,' Tyrone says. 'This is the Ziggurat of the False Ego. Read the sign.'

Sure enough, there at the base is a rotten old sign that says FALSE EGO. WATCH YOUR STEP.

I shade my eyes and look towards the top of the ziggurat. 'Don't suppose there's an elevator?'

'Typical Conscious Self,' Richard says, as he puts a booted foot on to the first step. 'Always looking for short cuts.'

I grab Chester and follow the glinting procession of pastels and rhinestones up the stairs. The little bow-tied dog licks my face and then snuggles down into my arms. I know I'm supposed to find my True Self. In fact, the Witch made it plain that it's more important than ever now that I'm going out into the field with Ronin. It doesn't make walking up a ziggurat with a funk band seem like any less of a crazy waste of time.

'Beware the Boomslang,' I read from a sign on the stairs halfway up. 'There are snakes here?'

'A snake, honey,' Junebug says with a nervous grin. 'Just the one.'

Dream sweat may be sparkly and multicoloured, but it sticks to you just like real sweat, and I use my forearm to wipe it off my face and then on to my jeans.

We get to the top of the ziggurat and I put Chester down. He barks happily and runs back and forth on the flat platform.

'So,' I say. 'Where's this False Ego of mine?'

Tyrone taps my shoulder and points to the other side of the platform. A huge jewelled snake slithers across to us. It stops and rises up, swaying back and forth, eyes swirling and spitting like pools of hydrochloric acid.

'Boom,' it says. A bass like a tsunami of titanic Tibetan gongs rattles my bones. My eyeballs vibrate in their sockets.

'That's the False Ego?'

'Have you ever heard that biblical stuff about the serpent rising up … yada yada … number of the beast, et cetera and so forth?' Tyrone says.

'Yeah.'

He taps me on my forehead. 'Well, those holy mofos were talking about what goes on inside people's heads.'

'Is it dangerous?'

'Dangerous?' Tyrone rubs his soul patch. 'Well, only in the way that YOUR OWN PERSONAL SATAN is dangerous.'

'Right.' I eye the jewelled serpent nervously. 'So what do we do?'

'We need funk,' Tyrone says. 'Stat.'

'He's right, honey,' agrees Junebug. 'A unified psyche will drive it away.'

'OK,' I say. 'Knock yourselves out. I'll stand back and watch.'

'I said "a unified psyche", honey.' Junebug primps her beehive hair. 'That means the Conscious Self.'

'You want me to play in a funk band?'

'No, no,' Junebug says. 'That'd be ridiculous. You're the Conscious Self. You have to be the lead singer.'

'You're joking. Please tell me you're joking.'

They're not. Musical instruments appear out of thin air and they begin strapping them on. Tyrone has a red Flying v guitar that he plugs directly into the spongy organic material of the ziggurat. Richard is on drums, Cabales on bass and Junebug has a set of keyboards that look like the controls of a spaceship. Even Chester has a shaker in his mouth.

'I don't sing,' I protest.

'Well, that's strange, honey,' Junebug says. 'Because you sure look the part.'

I look down to see that my clothes have changed to a white jumpsuit with a red lightning bolt down the middle that ends at my crotch. There are tassels hanging from the arms and the shoulders are heavy with sequins.

An old microphone appears on a stand in front of me.

The snake watches us, those terrible eyes swirling, then without warning it lunges forward. Tyrone raises his guitar and sends a chord at it like a flight of shurikens. It recoils, furious, and turns to hiss at us.

'Any time now,' Richard says, raising his drumsticks. 'We can't hold him indefinitely.'

I sigh and step up to the mike. The band breaks into a funky riff, all bouncing bass, psychedelic wah-wah guitar and spacey keyboard effects.

'Get on up,' I mumble into the mike.

The snake strikes again and Richard sees it off with a wild drum solo.

'Come on,' Tyrone urges. 'We need a wall of sound. It's going to keep attacking harder.'

'Boom,' says the Boomslang, and it collides with the music. I feel myself shaking with the G-force of a space shuttle flight. Reality itself rattles.

So I sing. I sing half-remembered lyrics and TV theme songs. I sing jingles from commercials, bits of poems from English class, and parody songs from YouTube. I sing rock, hip hop, pop, reggae and, yes, funk. I scream like a death-metal demon and wail like an opera soprano. I sing with everything I have. I pace up and down with the mike in my hand. 'Is everyone having a good time?' I scream from the edge of the ziggurat. Tyrone puts his back to mine and shimmies, ripping a jagged speed-metal chord across the ziggurat. 'Let Cabales finish him off,' he whispers into my ear. 'When he slaps, the motherfucker SLAPS.'

Cabales slides on to his knees, his head back, the bone through his nose shaking. A bass chord like a phalanx of armoured lions leaps from his guitar and slams into the snake. The Boomslang shudders violently, whips around, catches its own tail in its mouth. It solidifies and forms a perfect circle of gold on top of the ziggurat.

We step through it to the other side of the platform.

'Now that's what I call funk,' Tyrone says, putting his arm around my shoulder.

I wake up in the back seat of the Cortina with my face squished into the pages of an old magazine. 'Whaa …' I say, wiping the drool from my lip and squinting into the bright light.

'Morning, sparky,' Ronin mumbles. He has his beanie perched on the top of his head and is sucking at a cigarette. His eyes are bloodshot, he's still a horrible grey-white, sweat drips from his face and the rings around his eyes are so dark that he looks like he's been punched. The glaring red scar from where the Halzig tenderised his face is bright against his pale skin.

We left Hexpoort the previous night in a rush. I walked down to the Draken pens with Nom to say goodbye to Gigli. Gigli pushed his head against mine and emitted a series of hisses and growls.

'He says he should be going with you,' Nom said. 'He has a duty to protect you.'

'Tell him he's done enough.'

Gigli responded with a growl and ripped a piece of my hoodie off with his teeth.

'He says it's in case he needs to find you,' Nom said.

'Crazy bastard.' I hugged his thick pink neck.

'You OK?' Ronin says. 'You were making some weird noises back there.'

'Yeah.' I rub the sand out of my eyes and sit up. 'Just dreamt I was in a band.' I look out of the window. 'Where are we?' We're hurtling past empty scrubland. 'And aren't you going a little fast?'

'The open road, sparky,' he says and slams on the brakes. The car fishtails on to the side of the road and I'm flung against the seat.

'Fuck.' I rub my neck. 'Was that really necessary?'

'We need to find Squirrelskull,' he says. 'How's your brain mojo feeling? Think you can find them?'

'I don't know,' I reply. 'I haven't done anything like that since Basson.'

'The Witch says you have some kind of magical block?' He turns around to look at me.

'Yeah,' I say. 'I'm not exactly rocking my magical education.'

'What's wrong?' he says. 'You've got the ability.'

'Remember what you said about magic having a genetic component? That your genes can determine what type of magic you're good at?'

'Uh-uh.'

'I think the Siener part of me and the Crow part of me are trying to figure out who gets a say in that. They're just so different. The stuff I saw during the bonding ritual ...'

Ronin looks at me warily. He knows I've seen his history and he doesn't like it. 'You need to figure out who you are, sparky,' he says. 'Nobody can do that for you.'

'Find my True Self. Yeah, that's what everyone keeps telling me.'

He claps his hands together. 'So you going to give this a try or what?'

I nod and reach for the beads in my mojo bag. I pull them out, start weaving them between my fingers and then fumble them on to the car seat.

'Jesus Christ, it's like watching my mother trying to send an email,' Ronin says.

'You have a mother?'

'Never mind about the days of my life,' Ronin says. 'Magic us some GPS coordinates.'

I weave the beads through my fingers and focus on finding the Squirrelskull clan. I repeat the word over and over in my head. Squirrelskull. Squirrelskull. Squirrelskull. I hit a kind of invisible barrier. It's like penetrating a giant bowl of jelly. I'm breathing hard and sweating but I can't push through.

I open my eyes and shake my head. 'Some kind of barrier.'

'Enchantments,' Ronin says. 'Probably pretty rudimentary, but you're not strong enough to get through them.'

'And now?'

Ronin smiles. 'We do this the old-fashioned way.'

It's a relief to get away from the dark walls of Hexpoort, but Ronin is even worse company than usual. It doesn't help that he's cagey about what I saw during the bonding ritual. I can feel the bond hanging between us like a length of magical fibre-optic cable. His presence is a tangible feeling; it occupies a certain part of my mind and nothing I do can get rid of it. It's there, both of us can feel it, and neither of us knows exactly what to do with it.

Ronin responds by barely talking during the time it takes us to drive the hundred kilometres to the small town of Eenkuil. We coast through the town's high street. The place is a drab, pebbled wasteland of vibracrete walls, dry lawns and deserted petrol stations.

We turn off the high street and pull up outside a shebeen plastered with Coke signs.

'You armed?' Ronin turns off the engine.

'No,' I say. The Boer was meticulous in making sure our assault rifles and handguns were returned to the armoury.

'Well, you're going to have to get something of your own,' he growls. 'I'm not lending you weapons every time we go somewhere.'

'Fine,' I say. 'I'll put "handgun" on the list of things for my parents to get me next term.'

'Well, it's the sort of thing you want to choose for yourself,' Ronin says. 'The bond between you and your weapon is—'

'I was joking. Jesus, I'll get a gun, OK?'

He opens the glove compartment and pulls out the same heavy gun he gave me when we were searching for Basson. I don't remind him that I shot him with it and he doesn't say anything. I stuff it into the back of my jeans and pull my hoodie over it, then follow him into the shebeen.

Bright fluorescent lights highlight the blue plumes of cigarette smoke that hang on the low ceiling. There are several long benches running the length of the room where groups of men drink beer and watch soccer on a small TV. Everyone ignores us except a burly guy at the bar. He wears a tweed flat cap, a sleeveless Kaizer Chiefs T-shirt and a revolver tucked into a belt with a huge dollar-sign buckle.

He puts his hand on the revolver. Ronin whips back his coat, shows him the Blackfish and shakes his head. I try to nonchalantly put my hand behind my back on the handle of the gun.

'I'm looking for Hoxie van Rooyen,' Ronin says to the burly guy. 'Hoxie van Rooyen,' he repeats.

The guy does a quick mental calculation and decides that he's not in the mood for a gunfight. Which suits me fine. He jerks his head towards the back door.

'Good call, bud,' Ronin says.

I follow him through the door. The back room is packed with people, and it smells of sweat, blood and dog. Pit bulls tear at each other in a frenzy of blood, teeth and saliva. The savagery of it stops me in my tracks, but it doesn't take long before one of the dogs limps away a few steps and then drops to the floor, shivering and mewling. A guy in a suit and tie with a floppy green felt hat accessorised with an orange feather taps his cane against the ground and clenches a jubilant fist.

'Hoxie,' Ronin says.

'Ronin.' Hoxie flashes us a smile full of gold teeth and menace. 'Well, well. This is a surprise.'

Hoxie looks about sixty, his long grey hair augmented by colourful braids. A pointed ear sticks out from behind his hair, and his forest-green eyes are widely set and almond-shaped. He leans on his cane and watches us like a spider.

'A reunion of old friends,' Ronin says. 'So heart-warming.'

'Old friends, is it? I don't seem to recall any friendship between us.'

'Friends, enemies, I can never remember which is which.'

'Funny, I've never had a problem with that,' Hoxie replies.

'I need to know where Squirrelskull is,' Ronin says. 'You've been known to trade with them.'

Hoxie nods slowly and looks across to where two more dogs are being set at each other. 'So I have, so I have. The thing is, I've got worries weighing on my mind and I don't think I'll be able to remember where they are until those worries are laid to rest.'

'You always were so unbelievably subtle,' Ronin says. 'Please, by all means, tell me your worries.'

Hoxie leans in and whispers, 'My people are concerned. This Muti Man is stirring up the younger crowd and there has been violence.'

'You're supposed to keep your community under control,' Ronin says. 'That's always the way it's been.'

Hoxie snorts. 'Tell the younger generation that. They smoke their tik, chew their khat and wave their fucking guns in the air like they're cowboys. They've had a few run-ins with the Dwarven Legion and there's talk of open rebellion. That's not going to be good for us, Ronin.'

'Can't say I'm surprised. Dwarves and elves have never exactly seen eye to eye.'

'Azikem, please,' Hoxie says. 'The Legion may have embraced human mythology in their relentless PR campaign over the last few hundred years, but we still have a little dignity.'

'So what do the Azikem want from us?' Ronin asks.

'Speak to the Blood Kraal,' Hoxie says. 'Stop the Legion from hounding us. If I can get the young ones to calm down, perhaps I can stop the bloodshed that's coming.'

'I'll try. But you know humans are supposed to stay out of Hidden affairs.'

Hoxie pulls back his hair and shows us his other ear. The top has been shorn off, leaving an ugly mess of scar tissue. 'Oh, don't worry, I've experienced humans "staying out of our affairs" first-hand.'

Light brown, dark brown, beige, cream. We drive through the uninspired palette of the empty scrubland. I try to call Kyle and Esmé a couple of times, on a spare phone that I had to beg Ronin to let me borrow, but neither of them picks up. With each stupid, stuttering voicemail message I leave, my mood darkens a little more.

I'm in good company. Hoxie pointed out Squirrelskull's location on a map, but it hasn't improved Ronin's state of mind at all. He chain-smokes his way down the highway, swearing to himself and pounding relentlessly on the steering wheel.

'You OK?' I say.

'Sure, sure,' he replies. 'Hand me a stick of gum.'

I pass him the packet and he takes the cigarette out of his mouth long enough to stuff in a few sticks.

'You look different,' he says, his voice muffled through his gum and cigarette.

'Yeah. Must admit I never thought I'd be doing push-ups on my knuckles,' I say, looking down at the scars on the back of my hands from training with the Boer.

'Wait until they make you do knuckle push-ups on broken glass,' he replies.

'Can't wait,' I say. I look at his craggy, hardened face trying to smoke and chew the pain away and I can't help but think about the fresh-faced young guy I saw. 'Ronin, listen, I'm sorry.'

'Why, what did you do?'

'I mean about the Border … what happened to you.'

He's silent.

'I mean, it was—'

'Shut the fuck up, sparky,' Ronin says viciously, spitting smoke and gum from his mouth. He brakes hard and I'm thrown forward against my seat belt. 'It's part of the initiation, OK? It's part of the fucking burden of magic. You get to see parts of your master's life, stuff that you should never have access to. It doesn't mean you get to play amateur fucking psychologist.' He retrieves his cigarette from the dashboard and shoves it back into his mouth.

'I was just—'

'You were just sticking your nose into my business,' Ronin says. 'I don't need some teenager trying to explain to me why wiping out entire villages was actually OK and that I just need to forgive myself and sing "Kumbaya" and go frolicking through meadows.'

'Well, it is in the past,' I say.

'No.' Ronin raps on his temple with his knuckles. 'It's in here and it's not going anywhere. I drink to keep it away and now I've stopped doing that, so the last fucking thing I need is a little punk like you going all Dr Phil on me.'

'Fine,' I say, sitting back in my seat and crossing my arms sulkily. 'I hope you and your post-traumatic stress disorder are happy together.'

'Go fuck yourself,' Ronin grunts.

'Right back at you,' I reply.

All in all, I think my first day as a magician's apprentice has gone pretty much as expected.

We pull off the highway and follow a series of bad dirt roads until we land up in front of a hotel called The Zulu Regent. It's a monstrosity of a building, an ancient Gothic mansion complete with gargoyles and peeling paint. Basically it screams 'murder dungeon' to anyone with any kind of common sense. Ronin obviously likes it.

'We're not seriously staying here, are we?' I ask.

'Relax,' he says. 'We're safer here than we'd be camping outside. The guy who runs this place is an agent.'

A muscular black man in a faded pair of jeans and a white T-shirt walks down the steps and pulls Ronin into a bear hug. The sangoma beads on his forearms rattle as he shakes the bounty hunter from side to side.

'OK, OK,' Ronin growls.

'Oh come on, Ronin,' the guy says in a deep, pleasant voice. 'How many years has it been?'

'Only five or six.'

'Five or six?' He laughs as he puts Ronin back down. 'It was sometime in the nineties.'

'Yeah, well, time flies.'

'I'm sorry, but I refuse to accept that as an excuse. Never mind, it's good to see you anyway.'

'Good to see you too, old man,' Ronin says. 'This is my apprentice, Baxter. Baxter, Sandile.'

Sandile raises an eyebrow. 'I didn't think anyone would EVER be stupid enough to become Ronin's apprentice.'

'You underestimate the stupidity of the kids of today,' Ronin replies.

Sandile laughs a huge, booming laugh and crushes my hand in a vice grip. 'Good to meet you, Baxter. My condolences on your apprenticeship.'

'Thanks.' I put on a grieving face. 'I'm dealing with it as best I can.'

'Fuck you both,' Ronin says and strides up the stairs to the hotel.

The interior is as Gothic as the outside. The massive entrance hall is all dark wood, antique armour and velvet drapes.

'Not bad for a gay Zulu guy from Mthatha, eh?' Sandile says.

'Huh. How did you get the dough for all this? Last time I looked, MK pay cheques weren't exactly blowing anyone's mind.'

Sandile's face crumples. 'Well, the divorce. Michael always had money ...'

Ronin puts his hand on the big man's shoulder. 'Sorry, I heard about that from Pat.'

Sandile forces a smile on to his face. 'No matter. It's in the past. Get you a Scotch, old man?'

A flash of indescribable pain passes across Ronin's face. 'I, um, don't drink any more,' he mumbles.

'I must have misheard. It almost sounded like you said you don't drink any more.'

'That's what I said,' Ronin replies hoarsely.

Sandile shakes his head. 'The world has turned upside down. Basson dead, MK6 operatives getting picked off all over the place and Jackie Ronin turns down a Scotch.' He shrugs. 'Well, come and sit anyway. I'll make you a virgin cocktail.'

'Just shoot me now,' Ronin says morosely as we follow Sandile into a voluminous room housing a shiny mahogany bar and several dusty blackjack, roulette and poker tables that look like they were last used in the eighties.

'Welcome to the casino capital of South Africa,' Sandile says ruefully as he pours himself a massive tumbler of Scotch.

'Business not going well?' Ronin accepts a lemonade with a look of disgust.

'Understatement,' Sandile says, offering me a tumbler. I take it gratefully. 'Michael was right. I am a useless hotelier. So here I sit in this huge decaying house, all alone and waiting to be the next one to have my teeth pulled by the Muti Man.'

'Is it really bad?' I say. 'I mean the agents getting targeted?'

Sandile shrugs. 'Kramer got taken out on his farm two weeks ago. All his teeth, *zzzzip*, gone.'

'Damn,' Ronin says. 'They got a crazy motherfucker like Kramer?'

'Yeah,' Sandile says. 'And Goldberg, Mthewa and Jacobs. They're taking out the big guns and the Blood Kraal aren't doing anything about it.'

'They gave the Legion control of Hexpoort,' Ronin says. 'After the attack.'

Sandile gives him a startled look. 'They attacked the Poort?

What kind of lunatic would attack the Witch at home?'

'My apprentice here says the Muti Man is a Tengu.'

'A Crow shaman? I thought most of them were rounded up in the '82 purge? They were the Legion's public enemy number one.'

'Apparently not. And this one is pissed.'

Sandile grabs the bottle of Scotch and takes a swig from it. 'Well, fuck me. This just goes from bad to worse.'

Ronin eyes the bottle like he's a vampire looking at a vial of blood. 'Bottom line is that we're at war whether it's official or not. Any unusual activity around this area?'

'A coven of Semish in caves about twenty ks away. But they don't look for shit unless something pisses them off. I've capped one or two of them for hunting humans and now they stick to cattle.'

'Well, it's probably not a bad idea to be prepared. Like you said, things are turned on their head. You still have your collection?'

Sandile chuckles. 'Oh, a man does not get rid of a collection like mine.'

'Anything you'd be willing to sell the boy? He needs a weapon. The pig-iron I've lent him doesn't suit him.'

'I'm offended. You may as well ask me to sell him an organ.'

'OK.' Ronin turns his glass in his hand and stares at the lemonade. 'Just asking.'

Sandile looks at me. 'But I hear our boy here is a Dreamwalker.'

'Where did you hear that?' I say.

'The first Dreamwalker at Hexpoort in fifty years? News like that travels.' He taps his fingers on the glossy mahogany of the bar. 'So … what exactly can you do? How extensive are those Dreamwalking skills?'

'Stop beating around the bush. If you want something from him, just ask.'

Sandile sighs. 'It's my ex-husband, Michael. He won't answer my calls. He won't let me see our son. I just want to find out what they're up to.'

'You want me to spy on your ex for you?'

'Not spy exactly. Just make sure they're OK,' he says. 'He's threatened to take our son overseas if he catches me surveilling him.'

'So you want me to surveil him.'

'Do it and you can have anything from my collection you want.'

I look at Ronin. He shrugs. 'Let's just say I would do unspeakable things for something from his collection.'

'You'd do unspeakable things for a cigarette,' I say. 'But OK. I'm in. Have you got anything of his? I think it'll be easier that way.'

Sandile holds up a hand and disappears into the entrance hall. I hear his heavy footsteps going up the stairs. He appears a few minutes later holding up a denim shirt.

'Haven't washed it,' he says. 'Sentimental fool that I am.'

'This'll work.' I take the shirt and sit down on the floor in the middle of the room. As I weave the beads between my fingers, the cloth of the shirt throbs with something, a vibe, an essence, a unique marker that I follow back to its source.

I see a tall man in a blazer and jeans reading a small boy a bedtime story. The image shifts and I'm exposed to the man's dreams. Great swathes of ambition run through him, images of yachts, parties, a childhood obsession with old cars. And meeting Sandile. A single word of immense significance to the two of them throbs in my head.

I open my eyes. 'He still dreams about you,' I say.

Sandile stares at me. 'How can I tell this is real?'

'Does the word "Lotus" mean anything to you?'

'My God,' he says, clenching and unclenching a huge fist.

Ronin puts a hand on his arm. 'Steady there, old man.'

Sandile hangs his head, but when he lifts it he's smiling. 'I'm OK. This is a positive thing, right? Maybe I can still get him back?'

'I really don't know,' I say.

He shakes his head. 'So stupid. Love, right?'

I nod. So damn stupid.

Sandile downs his Scotch and then puts a hand on my shoulder. 'But let's talk about something a little less ambiguous. Let's talk about weapons.'

'Now you're speaking my language,' Ronin says.

We follow Sandile into a large sitting room. He taps numbers into a panel underneath a painting of a man in uniform stroking a greyhound, and a whole wall slides away to reveal a large steel display room filled with racks.

'Projectile weapons, bladed weapons, impact weapons,' Sandile says, brushing his fingers along a row of guns. 'You can pick one of each.'

Ronin shakes his head in wonder. 'I'll spy on anyone you want for as long as you want for one of these beauties.'

I look from rack to rack. There are so many different kinds that I don't know where to start.

'Any tips?' I ask Ronin.

'Logically, there are all kinds of things you should factor in: reach, range, magazine capacity, susceptibility to jamming. But the best advice I can give you is just pick the items that feel right.'

'Let's give him some space,' Sandile says, stepping back out of the room. Ronin reluctantly follows, and I'm left alone with the instruments of death.

I've always liked the concept of weapons better than the reality. In movies and games they seem so cool. Up close you can't help but become aware of their terrible lethal capacity. These are tools with no other purpose than that of ending life, and there's something terrifying about that.

I browse the long racks and decide to be systematic about it. Impact weapons first. There are iron-shod sticks, baseball bats, canes, batons, staffs, maces. There are nunchaku and tonfa and some kind of weird gnarled stick weighted with lead.

I pick up a heavy baton and immediately feel ill. The violence in it throbs against my palm and I can feel the heads that have been cracked open, the limbs broken, the bones shattered. I replace it carefully on the rack. As I go through the weapons I start to get a sense of what Ronin means. They all have personalities: snarling and rabid or lethally calm. There's a staff that feels like a snake in my hands, and a cane that I swear is laughing at me.

I happen on one that feels light to the touch. It's a spring-loaded baton that lengthens into a longer quarterstaff at the touch of a button. It's made of a faded grey wood carved with spidery sigils. Rather than the heavy, bloody, primal character of some of the others, it has a thoughtful, strategic, and maybe slightly snarky, sarcastic feel to it. It's the kind of weapon that would crack a joke as it's shoved into your solar plexus. I like it already.

I place it carefully on the floor next to me.

The bladed weapons are something altogether different. Arrogant, vain and narcissistic, the cutlasses, katanas, sabres, rapiers, longswords, knives and daggers seem to revel in their own sharpness. An ornate scimitar I take off the rack feels immediately like the worst kind of blowhard. I take a couple of test swings and it almost seems like I'm being forced to sit through some financier sounding off about how awesome he is. I put it back.

I pick up a short sword with a polished wooden handle. It feels solid, dependable, long-suffering. It's the Eeyore of blades, seeming to sigh through the air, stoically accepting that it's a sword and that's what it does. It's the kind of weapon that will cut through a thousand enemies and carry on going because that's the fate it has accepted.

I place it on the floor next to the baton.

The guns feel calculated and lethal, the stolid personalities of Marine Corps sergeants and Army Rangers. This time I take a total chance and pick something different. In contrast to my other choices, this one is pure ego: a shiny chrome handgun with an image of the Wheel of Fortune tarot card inlaid on the handle in mother-of-pearl and semi-precious stones. It feels comfortable in my hand, wild, untamed, a gun that'll blow between red hot and ice cold in a couple of seconds. It's a mobster's gun, a gambler's gun, a gun that's not afraid when the dice are thrown.

I place it next to my two other choices.

'Knock, knock.'

I turn to see Sandile standing in the room with a smile on his face and a jacket slung over his arm.

'You done?' Ronin asks.

I nod.

They look at the weapons I've chosen, like breeders studying thoroughbred horses. 'Excellent,' Sandile says. 'I'm very impressed by your choices.' He looks at Ronin with a raised eyebrow.

'Not my style.' Ronin grimaces.

'That's why I like them so much,' I say.

Sandile bursts out laughing. 'I think you two are going to be perfect together. Just perfect.'

He hands me a shoulder strap and holster for the gun and baton, and a belt and sheath for the short sword, and then presents me with the jacket he has over his arm.

'This is a gift,' he says. 'It stopped fitting me a long time ago.'

'Let's be honest,' Ronin says. 'It never fitted you.'

'You're probably right.'

I strap the sword around my waist and slide the baton and the handgun into the shoulder harness, then shrug the jacket on. It fits perfectly, like it's been tailored, seemingly moulding to my body.

Ronin seems less than impressed, but Sandile nods approvingly.

'He has potential, Ronin.' He puts his hands on his hips and looks at me. 'Real potential.'

'Yeah, we'll see,' Ronin says gruffly.

'Welcome to the agent's life,' Sandile says. 'It's not pretty, but it's something, I suppose.'

'Well, you look ridiculous,' Ronin says as I enter the room he's staying in for the night. I'm glad he's the one that got the Safari Room. A really badly taxidermied eland stares cross-eyed across the room, and the faux lion rug looks a little too well used.

Ronin sits at an old wooden writing desk with a cup of tea and an expression of utter defeat on his face. He's sweating again and he looks red and feverish. I'm starting to wonder whether he's ever going to break the back of his addiction.

'I look like you,' I say, unstrapping my weapons and laying them down carefully on the couch. 'So yeah, I guess you're right.'

'Lemon, ginger and honey,' Ronin says, looking into the teacup. 'Mmmmm.'

I sit down at the desk and Ronin grabs a piece of paper, turns it over and slides it away from me.

'What's that?' I say.

'Mind your own business,' he growls. 'Don't you have to go practise looking tough in a mirror or something?'

'Come on,' I say. 'What is it?'

He sighs. 'OK, I'll tell you. But you've got to promise not to laugh.'

'OK,' I say. 'I promise.'

'Well, in the book I'm reading, the doctor recommends writing a letter to your addiction as if it were a person.'

I burst out laughing.

'Whatever, porno boy,' he says.

'Sorry.' I try to suppress a giggle. 'Sorry. So you're writing a letter to alcohol?'

'Well, he says it works better if you're specific, so I'm writing a letter to Scotch. "Dear Scotch. You are a beautiful lady. You are the colour of copper. You are the taste of water to a man dying of thirst. We can't be together any more. It's not you, it's me. Be happy without me. Ronin."'

'That's beautiful,' I say. 'Real poetry.'

'It's not helping,' Ronin says, sipping his tea desperately.

We sit for a while and listen to the crickets chirping outside.

'That speech you made back at Hexpoort. About being an agent. Did you mean it?'

'Yeah, mostly.' Ronin takes another sip of his tea. 'It's a hard life at the best of times.'

'I've just been thinking,' I say. 'Are we really doing the right thing for the Hidden?'

'You're getting all political on me now, sparky?'

'It's just that maybe I don't want to be the prison guard,' I say.

'Sometimes you don't get to choose,' Ronin replies.

The next morning we pack our stuff into the Cortina and say goodbye to Sandile.

'Ronin tell you how we met?'

'No,' I say.

He rubs his chin. 'My village was destroyed by Gogs, real mean ones—'

'No other kind,' Ronin interrupts.

'Yeah, well. Me and some of the other kids escaped by hiding in a tree. The Gogs cleared out and days later Ronin's unit found us. His unit commander wanted to execute all of the survivors and Ronin knocked him the fuck out.'

'Yeah, what a hero,' Ronin growls. 'You neglect to mention that it was our Gog unit that destroyed your village.'

Sandile leans in. 'Don't let Ronin fool you with his whole poor-evil-me routine. He's done some really good things in his time.'

Ronin pats him on the shoulder. 'It's cute how you keep believing in something despite all evidence to the contrary.'

One hundred and forty-five white cars, ninety-five black cars, seventy-eight silver cars, seventy red cars, thirty-four green cars, one pink car with the words REAL FANDANGO emblazoned on it in lurid yellow, twenty-five cows, thirteen goats, one ostrich, one man dressed in a plastic bag holding a TV antenna on his head. These are the things I count on the endless road as I'm lulled into a vacant trance.

An infinite amount of time later, I regain a semi-conscious awareness of the car bumping down the road. Then I'm catapulted back into reality by Ronin mercilessly flicking my ear with his thick fingers.

'Stop.' I reach up to push his hand away.

'We're here,' he says.

I rub my eyes. 'Where's here?'

'Forest in Elgin,' Ronin replies, lighting up a cigarette and getting out of the car. 'Take a look.' I open the door and follow him.

A fine mist shifts and coils among the silent trees. Ronin gestures with his cigarette towards a tree stump in the centre of a clearing. We walk through the mist and I breathe in the cold, ghostlike wisps. Venus hangs in the sky like tacky pink costume jewellery.

The burnt, blackened stump is etched with symbols in gold and silver that are so faint you wouldn't see them if you weren't looking for them. Ronin drops to one knee and runs his fingers across the dark wood, then spits on to the pine-needle floor of the clearing.

'Obayifo ring,' he says. 'It marks the edges of their territory.'

'What are Obayifo anyway?' I ask.

'Well, they're really two distinct creatures: the queen and her offspring. The offspring are what would commonly be called faeries.'

'Faeries? Don't they just fly around and grant people's wishes and shit?'

'That's the Disney version,' Ronin says. 'The world that these faeries inhabit is the Brothers Grimm version, the one where Sleeping Beauty gets nailed in her sleep by the prince and wakes up having already borne three kids.'

'Right,' I say, feeling that familiar sinking feeling that accompanies going anywhere with Ronin. 'Well, let's get this over with then, I guess.'

Ronin claps me on the shoulder. 'Now you're starting to get into the spirit of being an agent.'

THE AGENTS GRIM

We walk through dense, silent forest. There's an ancient feeling hanging in the air. My magical senses are much more attuned to that kind of thing now, and the tingling sensation in my hands makes it seem like I'm clawing and kneading the air like a cat playing with yarn. My lungs fill with oxygen and I feel exhilarated as we walk. This is a beautiful, sacred space. If you spent enough time here you could really get in touch with yourself. The outer world would melt away and you'd be contained in a bubble of peace that—

My epiphany is interrupted by the sight of tiny figures up ahead. Tiny figures with wings. Slaughtering each other. We have walked into the middle of Faerie Armageddon.

The battle rages around us. A bloody, terrified faerie flies past me screaming, chased by two faerie warriors in armour. They catch and quickly dismember him. The forest floor is covered by faeries mounted on animals. An armoured squirrel rips the head off an angelic blonde faerie before it in turn is brained by a wild barbarian faerie with a spiked mace.

From what I can tell, the battle can be roughly divided into two sides: heavily armoured faeries flying banners with animal-skull heraldry, and wild-looking barbarian faeries consumed by berserker battle rage. Tiny whoops of bloodlust and the screams of the dying ring through the forest. The barbarians fight well, but they're outnumbered, and the well-armed regiment of trained battle faeries are brutally methodical. The barbarian force is abruptly broken and they scatter and flee. Lancers on the back of large angry rats run them down and skewer them.

A female faerie directs her golden-armoured baboon mount towards us and removes her blood-spattered helm. She flicks her long dark plait and stares at us with the hard eyes of a killer, their coldness accentuated by sharp lines of blue paint that curve across her cheekbones.

'I am Bodhi, Prime Enforcer of the Squirrelskull Cartel,' she says in a high-pitched voice. 'You are trespassing on our lands, humans. Why are you here?'

'Greetings.' Ronin bows with a flourish. 'We mean no offence to the esteemed Squirrelskull Cartel, who are known far and wide for their battle prowess.'

'Get to the point,' Bodhi says, wiping the blood from her helm with a hand and bringing it to her lips to taste. 'Or have the flesh stripped from your bones.' The faerie battalion encircles us. They're small but there are lots of them and their weapons are very sharp. They'd cut like surgical scalpels. One or two of those in the eye or neck …

'We request a meeting with your Slugmother,' Ronin says. 'And I ask you to consider carefully the fact that we are here under the protection of MK6.'

Bodhi laughs, a shrill little squeak. 'I'm afraid you'll find that that is no protection at all, human. The Slugmother has been expecting the human plague to send their little germs into our kingdom. I will take you to her mercy, but first, I have cartel matters to deal with.'

Ronin bows again graciously. 'At your leisure, brave and noble Enforcer.'

As it turns out, 'cartel matters' consist mainly of the impaling of captured prisoners on sharp sticks. Bodhi's eyes burn brightly as she oversees the skewering, calling out tips and suggestions to soldiers as they position the vanquished and terrified faeries on the sharpened ends of poles. Ronin sits smoking as tiny faerie screams rend the quiet of the forest. I close my eyes and think of Tinker Bell.

Cartel matters concluded, we're hemmed in by a guard of flying faeries, their wings fluttering like hummingbirds', and marched through the forest. The faeries speak to each other in a supersonic dialect, part English, part Afrikaans, part bird call and insect hymn.

'Quick cultural briefing,' Ronin whispers. 'The Slugmother is their queen. Actually more like king *and* queen, because all Slug-mothers are hermaphrodites, but always referred to as feminine. She gives birth to the entire cartel.'

'Great,' I whisper back. 'So what are the chances that this will end up with us being slaughtered?'

Ronin thinks for a second. 'About fifty-fifty.'

'If I'm going to be your apprentice, we seriously need to discuss strategy,' I say.

Ronin raises an eyebrow. 'We've survived this far, haven't we?'

'Only because you're harder to kill than a cockroach.'

'I'm going to take that as a compliment.'

We are finally ushered into a deep granite furrow. 'Scorpion Gully,' Bodhi announces.

Scorpion Gully is where the Squirrelskull Cartel hang their hats after a hard day of killing and pillaging. Thousands of nests, like those of weaver birds, are attached to the walls of the gully with a grey goo that Ronin says is Slugmother vomit. We take a winding path between them, passing rows of faeries sitting and drinking out of broken sparrow's eggs and acorn cups. It might have been charming if they didn't spit in our path as we pass.

In the centre of the gully is a huge sinkhole that has been turned into a giant faerie drug lab. Thousands of sweating faeries wearing face masks use their deft little fingers to mould pink powder into pills.

'What are they making?' I ask.

'MDMA maybe,' Ronin says. 'But whatever it is, it's weird. Squirrelskull have always manufactured counterfeit goods. For them to suddenly go into pharmaceuticals is a major fuck-you to the other Obayifo cartels.'

'You think the Muti Man is involved?'

'Selling drugs to fund a revolution? Very possible. We need to get a team in here to test those pills. Or take some with us.'

Bodhi leads us to the entrance of a huge woven dome at the end of the gully. Ronin and I stoop to enter, and then straighten up into a long room lined with squirrel skeletons wired together with gold thread.

An envoy appears in front of us, a stooped, sickly-looking Obayifo dressed in garish silks and a tall purple hat. He rubs his little hands together nervously. 'I am Demna, High Priest to the Blessed Slugmother Meptu.'

'Greetings, High Priest,' Ronin says with a bow. 'We are—'

'The Blessed Slugmother will decide what you are,' Demna says with a wave of his tiny hand. 'It is my duty to inform you of the rules.'

We are to speak only when spoken to. If she decides we are not worthy, we are to submit to execution without making a fuss. We both nod, although it's a bit like clicking on 'agree' on a website's terms and conditions. I mentally commit to killing as many of these bloodthirsty little bastards as possible if it comes down to it. Starting with the High Priest.

'The Infinite Slugmother Dogran Meptu,' Demna says, leading us into an alcove where a beautiful woman lounges attended by several shirtless male models. Except she's not really. Beautiful, I mean. There's something wrong with her, as if the air around her semi-naked body is being forced into doing something it really doesn't want to do. I blink my eyes, trying to get a fix on her.

'What's wrong with her?' I whisper.

Ronin raises an eyebrow at me. 'Obviously not all your training has been a waste.' He turns to the woman. 'Nice outfit,' he says. 'But why don't you slip into something a little more comfortable? Really, there's no need to dress up on our account.'

The woman smiles, shimmers and pops like a bubble, leaving an obese slug creature lounging in her place. It's roughly the size of a human, but big and lumpy like an old beanbag. Its skin is an uneven blue – dark at the head and tapering into a baby blue – and is carpeted in fine white hairs that sway and move like feelers. It rubs its spotted blue belly contemplatively with short T. rex arms and looks up at us with big, drowsy yellow eyes.

The Obayifo warriors squeal and swarm around her, suckling at a dark, oily liquid that pours from her. I've seen a lot of disgusting things since I met Ronin. This ranks pretty close to the top.

'I hope you have no objection to me feeding in public,' the Slugmother says, the little warriors struggling against each other for prime spots to slurp the black liquid. 'It really is the most natural thing in the world.'

The male models have also dissolved to reveal hideous giant stick insects that twitch and hiss at us. The Slugmother waves a stumpy arm and they settle a little.

'My Skinsects do love humans,' she says. 'But don't mind them. They just want to play.'

One of them extends a long proboscis covered in thousands

of needle-sharp spikes. I quickly update my nightmare list to include Skinsects.

'Humans in my kingdom,' the Slugmother says. 'How thrilling. I assume this is not a social call, considering the penalties for trespassing on our territory?' Penalties. Must have slipped Ronin's mind to tell me about those.

'Slugmother,' Ronin begins carefully. 'The cartels have always worked within the boundaries that MK6 has set for them.'

The Slugmother laughs. 'Those boundaries once coincided with our interests.'

'Your interests will be best served if you tell us about any communication you've had with the individual calling himself the Muti Man.'

The giant slug shakes her body and Obayifo fly from her in unison, like a flock of pigeons that has been disturbed.

'The agreement with the humans is null and void. A contract between master and slave is not a contract! We are tired of bowing our heads. You are the very definition of human arrogance, wandering into our territory and then demanding answers from ME! Send a message, the Muti Man says.' The Slugmother rubs her oily belly. 'Yes, we will send a message. A message that says that the age of human and dwarven exceptionalism is at an end.'

Demna hovers in front of us, his little eyes wide with outrage. 'Slugmother, I ask permission to deal with these humans who are defiling this sacred space with their presence.'

Ronin's hand slowly slinks down to where the Blackfish hangs under his coat. I pretend to stretch, and slip my hand under my coat and on to the grip of my new gun.

'Well, High Priest,' the Slugmother says, licking her thick grey lips. 'What do you think I should do?'

'The rules are quite clear, Blessed Slugmother: intruders to the realm are subject to the Grim,' the little bastard says.

'The Grim, yes. Very good.'

'An excellent choice, Slugmother,' Demna says with a bow.

Ronin whips his coat open and I'm about to grab Demna and blow his little head off when there's a pinch in my neck. I try to lift a hand to slap at it but I can't move. My body is completely numb. Judging by Ronin's posture, he's either decided to play an impromptu game of musical statues or he too is experiencing inexplicable paralysis.

Two little warriors with blowguns descend from where they were hovering.

'Obayifo poison,' the Slugmother says. 'The human body is not a fan.'

My entire body feels like how your arm feels when you've slept on it. My eyes and eyebrows can move but that's about the extent of my body's functionality. I slide my eyes across to Ronin and see him swearing as much as he can with his eyebrows. Our eyes meet and his ridiculous red eyebrows shrug. I try to tell him with my eyebrows to go fuck himself, but it probably comes across more like I'm having a seizure.

We're bound with strong silk and then airlifted out of the palace by dozens of faeries like we're statues being transported by helicopter. We're rudely dropped in the middle of a clearing and the silk is cut away by little swords. The faeries leave and I breathe in deeply. My body feels like I've been sleeping in an awkward position but it's regaining feeling fast. I feel a resurgence of hope. Perhaps the Grim is nothing worse than being carried through an Obayifo village.

Ronin is regaining movement too. He groans and looks across at me, and then shakes his head. 'This is just the start. The Grim is like a foxhunt. We'll run and the battalion will hunt us. They'll attack slowly, wearing us down and bleeding us out like animals.'

'So tell me, have the chances of us being slaughtered changed?'

He moves his head from side to side, weighing it up. 'I'd say they've dropped to about seventy-thirty.'

I sigh and put my head in my hands. 'You're like a bad joke, Ronin. You know that?'

'Yeah, knock, knock. Who's there? Fuck you, sparky. That's who.'

I shake my head in disgust. 'What now?'

'I'd suggest stretching. We're going to be doing a lot of running.'

A soft hum breaks the quiet. Bees, maybe? I should be so lucky. We pick up our pace, moving through the forest at a brisk jog. Weapons jostle for space under my jacket and sweat prickles my forehead.

With a sharp *zzzzzzzzzuuuuuuu* something flies past my face and I flail madly at it. A pinprick pain slices my neck.

'Ah!' Ronin shouts, clutching at his face. A droplet of blood appears on his cheek. He pulls the Blackfish from his coat and points it into the forest. I scrabble for my short sword and hold it in front of me. Back to back we circle around in the mist, the humming sound growing like a plague of insects.

Suddenly the mist erupts with the whoop of a hundred faerie warriors in full battle armour. A faerie with a lance flies past and impales my hand. I shout in pain and swing my sword in a wide arc, failing to hit anything. Ronin fires the Blackfish wildly into the air, but Bodhi's battalion are just too quick. He's hit by a faerie with a poleaxe. I flail around with the sword and grunt with satisfaction as the flat side thwacks one of the little bastards from the air like a fly swatter.

It's not enough. I'm getting cut. A lot. The cuts are small, like paper cuts, but when you've been hit ten times in ten seconds they begin to take their toll. Little droplets of blood ooze from me like sweat. Ronin is also bleeding from a dozen small cuts.

He pulls a disgusted face just as three small faerie arrows zip into his cheek. I give up trying to hit anything. 'Run,' I shout, 'up the path!'

He looks down towards where the Cortina is parked, but it is cut off by a wall of frantically buzzing faeries.

'UP!' I shout.

We sprint up the orange gravel path. It's steep and difficult, even if I wasn't bleeding from tiny lacerations. Ronin swears constantly as we struggle up the hill, swatting at the winged warriors that dart in at us at regular intervals. If we manage to loop around the path back to the Cortina we might be able to make it. If we can stave off exhaustion and blood loss for long enough.

That's when we see the battle squirrels up ahead, line after line of armoured grey tree rats glaring at us with red eyes. The faeries weren't mounting a concerted attack; they were just herding us towards the main attraction: being dismembered by the woodland family.

We swerve off the path and on to the pine-needle-strewn floor of the forest.

'We can't fight. We need to hide,' I gasp as we struggle through the trees, the terrifying chittering of a hundred rabid squirrels following us.

'Great idea,' Ronin gasps back. 'Where?'

He spins on his heel and blasts a leaping attack squirrel out of the air. We flatten ourselves against a granite boulder and he pulls another shell from his bandolier to shove into the Blackfish. He snaps the gun shut and we clamber over a gully of sharp boulders. I pick up a handful of little rocks as I run. Several squirrels appear at the treeline and hiss menacingly. Ronin fires another shot, scattering them. At the end of the gully I see faeries approaching fast, wings whirring and eyes filled with hate.

A dozen more squirrels appear at the treeline and begin to

advance in formation. I draw my handgun smoothly from its holster and fire. One of the squirrels leaps from a rock, sailing gracefully through the air and clamping its teeth on Ronin's neck.

'Errraaaiiii!' Ronin shouts, trying to disengage the little jaws from his flesh. He spins wildly, lifting the Blackfish and firing a shot that sends squirrel meat splattering everywhere.

We clamber up the rocks and break through the treeline and on to a path. An old lady walking her Labrador stands absolutely still as two gun-wielding maniacs, both bloody, one with tiny arrows jutting from his face, stumble wildly on to the track in front of her.

'Afternoon,' Ronin says, as we walk towards her. 'Lovely day.'

Once past her, we break into a wild run again. Running on level ground is gloriously easy, even though my legs are aching and my breath is coming in short, asthmatic gasps. We barrel along the path. Here at least the faeries seem reluctant to attack, falling back into the forest as we make our way among the bald, sweaty joggers and families guiding pushchairs carefully along the track. But the chittering of war squirrels and the hum of faerie wings doesn't disappear. It sounds like they're massing for another assault.

I look across at Ronin and stop abruptly, my sneakers skidding in the dirt.

'What?' Ronin says, stopping too and looking around.

I've stopped because there's something wrong with Ronin's face. The area around where the three small faerie arrows are lodged is dropping and sagging, making him look like a stroke victim.

'What?' he repeats, swinging around wildly.

'I think those arrows in your face were poisoned,' I say.

Ronin touches his face gingerly.

'Oh,' he says simply and then points shakily at my arm.

I look down to see a little arrow jutting from a bloody patch on the fabric. With all the cuts I received in the melee, I didn't notice it. Now, though, I begin to feel my arm tingling.

I look desperately at Ronin. He shrugs, his sagging face resigned. 'We carry on,' he says gruffly.

We continue moving swiftly. The tingling in my arm has become a deep numbness, which begins to ache. I try to lift it and barely manage to get it up to my shoulder. Ronin's left eye has closed completely and the left corner of his mouth is dribbling saliva uncontrollably.

The track ends in a large rolling lawn. We stumble past lounging picnickers and little cherub children chasing after guinea fowl. It's idyllic. If you're not poisoned by faerie arrows and running desperately for your life. We send the flock of guinea fowl scattering, making the children wail with fright. Ronin, one eye now completely useless, veers on to a checked picnic blanket and puts a large military boot into a gourmet arrangement of cheeses. Mothers pull their babies to them, and fathers stand protectively in front of their broods.

I stagger wheezing past a group of picnickers and grab a pastry from a plate. Ronin rips a champagne bottle from a couple and downs it, half of it foaming out of his poisoned, near-useless lips. He hands me the bottle and I swig the bubbly liquid.

'Sorry!' I shout as we carry on through the gardens and back into the forest. My sneakers slip on pine needles as we lurch exhausted, bleeding and poisoned through the trees. We tumble into the bed of a river and slosh upstream through the trickling water.

A telltale hum alerts us to the fact that our little executioners are back. I hear buzzing to my right and I spin, slinging the handful of stones in the direction of the noise with my good arm. A single faerie archer is battered by the onslaught, my sharp granite missiles ripping into him.

We climb up the bank and on to another path.

'Left or right?' I say as the faeries and their animals crowd into the riverbed below.

Ronin looks at me, a string of saliva hanging from his lip. 'Right.'

'You're sure?'

He grabs my arm and pulls me down the path to the right. We turn the corner and run straight into a dead end. There's a small cliff ahead of us, just too tall for us to climb.

'We're trapped,' I say.

Ronin turns and fires a round as the first of the armoured squirrels reach us. In my peripheral vision I see furry body parts hit a pine tree. More squirrels and faeries appear and we level our guns at them.

'Chances of us getting slaughtered now?' I hiss.

'A cautiously optimistic ninety-ten,' Ronin whispers back. 'I didn't entirely expect this …'

'Just shut up,' I say. 'You're the one that got us killed. Just remember that in these last ten seconds of your life.'

A rope drops from the cliff above us and hits me on the head. We glance up to see a curious face looking down at us, nose twitching.

'Hey, Big Ones, hey,' Klipspringer says. 'You looksosososososo-sosoterrible. I been following you for aggggeeesss.'

'Klipspringer!' I say. Half-human, half-bok, all nervous excitement, Klipspringer gives me a smile and bounces up and down. The last time I saw him was at the Haven, Pat's refuge for the Hidden, and he's grown a couple of inches. His bok hindquarters are longer and his human torso has a little bit more muscle.

'Well whatyouwaitingforhey? Come on away from those faeriedummies,' he calls.

I grab the rope and scramble up the cliff face. Ronin fires several times into the mass of winged and furry bodies, and then follows me up. I reach the top and turn around to look down over the edge. Ronin is shouting like a maniac and swinging wildly on the rope, trying to simultaneously shoot faeries and climb. Several squirrels have attached themselves to his trousers, and a faerie has a handful of his hair and is stabbing him repeatedly in the ear.

I pull my gun from its holster and aim over the side. The last time I tried to help Ronin like this I ended up shooting him, and this time the odds are much worse. I breathe out slowly and feel the giddy sense of risk. It's possible that I will help him, but it's also entirely possible that I will accidentally shoot him in the face. The thrill of it, the gun in my hands holding the power of life and death. I see the odds: the movement of the wind, the swinging back and forth of the target, my own inner condition. For a split second those things align in a microscopic window of opportunity. I squeeze the trigger and the faerie in Ronin's hair explodes.

Ronin looks up at me in horror. He kicks his legs and squashes two squirrels against the cliff, then, grunting, scrambles up the rope.

His ear is bleeding and the side of his face is completely paralysed. 'Whaa the fuuuu,' he says, the left side of his lip slopping about like a fish out of water.

'Come on, Big Ones, hey hey,' Klipspringer says and raises an eyebrow like we're naughty kids. 'No time to talktalk now.'

We follow him across the rocks to a cave.

'We can't stay here, Klipspringer,' I say. 'They'll find us.'

'They can't come in here, duh. Ndiru magic, hey, Big One, it's the powerfullest.'

Well, we certainly can't run any more. My arm has gone completely numb and Ronin looks like he's about to collapse.

'OK,' I say, slumping down against the cave wall. 'I guess I'll just have to trust you, bok-boy.'

The cave is filled with junk. There's a cardboard cut-out of Phil Collins, and the walls are covered with posters of action stars that I remember from when Kyle and I downloaded an entire eighties action movie library. Those old geezers on Internet forums can be as nostalgic as they want, but the films were all shit.

'What are you doing here, Klipspringer?' I ask. 'Why aren't you at Pat's?'

'This is my secret place, duh,' he says. 'The Ndiru have to be in the naturenature when the Bright Star is out. To talk to the ancestorguys, hey?'

Ronin groans. He's sprawled against the cave wall and he doesn't look good. His face is slightly green and the black rings around his eyes have gone purple. Drool drips from the side of his hanging lip and one of his eyes is twitching. 'You fuuu,' he murmurs and then shakes his head. I kneel down next to him and dab at the blood with a Ninja Turtles face cloth that I find on a crate full of Tamagotchis.

'He needs help, Klipspringer,' I say. 'Do you have an anti-venom kit?'

The bok-boy snorts with contempt. 'Anti-venomoms don't work. I'll make the magic tea.'

He whistles to himself as he rounds up a handful of blue M&Ms, some scraggly weeds and a packet of plastic army figurines, dumping the lot in a pot on top of a gas cooker. He murmurs something in another language as the pot begins to boil.

He hands me a *Who's the Boss?* mug. 'Thanks, Klipspringer,' I say, looking at Tony Danza's chipped ceramic face. 'But I don't think this is going to work. We really need anti-venom.'

'Drink,' he says sternly and puts his hands on his springbok hindquarters.

'OK, OK.' I sip the disgusting mixture. 'There, I can almost taste the magic. Now we need to get an anti-venom ki—'

My shoulder begins to tingle and the numbness slides off my arm.

'It works!'

'Duh,' he says, rolling his eyes. 'Ndiru magic is the powerfullest, you must listen better, hey?'

I refill the mug from the pot. Ronin is slipping in and out of consciousness as I hold it to his lips and make him sip. His face begins to twitch and then his eyes shoot open. He gasps and looks around wildly.

'It's OK,' I say.

He turns to look at me. 'You.'

'It wasn't just me,' I say with a smile. 'It was Klipspringer. We both saved you.'

'You fucking shot at me. One millimetre off and it would have blown a hole through my eye.' He shoves me away and pushes himself to his feet. 'What were you thinking?'

'Hey!' I say. 'A little frikken gratitude would be great.'

'It was one faerie. I could have got to the top,' he says.

'Right,' I say. 'Sure. You know, I'm sick of this. I save you, no gratitude, you don't give a shit. I save the world, no gratitude, nobody gives a shit.'

'YOU saved the world?' Ronin says, his eyes wide. 'If it wasn't for me, you'd still be wandering around looking for your girlfriend, and you would never find her BECAUSE SHE'D BE SPIDER FOOD.'

'HEY!' The shout from Klipspringer is so unexpected that we both shut up.

'Stopshoutingithurtsmyears,' Klipspringer says with an anxious twitch of his nose.

'Sorry,' I say.

'He's right, we've got better things to do than listen to you bellyaching about how poor widdle you is so underappreciated.'

Ronin limps over to the mouth of the cave. 'Ndiru magic might be keeping them away, but as soon as we step outside we're going to be cut to shreds. How are we going to get out of here?'

The bok-boy capers up and down excitedly. 'I'll show you, Big Ones, duh, the way only Klipspringer knows. You gonna be amazeded.'

Ronin gives me a dirty look as he follows Klipspringer to the back of the cave. I pull a face at him and pop the middle finger at his back. Asshole.

'Alittlehelpwouldbenice,' Klipspringer says, putting his back to an old fridge filled with tiny plastic trolls with bright blue hair. We help him push the fridge aside to reveal a small opening in the cave wall.

'Comenowhurryup,' he says, and ducks into the opening.

'You go first,' Ronin says. 'I don't want you shooting me in the back.'

'Yeah, I will,' I reply. 'I don't want you accidentally leading us into another fucking catastrophe.'

I climb through the opening and follow Klipspringer along a tunnel. Ronin swears and grunts behind me as we fumble our way through the darkness. Luckily the tunnel quickly opens up into a cavern filled with crystal stalactites and stalagmites. Red clay cave paintings of bok-people cover the walls.

'This is the secretsacredsecret place, Big Ones, so sshhhh,' Klipspringer says, putting his finger to his lips.

In the centre of the cave are bones, hundreds of them, bleached white by time.

'Ndiruboneyard,' Klipspringer says reverently. 'The ancestor-guys are here. You can't cross without the ancestorblessing, hey? If you try, it's badbadbadbad.'

He holds up a hand and begins to sing in his strange language, high and sweet like he's part of a boys' choir. In my mind's eye I can see generations of bok-people stretching back through the centuries, their noses twitching, their eyes bright and dewy, all collecting some serious bric-a-brac from across the ages.

An apparition appears in the centre of the bones, a misty bok-person who raises a hand in greeting. He is very old, his wild hair is long, and he has an impressive beard that stretches down to his hooves.

'The ancestorguy,' whispers Klipspringer. 'You have to trade him something to pass.'

'You have anything, Ronin?' I say.

He searches through his pockets and pulls out cigarettes, a lighter, a penknife, some mints and an old ticket for a roller coaster.

I go through my own pockets and find a couple of coins, a red Life Saver covered in lint and hair and the yellow Pornography Anonymous key ring.

The old ancestorguy points a shimmering finger at the key ring.

'Your trade is good, good,' Klipspringer says, nodding his head, clearly impressed. 'He's giving you something in return.'

The ancestorguy points again. There in the bones, an old spoon lies wedged between a femur and a patella. The handle has been shaped into the wavy tail of a bok.

'Er, thanks,' I say.

'Getit, hey,' Klipspringer says.

I walk across, kneel down and free the spoon from the bones. A flash of recognition jolts through me and I intuitively know it's one of the items for my mojo bag. I slide it carefully into the canvas pocket and nod in thanks to the ancestorguy. I look around for some indication that I've unlocked an achievement or levelled up, but there's only silence.

* * *

'Bye, hey, Big Ones, bye now,' Klipspringer says as we get into the car. He's led us across the boneyard and through the forest without a single faerie attacking. I wave to him as he disappears among the trees, jumping from rock to rock and humming softly to himself.

I look at Ronin. We're both bloody and bruised. Ronin's face seems to be regaining some movement, but he still looks like he's recovering from a stroke. On the plus side, the Obayifo poison seems to have relieved his alcohol cravings. Despite the cuts and bruises on every inch of flesh, he actually looks slightly better.

We drive in silence. I expect to be happy to get home, but when I see Table Mountain I feel more anxious and irritated than ever. Something hangs over Cape Town like an invisible smog, dark and noxious. There's an irritability in the air, like before a storm, and I feel like I want to scratch at my forehead.

'I feel it,' Ronin says through the side of his mouth.

'What is it?' I ask.

'Nothing good,' he replies.

Back at his apartment, we're silent as we treat our wounds. I'm pissed off. I have the feeling that getting shot up with faerie poison was eminently avoidable if we had just thought about it before running head first into Scorpion Gully. A dark feeling of loathing runs over me like oil and I glare at Ronin.

'You got something to say?' he asks, returning the glare with interest.

'I'm your partner, Ronin,' I say. 'I'm no longer that kid who hired you to find his girlfriend.'

'Apprentice.'

'What?'

'You're not my partner, you're my apprentice.'

'Seriously?' I say. 'You've got deep-seated psychological issues. You knew that waltzing into Squirrelskull like that was an invitation to get us fucked up, and you did it anyway. It's like you're trying to punish yourself for something and you're dragging me into it with you.'

Ronin turns on me. 'So I'm the one with deep-seated psychological issues? You're fucking half Crow.'

'Oh, now you're a xenophobe too?'

'Have you not been listening to me? I've always been a xenophobe when it comes to the Hidden. And unless it has escaped your attention, a Crow shaman was leading the attack on Hexpoort.'

'You think I'm somehow in cahoots with that thing?'

Ronin pulls out a first-aid kit from under his kitchen sink and throws me some antiseptic and bandages. I grab them and start dabbing at my wounds, wincing as the antiseptic burns each tiny little cut.

'No,' he says. 'First off because I'd never use the word "cahoots", and second because I think you proved in our last little adventure trying to find your girlfriend that you're not going over to the dark side. What I don't understand is why he didn't kill you when he had the chance.'

He has a point. The Tengu was there standing over me. It could have crushed me. But it didn't.

'I don't know,' I say. 'And I don't like the fact that I'm half Crow any more than you do. So back the fuck off.'

The dark feeling rises, wrapping around me. I feel like I'm sweating hatred and malice. We stare into each other's eyes like two animals on the brink of violence. And then before I know it we've both drawn our guns and are pointing them at each other. The Blackfish is centred on my chest and Ronin's eyes bore into me. The gun in my hand feels warm and I visualise the odds of getting out of this alive. They're not good.

'Ronin,' I say softly. 'This is ridiculous. Something's not right.'

'I know,' he replies, eyes not leaving me. 'The city is … off. There's something, something violent, in the air.'

'So put down your gun,' I say.

'You first.'

We stand for a long moment with guns pointed before I sigh and show him that I've taken my finger off the trigger. I slide the handgun back into its holster. The Blackfish disappears beneath Ronin's coat. We sit at the table in the kitchen and stare at each other.

'Well, that was weird,' I say eventually. 'What the fuck happened?'

'I don't know,' he says, putting his hands to his temples and rubbing them. 'We need to speak to the Blood Kraal. Whatever's going on, they have to know what it is.'

'OK,' I say.

'Oh, and sparky?'

'Yeah?'

'Don't ever draw your gun on me again.'

HATE COUTURE

'This is a bit touristy,' I say as the boat ploughs through the waves towards Robben Island.

Ronin turns his back and walks away. I think I liked him better when he was a drunk.

I watch the island grow in front of us and look at my borrowed phone for the thousandth time today. No missed calls. No messages. Esmé and Kyle have both gone dark. I sigh and lean over the prow to look at the grey-green sea.

I deserve it. I deserve to be dumped. I deserve to be unfriended. I was so caught up in Hexpoort, like a fly in a spider's web, that I put my old life on the back burner. I resist the urge to call either of them. I've left dozens of messages on both of their phones. They don't want to speak to me.

The boat coasts around Robben Island and pulls in to a small dock. I follow Ronin down the gangplank and across to a small service building. There's a piece of graffiti on the wall and he traces it with his finger, mutters a few words in Xhosa, and then places his hand against the door. It slides open to reveal an elevator. 'Welcome to the home of freedom,' Ronin says, as he steps inside.

The elevator drops rapidly below sea level and my stomach lurches. When it stops, we step out into a bright, high-tech bunker. The entrance is a huge bubble-like room with giant windows that look out into the sea. Fish, seals and the occasional shark swim into view and then disappear. Through the window I can see that the facility stretches beneath the island like a barnacle clamped to a rock. In the distance, submarines marked with red dwarven runes are docked against airlocks.

Ronin checks us through a security gate guarded by two uniformed golems and we walk along the main thoroughfare. I see two dwarves drag a man with a black hood over his head into an area marked with the Forked Tongue sigil.

'Dwarven Legion black ops,' Ronin whispers. 'Probably brought that poor bastard in by sub from Somalia or the DRC.'

'Who is this Malachi asshole anyway?' I say. 'He waltzed into the Poort like he owned it.'

'He's the Samnite that heads up the black ops unit. You're right. He's a real asshole. One of Basson's allies, but when Basson went down, nothing could tie them together. I would have loved to have seen him rot in one of his own cells.'

'Hey, sugars. You look a little roughed up.'

We turn to see Katinka lounging in a chair flanked by two stern sangomas in suits, white beads and dark glasses. She is wearing neon-pink hotpants that highlight the darkness of her skin, and her platinum hair is tied up in a side ponytail.

'Obayifo,' Ronin says, plucking at the bandages wrapped around his arms. 'What's a girl like you doing classing up a place like this?'

'Protective detail.' She flicks her head at the sangomas. 'Naebril is on the warpath and only my head on a spike will satisfy her.'

'Hey, Tinks,' I say with a grin. 'Yeah, I saw the esteemed leader of the Flock at Hexpoort. She looked pissed.'

Katinka rolls her heavily mascaraed eyes. 'She's always pissed. But once again she comes back to her favourite topic: killing the abomination that escaped.'

'Cheer up,' Ronin says, leaning down and giving her a kiss on the cheek. 'At least you've got these two rays of sunshine to protect you and brighten up your day.'

'Ugh.' Katinka leans on her hands. 'These two are about as exciting as a dialling tone. Aren't you, boys?' The sangomas stare straight ahead. 'You better get in there,' she says, nodding to a set of sliding doors up ahead. 'The Blood Kraal are at each other's throats.'

'See ya, Tinks,' Ronin says. 'Here's hoping the safe house they put you in won't be too awful.'

Katinka blows us a kiss. 'Shampoo and conditioner in one bottle. That's the kind of savagery I have to put up with.'

We walk through the sliding doors. Inside is a dark antechamber with a glowing red omnidirectional camera on the ceiling, and a huge vault-like set of metal doors taking up an entire wall. Dwarven black ops guards move up silently to pat us down and remove our weapons. The *swwhuuuu* of a hand-held metal detector and my own breathing are the only things I can hear.

The guards indicate for us to wait on a line of low metal chairs.

'You killed that faerie that you shot?' Ronin asks and lifts a cigarette to his mouth. A dwarven guard gives a terse shake of his head and then goes back to looking intimidating. Ronin sighs and replaces the cigarette in his pocket.

'Yeah,' I say. 'I killed it.'

'Then you should name your gun. It's traditional to name a weapon after its first kill.'

'Well, maybe I'm not psycho like that,' I say. I'm still freaked out about our whole stand-off in the kitchen. What the hell was I thinking? That tense, itchy feeling of violence hasn't gone away. I feel it crawling over my body like insects.

'Yeah, maybe,' Ronin says, unconvinced. 'It's just something that agents do.' He shrugs. 'Suit yourself.'

I look at the handle of the gun sticking out from the pile of weapons on the floor in front of the guards. Name that gun! Something epic like Faeriesbane? So lame. How about something mysterious like Darkfyre? Jeez, I may as well just call it Ubernerd and get it over with.

Then I remember something from Magical Design about the Vodoun god of the crossroads. A trickster who played with the same forces of chance and uncertainty that I felt when the mother-of-pearl grip was pressed against my palm.

'Legba,' I say.

Ronin nods contemplatively and scratches his beard. 'Good name, sparky. Good name.'

'The Kraal will see you,' one of the dwarves says in a low voice.

The huge doors unfold like metallic origami. We walk through into a circular chamber. A raised stone platform like a judge's bench curves in a semicircle around one half of the room, a red pennant with a black leopard's head over crossed spears hanging above it. Sangomas sit at regular intervals around the bench: I see the Red Witch, Tone, Malachi and many others I don't know, thirteen in all, staring down at us like we're the accused at Judgement Day.

'Thanks for the warm welcome.' Ronin turns his head to look at each of the sangomas. 'Should I put my keys in the bowl?'

'Agent Ronin,' Malachi says. 'Your reputation precedes you.'

'Why you got to play like that, Mal? You remember me. The Border, '82. You may recall the blood and screaming?'

'Ronin,' Tone says, his voice filled with iron. His grey cornrows have been pulled back and stuck through with two porcupine quills, and his suit has been replaced by an orange dashiki fringed with gold. 'You will accord this kraal the respect it is due.'

'Of course.' Ronin dips his head comically.

'What did you find out, Ronin?' The Witch sounds tired, as if she's been fighting a series of losing battles.

'Squirrelskull are working for him,' Ronin says. 'And they're not just ideological supporters. They're producing some kind of narcotic, possibly to fund this rebellion he's planning.'

'What narcotic?' Malachi asks.

Ronin reaches into his pocket and pulls out one of the small pink pills.

'You snagged one of them?' I whisper. 'How?'

'Strategy, sparky,' he says. 'But what the hell do I know about that, right?' He looks at the sangomas. 'We need to test what's in this pill. We need to—'

'What does it matter what drugs the Obayifo are peddling?' Malachi interrupts. 'They are rebelling. They will be stopped.'

'It matters because it's a fundamental break with their previous behaviour,' Ronin says. 'That adds them to the goblins and Crows who have given up their former ways to link with this madman.'

'Goblins are mercenaries. They'll fight for whoever pays them.'

'Sounds familiar,' Ronin says.

Malachi stands up and slams a fist like a hammer on to the stone bench.

'Your insubordination will not be tolerated, agent.'

'Perhaps we had best return to the matter at hand,' the Witch says. 'We will have the pill tested, but it is the least of our worries. There has been a dramatic rise in violence across the Western Cape.'

'We've felt something,' Ronin says. 'Any ideas what it is?'

'We believe it's an egregore,' Tone replies.

That shuts Ronin up. He grits his teeth.

'What's an egregore?' I pipe up, my voice sounding reedy in the big chamber.

'Every city has a common headspace, a sum total of all the

thoughts, feelings and emotions of a group of people. This commonality has an effect on every individual member; think of it like psychic weather. It can be influenced by things like physical weather, group activities like big sporting events or concerts. Even architecture can have an impact,' the Witch says.

'OK,' I say. 'So if it's always there, what's the problem?'

'An egregore is a conscious influencing of this group mind through magical means, and it can have disastrous results. Stock-market crashes, riots, massacres; throughout history egregores have been used to create terrible, unstoppable chain reactions in groups of people,' the Witch says.

'So what do we do?' I say.

'Creating an egregore is magically very taxing. In order to control it, he'll need some item to focus it on. We need to destroy that item.'

'What is the item?'

'It could be anything,' Tone replies. 'A weapon, a piece of clothing or jewellery ...'

'The Tengu was carrying a staff,' I say.

'The Tengu,' Malachi says. 'This boy, hardly even an apprentice, claims that the Muti Man is the Tengu who led the attack on Hexpoort.'

'Why would he lie?' Ronin asks.

Malachi smiles, a nasty, smug little smile. 'He's part Crow himself. Crows lie. Questioning him would be the proper course of action.'

'You mean torturing?' Ronin says. 'Not while he's my apprentice, Samnite.'

They stare at each other like gunfighters ready to draw.

'Put your dicks away,' the Witch says with a disgusted shake of her head. 'We're at war and I refuse to let MK6 splinter at the first sign of opposition. The other Obayifo families have indicated that they are willing to help us track Slugmother Dogran Meptu. If we can monitor her meetings, we can find the Muti Man.'

Malachi looks at the two of us like we're worms squirming underneath his raised boot.

'When this is over, you will both be held to account.'

Ronin winks and gives him double-finger guns. 'We'll be there or be square.'

There's a thick, noxious-smelling yellow mist hanging over the docks. Korean sailors are lounging on the deck of a blue trawler, smoking and flicking between pornos and soccer on a small portable TV. A mangy dog sniffs at my shoe and I shake my leg to get rid of it. It growls menacingly and I put my hand on Legba's handle. Go ahead, dog, make my day. It bares its teeth at me and then slinks away.

We meet a group of immaculately dressed men and women at the end of a pier. They emerge from the mist like phantoms and stand looking warily at us. The MK6 contingent consists of Tone, Ronin, me, and two female sangomas in severe black suits and white beads.

Tone leans on his cane and surveys the group in front of us.

'Drop them,' he says like he expects to be obeyed.

The group dissolves to reveal two Slugmothers and several Skinsects.

'Well, agent,' says one of the Slugmothers, a huge specimen even bigger than Meptu. Her fat toothless mouth is working like a baby chewing puréed vegetables. 'What can you tell us about our errant sibling?' Her eyes are grey and speckled and she sways back and forth as she speaks.

'Slugmother Tangris, we have proof that Slugmother Meptu

is producing pharmaceuticals in order to finance a Hidden rebellion with the Muti Man at its head.'

'Well, I speak for the rest of the cartels when I say we have no interest in rebellion,' Tangris replies. 'Who can judge where the axe will fall next, and they are bad for business. This Muti Man must be stopped and Meptu must be brought back into the fold.' The way she says it makes me think that she doesn't mean a quiet talking-to.

'Then we are on the same page,' Tone says. 'Do you have any intelligence on the Muti Man? Or any engagements that Meptu may have?'

'We only have a name. Lefkin. It has shown up in reports from several quarters. Media, fashion, advertising. Nobody knows who he is, only that he has his hands under the skirts of several of our media competitors. He has favoured Meptu from the beginning. And we know where he will be.' Tangris flashes a disgusting smile.

'Then I'd encourage you to share that information,' Tone says.

'Have you ever been to Cape Town Fashion Week, agent?' Tangris asks. 'It really is an essential cultural experience.'

Ronin and I go back to his apartment to wait while the Blood Kraal figure out a plan. Ronin slumps down on to his couch and quickly falls into a restless sleep. He twitches and shudders, shaking his head and mumbling 'no, no, no' several times. The wolf is still hunting him.

I sit down in one of the musty armchairs and browse social media on the borrowed phone. The mundanity of it all is comforting – selfies, cat photos and petitions about animal trafficking – and I scroll through with a sense of nostalgia.

Then Esmé posts a picture from a trendy market just down the road. A picture with Troy in it. No. No, Baxter. No. Again: no.

CrowBax: You are armed. Just saying.

SienerBax: You really think killing Troy is going to solve things?

Yes, yes I do.

I slip out of the apartment and weave my way past the drug dealers and crack dens that surround Ronin's office to the part of Woodstock that has been gentrified. My new weapons are pressed comfortably against my body under my new jacket. ok, maybe I won't kill him. I'll start with a friendly kneecapping and then take it from there.

I duck into the industrial building that houses the market and walk past cheeses, breads, preserves, their varieties written up on chalkboards. This produce is moist, tender, juicy, succulent, dreamy; that one has been kneaded, rolled, massaged. I swear there's salami that has been cuddled and given acupuncture and cognitive behavioural therapy, and chocolate that has been licked by kittens who have achieved enlightenment.

Through the crowd I catch a glimpse of Esmé walking with a guy with a beard. A beard! He looks about nineteen and is wearing a lumberjack jacket, and has a skateboard under his arm.

'Fuck,' I say.

I can feel my hands twitching and my body straining towards them. My new tough and muscled body. I reach into my coat and feel the reassuring pressure of Legba's handle.

Baxter.

I turn around.

'Rafe?'

My brother is standing in his orange onesie, an island of calm among the bustle of the market.

Stop.

I curl my face into a snarl. Fuck that. I went through hell to find Esmé. Sure, it may have been my fault to begin with, but not everybody would have done that. I don't deserve to be dumped like this … I don't

Baxter, chill the hell out.

I'm shaking now. Shaking with fury. I swear I'm going to kill everyone here. Shoot and hack and bludgeon every one of these pasty motherfuckers.

Rafe is in front of me and staring at me with the knowing eye.

CALM. THE. FUCK. DOWN.

I feel the rage slip away from me. He grabs my arm and leads me away from the market. There's a fire escape on the side of the building and he pulls me on to it. We go three flights up and then sit with our legs hanging over the edge.

She doesn't owe you anything, Bax.

For the first time since we were kids, I cry in front of my brother. Hot tears splash down my face. Rafe puts an arm around my shoulder.

'How'd you even find me?' I say between sobs

I'm the best damn Dreamwalker in the world, that's how.

'I was so angry.' The words spill out of my mouth. 'I wanted to kill that guy.'

It's this thing in the air. It's driving people crazy.

'The egregore,' I say, and flex my hands to try and relieve some of the tension in my body.

It's getting stronger. Your friends aren't going to be able to destroy it. The closer you get to the source, the worse the effects will be.

'So what do we do?'

You have to find your True Will. Knowing yourself, who you really are, will protect you from it.

'More Dreamwalking? There's a lot going on at the moment. I'm not sure I can—'

You'll have death going on unless you listen to me.

I sigh. 'Fine, I'll find my True Self. But you've got to promise me something too.'

What?

'You'll get out of your head and start giving Mom and Dad a little of what they need.'

He stares at me and then nods.

We sit in silence for ages, two brothers, both of us assholes, watching people in vintage clothes overcharging for hummus.

As it turns out, I have no time for Dreamwalking. I get back to the apartment and find Ronin on the phone.

'Uh-uh,' he says into his huge brick of a cell phone. He says he prefers it to the one he lent me because it makes a better improvised weapon. 'Roger that.' He shoves the phone back into his trench-coat pocket and looks at me. 'While you were on your stroll, we got confirmation from the Blood Kraal. Operation Fashion Victim is a go. We meet at an MK safe house in the city in fifteen minutes.'

'That's a big ten-four,' I say. 'Any idea what it'll entail?'

He shrugs. 'But it sounds like they're not fucking around. They're pulling a lot of people into this.'

'How you feeling?' I ask. 'And I'm not trying to play amateur psychologist, I promise.'

He rubs at his nose and considers me for a second. 'Still got the jitters,' he concedes. 'But I guess I'm feeling a bit better. I think I've got this thing beat.'

'That's really great,' I say.

He awkwardly puts his hands in his pockets and scuffs at the floor with his boot. 'How you doing with the whole noble and pure thing?'

I shrug. 'OK, I guess. I was going to maim Esmé's new boyfriend but I was persuaded not to.'

'Yay, progress for both of us,' Ronin says.

'Yeah.'

'So shall we go take out our frustrations on some real bad guys?'

'Yeah, let's.'

We drive through town in silence. The atmosphere has intensified, a steady hum of static that brings feelings of hate and rage floating to the surface. I find my mind drifting to thoughts of casual violence; vivid daydreams of drawing my gun and unloading into pedestrians as we drive, or of grabbing the wheel out of Ronin's hands and sending the car ploughing into a group of joggers. From the white-knuckled way that Ronin grips the wheel, he's fighting off similar thoughts.

The MK6 safe house is a laundry in the CBD called Cheerful Suds. The lady behind the counter is in curlers but she has white sangoma beads around her arms. She jerks her head to a door and then returns to reading the tabloids.

The same two sangomas in suits who were guarding Katinka are loitering in the back room.

'Hey, fellas,' Ronin says. 'Nice covert look you've got going on there. What's weird about two guys in black suits and sunglasses standing around in the back of a laundry, right?'

They give us several seconds of stony-faced disapproval before opening the front of an industrial washer-dryer to reveal a doorway into a high-tech command centre.

The Witch is in front of a bank of screens pointing out locations to Tone with a small beaded stylus. Katinka is sitting on a couch cleaning a handgun, and Nom is squatting down on the floor having a whispered conversation with a Christmas beetle.

'Nom, Tinks!' I say. 'What are you doing here?'

'Bax!' Nom gets up and trots across to me with the beetle on his finger. 'The Witch found out about my fashion blog. Turns out it's a good cover for this operation.' He nods to the beetle. 'This is X'ssrtthh. He has some pretty interesting ideas about geopolitics.'

'Uh, hey,' I say, nodding self-consciously to the beetle.

Katinka looks up from the disassembled Glock in her hand and gives me a smile. 'Thankfully I managed to convince them that I'm much more useful as an undercover agent than sitting in a safe house waiting for Naebril to find me. Those two dimwits were really starting to get on my nerves.'

The Witch turns in her chair to face us. 'Welcome to Operation Fashion Victim.'

'You giving us anything more than the catchy name?' Ronin sits down on the couch next to Katinka.

'The Dwarven Legion has assembled an assault team at a nearby location,' the Witch says. 'Our role is intelligence gathering: to find Meptu and the Muti Man and determine the nature and location of the object they're using to focus the egregore.'

'And how do we do that?' Ronin asks.

'Passes for Cape Town Fashion Week.' Tone holds up a handful of ID cards attached to red lanyards. 'Baxter and Ronin will be undercover as reporters. Katinka and Nom will go in as fashion bloggers. The Witch and I will coordinate from a mobile unit nearby.'

'Uh, small problem.' Ronin puts his hand up like a schoolkid asking a question. 'Meptu knows Baxter and me; it'll spook her if she sees us.'

'Spooking her is the point,' the Witch says. 'It'll force her to warn the Muti Man. We find him, we find the object, we destroy the egregore.'

'How do we know he's even here?' Katinka asks through a mouthful of gum. She snaps the pieces of the Glock together easily, and pulls back the slide with a menacing click.

'The cartels believe that Meptu has been planning for this event.' The Witch plants her palms on the desk and leans forward. 'Whatever she intends to achieve by running drugs for the Muti Man and the Bone Kraal, it culminates today. The Muti Man has to be there.' She looks around. 'Any other questions?'

Silence.

'Good. Stay focused out there. Being in the middle of an egregore is like being stuck in a psychic tornado. Remember your training and do not deviate from the plan.'

I've always wondered about the psychology of the type of man who owns a yellow Ferrari. Luxury sports car ownership takes a special sort of soul anyway, the type who isn't fazed by the sheer ridiculousness of revving his million-buck piece of racetrack engineering when stuck behind a Korean hatchback with a stick-figure family on the back window.

There are more yellow Ferraris parked outside the convention centre than I've ever seen before. Looking at them all makes me feel slightly nauseous.

I glance up at the sturdy concrete and glass of the building. Ronin shakes his head and sighs. 'Dwarven architects. Nobody could really accuse them of being tasteful.'

We find a parking spot in a dimly lit side alley next to a Somalian stallholder. He gives us a nod as we get out, and taps his ear twice. 'One of ours,' Ronin says.

'Nice outfit, by the way,' I say as we follow the crowd towards the entrance. He's wearing a white jacket with shoulder pads, a mauve tie, and has his hair pulled back into a tight ponytail.

'Timothy Tyson,' he says, flicking the ID card on the lanyard around his neck. 'From *Tigerbox* magazine.' He eyes my grey jacket, T-shirt and skinny jeans and gives a contemptuous sniff. 'At least I made an effort.'

TV crews and reporters are standing against the backdrop of the convention centre. They speak solemnly into their microphones, as if to communicate the extreme cultural gravity of this event. This is undermined somewhat by the truly hideous peacocking of the attendees.

The egregore is a palpable feeling in the air, and this amplifies the fashion world until it crackles and distorts. This is a place where malformed ideas are given birth to in a gush of fabric placenta and champagne amniotic fluid. Unhindered by the sober checking force of society, nothing is too impractical, too ridiculous or too mind-numbingly disgusting to be wrapped around a body and called fashion.

I see Nom and a small Asian guy in a lavender tuxedo, Katinka disguised using her abilities for illusion, entering the building.

'You have fun, Tinks,' Ronin whispers into the microphone at his cuff. The Obayifo and the Flock both have the ability to disguise themselves with illusion. King told me illusion is a common evolutionary trait among the Hidden. It helps them to avoid being killed by humans.

The Asian guy turns and gives us a salacious wink, then pretends to rub his chin as he speaks into his cuff. 'I always have fun under the covers, Jackie-boy.'

'What now?' I say.

'We find Meptu,' Ronin says. 'She'll be in disguise, so you're going to need to turn your mind-camera to maximum resolution. We find her and then send in Tinks and Nom to track her.'

We enter the brightly lit foyer and Ronin gives our undercover names to an efficient-looking lady with a clipboard.

'Your media passes,' she says, clipping another card to our lanyards. 'These will get you in everywhere except the VIP rooms.'

'Perfect, thanks,' I say.

'Your first interview is over here.' She takes my arm with a smile.

'Wha—'

'Designer Frenk Heidens,' she interrupts, ushering me expertly into the media enclosure. 'Let's not keep him waiting.'

I give Ronin a desperate look, but he just shrugs. The efficient lady deposits me in a bucket chair in front of a bored-looking man with grey hair and sharp eyebrows that make him look like an owl. He glances at his nails and then across at me.

'Who are you?' he asks with a German accent.

I glance down casually at my ID lanyard. 'Ermm, Daniel King. From *Fashion Fiend*.'

'Well, Daniel King,' he says. 'Are you going to ask me anything? Or shall we just stare at each other?'

'Yes, um, of course.'

My mind kicks into rerunning every bit of fashion TV I've ever watched, desperately searching for something to say. The problem is, every bit of fashion TV I've ever watched has been models walking down runways and people in Milan fanning themselves and looking bored.

'Clothes are important because they stop us from being naked,' I blurt out. Yeah, really good start, Baxter. 'How ... does that fit into your, um, work?'

He looks at me for a long moment, his owlish eyebrows raised. Well, that's that, then. I'm going to blow my first real MK6 assignment in the field within five minutes.

'That,' he says, 'is the most ... BRILLIANT question I have heard all day.' He claps his hands together in delight. 'Clothes protect our primal vulnerability. The inner core of tenderness is primary to my work and is obvious in the way I use pastel colours.'

'Obvious,' I say with a nod.

'It really goes back to when I was five years old and had an oddly intimate and spiritual experience with a cravat ...'

Twenty minutes later, I emerge from the media centre with my mind barely intact. Frenk's history and philosophy are so convoluted and nonsensical that I feel like I've been through a wormhole. I find Ronin at the buffet table.

'Well, thanks for that,' I say.

'Important for our cover,' he mumbles through a mouthful of mini quiche.

'What have you been doing?'

'Chatting to Sandile on the phone,' he says. 'Turns out your Draken visited at the African Regent last night.'

'Crazy bastard,' I say. 'He must be trying to follow me.'

'Can't worry about that now. He'll be fine. Nobody is going to fuck with a Draken.'

'Any sign of Meptu yet?'

He shakes his head.

'Frenk mentioned that there's a show on now. Meptu might be in there.'

Ronin grabs a handful of sushi from the buffet. 'Then let's go view some fashion, sparky.'

We stroll into the area that houses the main runway. I attempt to look like I belong by adopting an expression of smug superiority. We squeeze into a couple of the seats at the back and start scanning the crowd.

'I won't be able to tell what Meptu looks like,' Ronin whispers.

'Could be male, female, old, young. You're going to have to take point on this one.'

I make a sweep of the people closest to us; there are plenty of ill-advised hat choices, but no Obayifo beneath them. I look up as a house beat begins to pound from the speakers. A model appears and deadpans it down the runway. My stomach lurches as her lithe Eastern European body seems to shimmer, and I catch sight of the outline of the swaying insectile abomination beneath. Skinsect.

More models appear, all Skinsects. I tell Ronin.

'Not unusual,' he tells me. 'All the cartels use them.'

'Meptu has got to be here,' I say.

'How about you find her then? She must be in one of the front rows. Don't waste your time on the cheap seats.'

'Yes, boss,' I say acidly.

I continue to scrutinise the crowd as a monotone voice-over describes the clothes. This collection is called 'Theoretical Inversions' and has models in black sheets with upside-down lampshades on their heads. My scan of the front row yields no Meptu. It's only when the speakers announce the next collection, 'The Sorrow of the Existential Mist' – models in white sheets with bubble wrap covering their faces – that I see her.

Her disguise is a trendy older gentleman, immaculate grey hair gelled and parted on the left, thick hipster glasses and wearing a slim-fit grey suit. But beneath it I see the fat slug body of the Obayifo.

'Got her … him … it,' I whisper to Ronin. 'Front row. Older guy, grey hair, glasses.'

Ronin relays the description into his cuff.

'I've managed to access the attendance records and cross-reference them,' the Witch says into our earpieces a few minutes later. 'There are quite a few possible hits with that description.

Anything distinguishing about him?'

I strain my eyes and see a simple triangle tattoo on the back of his hand. I describe it.

'Constantine Dubreq, a fashion buyer,' the Witch says triumphantly. 'Good job. It'll be easier to track her now we know who she's disguised as. Keep an eye on her. Katinka and Nom will take over from you shortly.'

Which is easier said. The show ends, everyone stands up, and it becomes incredibly difficult to follow Meptu through the crowd. 'You go out the way we came,' Ronin says. 'I'll circle round and take another exit. Radio in if you find her.'

I slip out of the exit and catch a glimpse of the Obayifo disappearing into a cocktail bar on the other side of the auditorium. I weave my way through the crowd. And run straight into the back of Kyle.

'Kyle?' I say. 'Dude, what the hell are you doing here?' He's wearing a huge tweed jacket that engulfs his thin frame.

'Oh, so now I'm not allowed to enjoy fashion either? No magic, no fashion. Please, do make a list of things that I should avoid,' he says bitterly.

'C'mon, man,' I say. 'That's not what I meant at all.'

'Whatever. If you must know, I'm on a date.'

'A date?' I say, the surprise making my voice squeak. 'With a girl?'

'Yes, with a girl,' he says. 'I have a girlfriend. Which from what I've heard is more than you can say.'

Ouch. That really hurt and he can see it on my face.

'I'm sorry,' he says. 'That was a low blow.'

'Yeah,' I say. 'It was.'

There's a really long awkward silence. On the hierarchy of social awkwardness it's so far above a bungled handshake or a mistimed hug that it's almost another species.

'Anyway,' he says eventually. 'I've got to go.'

'Yeah,' I say. 'Me too.'

'Keep well, Bax,' Kyle says hoarsely.

'You too.'

I stumble after Meptu feeling like maybe I'd rather just let the Bone Kraal wipe humanity out.

'Here for the street-style blogging panel discussion?' asks the official at the entrance to the cocktail bar.

'Um, yep,' I say. 'Street-style blogging. Absolutely.'

He inspects my media pass and waves me inside.

The inside of the bar is all chrome and violet light. People with advanced degrees in looking and acting cool litter the place. A small stage with a line of microphones has been set up next to the bar and a couple of people are sitting at a table on it and sipping from bottles of water.

I find a table in the corner to hide at. Meptu is on stage, chatting casually to the people at the table.

'Found her,' I whisper into my lapel mike. 'In the cocktail bar, ground floor.'

The bar begins to fill up and Meptu taps on her microphone. 'Welcome to today's panel on street-style blogging,' she says. Her voice matches her smooth fashion designer persona perfectly, a masculine baritone with a clipped transatlantic accent. 'On stage we have Vintage Mindy, Clem9 and AngelaDevi, three of Cape Town's foremost fashion bloggers. Note that our hashtag will be #KILL for the duration of fashion week, so please follow our bloggers as they find the hottest street styles. Up first is Vintage Mindy and her take on the themes that define her generation.'

'Like, post-sincerity is the new irony,' Mindy proclaims into the microphone, her colourfully painted fingers moving incessantly as she speaks. 'Post-sincerity', I learn, is when something is worn, spoken about or displayed without any overt irony, because the irony is buried so deep that it actually looks sincere, but in no way is it to be mistaken for actual genuine sincerity, which had a revival in 2010 but is now again considered passé. 'In fact, I'm being post-sincere right now,' Mindy says with a smile.

'Any sign of the Muti Man?' Ronin says in my earpiece.

'Haven't seen him,' I murmur into my cuff.

The bloggers talk and my mind starts to drift. My eyes wander to a woman sitting in a booth across from me in conversation with a harassed-looking assistant. She's in her sixties, with grey hair that's gelled into a fifties ducktail. She's wearing a necklace made of laminated receipts and a tight white T-shirt that says GIRL BONER on it in electric blue lettering. Her assistant is a small man with huge round glasses and a waxed moustache.

'Cape Town,' she says in a posh British accent. 'What do we like in Cape Town?'

Her assistant flicks through a notepad. 'Penguins, lemon sorbet, small poor children, and one particular type of endangered grey fish. In that order.'

'Ah yes,' she says in a bored voice. 'I did like that grey fish. Find out if it's still alive and how much money I'll need to donate in order to eat it.' Her assistant nods once and writes something down in his notebook.

'Now, hand me my book of muses!'

He quickly passes her a fat black file. 'Boring,' she says, flicking through the pages. She holds up a picture of a blond-haired male stripper with, by my count, twenty-four-pack abs. 'It's like masculinity has given up on complexity and has decided rather to produce giant penises. And do you know what the ugliest thing on the planet is?'

'A giant penis,' her assistant says dutifully.

'Correct.' She sighs, thumps the file down on the table, and then turns her head. Her eyes fix on me and widen. 'That!' She points a bubble-gum-blue fingernail at me. 'I want that!' She leaps up and comes to stand in front of me. 'Such conflict on his face.' She strokes my chin tenderly. 'So flawed. It's like his soul has been chewed on by hyenas. I love it!'

'Um,' I say. 'I'm not a model.'

'Oh, everyone is constantly on display,' she says, as if she's revealing the secrets of the universe to me. 'We just don't all know it. Yes, you'll be my muse. My boy wonder. You'll ignite the passion in my loins and get the juices flowing.'

'I'm not sure I can …' I say, looking past her to where Meptu is wrapping up the panel discussion.

'Of course you can,' she says, chopping her right hand on to her left palm in a gesture of finality. 'That's done, then.'

Meptu and two of her Skinsects sweep through the crowd and out of the bar.

'Excuse me,' I say, leaping up. 'I've got to go.'

I follow Meptu at a distance, sliding in and out of the crowd and staying out of her line of vision. She strolls through into an area cordoned off by a velvet rope and manned by a huge bouncer, and gets into an elevator. I try to follow, but the bouncer stops me at the rope.

'vips only,' he says with a smirk.

Shit.

'Found Meptu,' I whisper into my cuff. 'But she's in a vip area.'

'Stay there,' Ronin says into my earpiece. 'I'm on my way.'

'Darling.' The grey-haired woman from the bar takes me by the arm and brushes past the bouncer. 'Let's get wasted.'

Her assistant scuttles after us and the three of us get into the elevator. The woman presses the button for the top floor.

'Thanks for getting me in,' I say. 'Um, who are you?'

'I'm Mermi Brock,' she says, extending her hand. 'Head designer for Imbramani.'

I shake it. It's cool and soft.

The elevator reaches the roof and we step out into an opulent rooftop party complete with ice sculptures, an infinity edge pool, fire dancers, and a white Bedouin tent stacked with cushions, hookah pipes and buckets of champagne on ice.

Mermi breezes into the party and immediately a pack of photographers surround her.

'This is my new muse,' she declares, and puts her arm through mine. A thousand camera flashes explode in my face. 'He is the artistic inspiration for my new collection,' she continues.

A guy in a lime-green corduroy suit pushes a dictaphone into my face. 'David X, from the street-style blog Fashionistaologist,' he says. 'Your personal style is clearly influenced by teenage ennui, but who or what would *you* say your biggest inspirations are?'

I don't easily get flustered, but the lights are flashing in my eyes and making my head throb.

'Um,' I mumble.

Mermi leans in close and I can feel her breath on my neck. 'Darling, it's easy. Just make something up.'

'Padlocks,' I blurt. There's a murmur of appreciation from the crowd. My mind is whirling and I just begin to free-associate. 'DVD piracy,' I continue. 'Poppy-seed muffins, the US gun control debate, that small piece of fingernail that always hurts to pull off, objectophiles, pigeon feathers and dial-up modems.'

The crowd breaks out in spontaneous applause and the crush forward is immense. Bloggers strain to hold their iPhones right in my face. Mermi drapes an arm around my shoulder and kisses me on the cheek. 'You've just started a new trend,' she whispers.

She leads me over to the Bedouin tent and pushes a glass of champagne into my hand. Out of the corner of my eye I see Meptu talking to a group of people. She takes a phone call, nods, and then heads towards an emergency exit.

'Just need the bathroom,' I say to Mermi, downing my glass of champagne.

She winks. 'Let me come with you to see if there's anything I can help you with.'

'No. It's OK,' I say, breaking into a run for the exit.

I push open the doors and look directly into the face of a goblin before he hits me in the solar plexus and drags a bag over my head.

TRUE WILL HUNTING

I'm hanging from chains that have been attached to ceiling bars in an upmarket private gym. Through the windows I can see the convention centre, leading me to believe that I'm being held in the centre's hotel complex. My headpiece, microphone and weapons are hanging from a bicep curl machine in the corner.

I am suddenly filled with the most terrible feeling of anxiety, and oddly enough it's not because I've been captured by goblins. I'm thinking about Kyle and Esmé.

'What's up, boy wonder? Why the long face?'

I look up to see that Mermi has been chained to a shoulder press machine. The look on her face seems to say that she meant to be kidnapped and beaten by goblins but will only tolerate it as long as she finds it amusing.

'I'm chained and bloody,' I blurt out.

'Darling, it's not a party until SOMEONE is chained and bloody,' she says. 'But that sadness is not just about getting beaten up, am I right?'

So I tell her about it. I tell her about Kyle and Esmé and how I can't hang on to my friends or my girlfriend. 'I'm trying to be a better person,' I say.

'Oh darling. Vanity is my favourite of all the vices. You're trying to be good, which is admirable, but you've become so invested in this image of yourself as a good person that you're ignoring common sense. That's just vain. Fashion is about liberation. Fashion is not about trying to be who you are, darling; it's about trying to be who you're not. Is there anything more liberating than that?'

'I've really fucked this all up, haven't I?'

'Quite, darling, quite. But how about we get out of this little predicament and then we can have our nails done and chat about it?'

She gives me a sly look, then vaults up on to her chains like a gymnast and uses her feet to manipulate the manacles until they pop free of her hands. She drops lithely down on to the ground and raises her arms like she's waiting for her final scores.

'Bravo,' I croak, and she gives a smile.

'You're not a fashion designer are you?' I say as she helps me out of my chains.

'Of course I am.' She pats my cheek. 'I just happen to have another job as well.'

I grab my earpiece and mike and call Ronin.

'Bloody hell, sparky,' he says. 'Where are you? Shit has kicked off here.' I can hear gunfire in the background.

'I'm OK. We're somewhere in the hotel, not sure where.'

'Goblins,' Ronin says. 'The whole upstairs is swarming with them. Something big is going down here, Bax. The Witch got back the lab report on that pill I took from the Obayifo.'

'Ecstasy?' I ask.

'About as far from it as is possible.'

I hear the popping of more gunfire in the background and Ronin breathing hard as he runs.

'Turns out it's an alchemical substance that makes you more susceptible to the egregore. I think he's been dosing people here with it. Are you feeling OK? Anything weird happening in your brain?'

'No more than usual,' I say. I can feel the egregore thudding against my head. 'You?'

'Yeah, I'm OK. Think I ate too much at the buffet, though.'

'Tell him to meet us at Room 454 in the hotel,' Mermi whispers into my ear. 'That's my suite.'

I relay the message.

'Perfect,' Ronin says. 'I can get there in about ten minutes. Be careful, sparky.'

Mermi puts a hand on my shoulder. 'You mind if I borrow one of your weapons, boy wonder?'

'Uh, OK,' I say.

Mermi grabs the short sword from its sheath and slashes the air with it. 'Interesting blade,' she says. She nods to Legba. 'How are your combat skills?'

I drag the gun from its holster. 'Just shoot something until it stops moving, right?'

'Quite, darling, I'm glad they're teaching you something at Hexpoort.'

'How'd you …'

'Wait until we get to my room. I'll tell you everything I know, I promise.'

We make our way to the foyer of the hotel, where all semblance of order and respectability has been abandoned. Fashion Week has been unexpectedly cancelled in favour of a vicious bout of supernatural terrorism. Heavily armed goblins in balaclavas stalk the hotel. Terrified people huddle together in groups, some of them nursing bloody wounds, and try to figure out exactly how their glamorous night of high fashion turned into this. A thick sense of rage and terror hangs over the area like a giant swirling storm cloud.

'It's growing,' Mermi says with a grim look.

'You can feel it?'

'Of course. THAT is what this whole thing is about.'

We huddle against a wall and Mermi puts an arm around me as if she's comforting me.

'Shit,' I whisper. 'How are we going to get to your room?'

'Subterfuge and then a little stabbing,' Mermi says. 'Hold still.' She wraps her arm around my neck and puts the sword against my throat.

'Whoa,' I say. 'I'm not sure if this is the best …'

She pulls me to my feet, the blade very close to the important veins in my neck, and marches me across to a goblin at the end of the corridor.

'I've got one of them,' she says. 'The boss is going to want to see him.'

The goblin looks confused, which is a particularly ugly expression for a goblin. 'One of …?' he grunts.

'One of them.' Mermi gives an exasperated sigh. 'THEM.'

The goblin understands that he's supposed to know who THEM refers to. But although he's racking his brain, he clearly can't quite get to a suitable answer. He reaches for a two-way radio at his belt. 'Let me call the boss.'

Mermi throws up her hands. 'Give it to me. I'll speak to the boss.'

The goblin passes her the radio and Mermi flashes him a winning smile. And then jabs the short sword through his eye. He drops to his knees with a stunned gurgle and looks up at her, suddenly understanding what this was all about. Mermi nods and drives the sword further into his head with the palm of her hand. As the goblin slumps, she grabs his assault rifle, slings it over her shoulder and then retrieves the sword from the goblin's skull, kicks open the door, and drags me through it.

Glass explodes around us. The other goblins clearly didn't miss the whole stabbing-in-the-face of one of their comrades. Mermi turns as she runs and strafes the auditorium with a line of automatic gunfire. I cover my head with my hands as we hurtle towards the elevators. A goblin up ahead brings his gun to bear on me and Legba jolts in my hands as I put a bullet through his shoulder.

The goblin roars, crosses the distance between us in one giant leap, grabs me around the waist and slams me into the hotel's soft carpet. The impact knocks the wind from me and Legba skitters out of my hand.

The Boer's training kicks in like a generator sputtering to life in a blackout. I wrap my legs around the goblin's waist to stop him from getting up, and jam my fingers into his eyes. His eyeballs are all gooey, like putty, and I have to force myself not to recoil from the sheer *ewww* factor. I drive my thumbs in deep and dig around as if I'm searching for lint in a navel. Fuck, this is disgusting.

Unfortunately, even blinded the motherfucker doesn't know when to quit. I'm right underneath him so he doesn't need to see much in order to pound the living snot out of me, which he proceeds to do.

I cover up with my elbows and weather the barrage of goblin fists as best I can before twisting him around so that we're both on our sides. I scramble away from him and stand up, which kinda foils his whole killing-me schtick, because now he has absolutely no idea where I am. He staggers to his feet. I snap the baton out of the harness around my chest, flick it open with a click and sweep the legs out from under him. He lands on his knees. I spin the baton around in my hands and take a running baseball swing at his head. That does the job.

Mermi is busy firing up at goblins on the first floor of the conference centre. Bullets whine around us and she jerks her head to the elevator. 'Let's get inside.'

She lays down a line of cover fire and we scuttle backwards through the foyer. The concierge has been decapitated and is lying in a pool of blood on the marble floor. The foyer has more chandeliers than is practical, and I can't tell if several of the paintings have been splattered with blood or whether they're just that ugly.

Mermi hands me a gun she stripped from the corpse of a goblin and we wait for the elevator. It pings and we step inside. One. Two. It stops at three, the doors open, and we empty our clips into a couple of goblins, who look surprised as they are aerated by bullets.

We reload. Four. Mermi pokes her head around the corner and gestures for me to follow her. We lope down the hallway and reach Room 454. She slides her card through the lock and barrels inside, slamming the door shut behind us.

The hotel room is chic – lots of glass and steel. The bed is all taut white linen and there are enough paintings of abstract shapes on the walls to teach a primary school geometry class. I slump down on the bed and Mermi throws me a water from the minibar.

'So what the hell is going on?' I say, lying back and prodding at my body to see if anything is broken. 'Who are you?'

She turns to me. 'Agent Mermi of the Bone Kraal. Pleasure to meet you, Apprentice Zevcenko.'

'You're part of the Bone Kraal?' I say, sitting up.

She smiles and holds up a hand. 'Guilty.'

My hand is on the handle of my gun. Mermi looks at me and gives me an angelic smile, the assault rifle hanging in her hand. 'You think you could draw before I could, apprentice?'

I lick my lips. 'I don't know.'

She lifts her hand off her gun. 'How about we don't find

out? I believe my partner, Radnick – he's the assistant you saw downstairs – is dead. You're in no better position than I am, so how about we don't shoot each other?'

I take my hand off Legba. 'ok. But you really need to explain what's going on.'

She sits down next to me. 'I'm from the Bone Kraal. The *real* Bone Kraal, Baxter, not the idea of the Bone Kraal that Lefkin has been using to bend the Hidden to his will.'

'So the Bone Kraal really exists?' I say.

'We always have.' She reaches up and pulls away part of her left ear, and then does the same for her right. She holds the prosthetic plastic in her hands. Her real ears jut from her head, proud and pointed.

'You're Azikem?' I say.

'Indeed.'

She stands up and retrieves a dossier from a briefcase under the bed. 'Lefkin Demishka. The Muti Man,' she says, handing me photos of a young Crow. 'The youngest Tengu ever to have risen in the Crow hierarchy. In 1987 he was captured by dwarven black ops and subjected to experiments.' She hands me another set of photos. It shows the thing I saw at Hexpoort, half human, half Crow, all twisted and deformed.

'They should have killed him. He was released as part of a deal between mk6 and the Crows that culminated in their misadventures with Basson. The failure of their operation, thanks to you, left a power void that Lefkin stepped into. His methods have gradually become more and more extreme, and he's used the name of the Bone Kraal as a way of securing support among the Hidden.'

'Why?' I say. 'To what end?'

'Revenge. He intends to punish dwarves and humans for what they did to him.'

'So why aren't you helping him?' I ask. 'Doesn't the Bone Kraal want the same thing?'

'The Bone Kraal, the *real* Bone Kraal, wants the power imbalance to be redressed. But the wanton bloodshed that Lefkin is aiming for won't do that. It'll tip everything into chaos.'

'So we stop him.'

'Yes,' she says.

She cleans the blood off my short sword on the white duvet and hands it back to me. 'A nicely balanced weapon,' she says.

I hold it in my hands. 'You killed a goblin with it. First kill. That means you get to name it.'

She looks at the blade. 'Anatole. It's the name of someone who was special to me.'

'Anatole it is.' I slide the sword back into its scabbard.

An explosion rocks the hotel and the windows in the room rattle. 'Ronin,' I say into my mike. 'You OK?'

'The Flock,' he says, breathing heavily. 'They're heading to your location. Get away from the win—'

There's an explosion of glass as several winged Amazons smash through the window of the room. Their faceplates are down and they have swords and handguns held in front of them.

'Get out of here, Baxter.' Mermi swings her assault rifle up. 'You have to find Lefkin and destroy the egregore.'

'You'll be OK?' I say.

She plants a kiss on my cheek and opens fire, punching one of the Flock across the room with a barrage of bullets, and sending the others scattering.

'Darling, I'm always OK.' She pushes me to the door and ducks behind the bed as return fire rips into the modern art on the wall.

I slam open the door and run into Ronin. Five goblins are coming down the corridor towards us. He grabs my arm and pulls me towards the stairs. We duck around the corner and I fire into the rapidly approaching grey shapes. One of them tumbles and the others return fire.

'You feeling all right?' I say, searching Ronin's eyes for any inclement psychological weather. No reply. 'Ronin! You OK?'

'OH GOD.' He has his back up against the wall, and rivulets of sweat are streaming down his face. 'It's here.'

'What?' I say, looking down the flight of stairs.

'The wolf.'

'There's nothing there,' I say. 'Seriously. You said that Lefkin was dosing people with that drug. You ate from the buffet. What if he poisoned that?'

'I knew it would come to get me.' He flattens himself against the wall. 'Eventually.' He draws the Blackfish and fires down into the empty stairwell.

'Ronin?'

'GET THE FUCK AWAY FROM ME!' he screams, and is up and running down the stairwell before I can stop him.

'RONIN!' I shout. 'Jesus, you insane motherfucker. Stop for a second. There's nothing there.'

He stops abruptly, turns and pins me to the wall. The knife is out of his boot and against my cheek before I can react. His eyes are no longer their usual calm, everyday insane. The pupils are huge and his left eye is twitching uncontrollably.

'You're working with it, aren't you? You and the wolf are partners.'

'Ronin,' I say softly, painfully aware of the knife that is poised below my eye. 'Ronin, it's me. You ate poisoned food. It's made you crazy. Well, more crazy.'

He looks up as if he's heard something. 'The howling. Why won't the howling stop?' Then he vaults up and sprints down the stairwell.

I take a deep breath and get up to follow him, but goblins appear above us in the stairwell and open fire. I press myself against the wall and empty Legba's clip upwards. There's silence as I reload, and I make a break for it. Gunfire follows me as I leap down the stairs, but I reach the ground floor alive. I sprint through the foyer and skid to a halt in front of the familiar figure I see hiding underneath an antique chaise longue.

'Kyle!' I say. 'Jesus, I'm so glad to see you.'

He crawls out from his hiding place and we hug for a length of time that would be completely awkward under any other circumstances.

'What. The. Fuck?' Kyle's hands are shaking with adrenalin and his eyes are wide.

'What happened to your date?' I say. 'Is she OK?'

'Er,' he says. 'OK, fine, I didn't have a date. But that's why I was here, I was working on it, OK?'

'Your NLP speed-seduction shit is never going to work,' I say with a grin.

'IT IS! I've almost isolated the formula. Any time now.' He gives me a rueful look and then breaks into a grin. 'So what do we do now?'

'We steal a car and get the hell out of here,' I say.

We steal a yellow Ferrari. Kyle is so excited that his extensive online car-stealing research has finally paid off that he can barely contain himself. He struggles with the door for a few minutes before popping it open, then gives a triumphant fist pump and gets into the driver's seat. He fiddles for another few moments before the car starts up with a throaty roar. The wheels squeal as we lurch off towards the entrance. The goblins in balaclavas manage to squeeze off a couple of rounds before Kyle ploughs through, and a bullet punches the windscreen between us. Kyle does a handbrake turn out into the road and pounds on the steering wheel with glee.

'Witch,' I say into my mike. 'Ronin has gone AWOL. Do you copy? Katinka, Nom. Anybody. Do you copy?'

Nothing but static.

Kyle's phone buzzes and he steers with one hand and holds it with the other.

'Oh shit,' he says, spinning the car around a corner. 'Look at this.'

'Oh shit,' I say. The hashtag for Fashion Week has changed thanks to a Vintage Mindy blog post. *#KILL is lame*, it states under a picture of me taken from Facebook. *The new hashtag is #KILLBAXTER. Put it on your blogs, your Twitterz, your Books of Face. If you see Baxter Zevcenko ... well ... give him a special Vintage Mindy high-five. To the face. With a chainsaw. LOL! Just kidding. No I'm not. Srsly. Kill Baxter Zevcenko.*

'Bloggers want to kill you?' Kyle says. 'That seems a little harsh, even for the Internet.'

I explain the situation to him.

'Damn,' he says. 'How many other people has this psycho dosed with the drug?'

'I don't know. I don't even know how we'll be able to tell who has been dosed and who hasn't.'

Kyle slams on the brakes. A group of kids – tweens and early teens – have blocked the road up ahead.

'Oh, I think we'll be able to tell,' Kyle says as he puts the car in reverse. 'Shit,' he adds, and I look over my shoulder. More of the little bastards have blocked the road behind us.

'Should I drive through them?' he says.

'What? No, fuck, Kyle, they're like eleven-year-olds.'

Kyle shrugs. 'Well, OK then, Mr Conscience, what do we do?'

'We get out and talk to them. They're kids. Even if their juice bottles have been dosed, we should be able to convince them that they're being conned. They're not really going to try to kill me.'

I get out, holding my hands up, a smile plastered across my face. The line of pre-teens move forward like troops on the front line. I notice that most of them are holding placards with pictures of pubescent males with coiffed hair: Heart System, the latest teen boy-band sensation.

BAXTER MADE HEART SYSTEM CRY, one of the placards reads; another one says: BAXTER WANTS TO HURT HEART SYSTEM.

'Hi,' I shout, making my voice as friendly as possible. 'Um, that's not true, you know? I didn't make anyone cry.'

The posse of girls, all in Heart System T-shirts, their faces painted with glitter hearts, move forward. I have seen and fought some seriously diabolical creatures. Never before have I felt such terror as looking into their dewy, evil eyes.

'THERE HE IS!' screams their leader, a freckly red-headed girl. 'KILL BAXTER.'

I turn and run, drawing Legba. Kyle sees me sprinting and turns to run too. The look in their eyes has ignited a primordial fear in my brain stem of being prey. So I run like I've never run before.

We take an alleyway between two buildings and sprint to the end. The hysterical screeching behind us has reached a terrifying peak and we don't even stop to catch our breath. I grab Kyle by the shirt and pull him towards a bunch of large recycling bins. We clamber inside one of them and I put a finger to my lips. Kyle nods.

The pitter-patter of tiny ballet pumps grows in volume and then dissipates as the posse disappears into the night.

'We're going to have to regroup with MK6,' I say.

'And try not to get killed by boy-band groupies,' Kyle replies.

'Exactly.'

We peek out of the recycling bin. The streets are empty except for a group of cyclists taking a night ride.

'Well, that was close,' I say.

'Um, Bax?'

'Fuck, I never, ever thought I'd be hunted down by a bunch of boy-band groupies. Can you think of anything more ri-goddamn-diculous than being assassinated by tweens?'

'Yeah,' Kyle says softly. 'I can. Cyclists.'

I look up and see that we have been encircled, hemmed in, laid siege to by the group of Lycra-clad cyclists. Along with their dorky helmets and water bottles, they have kitchen knives and garden implements.

'We saw you driving earlier,' a guy in lime-green Lycra says as he adjusts his tight shorts around his crotch area. 'You definitely weren't Thinking Bike.'

There's an angry murmur of agreement from the group.

'Is it really so difficult?' green Lycra says. 'You drivers are all the same.' He shakes his head. 'Some people just never learn. We're going to have to teach you.'

He pushes off from the pavement and pedals towards me. I lift my arms just in time to fend off a vicious blow from his bicycle pump. It glances off my forearm and a white-hot bolt of pain shoots up my arm.

'Arrgh!' I scream. 'Fucking hell!'

Kyle grabs me by the collar and pulls me out of the way as another cyclist whooshes past and narrowly misses braining me with her helmet.

'Time to get out of here,' I say, and Kyle nods enthusiastically. I draw Anatole and hand it to him. 'Here.'

'You're letting me use your sword?'

'Of course,' I say. 'You're my friend. You always will be.'

'Hell, yeah.' He swings it wildly. 'Let's Braveheart us some cyclists!'

'Don't celebrate yet,' I gasp, as we hop over a small wall and on to a large cobbled plaza filled with benches.

I can hear the whizzing of bicycle wheels in unison behind us. Overall, things are not looking positive. The cyclists are like pack animals hunting us as a finely tuned unit. Like sharks they flow through the night and neatly cut off our avenues of escape. They're in formation, a lethal peloton of knives, machetes, spades and hammers. We run again, but this time they have the advantage of speed. As they whizz past us, a cruelly serrated cheese knife cuts a gash across my face.

I aim a punch at a cyclist in purple Lycra, but he dips his head and my hand bounces off his massive helmet. Kyle picks up half a brick and hoists it at a rider in pink and orange with a bulbous mushroom helmet. It sails through the air, bounces off the oversize protective headgear and knocks him off his bike. Kyle blocks a hammer strike with Anatole and then jams the sword through the spikes of a bike. The rider is catapulted forward and lands on the tar with a wet thud.

'Climb!' I scream.

We scramble up a fire escape and look back to see that the cyclists aren't following. When we get to the third floor, Kyle unzips and pisses down on them. I grab his arm. 'We need to go.'

We break a window and make our way through a deserted office block. 'Let's try the back entrance,' I say.

We get out through a fire exit and run for as long as we can before stopping and taking some deep, gulping breaths. No cyclists have followed us.

'Nom, Katinka?' I say into my mike. Still nothing. 'We're going to have to find the Muti Man's lair ourselves.'

'Well, your …' Kyle waves his hands around his head, 'special powers or whatever should come in handy.'

'Yeah,' I say. 'We're close to the community centre. If I can get

Harold to let us in and lock the doors, I'll have enough time to do some Dreamwalking.'

'Cool,' Kyle says. 'You think you can find him?'

'If I can find my True Self, it should be a cinch.'

He shrugs. 'Good enough for me.'

We keep to the shadows. We're almost there. Almost home free. But a crunch of boots on gravel up ahead stops us, and a group steps out of the darkness: many guys in Spock outfits, a healthy chunk of people in Jedi knight robes, a few Lara Crofts, several Thundercats, a handful of Aragorns, a smattering of Wolverines, twelve or so Jokers.

'Fandom,' Kyle says. 'He's infected fandom. Bax, I can't fight my own people.'

'If we get to the community centre we can lock them out. That's all we need to do.'

Kyle breathes in. 'You won't make it to the community centre unless I draw them away.'

'Dude,' I say. 'You don't need to do that.'

'I've made up my mind. I may not have any special powers. No magic, no super sight. But I can do this. You're not going to stop me, Bax.'

I nod. 'OK. But listen to me first.'

He cocks an eyebrow.

'I'm sorry I made you feel like you didn't belong in this new world of mine. You're my best friend, you'll always be my best friend. No amount of magic, or lack of it, is going to change that. You understand that, you dumbass beanpole?'

Kyle smiles. 'You four-eyed jerkoff.' He hugs me again. 'I'm sorry for being such a dick. The death of the Spider hit me really hard and I guess I was just hurting.'

I smile. 'Yeah, I get that. Sorry I didn't see it sooner.'

'OK, let's do this.'

He emits a string of guttural yells. He's insulting them in Klingon. My Klingon has only ever been functional, but I recognise some pretty choice phrases. He switches to Black Speech and Sindarin and then back to Klingon, and then sprints off into the night. The assembled mass of geeks quivers with rage. One of the Thundercats raises an arm and they storm after Kyle whooping unintelligible battle cries.

I set off at a jog in the direction of the community centre. I make it through the remaining streets and alleyways without incident, but as I bang on the door, a whoop behind me spins me around.

Cyclists and Heart System groupies have joined forces like cavalry and infantry and move towards me methodically.

'Harold!' I scream. 'HAROLD!'

He opens the door. 'Baxter! I didn't realise you were back in town. Have you come to drop in on the meeting? The Fallen would love to see you!'

'Um, Harold,' I say, glancing over my shoulder. 'I'm in trouble. A lot of trouble.'

Harold grips the zodiac sign pendant around his neck tightly, looks at the growing crowd of armed cyclists and groupies, looks at me, and nods. 'Yes,' he says. 'It appears that you are. You had better come in.'

The Fallen are sitting around on their plastic chairs doing arts and crafts. They wave to me as I enter.

'What is happening, Baxter?' Harold puts a hand on my shoulder. 'Those people outside seem very angry.'

'There's sort of a group mind that is being created by magic. It's turning people insane.'

The doors to the community centre begin to rattle and the Fallen turn to look at them.

'Well, don't we all sometimes feel like the world is insane?' Harold begins.

'Harold,' I say. 'This is not a metaphor. The world, or most of Cape Town at least, has gone crazy. I need time to … well, basically I need to Dreamwalk across my own psyche. As far as I can tell, it's the only thing that's going to save us from certain annihilation.'

All credit to Harold, he takes this in his stride. 'Right,' he says. 'New creative project for the Fallen today. Please would everyone proceed in orderly fashion to the sports cupboard and arm themselves with whatever equipment they feel most comfortable fighting a melee battle with.'

The Fallen look at each other and shrug, and Darryl leads them to the sports cupboard. Sissy grabs a hockey stick and hefts it experimentally. Darryl picks up a couple of squash racquets and spins them in his hands. The rest of the group kit themselves out with helmets, cricket bats, croquet mallets and metal poles from volleyball nets. Harold stands in front of them wearing a hockey goalie's chest protector. He has a glass bottle in one hand and an aluminium softball bat in the other.

'Right,' he says. 'We have all come here, to this group, for different reasons. I commanded listeners. I was in the society pages. But that life was not to be. I hate those people outside.' He gestures with the bottle to the door, which is in the process of being kicked off its hinges by a bunch of cyclists. 'With their slacktivism, their moral outrage, their snide comments, their little jokes, their useless symbolic war against anything and everything.' He punctuates the last point by smashing the bottle on the floor. It shatters like dreams, ambitions and careers.

'They post their remixes and their memes and their jokes on the Internet.' Harold smiles. 'But now it's our turn. You are my people,' he roars. 'The forgotten, the fallen, the kicked-to-the-kerb, the addicted, the flawed. Are you with me?'

The group of weirdos roar back and raise their sporting paraphernalia in the air as the community centre door explodes inwards and cyclists and teenage groupies stream in.

'Rally to me!' Harold screams as the two sides clash bloodily. Eyes on fire, he swings the bat with clinical precision.

I run to the back of the building and lock myself in a supply cupboard. I'd better get this done quick. I retrieve my beads from my mojo bag, take a deep breath and weave them between my fingers into a suitable arrangement. The world shimmers, and I slip into the dream state.

'Hey, daddio,' Tyrone says. 'Where have you been? We've been sitting around like a game on pause waiting for you.'

'Guys.' The members of Psychosexual Development crowd around me. 'I need to find my True Self. Now. I'm in a lot of trouble.'

'No problem, honey,' Junebug says. 'Look where we are!'

I glance up and see the huge ornate pagoda rising into the lavender clouds. It is covered with carvings of tigers and dragons, and two ugly pig statues guard the entrance.

'We're here? OK, great. Let's find my True Self. Come on.'

'Tell him about the id,' Junebug says. She puts her hands on her hips and looks at Tyrone. 'He needs to know about the id.'

I shake my head. 'I'll deal with whatever comes along when I get to it. Come on, I don't have any time.'

I stride into the entrance of the pagoda and stop. A giant boar stands in the middle of the room, spilling a pool of dark congealed saliva on the floor. It has plaque-encrusted teeth and yellow tusks, and it smells like the morning of a hangover.

'Yeah.' Tyrone is standing next to me. 'Your id. Pure, undisciplined, instinctual urge. Killing you will plunge the psyche into total freefall. The id doesn't care. It'll kill you and eat your corpse if you let it, and you can't kill it or the same thing happens.'

I turn to look at him. 'So what am I supposed to do? Another song together?'

'No, daddio. We can't help you with this one. We're part of the *same psychic system as the id. Nothing we do can stop it. All our groovy, funky psychosexual energy just won't work. It'll probably make it more angry. Don't you have some other kind of artistic skill?'*

The id stands up on its hind legs and scratches itself, then defecates on the floor. It chews its own tongue until it bleeds and spits the magenta fluid at me. 'YOU,' it growls. 'KILL YOU.'

'I don't have any creative talents,' I whisper, stepping back.

'There must be something,' Tyrone says. 'Otherwise we're all going to die.'

I sigh. I have a terrible secret. The very thought makes me burn with shame. I did interpretive dance when I was a kid. My mom took me on the advice of one of her hippie friends. I did interpretive dance and I actually enjoyed it. There. I've said it. I've tried to bury this fact deep in my psyche, but now it's come floating back to the surface.

'Become a tree and sway with the wind,' I say, swirling my arms above me. 'I'm a tiger,' I whisper, holding my hands in front of me like claws. 'Rrrr.'

The id stops and looks at me quizzically, turning its oversized head from side to side.

'Keep going,' Tyrone says softly. 'It likes it.'

I kneel on the ground. 'A sunflower opening up to the rays of a new day.'

The id begins to growl, a long, low rumble that I can feel vibrating in my chest.

'Go back to the tiger, it liked that,' Tyrone says.

I jump to my feet, put my hands out like claws and pretend to lick them.

'Rrrrr,' the id says.

'I'm a sleepy cloud.' I yawn. 'A sleepy, sleepy cloud that is drifting deeper and deeper into a cosy, warm, soft sleep ...'

The id puts its vast head down on the floor of the pagoda and snuggles against it.

'Sleepy cloud,' I say. 'The sleepiest sleepy cloud in the whole sleepy world.'

The id begins to snore, a churning earthquake of sound that makes the floor shudder.

'Good job,' Tyrone whispers. He steps carefully around the id and gestures for the rest of the band to follow. We're almost past when Chester decides to sniff at the sleeping beast.

'Chester,' I hiss. 'Chester. Get back here.'

The little bow-tied dog pauses, wrinkles his nose and then comes trotting after us. We breathe a collective sigh of relief and make our way up the stairs.

We climb right to the top of the pagoda. With each step the sense of anticipation grows. I'm excited to meet my True Self, True Will, or whatever other names it goes by. It is, after all, the fundamental core of my existence, so I'm pretty sure it's going to rank pretty high up there in celebrity meetings.

Will it be impressive, like a giant flaming ball of consciousness? Or maybe something more staid, like a wise old man with eyes that stretch into eternity? Either way it's going to be incredible. I comb my hair to one side with my fingers and blow into my hands to check my breath.

I'm so excited that when I step out on to the top floor of the pagoda and see the middle-aged guy in a beige jumper playing with a model train set, I don't even think of the obvious.

'Excuse me,' I say. 'I'm looking for my True Self.'

He looks up, bewildered. He has one green eye and one blue. 'Um, and you are …?'

'Well, I know myself as Baxter … I mean, I realise that we're all Baxter in here.' I give him the kind of we're-all-in-this-together look that you give people in queues. 'But I'm the Conscious Self. And this is Psychosexual Development.'

He frowns. 'Oh yes, right, right. Sorry. I've been working on *getting my replica perfect.' He stands back and admires the little blue train. 'She's a beaut, isn't she?'*

'Yeah, lovely,' I say. 'Listen, I don't mean to rush you or anything, but a Crow shaman has created a group mind and put a bounty on my head, and accessing my True Self so that I can break through whatever enchantments he's used is the only thing that's going to save us. So could you show me to the ultimate source of power? Then you can go back to your train.'

'Certainly,' he says, picking at lint on his jersey. 'You're looking at him.'

I smile. 'No, misunderstanding, sorry. I'm looking for my fundamental essence, the burning core of my soul, the—'

'Yes, I understand,' the man says. 'I am all of that. But you can call me Norris.'

'You're … my True Self.'

'I'm your True Self.' He nods. 'You look disappointed.'

My True Will isn't a giant flaming condor. Or a pulsating ball of sentient light. My True Will is a middle-aged man in a lumpy jersey playing with toy trains.

'Model trains,' he corrects primly.

'I … didn't say anything.'

'He still hasn't grasped the fact that we are him,' Tyrone says, with an apologetic look. 'He's your True Will,' he whispers to me. 'He knows what you're thinking.'

Of course, as soon as he says this, I reflexively think of every embarrassing thing possible.

Norris blushes a deep red and backs away from me. 'I don't think that's physically feasible,' he says with a horrified look. 'Or at all hygienic.'

'Er, sorry. I can't help it. My mind won't stop.'

'A whale?' Norris puts his hand to his mouth. 'And a … no, that's not … really …'

'Sorry, sorry,' I say, trying to think of pleasant things. Rainbows, puppies, rainbow puppies. 'So you're my True Self, True Will, whatever. So what now?'

'I am not your True Will,' Norris says with a sniff. My True Will is also kinda patronising. 'You are merely the outer manifestation of a complex inner psychodynamic.'

'That's what she said,' I say.

'I beg your pardon?' He looks disapproving.

I sigh. 'Never mind.'

Finding out that my psyche was inhabited by a funk band was one thing, but finding out that my True Self is a model-train enthusiast named Norris has got to rank up there with one of the great disappointments in my life.

I sit down on my haunches. 'So what now? What words of wisdom do you have that will unlock my magical power?'

'Um,' Norris says. 'Well. There's this …'

We stare at each other. Norris looks at me with those different-coloured eyes and I can't look away. His pupils are like peepholes into reality, and through them I can see the swirling maelstrom of matter and antimatter in his eyes. This is the part of me forged in dying stars and spat out in their cataclysmic explosions. The part of me that views each passing moment as an eternity and ten million years as the blink of an eye. Norris remembers everything: every sound I've ever heard, everything I've ever felt. He could tell me in detail about every single breath I've taken like he was a sommelier describing a fine wine.

Norris is the union of the two parts of me. He is SienerBax and CrowBax, one part belonging to the Mantis god, the other belonging to the Octopus god. He contains the war between them; he is the vessel that trembles and shakes, a fault line running through him threatening to rip him, rip me, apart.

But he withstands, and I realise why my mind chose to show my

True Self as a boring model-train enthusiast. He is a blank spot, a greyness, a nothingness that contains everything. A giant flaming eye or an ancient sage couldn't possibly hold all the contradictions and flaws of my psyche in one place. But Norris can.

The split between Siener and Crow forms a rift through my psyche, and in that rift is magic, bone-raw energy that crackles and spits. Looking directly into that rift is madness, like looking directly at the sun. The rift is a tear, a flaw, a wound that bleeds into my psyche, and the only thing keeping my mind from tearing like tissue paper is Norris. He smiles at me, and in his mind-numbing boringness I see the industrial-strength grey putty that holds me together.

Because of him, I can reach into that rift and draw out energy. It shudders through me like howling winds made of fire. I scream, and my tongue is a flame that splits in two and coils through the air.

My eyes bulge to the size of plates, and I can feel the individual veins in them thickening like tree trunks; sinewy bulging vessels that thud with blood.

My bones melt, pools of marrow lava oozing over the floor in radiant mandalas. My muscles scatter like birds, my nerves wound like wool over a giant loom. My organs take vacations, waving goodbye to me, suitcases in hand. Bye, liver. Bon voyage, kidneys.

Such is the harrowing of a magician. Odin on the world tree, Jesus on the cross. I am left with nothing but the irreducible core. There are no blocks to magic because there is nothing but what I am, and what I am is what I am is what I am is what I am is what I am. If you know what I mean. I see now what I should have seen all along. I'm neither all good nor all bad, neither all Crow nor all Siener. I'm both: a grey smudge on a giant canvas. Relentlessly pursuing goodness is as stupid as relentlessly being an asshole. Both have their uses. The striving of this year falls away and I feel a deep breath fill me. I've been trying to suppress something that's part of me. But I can't any more.

Like pieces of a yin-yang my two sides fit together, and like a key in a lock it opens my mind.

I follow Norris's eyes through a spiralling furnace of consciousness. Fire and light intertwine into a spouting volcano of awareness. I can do nothing but drink it all in.

Lefkin appears like a point on a GPS, his enchantments falling away like burning paper. He's in some kind of military facility in a set of tunnels connected to the sewers under the city. He has focused the power of the egregore through the powerful muti collected from the bodies of his enemies. The crown. It glows with a sick, dark light.

In my mind I can see the egregore rearing up, twisting and spitting like a serpent. I instinctively move away from it. With the power of my True Self I'm stronger. The blocks to my magic have fallen away. But I'm not that strong. Not yet.

I spiral back down in cascading waves of perception. I need to destroy that crown.

I open my eyes. Kyle is standing over me, swinging Anatole wildly back and forth to keep a crowd of cyclists and geeks at bay. He holds out his hand, his face strained like he's constipated. He's trying to do magic.

'Kyle!' I hiss.

He looks down at me.

'I genuinely don't mean to put you down, or undermine you in any way. Seriously.'

He frowns.

'It's just that, you know, people are good at different things. I don't think you're ever going to …'

'What?' he says. 'Finish it, Bax. You don't think I'm ever going to do magic. I'm never going to throw fireballs, or levitate, or cross dimensions. Well, you know what? Maybe you're right. Maybe I'll never do any of those things …'

'Um, Kyle,' I say.

'No, Bax, I'm talking now. Maybe I'll be stuck as some humdrum ordinary guy. But I'm never going to stop trying, I'm never going to—'

'KYLE! Look at your finger.'

A tiny flame shimmers on the end of the index finger that he's pointing at the crowd. It sputters and flickers but stays there, tiny, miserable, but proud.

'BAX!' Kyle screams. 'I DID IT! I'M MAGIC!' He does a little jig, capering up and down like a full-blown lunatic. 'I'm magic, motherfuckers!' he screams at the crowd. 'I am going to force-choke each and every one of you assholes!'

'Kyle,' I hiss again. 'Kyle!' He turns to look at me, and despite our situation, I can't help but grin at the expression of glee on his face as he capers up and down. 'You probably won't be able to do that yet,' I say.

He shrugs. 'Yeah, but soon. Soon!'

The crowd are starting to overcome their fear of Kyle's erratic sword-swinging and tiny flame and start to push forward, a bristling wall of knives, hammers and spades.

An eerie, whooping battle cry that makes the hairs on my arms stand on end sounds through the community centre, and Harold appears, splattered in blood. His salmon polo shirt has turned maroon and he has a tie wrapped around his head like a bandanna. He raises his bloody hockey stick and whoops and yowls like a wolf. The Fallen swarm around him in a pack. The cyclists, geeks and boy-band groupies turn to meet him. Even jacked up on the insane power of the egregore, they look slightly uncertain at the prospect of facing Harold and his little army.

'Well,' says Harold, thumping the hockey stick into his palm.

'Lookie what we have here. Tell me again about how you signed an online petition to have me removed from broadcasting. Tell me again about the jokes you tweeted about me.' He holds up his hand and then chops it down decisively, and the Fallen whoop and rush to battle.

'Kyle,' I say as the brutal clash of bats, knives and hammers erupts around us like a storm. 'We need to get out of here. I know where his lair is and I know what he's using to focus the egregore.'

'Lead the way,' Kyle says. 'I'll protect you.'

We slip through the carnage and out on to the street. In the dim light I see a familiar figure walking towards us, his trench coat flapping in the breeze.

'Ronin!' I shout. 'Jesus, are you OK? Things are getting pretty crazy. I can't even begin to—'

Ronin strides up to us and bludgeons Kyle across the face with the back of his fist. My skinny best friend drops to the ground like he's been poleaxed.

'RONIN!' I scream. 'Don't make me shoot you!'

He swings a punch at me and I block it with my elbow by reflex. I look into his eyes and know that it's over. This is the bad part of him, the part of him that was unleashed on the Border, the part that he's been trying to shut the door on his whole life. The egregore has kicked that door wide open. He advances on me, serial-killer eyes bulging in his head, his face curled in an ecstasy of blind hatred.

'Oh, you run,' he says, nodding his head. 'That's what I tried to do. But the wolf caught me in the end. Like I'm going to catch you.'

Around us people are destroying things, killing, ripping each other's faces. I can feel the egregore writhing through the city like a mad dark cobra, twisting, spitting out hate and violence.

'Ronin,' I scream as I dodge behind a parked Smart Car.

'This isn't you. Remember all that stuff that happened before the Border?' The tiny car seems a flimsy shield between me and him. I feel what it is to be locked in the sights of this lethal and terrifying man, and it's not a good sensation.

He slides across the bonnet of the car and neatly drops me with an elbow to the chin. I hit the pavement and cover my face as he rains down punches, each one harder than the last.

In a desperate attempt to stop getting hit, I catch him in an armlock that the Boer taught me. We struggle. It's a testament to the Boer's teaching that I'm able to hold him at all. It's not going to last. Ronin is far too strong and far too skilled. He's going to break free and bludgeon me to death.

Something glints in the corner of my eye. I stretch out my hand, grab the hip flask that Ronin kept with him as a reverse psychology tactic, fumble to open it with one hand and then roll forward and hold it to his mouth. He breaks my grip and I cringe against the pavement and wait for death.

Instead I hear a gurgling like a baby that's found the breast. As he sucks at the flask, I watch his eyes change from extremely murderous to just mildly murderous and drunk. I look out at him and I see that alcohol has become his barrier, his protector, his insulator. It has shielded him from all the millions of tiny paper cuts that life deals on a daily basis. Sober he is vulnerable. Drunk he exists on a Ronin-shaped psychic island that not even an evil group mind amplified by drugs can touch.

'Sparky?' he says as I watch him.

'Yes?'

'Get the fuck off me.'

I roll off him and help him to his feet.

'Well.' He slaps his chest roughly. 'I feel much better.'

'That's great,' I say, nursing my jaw. 'Happy for you.'

I hear a groan and see Kyle struggling to stand. I walk over and help him up. He has a massive raised bruise on the side of his face. He looks at Ronin warily and clutches Anatole with both hands.

'He's sane again,' I say.

Kyle raises a sceptical eyebrow.

'Well, you know what I mean.'

'Sorry about … you know.' Ronin gestures to Kyle's face.

'That's OK,' Kyle says. 'Because I'm MAGIC!'

I tell Ronin about Lefkin, the crown and the tunnels.

He nods and takes another sip from the hip flask. 'We need to regroup with the others. Our rendezvous point is near the docks. Let's find them, and then we can figure out how we're going to get into the sewers.'

YUCK DRAGON

The city is crawling with various groups out for blood, so we have to stick to the back streets. We keep to the shadows and duck behind cars whenever anybody comes close. We huddle next to a Chinese shop called Happy Tom Tom and wait until a group of lawyers brandishing baseball bats pass. The egregore presses up against my skull, a dull thumping knocking at my brain.

I keep a watch on Ronin in my peripheral vision. He is humming happily, occasionally taking out his hip flask and looking at it like a proud father. So far so good.

We run and duck for another couple of hundred metres and I see the huge transport cranes at the docks up ahead. 'Almost there,' I whisper to Kyle. He gives me a thumbs-up. His ability to produce that tiny flame has faltered, but that hasn't affected his confidence. He makes a show of ducking behind things like he's a superhero. I smile. At least he's happy.

We step out into the road and Ronin curses and kicks a nearby car.

'What?' I say.

He points.

It's Meptu, flanked by four Skinsects, and with the air support of about two dozen faeries. Her fat slug body inches forward, leaving a trail of that viscous black liquid.

'Come out, boys,' she shouts. 'We've got something to finish. Nobody escapes the Grim.'

'What's a Grim?' Kyle asks.

'Oh,' I say. 'You really, really don't want to know.'

'Run!' Ronin shouts and fires a few shots at the advancing faeries.

I push Kyle ahead of me and we sprint back up the road. The faeries split into two groups, one flying up in formation and cutting in front of us in a pincer movement.

'Shit.' Ronin sprints across the road and kicks in the door of Happy Tom Tom. We follow him in, and I help Ronin shove a display case full of novelty lighters in front of the door. 'Well,' he says. 'I think we're safe in here for the moment.'

A hologram picture of Jesus flies off the wall and I duck as it whizzes by. A volley of faerie arrows thud into the face of a knock-off Barbie on the shelf above us. Acupunture Barbie, get her while stocks last.

Ronin smashes open a display case and grabs a pair of wooden nunchaku. He swings them over his head in a vicious arc and I'm splashed with faerie blood as he brains one of the little bastards. I fire a few shots into the air but the faeries are too quick. I reach into the display next to me, but the only weapon I can find is an electrified fly swatter in the shape of a tennis racquet. I feel something whizz past me and I lash out, to be rewarded with a satisfying *fzzzzzzt* as a faerie is barbecued.

We don't have time to celebrate. We're pelted with a barrage of heavy plastic paperweights, and one hits me in the cheek and reopens the cuts that were just beginning to heal. Kyle rips a couple of plastic kids' shields out of their packaging and hands me one.

'I hate Obayifo,' Ronin says as he ducks down behind the shelving next to us.

'Yeah, I must admit I'm not their biggest fan myself,' I reply.

I tell Kyle to cover his eyes, and then try to muster a combat spell that the Boer taught me. I chant in Xhosa, spit on the ground, and draw a symbol in the saliva with my shoe. Usually at this point the spell would fizzle out like a defective firecracker. But meeting my True Will, beige jumper and all, was like entering the correct password into my brain.

A flash spell explodes and burns like napalm, torching four faeries and sending them flaming and screaming into a giant box of bouncy balls.

'Booyah!' Kyle shouts as we run. 'That was great, Bax.'

'First time it's actually worked,' I say.

But the faeries don't back down. They've found a catapult, and two of the little bastards work in tandem to send heavy objects flying our way. I'm hit in the back by a flying snowglobe and tumble to the ground.

I look across to where Ronin is being strangled with the straps of a fake Hello Kitty bag. Kyle has ripped open a kids' bow and arrow set and pulled off the suction heads on the arrows, replacing them with tiny cocktail forks. He pins two of the faeries attacking Ronin to the wall.

I crouch and run quickly down an aisle filled with colourful stationery. I'm about to turn the corner into the clothing aisle when Meptu slams into me, her sheer bulk sending me sprawling into a display of mugs shaped like dogs. I'm cut by pieces of falling ceramic and lie entangled in a mess of broken mugs and shelving.

Meptu approaches, her T. rex arms holding a cheap katana in front of her. 'Well,' she says. 'So ends your participation in the Grim. The odds were never in your favour.'

She raises the katana and is about to stick it into me when the back of her head explodes. Her body collapses like a deflating balloon and oozes black liquid everywhere. I drag myself from the shelving and stand up.

Ronin hefts the Blackfish on to his shoulder and gives me a smile. 'That has got to rank in my top ten all-time favourite moments.' He turns around. 'The rest of the faeries will run. Time to—'

A Skinsect pounces on him and pins him to the ground.

'Ronin!' I shout, but another one of the giant stick insects grabs me in its spindly arms and slams me against the wall. Its mouth opens and the long, spiked proboscis extends, pushing forward like a needle towards my neck. I punch frantically at its arms, but it doesn't let go.

Then Kyle is there, with Meptu's katana in one hand and Anatole in the other. He slashes at the Skinsect's leg. It drops me, hissing and shrieking, whipping around and burying its teeth in Kyle's shoulder. He lops off one of its arms and then, clumsy and off-balance but still ultimately impressive, spins and decapitates it.

He holds his bloody swords above his head and gives me a grin. I pick myself up off the ground and limp towards him. There's a series of gunshots and then a blood-splattered Ronin joins us. He looks at Kyle and the grin drops off his face.

'Did that thing bite you?'

'Er, yeah,' Kyle says and touches his shoulder gingerly. 'But did you see how I decapitated it?'

'Shut up and listen. They're poisonous. Like deadly poisonous.'

Kyle frowns. 'Now that you mention it, I'm not feeling that well.' He stumbles, and I rush over and loop my arm around his shoulders.

'You're going to start feeling weird. Their poison is a psychedelic. It may be enjoyable, but don't succumb to it. It'll still kill you. We need to get you to King. Just don't give in to it, OK?'

'Things aren't so bad, you know?' Kyle grins hazily. 'Things are good.'

'ok,' I say. 'Just listen to Ronin. Don't give in to it.'

We stumble out through the doors of Happy Tom Tom, Kyle draped in between us, and drag him through the streets, Ronin and I both with guns out and ready to shoot anything that moves. Thankfully nothing tries to stop us and we make it to the docks. The door of a blue van parked in the shadows slides open and Tone and Katinka jump out to help us. We drag Kyle into the van and lie him down on the floor.

The Witch appears with an assault rifle slung over her shoulder.

'We need King,' Ronin says, checking Kyle's pulse. 'The kid's going to die without him.'

The Witch shakes her head. 'He's not part of this operation. Malachi has ordered a full investigation into him. My hands are tied.'

'For fuck's sake.' Ronin slams his hand into the door of the van. 'I can't believe you've turned into a yes-man. You used to stand for something.'

The Witch sniffs and shakes her head. 'Naivety. We do what we can.'

'You're going to let the Legion dictate to you whether some kid lives or dies? What about all those kids that died at Hexpoort? Would you go against Malachi to save them?'

The Witch's dark eyes shine moistly in the dim light. 'Those were my kids,' she says hoarsely.

'He's just like them,' I say, standing in front of her. 'He's just like me. I'm one of your kids. And I promise you that if you let that beanpole in there die, I will never, ever recover. You might as well shoot me, because I'll be dead too.'

She stares at me for a long moment and then nods. 'I'll call King.'

We sit and wait. I wedge myself in next to Kyle and hold his hand.

'Bax,' he says woozily. 'This shit is amazing. The fractals. Incredible.'

'Nice.' I put my hand on his forehead. 'Just stay with us. Don't give in to it.'

'I'm magic,' he says, and tries to waggle his fingers, but he struggles to lift his hand.

'Yeah. You are. I can't believe I ever doubted that.'

'What I said about Esmé,' he says, and looks up wide-eyed like he's staring at angels. 'I'm really sorry.'

'Don't worry about it. Don't worry about that now.'

'It wasn't easy for her, Bax, she told me that.'

'Thanks.'

'I need to sleep,' he says. 'This trip is way too wild.'

'No.' I slap his face. 'No, you don't.'

I hear the roar of a motorbike pulling up and turn to see King climbing off a Harley. He removes his black helmet and hurries over to us carrying an old leather medical bag.

He takes Kyle's pulse, opens his eyelids gently with his claws and shines a light into them, then nods. He produces a vial of blue liquid, forces Kyle's mouth open, and pours it in.

Kyle gurgles and thrashes, and then stiffens and lies completely still.

I rush over, but King stops me.

'Is he …?' I ask, tears prickling in my eyes.

'He's going to be OK,' King says with a smile. 'It was touch and go there for a second, but he'll pull through.'

Relief floods through me and I wrap my arms around King's furry bulk. He purrs and scratches his claws gently through my hair. 'It's OK,' he says. 'He's going to be fine.'

We leave Kyle sleeping on the floor of the van and join the group assembled outside under a low concrete overhang. Nom bounds up to me and grabs me in a hug. 'That was some crazy shit, Bax. Goblins everywhere shooting at us, then this group of tourists started attacking us. Then some of the agents went batshit insane and had to be restrained. Or killed.'

'That's terrible,' I say and catch Ronin's glance out of the corner of my eye. He pulls out his hip flask and refills it from a bottle in a brown bag.

King gives the Witch a terse nod.

'Thank you for your help,' she says. There's tension between them. I guess suspending a member of your staff at the command of the dwarven military doesn't exactly make for harmonious relations.

'Have we managed to ascertain where Lefkin is?' she asks, turning to me to get away from those large, accusing feline eyes.

'He's in the sewers,' I say.

The Witch frowns. 'Can you be more specific?'

'I'm not sure. I saw sewers, and some kind of facility beneath the city. It looked old and run-down.'

She scratches her chin. 'There are bunkers that the apartheid government built down there, long since sealed off.'

'It definitely looked military,' I say.

'It's the only lead we've got. Tone, establish contact with the dwarven assault team.'

Tone speaks a few phrases of dwarven into a two-way radio. A reply comes back and he grinds his teeth in frustration. 'The dwarven rendezvous point has been compromised,' he says. 'The Flock found them.'

Katinka swears and stubs out her cigarette in the dirt. 'I've never had much fondness for my murderous sisters, but going over to this madman is a new low.'

'A small team of dwarves escaped and will meet us at the old sewer entrance at the foreshore. There aren't enough of them to do it alone. They're going to need backup.'

The Witch gives us all a grim look. 'Welcome to the new assault team. We're going to need each one of you. King, I know I have no right to ask you to join us, but we could really do with your help.'

King crosses his hands in front of his belly. 'Well, I hardly think this is the time to hold grudges,' he says. 'I will join you.'

We pile into the blue van and head towards the foreshore. Kyle is conscious and he looks up at me with a smile. 'Hey, Bax. I had the most insane dreams.'

'I know how that feels,' I say with a smile. 'I'm glad you're OK.'

'We going to kick some ass?' he asks, sitting up groggily. 'I want to stab some more things.'

'Easy,' I say, holding him up. 'We need you here to radio back to us.'

'No way. I'm not sitting out while you have all the fun.'

If I thought it would have any effect, I would point out to him that diving into the sewers on the trail of a mutilated Crow wearing a crown of human teeth is not everyone's idea of fun.

'Listen.' I hold him by the shoulders. 'Remember when we were in the Spider and you trusted me? You trusted what I said and the decisions I made.'

'Yeah,' he says sullenly.

'Well, you have to trust me now. You have to stay here. Let us know if there's trouble topside so that we don't get trapped down in the sewers.'

'OK,' Kyle says with a sigh. 'I'll stay.'

I draw Anatole. 'You take this. You might need to protect yourself.'

We pull up in a dingy part of the foreshore next to six dwarves on four-wheeler bikes. They look like they've seen better days. All of them have wounds and one clutches his arm limply against his body.

'Fucking flying bitches,' says their leader, a squat auburn-haired dwarf wearing a black bandanna across his mouth. He looks across at Katinka. 'They took us by surprise. We killed them all eventually but we sustained heavy casualties.' He jerks his head to the five members of his team. 'This is all that's left.'

'It'll have to be enough,' the Witch says. 'If we don't stop this, the whole city is going to tear itself apart, and then God knows where it'll spread to.'

We leave Kyle at the van and follow a concrete ramp to where a large sewer leads out to sea. The dwarves manoeuvre their quad bikes down and blast away an old rusted gate.

'We'll scout ahead,' the dwarf leader says as we group together in front of the dark tunnel.

Their bikes rev and wheelspin in the shallow water and then they disappear. We follow, trudging through the watery grime, the high-powered torch that Tone carries illuminating the graffitied sewer. It smells of salt and rotting seaweed.

Headlights blind us as the dwarves return. 'We've got tracks. Goblins, a lot of them,' the lead dwarf says. 'Expect hostile engagement.'

'Always do, buddy.' Ronin slaps him on the shoulder. 'Always do.'

We move forward, the dwarves cutting through the grime in a spearhead formation. I have Legba clutched in my right hand and I look around nervously.

'How you doing, Kyle?' I whisper into my mike.

'ok,' he replies. 'Saw a group of old people attacking a security guard. It's getting crazy up here.'

'Well, down here is dirty and gross.' I step over a dead seagull.

'Good,' he says with a laugh. 'Shit. I've got to go. There's someone coming.'

'Be careful,' I whisper as the line goes dead.

I'm so lulled by the monotonous action of sloshing through the dirt and grime that when the first burst of gunfire erupts I almost drop Legba. The Witch holds up a fist and we spread out through the sewer, guns at the ready. The dwarves' assault rifles are lighting up in loud bursts but I can't see what they're shooting at. That is until what they're shooting at comes running towards us in a wild, loping group. Halzigs. Lots of them. They look grey in the torchlight but still menacing.

One of them bats aside the Witch's gun and throws her against the wall. Tone whistles and chirrups and his sonic magic slams into the back of the Witch's attacker and send him sprawling.

I bring my gun up, but it's knocked aside by another of the monsters and suddenly I'm in a fist fight with a Halzig. It's not a good place to be. He kicks and I block with my leg, a muay thai block, but the force of the blow shudders through my skeletal system like a jackhammer.

I bob and weave and slam a couple of jabs into his face, but they don't have much effect except pissing him off. A surge of confidence flows through me but is unfortunately cut short by a Halzig uppercut to the sternum that drops me to my knees. My fighting ability is reduced to cowering and covering up desperately as a volley of hard shots smash into me. I roll back, scissor his legs between mine and drag him to the floor.

I am grateful for every lesson that the Boer gave me, grateful for every shovel of dirt, every session on the heavy bag. Because it allows me to hold off the brutal attack. Not well, not gracefully, but I hold it off and stop myself from being killed. Which is enough for me.

The Halzig is sitting on top of me and trying to rain down crushing punches on my unprotected face. I wrap my legs around his waist and lock him in place, using my hands to try and control his wrists and stop him from pounding me. I punch him once in the groin, which gives me enough time to squirm out from underneath him. I catch his arm with my legs, grab the forearm with my hands and pull back. I strain, like I'm pulling the lever of a giant slot machine. The arm breaks with a satisfying crunch.

I draw the baton and snap it open. It seems to chuckle with glee in my hands. I spin it in my hands and circle the Halzig. One arm hangs uselessly at his side but he's far from defenceless. As if to prove this, he picks up a large sharp rock with his good hand and launches it at me with the force of a rocket.

It catches me full on in the chest and I catapult backwards into the wall. The wall hits even harder than a Halzig and I drop the baton. I don't see stars so much as an undulating wave of colours and shapes. At the same time I realise that the Halzig is heading towards me with unpleasant intentions.

His clawed hand grabs me around the neck and starts to choke me, and I scrabble for something to fight with. In desperation I reach into my mojo bag and pull out the spoon from Klipspringer's ancestorguy. I hold it up in front of me and use it as a focus point. The Halzig grins. I draw a symbol in the air, and the Halzig's face melts like acid has been poured on it. One of the Boer's nastier combat spells. The monster screams and I push him over and jab the spoon through his melted eye socket. He jerks and goes still.

'Nice,' says Ronin, standing next to me and breathing hard. He is cut, and there's a lump forming under his eye, but otherwise he's OK. I suddenly feel incredibly fatigued and I grab his shoulder before I topple over. 'You used a lot of energy with that spell.' Ronin props me up. 'Combined with the adrenalin of the fight, you're going to collapse. Don't use too much magic.'

'OK,' I say, breathing hard. I feel ill, like I've been running a marathon.

Ronin grins. 'That's why I prefer just to shoot them in the face.'

I fish my weapons out of the gunk of the tunnel and we regroup with the others. One of the dwarves was killed, and everyone has injuries.

'Well, that's probably the worst of it, then,' Ronin says. 'A bunch of Halzigs. Seriously, what else can he have?'

I sigh. 'You had to say that, didn't you?'

'What?'

'Well, we know what's going to happen now.'

'Oh for fuck's sake, sparky, you're being superstitious.'

'Every time you say something stupid like that, something awful happens.'

We wait for a few moments in silence, hands on weapons.

'You see?' Ronin says. 'You're being stupid and I'm going to prove it to you.

'THE WORST IS OVER!' he screams into the tunnel. 'Come on, universe. Do your worst! I challenge you – no, I dare you! Jackie Ronin dares you to throw something at us.'

He turns back to me with a grin. 'You see. Absolute bullshit. Try to think more logically. Science, not superstition, that's the way forward.'

There is a rumble, followed by a hissing slither. We all look up in horror. 'Oh,' I say. 'Well, that's just lovely, Ronin, really lovely.'

The sewer system is full of fat, congealed fat; our modern diet of greasy food clogs our sewers as badly as it clogs our arteries. Rivers of the stuff begin to pour into the tunnels ahead of us, bringing parts of the city with it. Broken glass, pieces of metal, and other things that don't dissolve when thrown down sinks and toilets, embedded in the swirling yellow, grey and beige mass.

'Oh God,' I say. 'What's happening? It's something bad, isn't it?'

'Well, to unpack your question,' King starts, 'it's not so much just blindly happening as—'

'The short version, please,' Ronin growls.

King sighs. 'Yes, bad. The egregore has reached a critical mass and he's using it to create nightmares.'

The fat continues to pour from the sewers into the tunnels. It seems to be held together by some kind of invisible force.

'Can we destroy it?' asks the Witch.

'We can goddamn try,' Ronin replies, and he sweeps the Blackfish from under his coat and fires in one smooth motion. The sound of the gunshot goes through my skull like a hammer and the intense ringing in my ears causes me to lose balance for a second.

'We're in a confined space,' I say, shaking my head to try and get rid of the sound. 'Some warning would have been great.'

Ronin grunts his indifference, his eyes on the fat. It seems entirely unperturbed at having been shot.

'We're going to have to hit it harder than that.' The Witch's voice is grim.

'We need blood to channel enough magic to gut-punch that thing,' Ronin says.

'Well, don't look at me,' I protest. 'I'm an apprentice, not a blood sacrifice.'

'Rats,' Ronin says. 'Or birds. There must be something in these sewers we can use.'

'Actually there are several tribes of rat living here,' Nom says matter-of-factly. 'A complex socio-economic system. They use bottle caps as currency to—'

'We need to catch some of them and bleed them dry,' Ronin interrupts.

Nom's nose seems to twitch like a bok-boy's. 'I will put your proposal to them,' he says.

He rests his head against the wall and emits a series of squeaks. There's a scratching sound, and dozens of rats squeeze themselves from a crack and assemble in front of us. Their spokesperson, a large grey rat with red eyes and a scar on its face, stands on its hind legs and addresses us.

'Ambassador Sadler from the Seventh Tribe of Dust and Mud welcomes you. The Seventh Tribe has heard your pleas and graciously responds,' Nom translates.

'I could just grab them,' Ronin whispers, eyeing the fat pooling in the tunnels ahead. 'Stop yapping and let me grab them.'

Nom glares at him and chitters to the rats. The leader responds.

'They say that they have felt the presence of the intruder in their realm. They have martyrs willing to sacrifice their lives for the greater good.'

The rats present themselves to us, their necks bowed. It doesn't exactly feel right, but the sangomas have no such qualms. Magic is a dirty and dangerous discipline.

Ronin grabs a handful of rats, slashes them open and drips blood on to the floor of the tunnels. He hands me a couple. 'Take them,' he says. 'You're going to need them for later.' My nose crinkles in disgust.

Ambassador Sadler chirps angrily. 'He says you dishonour their souls and deny them access to the Great Sewer if you do not use them,' Nom says.

I take the dead rats and tie them by their tails to my belt.

The Witch opens her mojo bag and pulls out a rattling string of beads. She ties it to her ankle and stomps on the ground, and the beads snap sharply like a snare drum. She sets the beat and Tone picks it up by clapping his hands, a sharp, syncopated rhythm that echoes off the tunnel's walls. Ronin nods his head, swaying from side to side like a gnarly old red tree in the breeze. They begin a droning call-and-response song, chanting in Xhosa, Zulu and Afrikaans. Their voices complement each other, not exactly harmonious, but strong and commanding.

A coiling mess of dirty yellow energy rises up from the rat

blood and rushes towards the fat. When it hits, the mass is pulled apart, and for several seconds lumps of fat hang in the air like they're suspended on a giant loom. Then it's sucked back into shape again and the energy snaps out of existence with a high-pitched metallic ringing sound.

Ronin leans on his knees panting heavily and spits on the tunnel floor. Tone does some kind of breathing exercise, and even the Witch looks unsteady on her feet.

The pooling mass of fat, on the other hand, hardly seems to have noticed. In fact it's starting to turn into a clearly defined shape: a massive head with whiskers, a sinuous body with patchy scales of glass and metal, and legs with claws made of rusty nails. A dragon made of fat. A fatdragon.

'If that spell didn't do it, then nothing else we have will stop it,' the Witch says with a grimace.

'So what do we do?'

'May I suggest running?' King says, lifting his kaftan gingerly up around his ankles.

Running. Always running. Still, it's a solid plan and I like it. We turn and sprint just as the fatdragon becomes aware of our presence and lurches towards us. A warm, mucusy blast of breath follows us as we tumble down the corridor.

I shoot a look over my shoulder. The dragon is squeezing its way through the tunnel like toothpaste from a tube. Its snout writhes from side to side and a deep, squelching roar erupts from its mouth, bringing with it a river of diapers and sanitary towels. It looks up at me with strange multifaceted eyes, dozens of globules of fat like jellyfish stuck together, and seems to give me a gormless smile.

Just for the record: there is no way I'm getting eaten by that thing. Beaten to death by goblins? Fine. Decapitated by Crows? I'll take it. But going anywhere near that clearly unhygienic maw is completely out of the question. Non-negotiable. I run faster than I have ever run before.

The dim concrete tunnels rush past us as we sprint. The fluorescent lights begin to flicker, making everything look like it's happening in slow motion. Sweat prickles on my face and starts to burn my eyes. I trip on a rusty bicycle frame and pitch head first into the gunk.

'Come on, sparky,' Ronin shouts over his shoulder.

'Thanks for the encouragement.' I wipe sewer grime from my glasses, push myself up on to my haunches and look behind me.

The fatdragon is dragging itself through the tunnel with gooey squelching and sucking noises. It smiles again, and the jagged brown glass shards of its teeth glint. I leap to my feet and run. There's heavy gunfire up ahead, but I can't turn back.

'No retreat, no surrender,' I whisper to myself, pushing my glasses firmly back on to my face.

I blunder out into a vast circular concourse where several tunnels meet. Ronin and the rest of our team have dug in behind a huge sewage tank. They're being pinned down by a platoon of goblins with automatic weapons.

I dive behind a rusted staircase that leads up towards some sort of control station, just as a line of gunfire chews into the wall behind where I was standing. Another sewer grime facial. I look across to Ronin and the others. Trying to reach them will get me ventilated by goblin bullets, but an old staircase is hardly what I'd called a primo bullet shield. Already a couple of rounds are zinging past my head, and I don't really want to wait until the goblins' aim gets more accurate.

That's when I come up with the brilliant idea of *making a break for it.* I dart out from behind the staircase, and immediately a bullet clips my scalp and spins me to the ground. I scrape my hands breaking my fall but my jaw still thuds painfully into the concrete. The searing pain from the head wound is white-hot, and I scream. A sticky wetness runs into my eyes and I try to wipe it away with my sleeve.

Another scream fills the concourse as if parodying mine. I stop screaming and look up. Through a veil of my own blood I see the fatdragon coiling above me. Pieces of goblin drip from its smirking mouth, and it stares at me with those bubbling translucent eyes.

I'm pulled to my feet and propelled forward into a run by a pair of hands.

'Hope I didn't interrupt a special moment,' Ronin says. 'But time to move.'

We duck through into one of the tunnels at random. A dead dwarf lies slumped over the handlebars of his four-wheeler, a bullet hole through his cheek.

'Gremesh nasta ek.' Ronin touches the dwarf's forehead and then pushes him off the bike and into the muck. 'Get on, sparky,' he says, clambering on to the bike.

I slide on to the seat behind him and wrap my arms around his waist.

'Please be advised that we might experience some mild turbulence,' Ronin recites in an air-hostess voice.

'Oh God,' I say.

He fires up the engine and the wheels spin, sending a barrage of muck everywhere. My arms are almost pulled from their sockets as we roar off. I can feel the maggoty moistness of the fatdragon's breath on my neck.

'Faster,' I shout to Ronin.

'What's that?' he shouts back. 'You want me to slow down?'

'Oh for fuck's sake,' I say. 'Can we not do this now?'

He slows the bike down.

'Maybe I should take it easy,' he says. 'Laws ARE there for a reason.'

'OK, you're a good driver, is that what you want to hear? You drive fantastically, you should be a driving instructor.'

He guns the engine and my arms are jolted again.

'You're such a fucking child,' I shout as we hurtle around a corner.

The dragon gains on us slowly. Ronin's trench coat flaps against me as we speed through the tunnel, a rhythmic *dapdapdap* that for a second is in perfect rhythm with the slapping of fat behind us.

'Do something,' Ronin says. 'Try to slow it down.'

I sigh, untie a dead rat from my belt and look at it. There's a horrible spell that the Boer taught us. Not pleasant at all. I really don't want to do it.

'Sparky,' Ronin calls. 'Running out of time here.'

I steel myself and then bite into the little rat body. Blood, dark, obscene and metallic, rushes into my mouth. I gag several times but manage to stop myself from either swallowing or spitting it out. I drag the bok spoon from my mojo bag and use it as a focus point, and then turn and spit the blood out behind me in a dark fountain.

The blood starts to shriek and transforms into a huge throbbing net across the mouth of the tunnel. The fatdragon slams into it and is momentarily stopped. It thrashes and whines, infuriated by the sticky obstacle that is stopping it from devouring us.

We careen up the curved side of the tunnel wall to avoid a pile of debris and then swing madly back the other way, Ronin only managing to maintain control of the bike with his superhuman drunk reflexes.

'Up ahead,' he shouts. 'There's a ramp.'

Sure enough, I can make out the outline of a ramp leading upwards to where construction work has opened a ragged hole in the tunnel ceiling. I immediately know what Ronin is thinking.

'No!' I shout. 'Ronin …'

He guns the engine and sends the bike towards the ramp

with the precision of a kamikaze pilot. I lock my hands together around his waist and brace my head against his back.

My stomach hops as we hit the ramp, does a double backflip as we ascend it, and pikes as we sail through the hole in the ceiling, hanging gracefully for a moment in my abdomen before plunging into my intestine as we hit the ground above. The wheels slide along the dirt of the construction site as if on ice, then lock and tip the bike over. I'm plucked from around Ronin's waist and flung across the empty lot in a flailing tangle of limbs before slamming into a large mound of sand.

Ooooooooof! Air. That's what I need. Lots of it. Unfortunately my lungs have been shocked into forgetting how to breathe. I suck vainly at the atmosphere around me like a goldfish out of its bowl before finally sweet, beautiful oxygen rushes into me.

I have sand in the bullet wound in my head, blood and dirt mixing together into a gruesome failed toddler art project on the side of my face. My mouth tastes of rat blood and I retch several times.

Next to the mangled corpse of the bike, Ronin is picking himself up out of the dirt and brushing off his trench coat. He limps to the edge of the hole and looks down into the tunnel.

'It can't get up,' he says, and gingerly walks over to me, clutching his leg. He slumps against the pile of sand next to me, fishes around in his coat pocket and hands me a grimy bandanna. I press it lightly to my head and wince.

'Just a scratch, sparky.' He takes a swig from his hip flask.

'Yeah,' I say. 'You OK?'

He nods, smacks his lips together and contemplates the flask.

'Can't believe drinking is actually a positive thing,' he says. 'Kinda takes some of the enjoyment out of it.'

'You're an idiot.'

'Yeah,' he agrees. 'True.'

We sit for a while and nurse our wounds.

'Back there, when I was trying to kill you …' he starts.

'Hey,' I say. 'It's OK. Thanking each other is not really our thing.'

'Who said anything about thanking you?' He takes another swig. 'You've turned me back into an alcoholic. You're an enabler.'

'I've decided I'm no longer going to try and be good,' I say. 'It's not really who I am.'

'Well, we've both failed then.'

'Yep.'

'Feels pretty good, doesn't it?'

I look at him and smile. 'It's the best thing ever.'

I grab the flask out of his hand and wash out the taste of rat blood with the bitter alcohol. Ronin stands up and holds out his hand. I grab it and he pulls me to my feet.

We locate a manhole a few blocks away and Ronin wedges the cover open. We climb down in the dim, flickering light. The tunnels are older here, crumbling and permeated by a dank and musty smell that clings to my skin. Scrawled graffiti covers the walls. Ronin runs his fingers over some of the Afrikaans words.

'From the eighties. Army kids on guard duty did this,' he says. 'I think we're near the old bunkers.'

We follow the tunnel to where it ends in a thick, rusting steel door with the Forked Tongue sigil painted on it.

'Dwarven black ops?' I say.

'Project Staal. I used to hear about this place when I was on the Border,' Ronin replies. 'This is where Basson and the Legion did their dirty work.'

I push the door. It creaks as it opens and we step into a lab filled with old vats, jars and hastily destroyed equipment. The floor is a mess of shredded documents and burnt files.

'They wanted to get rid of all this stuff when the government changed,' Ronin says.

We look around. A mouldy old South African flag adorns the wall, along with gold-framed photos of stern-looking uniformed men with moustaches.

'C12,' he says, picking up a half-burnt document and pointing to the letterhead. 'What MK6 used to be called.'

'MK6 used to be called something else?'

'Yeah, genius. The MK designation is from Umkhonto we Sizwe. Hardly something the old fascists would have used.'

He sits down in an old swivel chair and takes another swig from his hip flask. His eyes are hard as he kicks some of the files from the desk.

'What's the matter?' I say. 'Are you freaking out again?'

'Memories from the old days. Really bad memories. It's weird how you can start to pretend that none of this shit existed.'

'Project Staal,' I say, leaning against the desk. 'What was it?'

'I don't know much about it. Way above my pay grade. I know it was linked to Basson's weapons project, but it was mostly run by the Dwarven Legion.'

I shift through shredded documents and find a few untouched pages. It features diagrams of the biology of bok-people, detailed notes about horrific experimentation, and a single grainy black-and-white photo of a bok-boy just like Klipspringer. He has been opened up, his torso splayed open and his organs visible, but his innocent eyes are wide with horror. He is still very much alive.

A sour, sick feeling creeps down my throat. 'They're still doing this?'

'I don't know, sparky. I've heard rumours ...' Ronin says.

I read from another page. '"The Hidden are a fundamental threat to safety and stability. Learning to exploit their vulnerabilities is essential."' I look up at him. 'This is sick. I've given up being needlessly good, but this is way beyond good or bad. This is plain evil.'

He sighs and nods. 'I know.'

'So why haven't you done anything about it?'

'Like what? Let Lefkin win?'

'No,' I reply. 'He's just using this as an excuse to kill people.'

'Listen to me,' Ronin says. 'The Legion is rich beyond comprehension. They have mercenary armies in all the major conflict zones in the world. The superpowers *depend* on them. Stopping them will take more than saying, "Like hey dude, this is like way uncool."'

'Then what will it take?'

He claps me on the shoulder. 'That's what I like about you, sparky. You're barely into being an apprentice and you're not satisfied with fighting a Crow shaman. You want to take on one of the most powerful organisations in the world at the same time.'

'Well, what can I say? I'm an overachiever.'

He nods. 'You're right. What they're doing is wrong. There are agents … not all of them, but some who want things changed.'

'OK,' I say. 'That's a start.'

'A start we can build on if we stop Lefkin.'

I nod.

'Don't look so depressed,' he says. 'We could still get killed.'

We wade through the debris in the old bunker. The lab branches off into a series of offices, apartments, and an old apartheid-era nuclear fallout shelter. I'm peering through dirty reinforced glass into a room plastered with nudie pics and posters from eighties magazines when the fatdragon pulls itself through a huge vent in the lab and grins at us with glee.

We turn and run, but the dragon wriggles after us like a viper.

'No, no, no …' I scream, feeling its toxic gassy breath on me. It's too late. We're slurped up. My jacket is caught on one of its glass-shard teeth and I thrash and kick, screaming soundlessly to try to escape the horror of it all. Nope.

I tumble after Ronin into its gullet and cringe into a little whimpering ball as its oesophageal movements push me through its wet and gooey insides. I scramble blindly for my gun but I can't move my hands through the stinking froth of its stomach. I gasp and hold my breath, not sure whether to be more afraid of being digested or of drowning.

Neither should have been my primary worry. There's a sudden retching sound and I'm sucked upwards and spat out on to a hard concrete floor. I lie shivering, soaked in sewer fat and unable to see anything around me.

'Ronin!' I scream. 'Ronin, I can't see.'

Something grabs my head and wipes at my glasses, revealing Ronin standing over me shaking fat from his hands.

'Well, we found the place,' he says, flicking his wet hair out of his face.

We're standing in a blue-carpeted corporate office. There's a fax machine, a water cooler, and a giant whiteboard filled with motivational messages. FOLLOW YOUR PASSION AND YOU'LL NEVER WORK A DAY IN YOUR LIFE, I read before I'm dragged across the floor by strong hands. I manage to headbutt one of my assailants, but three more overpower me, force me into a chokehold and manhandle me into a glass-fronted boardroom. I'm knocked to the floor with a swift kick to my patella. Next to me, Ronin is being forced to kneel by a sizeable group of goblins. Hands reach into my jacket to relieve me of my weapons, and my mojo bag is pulled from my belt. They even take the dead rats. Ronin swears as an assault rifle is jammed against his temple and the Blackfish is torn from his hands.

A figure in a blue pinstriped suit, a starched white shirt and a thin black tie sits in a leather chair at the head of the board table, his hands behind his head. He is wearing a huge crown of teeth.

'Welcome to the office,' Lefkin says. 'Can I get you anything? Tea, coffee?'

'How about a shower and all the disinfectant you have?' I'm still trying to scrub the fat from my face.

Lefkin smiles, his twisted beak and half-human face curling into a rictus of triumph. 'Hygiene should be the least of your worries.'

'What happened to your cloak and staff?' I croak. 'I like that look better.'

He waves a hand. 'That was theatrics. People expect that sort of thing from the Muti Man.'

'This from a guy with a crown made of teeth,' I say.

He laughs. 'Muti is muti.' He holds one of the dead rats taken from my belt. 'Sacrifice is part of magic. You are only just beginning to learn this.'

'Oh fuck off,' I say. 'Don't start with this you-and-I-are-alike bullshit.'

'You misunderstand. I don't think we're alike at all. You're human. That makes you completely foreign to me: an alien, a parasite. But it doesn't mean I don't understand you. The egregore is nothing but humanity amplified. When I was captured and brought to this place, I realised something about my tormentors, the men and women who attached me to probes and killed my Crows in front of me to test whether we feel the same way humans do. I realised that it's not some kind of moral bias that stops people from doing evil, but rather a certain social pressure. To maim, kill, dismember only requires encouraging the natural human to come out.'

He gets out of his chair and walks across to Ronin. He reaches down and grips him by the throat. 'Let me tell you this, agent. We feel just as vividly as you do. Monitoring me as a Crow child was killed in front of me convinced them of that.'

He turns to me. 'So I'll offer you a deal. Kill yourself and I'll let him go.'

'Don't give him a fucking thing,' Ronin shouts, struggling against the hand at his throat.

I force myself to look Lefkin in the eyes. 'I'm not going to kill myself.'

'Oh yes,' he says. 'I think you are.'

He weaves his fingers together in an intricate pattern and then points at me.

'What are you doing?' I croak.

'Something you would have learnt to do if you'd had a decent teacher,' he says, and crooks a finger at me in a beckoning motion.

I feel a force sucking at my psyche. An incredible pressure hits me in the temples and I collapse with a gasp. The room flickers in and out of focus for several seconds before I lose consciousness.

'What the hell?' I say, looking around the pagoda.

Psychosexual Development and my beige-jumpered True Self are staring at Lefkin in horror.

'I dragged you into your own psyche.' Lefkin shrugs. 'It's not difficult when you know how.'

'He can't be here,' Tyrone says. 'Baxter, he really can't be here. This is your mind. Unless a part of you asks him, it's fundamentally impossible for him to—'

'A part of you asked me in,' Lefkin says. 'Well, technically it was someone who was press-ganged into being a part of you. He wasn't happy. I promised to help him.'

We turn as a unit to Cabales.

'Cabales?' Tyrone says. 'You?'

Cabales straightens himself up and faces us. He speaks in perfect English. 'This is not my mind. I have been away for too long from my family. I need to go back.'

'Cabales.' *Tyrone grips his afro with both hands.* 'You can't go back. Don't you get it? You detached from your body during that ayahuasca trip. You died. We took you in because you had nowhere else to go.'

Cabales turns to Lefkin. 'Tell them what you told me. Tell them that it's a lie. You can send me back.'

Lefkin laughs and puts an arm around my True Self's shoulders. 'No. He's right. I used you. You helped me to remove all the psychic defences necessary so that I could take complete control of his psyche. Not even the stupidest of amateur magicians do that.'

Cabales wails and clutches at his face.

Lefkin grips Norris by the throat and gives me a wink. 'No need for us to hang around.' *He jerks his head and the pressure slams into my temples again.*

I roll on to my back and look up at the boardroom ceiling.

'What happened?' I say. 'What did you do to my True Will?'

'Oh, I have him.' Lefkin looms over me. 'I have him nicely locked away. I put this question to you. Why bother? Why bother with all of this? Even if by some miracle you defeat me, if you carry on along this path, you're in for a world of living in the shadows, of fighting things most people have never heard of, for no thanks, no praise. You're not a hero, Baxter. Anybody can tell that just by looking at you.'

I've been in this situation before, of course. If I'm honest, I gave up the most powerful objects in the universe for Esmé. How pathetic is that? And if giving up world domination wasn't good enough for her, well then, I doubt flowers and chocolate were going to do it.

Lefkin is right. I'm not cut out for this world. 'Kill yourself,' he says and offers me Legba. I take the handgun. My head is split, but for once all parts of me agree on a singular course of action.

CrowBax: Shoot him!
SienerBax: Shoot him!
Lefkin: No. Kill yourself.

His voice in my head is unstoppable.

I place the barrel of the handgun in my mouth. I have lost everything and there's no real point in going on. Karma is a bitch. Karma doesn't care that I wanted to change my ways. Karma doesn't believe in good intentions.

I have failed miserably at being good. I couldn't even get that right. I'm the same nasty piece of work that I've always been, except now I can't be happy with it. What has been felt cannot be unfelt. Even having saved the world doesn't make me feel good about myself. Perhaps it's something you get habituated to; each new world-saving moment has to be bigger and better than the last to give you that same dopamine and serotonin kick. Maybe heroes are just junkies.

I've killed everything in this life worth living for, so the only thing left to do is kill Baxter. They say suicide is a selfish, egotistical thing to do. It suits me perfectly. It all seems so clear now. This is going to be great. The steely taste of the gun. The explosion. The oblivion. I can't wait.

Lefkin has Ronin's face in his hands and is forcing him to watch. 'What are you feeling, agent?' he says. 'Is it fear, anger, maybe indifference? Maybe you just don't care.'

I catch a glimpse of Gigli slinking in the door. He's filthy, injured and tired, but he has a maniacal grin on his piggy pink face that makes me smile.

'You find this funny?' Lefkin asks.

'Kinda,' I say.

Gigli leaps and crashes into Lefkin, locking his jaws around his wrist and shaking him from side to side.

Ronin tackles the nearest goblin and wrests the gun from his hands. He rolls and takes out several more goblins. I'm momentarily released from the thrall Lefkin has me in, though I can still feel him in my head.

Lefkin throws Gigli from him. The Draken catapults head over tail and slides across the floor. Lefkin stands up and I swing the gun round to draw a bead on him. The forces of chance align, and I fire, putting a haphazard pattern of bullets in his back. He topples forward on to one knee, but pushes himself back up. He's tough, but he doesn't have the same immunity to injury as a normal Crow. He's hurt.

He stumbles forward and rips the crown from his head. The fatdragon coils around him and Lefkin puts the crown into its mouth. 'Don't let them have it,' he shouts. 'Never let them have it.'

The fatdragon, the crown in its mouth, turns and disappears down a tunnel. Lefkin is helped up by the remaining goblins. They fire on us, and I'm forced to cower behind a row of desks. I hear Ronin returning fire, and a scream rips through the air as someone or something goes down.

I peek around the corner with Legba in my hand and see Lefkin and a goblin disappearing down another tunnel. I sprint out from behind the desk and fire after them. Ronin appears at my shoulder and we stand at the crossroads where the tunnels meet and look down each one. 'Get the crown,' I say to Ronin. 'I'll go after Lefkin.' He hesitates for a second and then sprints after the fatty tail as it disappears into the sewers.

'Gigli!' I shout.

The Draken kills a badly injured goblin and then trots over to me with a bloody grin. I climb on to his back and clutch his neck as he hurtles after Lefkin. He smells of sewer and blood.

'You found me, you crazy old dog,' I say into his ear as he runs. 'I told you not to follow me.'

He shakes his head in disgust. Even without Nom to translate, his meaning is clear: you don't tell a Draken what to do. We turn a corner and are greeted by a hail of bullets.

I tumble from Gigli's back, fire once, and then *click click click.* I'm out of bullets.

Gigli is up and running. He hits the goblin full on in the chest and they tumble to the ground. The goblin has Gigli around the neck and is struggling to keep those jaws from his face.

Lefkin is slumped, wheezing, against the tunnel wall.

'Just give up,' I shout to him. 'You're hurt.'

He smiles and crooks a finger, and that sucking feeling grips my brain and pulls me into blackness again.

We float above a mountainous field, facing each other.

'I presume you've never commanded an army before?' Lefkin says. He waves his hand and an army appears beneath him: thousands of ninjas in formation. 'They're going to rip your psyche to shreds. All that will be left of you will be a quivering outer shell, a body with nothing inside.'

'Tyrone?' I shout into my psyche. 'Junebug?'

Nothing. I'm all alone here facing Lefkin. I feel my will fading. I can't fight this.

Lefkin sees it on my face. 'I tried to give you an easy way out,' he says, that cruel smile playing across his twisted features. 'A bullet through the brain, a clean death. Now you will suffer like I suffered. Come on, Baxter.' He points down to where Norris, my True Self, is being held captive by a bunch of ninjas. 'All you have to do to save your True Will is beat me.'

Suddenly Rafe is there next to me, floating in mid-air with his arms crossed in front of him and his red hair streaming behind him like flames.

'Who the hell are you?' Lefkin hisses.

Rafe smiles. 'Me? Oh, I'm the best Dreamwalker in the whole world.' He waves his hand and an army appears on the field to match Lefkin's: mech warriors, giant bears, troops in shining armour.

The dream armies clash with a soundtrack full of battle cries and screams. Each of those soldiers is a part of my psyche, and I can feel their dying reverberate through me. If enough of the little bastards die, I'm pretty sure I'll become a blubbering idiot in the real world.

Lefkin is aggressive and he's powerful. But he hasn't balanced his forces. Rafe draws his infantry into an ambush and decimates them with archers. Rookie mistake. Lefkin retaliates with a platoon of black-masked trolls that smash into Rafe's warriors. My psyche shakes with the impact.

Rafe's eyes are focused on the battlefield. It's the classic strategy-game dilemma. Building units requires concentration, which takes your focus away from the actual fighting.

'Go get your True Will,' he says.

I fly down awkwardly to where Norris is standing looking bewildered. He clutches his little blue train to his chest. I crash-land on the ground and foot soldiers immediately swarm me. I manage to manifest a shield just in time to block a vicious slash from a ninja with an ugly poleaxe. I stumble backwards and raise the shield above my head, blocking another slash. I'm forced to my knees by the impact of the blow.

I manifest a large handgun, slip the barrel under the shield and shoot the ninja in the crotch. I try to aim again, but I lose concentration and the gun disappears in my hand like smoke. I manifest a sword and attempt to stave off more attackers.

'Focus,' I whisper to myself. 'Focus.'

I change the sword to a battleaxe and take out several soldiers. I swing hard and methodically, mowing through them like a Spartan, battleaxe red with blood and gore. A ninja throws two shuriken, but I bat them out of the air and launch myself forward to decapitate the man.

I reach Norris. He looks at me with big eyes.

'I want to go home,' he says.

I grab his jersey and pull him up with me. We float up to the lavender clouds, where Rafe is commanding the army below with grim determination. I watch as he destroys Lefkin's ninja cavalry, wiping each unit out with scary precision. It's like witnessing a genocide.

'I have mastered every strategy game ever made,' Rafe booms across to Lefkin. 'On the hardest level. Kids in Korea ask me for gaming advice. I am Rafe378 and you are mine.'

Lefkin screams, a long, anguished howl full of pain and suffering.

I'm jolted back to reality with a sickening lurch. The room swims around me and I clamp my hand to my mouth to stop from throwing up.

Lefkin has slumped to his knees, gurgling. Those dark eyes are unfocused and seem to roll around randomly in his skull. He's nothing but a poor twisted soul who had the right intentions but the wrong methods of achieving them.

He doesn't scream or struggle as he dies. He just looks at me with empty eyes, terrible eyes. Is Lefkin a hero, a martyr, or a villain? And what are we, what am I? Who the hell knows. But I'm covered in fat, so my mind is on other things right now. Like a shower.

Ronin appears, limping, covered in grime and fat but clutching the crown of teeth in his hand.

'Lost that thing in the tunnels,' he gasps. 'But it'll be back.'

'So destroy the crown,' I say. 'Ronin, c'mon!'

'I tried.' He turns it over in his hands. 'It's just ... the power ... I can't bring myself to do it. I don't want to do it.' His eyes are slipping towards that dark psychosis again. The wolf is back and it's hungrier than ever. Up close the muti is too powerful, and it's dragging him back down.

'No problem,' I say. 'Just hang on to it for a while.' I edge closer. 'No need to destroy it just yet.'

He clutches the crown and looks up at me with bright eyes. 'Just for a while,' he says. 'Just a little while longer.'

I smile and make as if to pat his shoulder, then quickly change direction and grab the thing out of his arms. He roars with pain but I dance back out of his grasp.

The power of the crown is immense. It's like being hard-wired into the city with all its rage and hate, its petty irritations and small defeats concentrated in one place. My whole body thrums with the power of it. The pressure builds but it doesn't crush me. The thing is, I've seen my mind. I've mapped the contours. The bad part of myself, the part that the crown amplifies, is not a bogeyman in the closet that I'm trying to repress any more. Finding my True Will taught me that.

I raise the crown above my head and for a moment I feel like I'm part of a royal ceremony. Then I bring it down with all the force my tired body can muster and smash it on the ground. It shatters, teeth spraying everywhere, skittering across the floor. I stomp on the remains for good measure.

Ronin looks at me, blinking as some of the sanity returns to his eyes. The wolf recedes to a far-off howling in his mind, always there, but safe in the distance for now.

'Thanks,' he says, flicking some of the lard from his hands. 'Now let's find a hosepipe and all the soap we can carry.'

NICE GUYS FINISH LAST

*C*abales sits against an orange tree that gurgles like a baby as it sways in the wind. When I entered my psyche that evening, Tyrone told me that they couldn't get the Peruvian shaman to do anything. Not even play bass. I found him sitting in a colourful field, picking listlessly at the giggling grass.

I sit down next to him and we watch the lavender clouds play in the sky.

'I'm sorry, my friend,' Cabales says, eventually. His long dark hair hangs over his face and the bone in his nose twitches as he speaks. 'I've betrayed you.'

'You were trapped in someone's psyche and forced to perform as one of its developmental stages,' I say. 'I'm pretty sure we can allow you some leeway here. Remember what you told me in the Asphodel Meadows?'

'Yes,' he replies. 'I was trying to get you to your True Self. That Crow said he would only help me if I got you there.'

'It doesn't matter. It worked. You pulled me out of that depression. I want to do the same for you.'

'It's too late.' He looks at his hands. 'I'm nothing. I'm nobody.'

'Dude, when the False Ego came slithering out to finish us, you *slapped that bass like nobody I've ever seen.'*

His mouth quirks into a smile. 'The bass keeps me going.'

'Focus on that,' I say. 'Focus on the funk. We need you, Cabales, we need you as part of this psyche.'

He sighs and looks up at the sky. 'Being part of you is not easy.'

'I know.' I laugh. 'Trust me.'

'Do you know what the anal phase actually is?' he says. 'What its function is in the psyche?'

'Um, potty training?'

'Yes, on the physical level it's obvious. Really, your body is one big metaphor. On a more subtle level, potty training is about learning when to hold on and when to release.'

'Right.'

'Sometimes you have to learn to let go,' he says, looking at me with his dark, almond-shaped eyes.

'Right,' I repeat. 'You're talking about Esmé.'

'I'm talking about whatever you think I'm talking about.' He stands up and offers me his hand. I take it and he pulls me to my feet.

'You do need me,' he says. 'I will never betray you again.'

We walk back to where Tyrone and the rest of the band are waiting outside the pagoda. Cabales takes his place among them.

'It's time for us to continue our journey through the psyche,' Tyrone says.

'See you, honey.' Junebug plants a kiss on my cheek. Richard gives me a macho man-hug with a pat on the back.

I pick up Chester and he licks my face.

'Well,' I say, putting the little bow-tied dog back on the ground. 'Finding out that my libido is a funk band and my True Self is a suburban dad has been pretty weird.'

'We are really just reflections of what you want to see,' Tyrone says with a smile.

'Don't ever change.' I return the smile. 'Will I see you guys again?'

Tyrone sighs. 'We ARE you, Baxter. I don't know how many times I need to tell you that.'

With a final wave they disappear into the lime-green sunset, a band and their dog, on a quest to bring funk to the rest of my psyche. Godspeed and good luck, you ridiculous weirdos.

'An explosion in the sewers killed dozens of people and covered the city in human waste today. Political parties have hit out at each other, saying the loss of human life was avoidable.'

Ronin presses the mute button on the remote control. I've just woken up on his couch and found him with his feet up watching the TV and gulping down a huge mug of coffee. I breathe in and almost gag at the sewer smell that's leaking from my pores.

When we arrived back at Ronin's apartment last night, I scrubbed myself until my skin was red and raw, but it wasn't enough. I can still smell it on me. My whole body hurts and the bullet graze on my scalp is burning like hell, despite the field dressing that King applied.

'Tone has been spinning this shit all night,' Ronin says, gesturing at the TV with his coffee mug. 'In lieu of any credible explanation, people are actually believing him.'

'And the ones that don't?'

'Rattlebone,' Ronin says. 'Or a nice little vacation in a dwarven re-education facility. Either way, it's business as usual.'

'Tell me you don't think that's fucked up,' I say.

He nods slowly. 'Did I ever tell you about art school?'

'You don't need to do that. You're right, I have no business playing amateur psychologist.'

'You're my apprentice,' he says. 'My past is part of who I am and it's the reason I do some of the things I do. That affects you.'

'That from your motivational book?'

He reaches across and grabs the yellow book from the table next to the couch. He smoothly pulls a knife from his boot and jams it through the smiling, smug face of the guy on the cover.

'Fuck that,' he says. 'Positive thinking just isn't for me.'

I laugh. 'I could have told you that.'

'You're the next generation of magic in South Africa, which is a scary thought by the way, but who knows, maybe you can change things. They'll fight you tooth and nail. But if you do decide to grow a social conscience, then I'll back you up,' he says. 'I hate those fuckers as much as you do.'

'Thanks, Ronin.'

'Maybe you haven't failed. Maybe you *have* become a better person, sparky,' he says, looking at me with his clear blue eyes.

I smile. 'No,' I say. 'I really haven't.'

I have the day to myself before we reconvene at the MK6 headquarters beneath Robben Island for a debriefing. Whatever that means. My body is aching and I just want to lie in, but I have several people I want to see. Starting with Esmé.

I'm walking down to the taxi rank from Ronin's apartment when a big silver SUV pulls up in front of me. 'Tsk!' A rich suburban woman leans through the open window, lowers her sunglasses and gives me a wink.

'Mermi?'

'Hey, boy wonder,' she says. 'Climb in. I'll give you a ride.'

I climb in and buckle my seat belt. 'You made it through that fire fight! What are you doing here?' I say as she pulls away from the kerb.

'Giving you a heads-up. Your debriefing today isn't a debriefing.

It's an interrogation. They want to know how much you know about the Bone Kraal.'

'What are you talking about? I don't know anything about the Bone Kraal. And I'm the one who stopped Lefkin.'

'You know about me,' she says, tapping the car's dashboard and turning on a Josh Groban song. 'You worked with me. That's enough. They're on high alert. The world of the Hidden is now officially under martial law. The Dwarven Legion has been given the power to search, seize and detain any of the Hidden for any reason.'

'That's bullshit.'

'That's the kind of traitorous attitude they'll be trying to ferret out during your "debriefing".'

'So what do I do?' I say.

'Two options. You tell them everything. You tell them about me, you tell them that you have Hidden sympathies.'

'Or?'

'Or you lie to them. You beat the interrogation. You'll need a mental block, something you can think about or recite in your mind to blank out their methods. These guys are pros, so it'll have to be powerful.'

'Jesus,' I say. 'I can't get involved in this.'

She turns to me. 'That's your choice, Baxter. I'm not going to force it on you. I have committed myself and there's no going back now. You have to decide where you stand.'

'What are you trying to do here?' I ask. 'If you don't want to destroy us like Lefkin, what's your game?'

'The next generation,' she says. 'Kids with magical power. I want to find them so that they can be trained in a way that doesn't make them part of the system.'

'They'll hunt you down.'

'They already are. But the alternative is worse. You're one of us, Baxter,' she says. 'However much you try to pretend, your Crow heritage makes you different. That and the fact that you're a Dreamwalker. They're not going to let you forge your own path. They're going to try to break you and mould you.'

I know she's right. I think of Ronin, crushed and battered by the system and forever running away from his past, with the wolf chasing him.

'Fuck that,' I say.

She nods. 'Then help me. Help the Bone Kraal.'

'I'll think about it.'

She smiles. 'That's all I can ask of you, boy wonder.'

I meet Esmé at a coffee shop in Woodstock. She's sitting at a wooden bench with a ceramic teapot centrepiece, sipping a latte. She's wearing a military jacket with the collar turned up and little silver dagger earrings. She looks beautiful.

She gives me a smile when she sees me, but tries to twist away from me when I sweep back her hair with my hand.

'Easy, just checking for mind-controlling spiders,' I say as I sit down across from her.

She gives me a small smile. 'Not this time.'

'So why?' I ask. No sense in pretending that that isn't what this is about.

She sighs and cups her hands around her latte. 'I don't know. We're young, Bax. I want to go out and meet people. I don't want to be sitting at home pining for someone who is somewhere else, doing things that I don't get.'

'You don't have to pine,' I say. 'And I could explain it to you.'

'The thing is, I'm not sure I want to know. I honestly thought I was the type of person who would. I love the idea of monsters and demons and shit. But the reality ...' She trails off, and in that moment I know how stupid I've been. I haven't seen the effect that her experience with Basson has had on her. 'I hate to admit it,' she says, 'but I was terrified. Completely terrified.'

'I know the feeling.'

'That's the thing, Bax,' she says. 'You're weirdly suited for this. A year ago, if someone had asked me who I thought the least likely person to be off being heroic was, I'd have said you.'

'Wow, thanks.'

'But it turns out you've got some kind of knack for it.'

'I'm just too stupid to not get involved, clearly.'

'I don't believe that. Destiny is bullshit and nobody will convince me otherwise, but you've always had a darkness and this shit somehow suits you. But it doesn't suit me.'

'I get that,' I say. 'I really do. And it's not that you're not heroic. You're so fucking brave. You're just smart enough to look ahead and see that this is the kind of path you don't come back from. The more I get to know Ronin, the more I see that.'

We sit in silence.

'So this guy you've met ...' I say.

'He's cool. I mean, he can be a bit of an idiot, but he makes me laugh and we have fun together.'

'That's great,' I say, my voice thick with emotion. 'I'm happy for you.' I'm really not, but I get it. Meeting my True Self changed me as irrevocably as that day I woke up and realised I had a heart. Esmé set that in motion, she opened the little doorway in my chest, but that doesn't mean she has to stand there and be the door person for the rest of her life. She has her own journey. It may not involve goblins or Obayifo, but it's every bit as scary, every bit as crazy and every bit as important. I can see that when I look at her. She's searching for her True Self as desperately as I searched for Norris, and she deserves to find it. Even if that search doesn't include me.

Her phone buzzes and she looks at it. 'Troy is here.' She stands up. 'I've got to go.'

'OK,' I say.

We hug awkwardly in that way broken-up couples do, and then she walks out of the coffee shop. No tears, no anger. Just a dull sense of longing for something I'll never get back.

Everyone is being debriefed about their part in the mission. Nom, Faith and Chastity and Stevo are waiting outside the Blood Kraal's chamber, fidgeting nervously. I give them a wave but am led by a dwarf to another part of MK6 headquarters. We stop outside a door with the Forked Tongue sigil emblazoned on it and the dwarven guard leans down to have his retina scanned. The door opens and I'm ushered inside.

Vats. Dozens of them, filled with unfortunate creatures too slow or too naive to escape the clutches of MK6 and the Dwarven Legion. This lab is more high-tech, but is otherwise a replica of the one in the bunkers. A bok-boy, thankfully not Klipspringer, is floating, his eyes closed and his body connected to a series of tubes. I put my hand against his vat and look at him with horrified fascination. A hand grabs the back of my head and pushes my face up against the tank. 'Look, boy,' Malachi says. 'Take it all in.'

'Get the fuck off me,' I hiss and struggle against him. I've fought goblins but apparently you don't get to be a Samnite for nothing. His arms are like iron bands.

'You need to see this,' he says, his breath hot on my ear. 'You need to see what you're part of.'

'What a big man you are,' I spit out. 'That Ndiru looks like he could destroy whole cities.'

'Knowledge is what I gather, more valuable than gold, more

dangerous than nuclear warheads. Individually this thing is unimportant. But together it is all significant.'

'Right, you're all about knowledge,' I say. 'Oh, and murderous oppression. Let's not forget about the murderous oppression.'

He punches me in the kidneys and I slump to my knees in front of the vat.

'Make no mistake, boy, you are part of this. You are complicit. We live in a difficult age and you don't want people wondering whether you fight on the side of good or the side of evil.'

'I forget, which side is MK6 on again?'

'You've wormed your way into the big league now, boy. There is no space here for your squeamishness.'

I turn around to look at him. Cold hatred burns. If I thought I could kill him, I'd try right now. Then and there I decide I'm going to help Mermi. I'm committed: anything and everything I can do to fuck with this dwarf.

He sees the look in my eyes and nods. 'Good. I don't consider my day complete until I have someone or something hating me with every fibre of their being.' He grabs me by the T-shirt and lifts me up. 'Your debriefing awaits.'

He pushes me into a room that holds nothing but two steel chairs and a steel table. In one chair sits a dirty old man in a tattered and stained white robe. He's completely blind and he holds his hands up to me as I enter.

'Who is this?' I ask.

'A truthsayer,' says Malachi, shoving me into the chair in front of the old man. 'Answer my questions truthfully, boy, or he will know.'

The old man places his hands on my temples and I feel a sickly, cool presence in my mind.

'What do you know about the Bone Kraal?' Malachi demands.

O koud is die windjie. I begin the recitation in my mind. The

Afrikaans words hum in my head and the cold, empty feeling of the veld rushes into me.

'Nothing except that they oppose MK6,' I say.

The truthsayer nods.

'Are you in any way affiliated with Lefkin Demishka or the Bone Kraal?' Malachi says.

en skraal. En blink in die dof-lig. I can feel Grandpa Zev's presence.

'No,' I say.

The truthsayer nods.

'Do you harbour any beliefs or ideologies that could be construed as being at odds with those of MK6?'

en kaal, so wyd as die Heer se genade, lê die velde in sterlig en skade. For these moments I am a Siener, and nothing can touch me.

I force down the disgust I feel for Malachi and his projects. The bok-boy in the tank and the hundreds, thousands that have gone before him. 'No,' I say.

The truthsayer hesitates for a long moment, and then nods.

The interrogation lasts for an hour and I repeat the poem dozens of times in my head. Nothing Malachi says can reach me. He watches me as I leave, his hands clasped behind his back. I feel a chill run down my spine and I know with a cold certainty that this isn't the end of it.

Seeing my family is like a balm. We've organised a civilised game of boule in the park, and as we stand and throw the silver balls, it's almost like old times. Well, except for my bandaged head and dozens of small bruises and cuts that I've tried to hide with a long shirt. My mother looks at me suspiciously. I'm not sure if she's buying my 'soccer injury' story.

My mom and dad are hyper-competitive and end up having a massive fight about whose ball is closer. My mom bursts into a string of vitriol that makes even me blush.

Rafe stands next to me and stares at the grass. His voice pops into my head.

You OK?

'Yeah,' I say. 'I need to ask you something.'

Go ahead.

'What's your game, Rafe? What you did to Lefkin was incredible. You destroyed him. You're a far better Dreamwalker than I am. Yet you're not at Hexpoort. What are you doing?'

You think you're the only one who is on a journey? I've been doing this for a long time, Bax, the poor special kid who everyone ignores and forgets about. I am walking my own path and it doesn't include Hexpoort or MK6. There are things out there, beings, organisations, dimensions, that are beyond them.

'Well, do me a favour,' I say. 'Don't try to do it alone. Let me in.'

Maybe one day I will.

My dad takes Rafe for a go on the skateboard ramp while my mom cools off. I sit next to her on the grass. We get dirty looks from the parents who are taking their toddlers for a stroll. They clearly didn't appreciate my mom's creative approach to swearing.

'You spoke to Rafe, didn't you?' she says.

'Yeah.'

'I can tell. He's doing much better, being much more social. Thank you, Baxter.'

'What can I say? I'm a natural-born philanthropist.'

She laughs and ruffles my hair.

'How is your new school?' she asks.

'It's different,' I say.

'How?'

'Oh, you know, just different.'

* * *

We meet on the platform. Faith, Chastity, Nom and Stevo on one side; Kyle, Zikhona and the Inhalant Kid on the other. They look at each warily, like rival gangs. Kyle has his suitcases with him. He managed to convince his parents to take him abruptly out of Westridge and send him to Hexpoort. A faked letter saying that Kyle had been chosen to take part in an elite academic programme didn't hurt with that.

I stand and look at my friends, old and new.

'Things have changed. I'm reinstating the Spider,' I say. There's a small sob and I look up to see a single tear of joy running down Kyle's face. 'Zikhona and the Inhalant Kid will run things here in my absence. And I'm creating a new satellite organisation called the Web at Hexpoort.'

'What are we going to be doing?' Zikhona asks through her gum. 'The porn trade has been taken over by Anwar.'

I open my hand and show them a palmful of Mumblerock crystals. 'We'll be transporting Runeshine and Mumblerock to Cape Town, where you'll distribute it. We'll be moving in on Anwar's territory, so we're going to have to recruit more members. Especially ones with magical ability. This isn't purely a commercial endeavour. We're looking to build an organisation with talented kids, magical and non-magical.'

'I'm going to be part of a teenage underground revolutionary organisation AND a drug dealer. That is so damn cool,' Kyle says, rubbing his hands together.

Chastity gives him a look. 'Is he always this weird?'

'Always,' I say, clapping him on the back. 'And I wouldn't want him any other way.'

I say goodbye to Zikhona and the Inhalant Kid and we sit waiting for the train to take us back to Hexpoort. It eventually comes and I help Kyle with his bags. We're walking down the corridor when someone slams into my shoulder and pushes me against the wall.

'Hey, asshole,' Hekka says as he passes me. 'Ready to get back to where we left off?'

I move my neck from side to side and crack my knuckles. 'Ready?' I say to Kyle.

He smiles. 'Ready.'

'Let's go destroy this kid.'

Kyle puts his hand on my shoulder. 'Welcome back, Bax,' he says and we set off after Hekka.

ACKNOWLEDGMENTS

Thank you to South Africa's writers, publishers, designers, comic-book artists, game developers and filmmakers for all the creative camaraderie and inspiration.

And to the international network of strange and wonderful creatures who recognised something of themselves in Baxter and told me so. Thank you.

ABOUT THE AUTHOR

Charlie Human is a graduate of the University of Cape Town's creative writing programme and has contributed short pieces to print and online publications. He works in online media, is married and lives in Cape Town.

Follow him on Twitter @charliehuman.

APOCALYPSE NOW NOW
CHARLIE HUMAN

Baxter Zevcenko's life is pretty sweet. He's making a name for himself as the kingpin of his smut-peddling high-school syndicate, the other gangs are staying out of his business, and he's dating the girl of his dreams, Esme.

But when Esme gets kidnapped, things start to get seriously weird, and the only man drunk enough to help is a bearded, booze-soaked, supernatural bounty hunter that goes by the name of Jackson 'Jackie' Ronin.

Plunged into the increasingly bizarre landscape of Cape Town's supernatural underworld, Baxter and Ronin team up to save Esme. On a journey that takes them through the realms of impossibility, they must face every conceivable nightmare to get her back, including the odd brush with the Apocalypse.

KOKO TAKES A HOLIDAY
KIERAN SHEA

Five hundred years from now, ex-corporate mercenary Koko
Martstellar is swaggering through an early retirement as a brothel
owner on The Sixty Islands, a manufactured tropical resort
archipelago known for its sex and simulated violence. Surrounded
by slang-drooling boywhores and synthetic komodo dragons, the
most challenging part of Koko's day is deciding on her next drink.
That is, until her old comrade Portia Delacompte sends a squad of
security personnel to murder her.

KOKO THE MIGHTY
KIERAN SHEA

After narrowly escaping death, Koko Martstellar (ex-corporate mercenary) and Jedidiah Flynn (depressed former sky-cop) are busy putting their lives back together, running a saloon/brothel on The Sixty Islands—the world's most violent and decadent resort. But when bounty agent Jackie Wire comes to collect the outstanding price on Koko's head, it's time again for Koko and Flynn to make tracks. Fleeing pell-mell across the Pacific and shipwrecking along a thought-to-be uninhabitable coast, things only go from bad to worse for our heroes... but, hey, that's the 26th century for you. Buckle up, buttercup. Only the mighty survive.

TURBULENCE
SAMIT BASU

Aman Sen is smart, young, ambitious and going nowhere. But then he gets off a plane from London to Delhi and discovers that he has turned into a communications demigod. Indeed, everyone on Aman's flight now has extraordinary abilities. Aman wants to heal the planet but with each step he takes, he finds helping some means harming others.

Will it all end, as eighty years of superhero fiction suggest, in a meaningless, explosive slugfest?

For more fantastic fiction, author events, exclusive
excerpts, competitions, limited editions and more

VISIT OUR WEBSITE
titanbooks.com

LIKE US ON FACEBOOK
facebook.com/titanbooks

FOLLOW US ON TWITTER
@TitanBooks

EMAIL US
readerfeedback@titanemail.com